MASS
MURDER

Previous novels by John Keith Drummond:

Thy Sting, Oh Death
'Tis The Season to Be Dying

JOHN KEITH DRUMMOND

MASS
MURDER

ST. MARTIN'S PRESS

Production Editor: David Stanford Burr

Design by Judy Dannecker

Library of Congress Cataloging-in-Publication Data

Drummond, John Keith.
    Mass murder / John Keith Drummond.
        p.   cm.
    "A Thomas Dunne book."
    ISBN 0-312-05467-X
    I. Title.
PS3554.R75M37   1991
813'.54—dc20   90-19459
                                                CIP

First Edition: May 1991

10 9 8 7 6 5 4 3 2 1

for
J. Michael Sutton
and a lifetime of friendship

. . . *hos tibi versiculos fidus transmisit amicus*
si de parte tua fidei stat fix catena
nunc precor ut valeas felix per saecula cuncta.

. . . thy loyal friend these minor verses sends
and should the chain of faith still bind us fast
I pray God grant thee everlasting joy.

—Walifrid Strabo, *Ad Amicum*

MASS
MURDER

PROLOGUE

1 Later—when it was all over and everyone knew who the murderer was and why—Miss Worthing finally allowed herself a bit of crowing: "Well, I think we've done very nicely, thank you. And not exactly the easiest case, either. Three broad avenues of inquiry, any one of which might have led to the quarry, and by sheer dumb luck we actually managed to trip down the right one!"

The bishop and Father Reggie promptly, piously, and properly demurred to that "sheer dumb luck."

"Oh, well, okay. I suppose you are right," grumbled Miss Worthing, before rallying and adding, with something of an edge to her voice: "Though, frankly, I fail to see how we deserved any divine intervention! I mean who would have dreamed that a church—a *church*, mind you!—would prove a breeding ground for such a disedifying spectacle of scandal and septic wickedness!"

His lordship and Father Reggie looked suitably abashed—and said nothing, being, as they were, in the ungrateful position of being enormously grateful to Miss Worthing for having, rather featly, saved their bacon. Furthermore, both men realized that sometimes allowances have to be made, even for censorious observations.

For both the bishop and Father Reggie knew what it had cost Miss Worthing and Miss Shaw to undertake the investigation and pursue it to its successful, if not very happy, conclusion; that during the investigation both women had been so tired they were practically bouncing off the walls; and that fatigue had done nothing to sweeten their tempers.

But neither man was to know for some time that that fatigue had also been the reason it took rather longer than perhaps it should have for Miss Worthing to recognize the importance of one simple little datum—a fact to which nobody else had paid the slightest attention but which turned out to be so glaringly obvious and so obviously significant. . . .

Not that either woman had the least notion their particular experience would prove so important.

In fact, at the time it all began, they had been doing nothing more than reveling in a hard and dirty job well done and finished. For the two solid weeks preceding the murders, Miss Worthing and Miss Shaw had been totally preoccupied with harvesting a record crop of fruit, vegetables, herbs, and aromatics from their jungle of a garden that stretches down to the banks of the Jolliston River behind the Victorian, and altogether absurd pile they live in at 875 Jasmine Avenue in Jolliston, California.

Four young men—stalwart sons of neighbors—had been hired to do most of the heavy work: climbing trees, bending over vine and set, doing all the picking, lugging the resulting buckets and flats into the kitchen.

Where the two women hovered over the range, stirring great, steaming, evil-smelling cauldrons, the contents of which, at just the right moment, were poured into jars and crocks, magically changed into jams and jellies, pickles and preserves.

And when they weren't busy in the kitchen, the two women were in the nethermost depths of the cellar.

There, in hushed and secret session, far from any prying eye, they prepared those herbal decoctions that would be crocked, blended, and, presently, transformed into the herbal wine they served up to universal delight at their annual Christmas open house—and for the secret of whose making every vintner in the Jolliston Valley would have cheerfully sold his soul!

Live yeast was placed on tiny boats of stale toast and set forth upon frothy and ebullient voyages. Then, when the fermentation had ceased, the two women had to clarify it and barrel it, heavy chores they had to do themselves—the lads being all of them sons of vintners and so all quivering eagerness for whatever intelligence might be gathered.

And then it was back to the sunlit world above (firmly locking the cellar door behind them) to direct their helpers where to shelve all those jars and bottles and crocks—meanwhile trying to keep the boys fed.

And no easy task that! But it was, after all, part of the deal: Miss Worthing had agreed, when contracting for their labor, that (teen-aged boys being what they are) feeding them would be only fair—though it had actually been upon Miss Shaw's ample shoulders that the responsibility fell.

Which was as it should be. Miss Shaw—who was quintessentially the Earth Mother type—took a profound joy in the chore of plying the lads with an endless supply of cakes, pastries, burritos, burgers, tacos, beer, iced tea, and, when they seemed to flag, espresso strong enough to dissolve the bowl of a spoon. . . .

After which it was back to simmering tomatoes, shredding zucchini, and blanching carrots, sugar peas, snap beans, Brussels sprouts (all for freezing), meanwhile keeping an eye on the trays of beans, onions, and garlic drying away in the summer sun.

The fierce summer sun.

For that year, making the job even harder than usual, there was lots and lots of sun.

At first it had seemed like nothing more than an unusually dry spell.

But then, for days on end, none of the usual soothing fogs

had come wafting over the western hills of the Valley—fended off, we were informed, by a high-pressure system that settled in and began to look as though it might very well stick around forever. Every day the heat, the barometer, and the humidity climbed higher, ever higher, until—by about ten o'clock every day—the temperature was somewhere in the nineties and stayed that way till well after dark. There was not the faintest breath of a breeze; leaves hung flaccid and listless on tree and shrub and vine; great clouds of gnats, flies, and no-see-'ems erupted out of nowhere, determined to dine on any piece of exposed flesh; and the sun shone unrelenting from a burnished sky empty of even the fleeciest wisp of a mare's tail.

Now, under ordinary circumstances, all of this would have been quite enough to send the ladies straight into the living room to pull the draperies to and, in the resulting gloom, fan themselves, absorb pitcher after pitcher of iced tea, and do nothing whatever for however long it lasted.

This time such a practical solution was out of the question. That very intensity of sunlight, which had brought all the fruits and vegetables in the garden to such a peak of ripeness all at once, had the entire Jolliston Valley in a tizzy of anticipation of an early grape harvest. And in the Valley everything takes a backseat to the grape harvest. Everything. And furthermore, as has been pointed out, those young men helping the two women were all sons of local vintners. Which meant that, if Miss Worthing and Miss Shaw were going to get their help, they were going to get it then or not at all.

Besides which their frugal souls would have shrunk in horror from the prospect of letting that incredible plethora of delicious foodstuffs all go to waste and the wasps.

Three and four showers a day helped, with complete changes of clothes and linen at least that often again. A quarter hour in that Turkish bath of a kitchen, however, was usually enough to make it all seem pretty useless as each

woman—rather more frequently than was altogether necessary—wondered aloud, "Why do we do this every year?"

But even the nastiest river wends somewhere home to
sea, and the worst job reaches a conclusion. And as that por-
tentous Saturday, August twenty-fifth, drew on toward evening, the last jar had been placed on its shelf, the new barrel
of wine was in the cellar next to its twin from the year before
and resting comfortably on its trestles of repose where it
would remain for the next sixteen months—and there was
nothing left to do. . . .

Miss Worthing handed around agreeable checks to the
lads, while Miss Shaw pressed packets of sandwiches and
cookies upon them lest the poor things perish of famine during the ten minutes it would take them to get home. Thanks
and farewells were shouted over and again while the young
men waved from the windows and the bed of their truck and
the two women waved from the shadows of the porch. An
ailing muffler roared into the fading afternoon and, in a
cloud of mephitic vapor, the ancient pickup rattled down the
drive and vanished into the distance.

2   At once, like a cautious cat, the great silence of a
    warm country evening came creeping stealthily back.
The only sounds were of a chain saw far off and damped by
distance to a not unpleasant buzz, while in the live oaks
across the road the resident mob of starlings held evening
confabulation.

And even though the sun yet remained several degrees of
arc above the rampart of the western hills and it was as hot
and still as ever, the evening scents of broom, jasmine, and
mock orange were already beginning to permeate the air,
borne upon those listless and momentary eddies of air even
the stillest day heads toward nightfall.

The two women looked at each other and, simultaneously uttering a ghost of a giggle, collapsed each against one of the porch pillars and gave herself up to silence, exhaustion—and sheer exultation.

Which was when they heard it and held their breath to listen:

From across the Valley, muted to velvet by the distance, came the sound of the great bawling bronze and silver bell of the Church of All Saints, bonging out the evening Angelus.

It was a rare sound to hear on Jasmine Avenue, and the hearing of it only underscored the stillness and quiet of the evening. Thrice times three they heard its deep bourdon summon the faithful to repeat the Angel's salutation to Mary and then, after a fraction of a pause, slowly toll during the time it might take one to say that great and wonderful prayer: "Pour forth thy grace into our hearts, we beseech thee, O Lord. . . ."

"My land!" said Miss Shaw, glancing at her wristwatch. "It's six o'clock. Let's go in."

Miss Worthing fetched a deep and happy sigh.

"Why, so it is," she muttered, responding to the first part of Miss Shaw's statement, ignoring the second part, and—defying heaven and earth to move her for the foreseeable future—gave herself up to a rather scatty attempt to remember the Latin of the prayer.

She had gotten as far as—and thoroughly stuck at—"ut qui angelo nuntiante," when, softened by the distance of well over a mile that it had to travel, came again the sound of the great bell, this time to announce to the world without and the faithful within the church that, once more, a priest was on his way to the altar to reoffer the only perfect sacrifice the world has ever known. . . .

This time, when Miss Shaw spoke, it was more forcefully. "Mattie! Come on! Let's go in! That was the bell for the six-fifteen Mass. We've been out here twenty minutes."

With a sigh of resignation Miss Worthing pushed against her pillar and stood upright.

"I suppose you're right, Martha," she muttered.

"Come on, now, Mattie," repeated Miss Shaw more gently, as to a fractious child. "Let's go in and get ourselves a nice cup of tea. After all, we didn't really have time for a decent cup all day."

"I know," said Miss Worthing, "or all week, for that matter!" and she turned to follow her friend indoors, suddenly longing for tea, yea verily as Israel in Babylon longed for the waters of Jordan.

3 And presently they were in the kitchen yet again—this time both women moving about their tasks in that languid, almost underwater kind of way so characteristic of the truly dead tired.

Miss Shaw stood at the stove, poised for the kettle to boil, teapot at the ready on the counter next to the stove with an open caddy of Earl Grey wafting the infinitely comforting scents of good tea and oil of bergamot into the moist air.

Miss Worthing, meanwhile, fetched cups and saucers from the china cabinet, stretching a bit to reach the cups down from their hooks.

Matilda Worthing was of rather less than even medium height, which was why she had to stretch so. Nevertheless, she always managed to give an impression of being taller than she was—an impression sustained by excellent posture as well as a self-confident composure that seldom failed her. Further, she had always been a trim, even athletic woman, though in recent years there had been a certain, perhaps inevitable spreading—which she fought like a fury in an ongoing if ultimately futile war.

She was, as she expressed it, in her late-middle-seventies and was never very forthcoming with particulars. Nor was she exactly overwhelmed with joy when most people were surprised that that was all she was. The depressing fact was she did look considerably older. Once upon a time, in her youth—right here in Jolliston—she had been rather the belle of the Valley. But time, unfortunately, stayeth not its course, and she was no longer by any means a handsome woman, having a face that had settled into an expression of determined disapprobation.

This expression, it must be said, had less to do with any native tendency to disapproval of the world at large as with the fact that, for forty-odd years of her life, she had been a shorthand court reporter, a peculiar profession that requires—for hours at a time and for days and even weeks on end—that one be completely and intently concentrated, to the exclusion of all else, on the phonic sounds of whatever the several parties might be prattling.

It is a very well-paying profession, but concomitantly stressful, and it takes its practitioners in varied ways: Some take to long and frequent holidays, others to curious hobbies, still others to drink. Matilda Worthing had taken it in the face, leaving her with the countenance of a morose dragon. Nor was her resemblance to the dread basilisk of yore one whit mitigated by the fact that, her eyes having always been weak, in her age she was compelled to wear great, thick, heavy spectacles that had the disconcerting effect of magnifying her China-blue eyes to large and baleful orbs. Her hair, finally, still remarkably auburn—if well-streaked throughout with iron-gray—was a mass of sprung curls and willful wisps, and though she dutifully ran a brush through it as often as she thought about it, it never did much to help anything.

Now Miss Worthing is usually the first to acknowledge that there are times when it is extremely useful to have a face that can curdle fresh milk. The fact remains that folks who get to know her learn early on that she is actually a mild-mannered, pleasant, altogether good-humored, and rather old-fashioned kind of lady—with a mind of razor sharpness and a certain wry appreciation of all those excesses so typical of humanity since Adam proved difficult. . . .

The kettle came to a boil. Before a nanosecond had passed, Miss Shaw had it off the fire, efficiently going through the ritualistic movements of the dedicated tea drinker—scalding the pot, pinching the right amount of tea out of the caddy into the pot, and, finally, flooding the leaves with water "just off the boil."

It always amazed Miss Worthing (and she was not the only one) at just how efficient, quick, and nimble on her feet Miss Shaw could be.

In the old days, when the two women had together owned and run a successful court reporting and secretarial services firm in San Francisco, Miss Worthing had been quite content to leave the daily managing of it to Miss Shaw; she had a way with people and—just as she had with their young helpers over the last couple of weeks—took a genuine, even maternal interest in their welfare.

Miss Shaw had been, in her youth, a remarkably beautiful woman with flaming red hair, luminous blue eyes, and a lustrous complexion. That exquisite complexion yet remained, and her eyes, of course, were still blue. All else, however, had changed. Her hair was now a cloud of the finest and snowiest cotton wool, and her eyes which (let us be frank) bulged somewhat, looked like nothing so much as azure headlights.

In spite of the fact that she was actually a bit older than Miss Worthing, she had a lot fewer wattles and lines, which was almost certainly due to the fact that she was appreciably, *ever* so appreciably, larger than Miss Worthing.

As she had grown to her present amplitude, her clothes, which she deftly constructed herself, had become more and more billowing, and she was floating around the kitchen in a pale blue cotton Arab burnoose-like thing that might well have been cut down from the same Arab's tent.

She was not, finally, in the least, an intellectual woman. And some, perceiving her an attractive and rollicking colleen, had made the unwarranted assumption that she must be, therefore, rather stupid. This could be very foolish indeed, as more than one person had found and to his cost. She was not stupid. And in her own way, she had quite as good a grasp of the peculiarities of people as ever did Miss Worthing.

She plunked the teapot down in the center of the plain pine kitchen table, and presently the two women sat opposite each other, large mugs of fragrant tea at their elbows.

"I don't suppose you're hungry," ventured Miss Shaw.

"Good God, no!" asseverated Miss Worthing. "I ate enough while trying to keep that little host of Pharoah's locusts fed to last me till Christmas."

"I know." Miss Shaw nodded and sighed. "I grazed like a cow all day long myself." She looked down briefly at her exuberant bosom. "I have got to go on a diet," she said mournfully. "I don't know why, but I just keep getting fatter and fatter."

Miss Worthing drank tea, deeming it far more politic to say nothing—and keep her face devoid of expression as well.

"And don't think for one minute I don't know what you're thinking, Matilda Worthing," said Miss Shaw crisply.

"I'm sure I don't know what you're talking about," said Miss Worthing indignantly.

"Stuff!" said Miss Shaw succinctly. "I've known you far too long not to know you're thinking very loudly indeed when you pull that poker face of yours." But she sighed resignedly and, after a second or two, uttered a weak little chuckle of defeat. "Oh, well, I suppose I should just stop deluding myself." She reached out and pulled the sugar bowl toward her. "And after all, what difference does it make anymore if I do look like the back end of a bus."

"You—we both—might live longer if we lost some weight," ventured Miss Worthing.

"Maybe," said Miss Shaw dubiously, standing up and pulling out the silver drawer to get a spoon. "But all I can think of is my grandmother who—at the age of ninety, mind you—was told by her physician that, if she gave up cream in her tea and all that butter on her toast and potatoes, she'd live a lot longer." She snorted, shook her head, and lapsed into a broad Irish brogue. "'Sure an' it wouldn't be livin',' said Grandmamma to the doctor, and I'm told that her last words, several years later, were something to the effect that she knew she shouldn't have eaten 'that damned pickle!'"

She reached a hand into the drawer, exclaimed, and withdrew her hand, holding a rather tatty piece of paper. "There it is!" she said, and tucked it into her bosom before reaching once more into the drawer and this time taking out a spoon.

"What is it?" asked Miss Worthing.

"My muffin recipe."

"I have a feeling I'm going to regret asking," Miss Worthing confided to the ambient air before demanding of Miss Shaw, "but why was your muffin recipe in the silver drawer?"

"Well, I *was* looking for it earlier today."

"Why?"

"Because Father Reggie called and said they want me to make buttered crumpets to sell at the intermission of the play. You just add twice the milk to the muffin recipe and . . . And what, may I inquire, is so funny?"

"Nothing, dear," said Miss Worthing, imperfectly restraining a perfectly natural impulse to grin, "but somehow it does seem typical of that church that they would actually serve up crumpets during the play."

"Well, they are my crumpets," said Miss Shaw complacently.

"But why in the silver drawer?"

"Damned if I know," said Miss Shaw cheerfully, resuming her seat and spooning several heaps of sugar into her tea.

Miss Worthing shuddered.

"How can you sweeten Earl Grey?" she said.

Miss Shaw shrugged and drank. "Much better," she said presently and, fetching a deep and happy sigh, stood up. "What shall we do now?"

"I don't want to do anything," said Miss Worthing. "I'm

exhausted. Why don't we just watch some television—you know, some thoroughly mindless movie—and then sleep till we wake up. We can go to Mass tomorrow night for a change."

"I think that's an excellent idea," said Miss Shaw approvingly, and, waddling to the counter, opened a cupboard from which she withdrew a largish mixing bowl.

"Oh!" she exclaimed. "Now I remember why I put that recipe in the silver drawer."

"You do?"

"Uh-huh. Because we don't have enough crumpet rings." Miss Worthing looked blankly at her.

"It's really very simple," said Miss Shaw. "It was the other day when I made crumpets for the boys' breakfast. You remember. And I only had the four crumpet rings we use, and which for us, of course, are quite sufficient, but which for the gaping maws of that quartet were woefully inadequate, and so I thought that we just have to buy some tuna fish—so I can make crumpet rings from the cans," she explained. "And so I put the muffin recipe in the drawer with the silver so that each time I took out a spoon or a fork I would remember—you know what my memory is!—that I need to pick up a dozen cans of tuna fish at the market this week. And it had better be soon, too, now that Father Reggie wants me to make crumpets for the play. So I do hope you won't mind if we have tuna noodle casserole this coming Friday. I know you don't much like it—who could?—but it's either that or tuna salad which always gives both of us the worst heartburn. So . . ."

She removed the recipe from her capacious bosom and, continuing to mutter half under her breath, began to assemble flour, sugar, yeast, and milk.

Her head spinning from this extraordinary explanation as well as this burst of renewed activity, Miss Worthing asked, rather weakly, "Martha, what are you doing?"

"I just thought I'd whomp up a mess of crumpet batter. It'll be yummy by the time we get up in the morning."

Miss Worthing cast her eyes toward the heavens and stood up.

"Well, then, I'm going to see what's on TV," she said firmly. "I refuse to sit in this kitchen and watch you doing utterly unnecessary work after the day we've already had. Besides," she groused, "you make me feel guilty."

"Nonsense, Mattie," said Miss Shaw, pitching ingredients into the bowl. "It won't take a minute."

"Nevertheless, I'm going into the living room and fix myself a highball," said Miss Worthing, opening the refrigerator and taking out an ice tray.

"Now *that's* a great idea," said Miss Shaw. "Fix me one, too. I'll only be a minute."

"You keep saying that," said Miss Worthing unreasonably.

She was halfway through the dining room when she heard the phone ring and Miss Shaw answer it.

Good heavens, she thought irritably, who can that be?

She proceeded the rest of the way into the living room, emptied the ice tray into the ice bucket, and stalked back toward the kitchen to refill the tray, all the while thinking how she did not want to speak to anyone, see anyone, or, for that matter, do anything but toss a strong highball down her throat, watch some idiotic horror flick on TV (it was, after all, Saturday night), then go to bed and sleep for a week.

Which made it all the more irritating when she reached the door into the kitchen to be able to hear—even across the breadth of that very large room—a cackle and a quack coming from the receiver that, to her all too practiced ear, indicated the party on the other end was none other than her venerable, redoubtable, and rather antic aunt, Eulalia, Lady Fairgrief.

"Oh, Lord!" she breathed. "Aunt Eulalia!"

Telephone conversations with her ancient relative were never short, and she was in no mood for the usual hour-long harangue from her ladyship in which the whole world would be arraigned, judged, and found wholly wanting.

She dashed across the kitchen, flailing her arms wildly in

an attempt to tell Miss Shaw that, for her aunt, she wasn't there.

Unfortunately, Miss Shaw turned away just as Miss Worthing made her mad dash into the kitchen. Miss Shaw, moreover—to judge from the sounds she was making—had been trying to break into the torrent for some time. "Just a *moment*, Lady Fairgrief! I'll get her. Wait! Please! Will you wait? I said she isn't here right now. She's in the living . . . *Will* you hold on! I'll tell her to pick up in there. Just a minute, won't you?"

She turned and saw Miss Worthing, and without further ado—and in spite of Miss Worthing's continued flailing—glared at her, shouted into the phone, "Here!" and pointedly held the instrument out to Miss Worthing.

With a profound sigh Miss Worthing accepted her fate and the phone.

"Hello, Aunt Eulalia."

Miss Shaw, snickering at the tone in Miss Worthing's voice, immediately repaired to her batter making—though, to be sure, all she had left to do was put a damp cloth over the bowl and stick it into the oven overnight; the pilot light would keep it just warm enough for the yeast to work nicely without overdoing things.

Preoccupied as she was, it took several minutes for it to register that very little was being contributed to that conversation by Miss Worthing. She turned to look at her friend and uttered a sharp little cry of alarm.

Miss Worthing had sagged against the wall. Perceiving Miss Shaw out of the corner of her eye, she glanced up and shook her head in an unhappy fashion.

"Very well, Aunt Eulalia," she said presently. "Yes, of course. Of course, we will. Though I don't really know what use I can be. . . . Yes, all right. . . . Yes, of course, I'll see what I can do."

She hung up and drew a long and ragged breath and then let it all out again in an equally long sigh, her eyes shut tight.

"Mattie?" said Miss Shaw. "What's wrong?"

Without answering, Miss Worthing leaned over the table and, lifting the lid of the teapot, peered within. She replaced the lid and, hefting the pot, filled her mug to the brim.

"Mattie!" protested Miss Shaw. "You won't be able to sleep."

Miss Worthing finished drinking deeply of the rasping brew before saying, "We aren't going to be able to do that anyway, are we? Well, I suppose we'd better get dressed."

"What! Mattie, what are you talking about?"

"Aunt Eulalia didn't tell you?"

"Tell me what?"

"Martha, we have to go to church."

"What for?" demanded Miss Shaw. "I thought we weren't going to go till tomorrow night."

"We weren't," said Miss Worthing grimly. "But that was before someone began murdering all the priests."

CHAPTER ONE

1   The two women said little as they drove the short distance. Indeed, to drive at all seemed strange. Normally, and certainly on a warm evening like that, they would have walked, allowing themselves pleasant interludes in which to prepare for, and on the way back to meditate upon, mercies received.

This time it was more important just to get there.

And that something major was going on was clear even before Miss Shaw turned their car into Church Street. Official vehicles either raced past them or careered wildly around them, sirens blaring, at intervals of what seemed no more than fifteen seconds. Then, at the intersection of Church and Dolores, just half a block short of their goal, they were stopped by a sheriff's car parked in the middle of the street, effectively blocking access to the church.

Miss Shaw pulled to a halt and rolled down the window— the air conditioning wheezing audibly at the blast of warm air penetrating the interior—as a young man in the tan uniform of a deputy and who had been leaning against the blocking car, pushed himself upright and sauntered over.

"Evening, Miss Shaw," he said, bending over and peering

within. "Miss Worthing. 'Fraid you're gonna have to turn 'round."

"Oh?" said Miss Worthing, leaning over a bit to peer up at the young man.

"Yes, ma'am. There's been a accident, so we're restrictin' access to thuh area."

"D'you mean the murders, Harry?" asked Miss Worthing. The deputy made a face.

"Mighta know'd you'd know already."

"Actually," said Miss Worthing consideringly, "I really think you ought to let us through."

"Can't. Sheriff said no one."

"I'm sure he did. But Father Reggie sent for me."

"He did?" The deputy seemed taken aback. "Well, okay, I guess," he said, and then hesitated. "Well? No! Tell you what. You two wait here. I better check first."

"You do that," muttered Miss Worthing, sitting back up and watching through the windshield as the deputy stalked back to the official car and, reaching inside, picked up his microphone.

"Damn!" she muttered.

"Did Father Reggie really send for you?" demanded Miss Shaw.

"Only in a manner of speaking."

"And what manner might that be?"

"Aunt Eulalia *was* calling from the church office."

Miss Shaw snorted. "Don't mean a thing. She'd call you if Michael the Archangel were standing guard at the door."

Further conversation was cut short by the deputy ambling back toward them, scratching his cheek in a thoughtful manner.

"Well, I guess it's okay," he said. "Sheriff said come on ahead."

He stood back.

"Harry?" said Miss Shaw.

"Yes'm?"

"Would you mind getting your car out of the way?"

"Oh, yeah! Sorry!"

He trotted back to the squad car, backed to the curb so they could get by, and then put it right back in the middle of the road.

"Curiouser and curiouser," observed Miss Shaw.

"Indeed," said Miss Worthing. "I really didn't think it would be that easy. What do you suppose is going on?"

As they pulled into the church parking lot, which was at least half full of cars, Miss Worthing murmured, half to herself, "Looks like whoever was here for the six-fifteen Mass is still here."

Miss Shaw said nothing as she negotiated into a space toward the back of the lot.

"As, of course, they would be," Miss Worthing continued to mutter as both women clambered out of the car, "especially if there really was a murder."

For a moment they lingered in the deep shadow of the hedgerow bordering the parking lot, trying to assess the situation.

Across the way, in front of the church, the street was lined with five of the ten cars Jolliston County provides its sheriff's department, red and white gum-ball lights flashing, while in the clergy parking lot an ambulance and several of the stripped-down gray Fords the county provides its other employees were idling.

Even as they watched, the lights of the ambulance began to spin and its siren to wail as it raced from the lot and headed down Church Street, preceded by one of the sheriff's cars similarly wailing.

Preoccupied men and women, both in uniform and in business suits, hurried back and forth in the west cloister colonnade that fronted the street. Some descended to the clergy parking lot and, opening the trunks of one car or another, lifted equipment from within and hastened back into the cloister—thence, presumably into the church—or disappeared into the open double doors of the church hall.

Miss Worthing sighed and shook her head. "I can't imagine what Aunt Eulalia was thinking of, calling me in."

Miss Shaw chuckled and waved a dismissing hand at all the scurrying officials. "I'll pit you against all that any day."

"Martha, that's nonsense and you know it. I haven't got the foggiest notion of what's been going on here, but if the professionals are involved, surely there's nothing we can do."

"Humph! You've solved any number of cases that stymied them."

"Any number!" said Miss Worthing with a click of the tongue. "Precisely one, if you'll recall. The others were just cases—well, that no one official was going to investigate. Looks to me as if they've got the whole posse out tonight."

"Uh-huh. And still they let us through the barricade."

"Hmm, yes; there is that. Well, let's see if we can find out what it's all about."

Ignored by bustling officialdom, they climbed up the four broad steps to the west side of the cloister.

"Did your aunt by any chance mention where she might be?" asked Miss Shaw.

"No, she didn't," replied Miss Worthing, "although I'd imagine they're probably keeping her cooped up with the rest. Wherever that might be. . . ."

"Well, you two certainly took your sweet time getting here!" a sharp voice barked at them from the deep gloom of the cloister garth.

Startled, Miss Worthing and Miss Shaw turned to face into the well of darkness in the garth just as a wheelchair was pushed forward into the light bleeding into the garden from the overhead bulbs in the cloister. Seated in the chair, regally erect and glaring malignantly, was Miss Worthing's ancient and improbable relative.

"Ah!" said Miss Shaw, recovering first from their momentary surprise. "*Dear* Lady Fairgrief! How *nice* to see you ever the same!"

Since the only possible response to that kind of thing is a derisive snort, Lady Fairgrief snorted derisively.

For Eulalia, Lady Fairgrief, relict of the late Sir Arthur Fairgrief, had long since reached an age at which she felt that, if a situation called for a snort, snort she would, and never mind what she might once have been taught was more "ladylike" behavior. She'd been around quite long enough to know better. Approximately a century old, she nevertheless firmly rebuffed all inquiry after particulars with a disdainful look through a tortoiseshell lorgnon, a haughty sniff, and a crushing, "Do please try to remember that I am, after all, a lady!"

She had been, eighty years and more ago, a great beauty in an age of great beauties, and it had been the dazzling young American who had walked away with the most eligible and sought-after bachelor of that London season of 1908. Returned now to the town whence she had begun all those years before, Lady Fairgrief had become a pillar of the community, a valued parishioner of the Church of All Saints—and a distinct embarrassment. Her ladyship was possessed of opinions, an income, and a tongue, none of which was she loath to spare.

Little remained now of her fabled beauty, except perhaps her eyes—black pools twinkling with intelligence, vast good humor, wisdom, and not a little innocent malice. Her skin, too, had been spared the wearing effects of makeup; in her day, maquillage had been all but unthinkable—a little powder, perhaps, or for midnight balls, a touch of rouge to a lower lip. Her complexion, therefore, was still freshly colored and soft as velvet, though now a labyrinth of those infinitesimally small lines of the truly old. Her long, determined chin was decorated with a fine collection of wattles and draperies of sagging skin, while her nose seemed to have grown with the years to a great parrotlike beak. Her hair was snow-white, baby fine, and never other than immaculately coiffed, over which she now wore, having been to church on a hot summer evening, a shawl of lace, and she was dressed in a simple and beautifully cut summer gown of purple silk, while a coverlet of silk the identical shade of her dress swaddled her useless lower limbs.

Pushing the chair, her face a mask of stony disapproval, was her ladyship's longtime companion, nurse, and maid-of-all-work, Maude Bennett.

Maude was an altogether different sort. Strongly built and of forbidding mien, she had been with Lady Fairgrief ever since that disastrous day, thirty-five years gone by, that had cost her ladyship her husband and the use of her legs.

Maude was by no means young herself, but she was definitely one of nature's blessed ones, hale, for the most part hearty, the only real difference between the Maude of today and the Maude of three and a half decades ago was that her hair had gone a little grayer. Which was about it. That and the expression that had come to seem almost stamped upon her rough, plain features.

It was a never-failing source of amusement to those who knew Lady Fairgrief and Maude Bennett (who, incidentally, deeply and dearly loved each other) that the latter was in a state of almost constant growling disapprobation because her ladyship *would* get mixed up in "unsavory goings-on." And since, unfortunately (at least from Maude's viewpoint), Lady Fairgrief was endlessly fascinated by all that was unsavory in humanity, poor Maude was in a taking most of the time.

"Evening, Matilda. Martha," said Maude stiffly. "Glad you finally got here. Now." She leaned forward and demanded of her employer, "Will you let me take you home?"

Lady Fairgrief sniffed.

"Don't be silly. The police wouldn't let me. I'm a witness. And so," she snipped over her shoulder, "are you. Besides"— she sat up straighter and seemed almost to preen—"have you forgotten that I'm to be the bishop's personal representative in all this?"

Miss Worthing and Miss Shaw exchanged a glance concocted, in about equal measure, of irritation and puzzlement.

"Bishop's representative?" repeated Miss Worthing.

"Indeed," rejoined Lady Fairgrief with a rather smug nod while Maude's scowl deepened appreciably.

At which point, justifiably roused, Miss Shaw angrily rapped out, and in a voice that would brook no denial, "Would anyone—anyone at all—mind telling us anything at all about just what the hell is going on here!"

The others all turned to look at her.

"And don't look at me as if you think I've gone funny," Miss Shaw continued in much the same tone of voice. "All we—Mattie and I—know at this point is that, out of the blue, you telephoned us to say that priests are being murdered."

"So they are," said Lady Fairgrief mildly.

"Martha," said Miss Worthing, "that will do. Calm down."

"Indeed," murmured Lady Fairgrief.

"No, Aunt Eulalia," said Miss Worthing to her aunt. "Martha's right. So far that is all we know. Of course, it's fairly obvious from all this"—she gestured vaguely toward the street—"that something's going on. But what?"

"And all we get from you," added Miss Shaw, "is that you're a witness and so is Maude. (Evening, Maude, how are you, my dear?) And then some other twaddle about you being the bishop's representative."

Somewhat testily her ladyship protested: "It isn't twaddle. It happens to be true. Nevertheless," she conceded, "you do have a point. How could you know?"

In reply, Miss Shaw snorted while Miss Worthing waited.

"Well?" Miss Worthing asked her aunt, presently.

"Maude," her ladyship barked over her shoulder, "if I get anything wrong, correct me."

"Very good, my lady," said Maude, resignedly.

And after a moment, Lady Fairgrief began. "The facts,

baldly, are these: This evening, while saying Mass, Father Hughie Barnes—"

"Excuse me?" interrupted Miss Shaw. "Father *Hughie* was saying Mass?"

"Yes. Father Hughie," replied her ladyship.

"But . . ."

"Yes, I know," said Lady Fairgrief grimly.

At which point Miss Worthing instructed, rather severely, "Aunt Eulalia, start at the beginning."

"Yes," her ladyship agreed with a sigh, "I suppose that is the only way to do it. Very well." She settled back and, turning to Maude, said, "And I meant that. If I forget anything or leave something out, chime in."

"Yes, my lady," agreed Maude.

"Well, I would imagine the best place to start," began her ladyship again, after another pause to collect her thoughts, "was when we arrived."

"Which was when?" asked Miss Worthing.

"It must have been right around five-thirty or so. No later than that because I realized that I had plenty of time to say my private prayers before Evensong was to begin at quarter to six. . . ."

2   "We are rather early this week, ma'am," said Maude, grunting a bit as she bounced her ladyship's chair up the steps from the street into the west cloister.

During that operation Lady Fairgrief said nothing, merely enduring. It may have been one of the daily indignities to which she had perforce grown accustomed, but the bump and grind (as she had been known to style it) of being bodily hauled up steps was not one she ever endured happily.

When, however, they paused a moment in the cloister for Maude to regain her breath, and Lady Fairgrief her equanimity, her ladyship observed, "Perhaps we are. But one suspects both of us can use the extra time profitably improving our immortal souls. Besides"—she groped amid the folds of her coverlet and presently snapped open an elegant little fan of paper-thin, lace-carved slats of sandalwood, which she began vigorously to ply—"we should also be grateful, on a day like today, for any time spent in a nice, cool stone church."

"Amen to that," muttered Maude, pushing the chair through the side door into the nave.

But if it was cooler inside the church, it was only that it was just not as hot as it was outdoors. In fact the interior of the church was redolent of that faintly acrid odor of sweating stone, a smell unutterably revolting to some and to others immensely comforting. To both women, attendant and termagant alike, it was the latter. Both, upon fetching up in Jolliston, had been grateful to have the Church of All Saints in place, looking almost as though one of the great churches of East Anglia or the South Downs had somehow fallen to earth in Northern California.

Which was what the founders had intended.

Constructed in the mid 1890s in that pseudoperpendicular Gothic the Victorian mind found so suitable for worship, the Church of All Saints was huge, larger, in fact, than many a diocesan cathedral.

And light. Great windows marched the length of the nave to conclude with the triptych surrounding the apse. The glass, furthermore, unlike the usual mid-Victorian scenery in translucent pigments, was of intricate Celtic-type designs, and colored in those subdued blues and greens and vermilions the artisans of the late nineteenth century grew so fond of as they relearned the ancient craft of true stained glass. With the pleasant result that the interior light, though plenteous, was subdued, dim, subaqueous.

The wood, too, good solid oak and polished walnut, after nearly a hundred years of rubbing with the old-fashioned petroleum and beeswax polish the Sisterhood of the parish still used, tended to a medieval black, while the brass, silver, and even gold wherewith the sanctuary was appointed gleamed richly in the soft light.

For the Church of All Saints was a parish very well-off indeed. Had been almost since its inception back in the days of the Gold Rush of 1849. Then, as the settlers in the Valley discovered that the climate and soil of the Jolliston flood plain was all but perfect for the growing of Chardonnays and Rieslings, and the middle uplands even better for Pinots and Gamays, the church had grown even more prosperous as the local agricultural population besought to induce, cajole, and, generally speaking, bribe the god of rain and sunshine into cooperating with them.

And even today—even after a number of suburban-type commuter subdevelopments had been built here and there in the Valley, the backbone of the parish remained that large percentage of the populace involved in the growth, manufacture, nurturing, and sale of wine.

Which was one of the reasons the sight that greeted them as Maude wheeled her ladyship up the south aisle took both of them aback: The church was full. Or so, at least, it seemed.

Actually, it was no such thing. There were, perhaps, a hundred people all told. Two or three were lined up outside of Father Reggie's confessional wearing suitably penitential expressions. But for the most part, the forgathered congregation was scattered broadcast throughout the nave. The candles on the altar had not yet been lit, so most quietly chatted with their neighbors or knelt in private prayer.

Nevertheless, there were altogether too many of them.

Saturday afternoon Evensong and Mass had never been a particularly popular service. Most of the people who, for one reason or another, had spent the day in the church compound were usually eager just to get on home. For the vintning populace, Saturday was just another long, hard-working day. And since the next day was Sunday, after all, there would have been little point in going to church in the evening. The usual attendees at this particular service had, therefore, historically been comprised of older people with a scattering of week-ending suburban types.

Not so this evening.

Many of those present nodded or smiled as Maude pushed the chair up the aisle to the front pew north, sacred by long-standing use to her ladyship's presence. Maude locked the brake of the chair, slipped into the pew beside the chair, and knelt to her own prayers while Lady Fairgrief bowed her head.

But such a very unusual circumstance was not to go unremarked for long. Not by Lady Fairgrief. Which meant it took no more than a minute to pass before she raised her head and her lorgnon and was peering around.

"What do you suppose they're all doing here?" she asked in a whisper that could have been heard in the narthex. "Why, there's Clyde Cartwright. Why isn't he at home in the fields? All this talk I've been hearing about early harvest, and here's the largest vintner in the Valley at Saturday Mass! And there's Stringer Yates, too. And Maria. And, bless my soul"—she craned farther around—"their whole brood is with them. What do you suppose . . . Maude!"

"What!" asked Maude, raising her own head and glaring at her employer.

"Well? What do you think?"

"I'm sure I don't know! Although, now you mention it"— she too looked around—"it is a bit odd. Especially considering," she went on in an altogether drier tone of voice, "I would have expected there to be even fewer people here tonight, not more."

"What? Oh! Oh, yes. I had forgotten. It is Dr. Cantrell's turn to preach, isn't it? You're right. I would have expected the place to be deserted. Don't know why, of course."

"Oh?"

"Oh, well, I do know he's not to everyone's liking."

"Like two-thirds of the people in the parish."

"Now, Maude. I concede he's a bit old-fashioned."

"He's a pedantic, opinionated, hypocritical, old poop."

"Maude Bennett, that is a most unchristian observation!"
"But an accurate one," retorted Maude.
"And we are in church."
"Yes, well, there is that. Sorry." Maude nodded briefly toward the altar, noting as she did that their conversation had hardly gone unnoticed, that a good many others were smiling—even grinning—in their direction.

"So," asked Miss Worthing, "did you find out why there were so many people in church?" She gestured toward the parking lot across the street. "Now you mention it, I can see there were more than usual."
"Not yet. I expect it's something you'll uncover. Just don't forget to tell me. I mention it now because I just thought you ought to know that I thought it unusual and why I found it so."
"Yes, all right. Go on."

. . . But presently it penetrated even Lady Fairgrief's busy mind that, whatever might have brought this peculiar situation about, the earliest she was going to be able to find out about it was when Mass was over.

Accordingly, once more, she bowed her head and gave herself over to thoughts more appropriate to the time and place. And was reasonably successful, too. Until, that is, several minutes later, there came the sound of the bell in the sacristy followed immediately by the sound, around and behind her, of the congregation rustling to its feet to welcome the priest-officiant for Evensong. At which point, who should emerge from the sacristy—all tricked out in cassock, surplice, and stole—but the Reverend Fiona MacLaren.

At which point curiosity passed from a pleasant tickle in her ladyship's mind into an all-engrossing itch. And not alone in her ladyship's mind, either. Interest was tangible all over the church. Even Maude was heard audibly to gasp.

Nor, for that matter, could anyone so reacting be blamed.
The Reverend Miss—excuse me, the Reverend *Dr*. Fiona

MacLaren, though a familiar enough sight about the purlieus of the Church of All Saints, was, nevertheless, something of a challenge to the serenity of that normally placid institution. In fact, the very mention of her name had been known to send Dr. Cantrell, the rector—and the very man whom she was, at the moment, replacing—into a seething rage. But then, Cantrell, in all things arch-conservative, found it difficult rationally to discuss the subject of women ordinands.

But whether Cantrell liked it or not (he didn't), Fiona MacLaren was engaged to marry the Reverend Mr. Hugh Barnes, assistant or third priest at the Church of All Saints. It only stood to reason, therefore, that inevitably she should be often about—and usually at loose ends.

For Dr. MacLaren was something of a problem in the parish and the diocese—and perhaps the entire body politic of the Church Militant. She was a woman of frightening intelligence, and Lady Fairgrief had heard (from several who were present) that the *viva voce* examination for her doctorate in the General Theological Union at Berkeley had been less examination than coronation. A clear, honest, and brilliant thinker, who was also, wonder of wonders, a good writer, she had moved, having achieved her doctorate, an unstoppable force toward ordination impelled by a vocation so strong and so obvious that great and hitherto impassable barriers had fallen like straw before it.

But the struggle had not been without cost: Few people did not admire Fiona MacLaren; hardly anyone liked her. She was by no means above bullying away with the fact of her doctorate and had used it more than once to bludgeon aside objections or obstacles to one thing or another she desired. Only one problem remained. And that was proving remarkably unyielding.

No one wanted her.

She stormed, she railed, she protested to anyone who would listen, and they grew fewer every day. And she wept. For she was not above using that ultimate tool of manipulation as well. It was all, however, to no effect.

Her applications for vacant livings around the diocese were always received with every courtesy, which always, in spite of her experience, caused her to hope again. And then the post always, always, went to someone else, and to someone, usually, considerably less qualified than she was—except for the simple fact that they got along rather better with people.

And so for many months now, since her engagement to Father Hughie, she had hung around the Church of All Saints.

It was also too bad—at least in Lady Fairgrief's opinion—that, for purposes of making whatever obscure political point it might be, Fiona made no effort to make the best of herself. Which, in a way, was rather sad; she could have been a fairly attractive person. She was a large woman, tall and definitely on the hefty side, and since she dressed almost exclusively in blue jeans, men's polo shirts, and clerical dickey and collar, she tended to bulk larger than she really was. She wore no makeup, had a habit of biting her nails, and wore her hair—of an ash-blond color and in desperate need of conditioning—pulled back and woven into a clublike queue from which split ends were constantly escaping. Her eyesight was not of the best, and she wore thick, bent-wire, and apparently inadequate spectacles through which she peered squint-eyed at the world. And though she could wax persuasive and eloquent on paper, she was not quick on her feet, so to speak, and there were those who thought her flat, unmusical speech a portent of stupidity. This was not only wrong, it was dangerous.

And Lady Fairgrief frankly detested her. It had nothing to do with her being woman and priest. Like most thinking members of her generation, her ladyship had early on recognized the inevitability of that—though, admittedly, she had been somewhat taken aback by its coming about in her lifetime. It was just that Fiona made so much of being a priest and so very little of being a woman. To her ladyship—who, after all, had spent the better part of a hundred years rejoicing in being a woman and working hard for women's equality—it seemed not only absurd, but faintly insulting. "What kind of triumph for women is this if she won't even take the time to be one?" Lady Fairgrief had inquired—which was not exactly fair, but there it was.

And now, as Fiona proceeded, droning through the collects and psalms, Lady Fairgrief found it difficult to keep her mind on the service.

Approximately a third of the way through Fiona's already hasty recitation of the office, above them in the tower the great bell bonged out the Angelus—which meant it was just on six o'clock. It was also clear that the ringing thereof rather startled Dr. MacLaren. She redoubled her pace, and if the concluding prayers were a bit muddled, she, nevertheless, soon retired to the vestry, reappearing a few minutes later clad as usual, her face set in an expression of bashful self-effacement as she emerged and proceeded to the aisle seat in the very pew where, at the north end, Lady Fairgrief was palpitating with curiosity. There Fiona knelt down, bowed her head, and covered her face in prayer.

Questions by the dozen crowded into her ladyship's head. Had Dr. Cantrell suddenly repented him of his stated position? And if so, what could have brought it about? Was Fiona now suddenly to be a priest of All Saints? Lord knew they could use one. Or was it going to happen after her marriage to Father Hughie? Was this, as it were, a dry run? What would Father Hughie—poor lamb that he was—have to say about it?

And suddenly, interrupting this spate of questions, once again the great bell in the tower began to ring, and from the sacristy emerged, first of all, the altar boy, hands folded, eyes downcast, expression meek, followed by Father Hughie Barnes, third priest of the Church of All Saints and Fiona MacLaren's solemn betrothed.

"Where do you suppose Dr. Cantrell is?" inconsequently demanded Lady Fairgrief of Maude.

Dr. Cantrell was supposed to take this Mass. Furthermore, by a custom of such long-standing it may well have been instituted at the founding of the parish, that the priest whose turn it was to preach in any given week was assigned the task of offering the six-fifteen Mass on Saturday evenings. Dr. Cantrell had been scheduled to preach this week. Or so it had been announced in the parish magazine. Ergo, Dr. Cantrell should be offering this Mass. He was not. Therefore, where was Dr. Cantrell?

Not that her ladyship was the only one asking the question. This time the reaction around the church, though decorous and more or less subdued, was distinctly audible.

Father Hughie himself was certainly aware of it. He looked up, flushed, and quickly lowered his eyes to the covered chalice and paten he carried, telegraphing apology to everyone in eyeshot.

As well he might, thought Lady Fairgrief, grimly settling herself for what must inevitably follow.

Actually, she was rather fond of Father Hughie. As were most of the parishioners. This did not, however, mean that they were unaware of the poor man's shortcomings. Indeed, one would have had to be pretty far gone oneself not to be aware of them.

The Reverend Mr. Hugh Barnes was a phenomenon to which churchfolk have necessarily become accustomed in recent years. The process by which one becomes a priest is not exactly an easy one. Deliberately so. It is a life of generally ill-paid and exhausting service, and Holy Church has gone, with great wisdom, to some lengths to try to protect souls not up to the responsibilities of the office from assuming it. Nevertheless, mistakes are made—or what seem like mistakes.

It would be unjust and pointlessly judgmental to say that Father Hughie was one of those mistakes. Indeed, there were those who, in a fit of exasperation, asked themselves and anyone who would listen, "What else could the man have become?" But such an attitude was unfair not only to Father Hughie but also to the priesthood he bore. He was just like so many others abroad in the modern world—earnest, willing, sentimental, neither particularly insightful nor intelligent nor articulate. And hopelessly incompetent at the increasingly arduous business of just living in that world.

And yet, as has been said, in spite of exasperation, irritation, and even despair at his general fatuity, hardly anyone really disliked the man. There was something about him that summoned the parent in one, and most people reacted by wanting to shelter this innocent from the vagaries of existence. He was in his early thirties but could easily have passed for a teenager. His coloring was brown: brown hair, sallow complexion, and a hairlessness of chin and arm that was positively boyish. With dark eyes. Dark brown eyes under a finely shaped brow that inevitably caused people to root out the old cliché about "puppy dog's eyes." Not especially tall, and thin withal, he gave a distinct impression of frailty, an orphan-in-the-storm manner, so to speak, which his general vagueness and indeterminacy ameliorated not a whit. Not even the man's blazing sincerity of belief in the doctrines of the Christian dispensation was able to make the slightest difference to his perpetual air of a somewhat wanting child lost in a world that would never make sense to him.

And now the church was full of people who—for whatever reason they might be present—had come expecting to hear a Mass celebrated by Dr. Cantrell, a task he would have accomplished with reverence, punctilio, and aplomb. And preach. And even if his manner and frequently his matter were not to everyone's liking, Dr. Cantrell was an accomplished preacher.

As for poor Father Hughie, he was not only a genuine klutz, but his *prepared* sermons were torture. If his appearance here was (as seemed likely) as a replacement for Dr. Cantrell, what, oh, what did it bode in the way of an *improvised* homily?

Presently, however, setting aside these thoughts as distinctly unworthy for one attending the mysteries, Lady Fairgrief turned her attention to the Action proceeding at the altar.

Antiphons were chanted, the Thrice Holy sung with reverent attention, the epistle read, the gospel, borne aloft, brought forth and proclaimed.

At which point one could almost feel the congregation holding its collective breath in trepidation. Then, mercifully, Father Hughie apparently decided not to preach at all.

And the relaxation of tension in the assembled was similarly almost tangible as Father Hughie proceeded directly to the recitation of the creed. The great admonitions were spoken, and the congregation was fervently chanting along with Father Hughie, "Holy, Holy, Holy, Lord God of hosts . . ."

They sang the words of the triumphant entry into Jerusalem, and all knelt while once again the words were spoken and the Spirit invoked to consecrate the elements, and all present bowed their heads as the great Epiclesis ended with the triple amen.

It had always struck Lady Fairgrief that there is a subtle relaxation of tension in any church at any liturgy after that most mystical moment of trust and faith is past. So, too, that evening at the Church of All Saints there was a certain rustling through the crowd as they all settled and, presently, stood to recite the praises of the Blessed Mother, invoked God's grace on the whole state of Christ's Church Universal, then knelt again to share in the recitation of the Lord's own prayer.

At the end of it, Father Hughie, as was his wont, chanted the doxology with a joy and a clarity that many in the congregation had wished more than once could somehow be transplanted into other areas of his life. For here was a man transformed by his statement of faith and praise: "For Thine is the kingdom, the power, and the glory, now and forever . . ."

And together with the congregation, Father Hughie recited the prayers before Communion, bent over, lifted the Host to his mouth, received the Body of Christ, and then, while still visibly masticating, raised the chalice and drank deeply.

After a moment Father Hughie set the chalice down and seemed to stare at it a second or two in a puzzled fashion. But no, it was nothing. He did pause rather longer than was perhaps usual, but was it surprising that a priest, upon receiving those most abundant gifts, would not pause for a moment in thanksgiving, worship, and honor?

Be that as it may, thirty seconds later, Father Hughie picked up a single host and the chalice and walked toward the altar boy and communicated him.

And this time there was no question that the lad faltered a bit, pulling his head back sharply from the chalice as though something had struck him.

And Lady Fairgrief made a note to herself to decline the chalice when Maude wheeled her up to Communion. The wine in the cruets had clearly gone "off"—not exactly surprising on such a searing day as this. In fact, she had to struggle a bit to keep from chuckling. What a horror for the poor priest! To have to consume a chalice of consecrated wine that was half vinegar!

Presently, however, the boy visibly steeled himself and, leaning forward, also drank.

Together, the boy and the priest recited a prayer of thanksgiving, whereupon Father Hughie stepped back, turned, went up the steps of the altar, and replaced the chalice thereon. At that point he once again made to pick up the paten.

Before he could do so, however, he swayed in his place. Quickly, he righted himself and, as quickly, put a hand out to steady himself on the altar, as though, had he not done so, he would have fallen.

It was then, his face drained of all color and twisted first in puzzlement and then in anguish and dismay, he looked up and in a horror-stricken voice announced, "Something is terribly wrong!"—and collapsed at the foot of the altar.

The acolyte leaped to his feet and ran to the recumbent

priest and bent over him. Suddenly, twitching and clutching at his own stomach, he struggled back to his feet and called out, his voice breaking in his emotion, "It was in the chalice! There was something in the chalice!" And he, too, fell groaning across the fallen priest.

3 "Do you mean someone poisoned the *chalice*?" demanded Miss Shaw in horror.

"I'm afraid that a chalice merely full of vinegar wouldn't have that kind of result," said Lady Fairgrief.

"But how could someone poison a chalice?" asked Miss Shaw.

"Just so," said her ladyship grimly, eyeing her niece, who said nothing. "But that's not all."

"What?"

"I only wish it were," observed her ladyship, getting an emphatic nod from Maude as well.

"It's bad enough!"

"Yes. Nevertheless . . ."

"Okay, Aunt Eulalia," said Miss Worthing. "What next?"

Needless to say, this was not the kind of thing one expects in church on a Saturday evening. It was perhaps understandable, therefore, that it took a few moments for the reality of the situation to penetrate the minds of those present.

When it did, the three galvanized into action were Father Reggie Tinsdale, Belinda Sue Morgan, and Dr. Rex de Castre—all three of whom leaped up from their seats in the nave and sprinted toward the altar and on up the three steps to the ambo.

Dr. de Castre, moving far faster than one might have expected his old legs could carry him, was actually the first to kneel at the side of the two forms and pull them over. Nor were Father Reggie and Belinda Sue much behind him.

They lent the doctor what assistance they could in separating the two victims and stretching them out on their backs. Miss Morgan took the vital signs of the boy, while the doctor did the same with the priest.

As he did so, Dr. de Castre yelled out, "Get an ambulance here and tell them to hurry. And tell 'em to have a stomach pump. And then call the poison control people and tell 'em to meet me at the hospital. Come on, people! Move! Anyone! Now!"

And a flurry of activity at the back of the church indicated that, in obedience, several people had already run out to dash across the cloister to the church office and the telephone.

That flurry at the back of the church perhaps can explain why, not a half minute later, another flurry occurred and no one paid any particular attention. At least, that is, until a third of the way up the aisle an absolutely frantic-looking Millicent Cantrell, wife of the rector, came to a halt in the middle of the church and shrieked in a voice that went through everyone, "Murder! There's been murder! Somebody's tried to poison my husband!"

CHAPTER TWO

1 For rather a long time after her ladyship's tale had reached its distressing conclusion, the four women remained in silence, the only sounds were the musical tinkle of drops of water falling into the basin of the fountain, and the passage of the occasional automobile in the street. The frenzied activity of county officials seemed to have tapered off, though every window of the church and the church hall still blazed with light.

"So three people are dead?" asked Miss Worthing presently.

"Oh, dear," said Lady Fairgrief. "Did I say that?"

"Well, I would say you rather strongly implied it."

"So sorry, dear. No, no one's dead. As far as I know. At least not yet."

"What!" said Miss Shaw.

"Which does not, however"—her ladyship ignored the exclamation—"detract in the least from the fact that murder's been tried."

Miss Worthing sighed and scowled. "Well, yes. Of course, that's true."

For a moment she and her ancient relative eyed each other wordlessly.

"You are thinking the same thing I am, aren't you?" said Lady Fairgrief.

"Very likely," said Miss Worthing. "The possibility does rather spring out at one, doesn't it?"

"It does. And naturally, we shall have to check it out."

"Check out what? What possibility?" asked Miss Shaw.

"What are you getting up to now?" demanded Maude.

Before either Miss Worthing or her aunt could reply, however, a voice called from behind them, "Lady Fairgrief? Are you in there?"

All four women turned to look toward the west cloister. A tall thin man dressed in faultlessly tailored black clericals, his sleek graying hair combed back from a high forehead, stood peering into the gloom.

"It's Ren d'Arcy," said Lady Fairgrief. "The bishop must be here. Yes, Renny"—she raised her voice—"I'm here."

The man tripped gracefully down the steps into the garth and then, his eyes still dazzled from the lights in the cloister, came forward with a rather more hesitant step.

"The bishop wants to see you— Oh! Is that Matilda Worthing there?"

"Yes, it is," said Miss Worthing. "Hello, Ren."

"Oh, but this is wonderful," said the man. "He wants to see you, too."

Miss Worthing nodded. "Very well," she said tranquilly. "So why don't you just tell him where we are. I know," Miss Worthing explained with a little chuckle at the man's slightly scandalized expression, "one does not usually summon a bishop like that. But that's not really what I'm doing. This place is positively crawling with people . . ."

"I know," murmured the priest.

". . . and I should think we could talk rather more privately out here."

"I see your point," Father d'Arcy conceded. "Okay, I'll tell him."

"Where is he at the moment?" asked Miss Worthing.

"With Father Reggie. The sheriff and the district attorney, are there, too."

"Okay. Then wait till he's through with them, would you?"

"That isn't necessary. They knew you were coming."

Miss Worthing turned toward the man in surprise, but he had already tripped off.

What on earth was that supposed to mean? she wondered. Oh, well, no doubt in due season she'd learn.

"Martha," she turned back to the others and instructed briskly, "I think it would be best if you could try to—well, find out what you can."

"Such as?"

"Like what people are saying. If anyone has any thoughts about this." She frowned. "No matter how wild it may sound. Find out if anyone else noticed Father Hughie flinching away from the chalice, for example. If he did. Find out what you can about the condition of the victims. Who was the altar boy? You know. Anything."

"Gotcha. Lady Fairgrief?"

"Yes, Martha?"

"Where are they keeping everyone? Do you know?"

"Yes, indeed. In the gymnasium. I suggested it."

"Why the gym?" asked Miss Worthing. "Why not the church hall? It would be far more comfortable."

"No doubt," replied her ladyship. "But if there's been poisoning going on, I didn't think it would be so wise to have a hundred miserable souls mucking about the kitchen."

"Good point."

"Thank you. Father Reggie had Sloan's deliver sandwiches and things to try to keep their spirits up somewhat."

"Very good. Okay, Martha?"

"Right."

Miss Shaw departed.

"And now, Maude," said her ladyship, "do you think you could fetch us up a cup of tea from the gymnasium? I could rather use one."

"None for me, Maude, thank you," said Miss Worthing hastily.

"I'll see what I can do, my lady, but if you want my opinion, you'd be a lot better off at home in your own bed. All this excitement and now stimulants late at night . . ."

"Maude?"

"Yes, my lady?"

"Tea."

"Yes, my lady."

When they were alone, Miss Worthing sighed. "Leo Cantrell definitely was supposed to preach this weekend, wasn't he?"

"Oh, yes."

"So we are assuming that Father Hughie took the six-fifteen Mass at the last minute . . ."

". . . and got what was intended for Leo Cantrell."

Miss Worthing frowned. "Well, yes. That certainly does seem to make the most sense. But there's a problem. If Leo was poisoned—Where was he? In his study?"

Lady Fairgrief shrugged. "I don't know. I would assume so. If for no other reason than where else would he be if he wasn't at Mass?"

"Do you have any idea how it was done, incidentally?"

"How what was done?"

This time Miss Worthing shrugged.

"I don't know! Either one?"

"Either one what?"

"Attempts at murdering Leo?"

"Of course I don't. But if I'm reading you correctly, you're worried about the fact that two different attempts were made on Leo."

Miss Worthing nodded.

"It's hardly a problem," said her ladyship. "Obviously, whoever poisoned the wine found out Leo wasn't going to say the Mass and simply took alternative measures."

"Rather cruel to leave it for Father Hughie."

"What was he—or she—going to do? Trip into the sacristy and say, 'Oh, dear me, you mustn't use *that* wine; that's been specially fixed up to kill Dr. Cantrell.'"

Miss Worthing sighed and stood up and began to pace back and forth. "Ruthless."

"Oh, quite!"

Miss Worthing stopped and looked at her aunt. "I don't know."

Lady Fairgrief chuckled. "Anything, right?"

"Anything," repeated Miss Worthing with a rueful laugh. "And I'm hot. And I'm tired. I have no data at all and haven't the foggiest notion about where to begin."

"Ah, yes!" a rich masculine voice spoke, causing both women to start. "But I have absolute faith that somehow you'll manage it admirably."

2 Miss Worthing and her aunt looked up to see striding toward them the Right Reverend Charles Winston Fisher, S.T.D., Bishop of Sacramento and North Central California.

At first glance the bishop seemed rather a youngish man for such a responsibility, until, that is, one looked a bit closer and saw that, though a youthful man, he was by no means young. Blessed with a full head of dark gray hair conventionally cut, his round and rather chubby face had something about it of a little boy—and one with more than a bit of the imp in him, perpetually on the lookout with those obsidian pebble eyes for what mischief he might get into next. And, in fact, it was probably that impish sense of humor that kept the man sane in his less than enviable job as father in God to an enormous diocese filled with a most bewildering diversity of people.

And yet anyone who had ever had occasion to see Bishop Fisher in action knew very well that when need be, he could deal intelligently, competently, compassionately, and incisively with whatever required his attention. He had risen within the hierarchy effortlessly as a bubble of oxygen rises in clear water, graced with a bluff manner and administrative genius. And part of that genius was an absolute belief in what he styled "holy laziness" (his own lighthearted translation of that *sacrum otium* the spiritual writers tell us is so useful), a concomitant of which was his strongly held conviction that the best rule was minimum rule. Arising logically from those principles was a cheerful willingness to turn over a job to whatever expert was on hand who could best get that job done.

"Hello, Bishop," said Miss Worthing, and immediately asked, "Am I to gather, then, that you want us—Aunt Eulalia, Martha, and me—involved in this?"

The bishop chuckled. "Why, Matilda! You don't sound very happy about it. I would have thought you'd be simply itching to get in there and find out Who Done It."

His response did nothing for Miss Worthing's already questionable hold on her patience.

She confronted her bishop and spoke very plainly, chin out and clenched fists akimbo. "Now see here, Dr. Fisher! There's nothing in the least funny about this. Besides, I can't see what in the name of all that is holy you want us to do."

"Oh, now really, Matilda!" remonstrated the bishop. "Of course, there's nothing funny about the situation. But I would very much appreciate it if you don't lose your equilibrium like everyone else seems to be doing. I need you, and what I need you for I think should be obvious."

"But, Bishop!" began Miss Worthing, only to be interrupted by an unutterably malignant chuckle emanating from her ladyship.

"Do calm yourselves, children!" Lady Fairgrief then instructed with Olympian disdain. "Matilda," she admonished, "get a hold of yourself. Bishop, sit down," she gestured to the ledge of the fountain. "The situation here is unpleasant enough without the two of you getting into it."

"Quite so," said Miss Worthing irritably. "Nevertheless, I still don't know what you think I could do."

"You do keep saying that, Matilda," observed her ladyship.

"Perhaps," said the bishop, "I can explain."

"Yes?"

"Father Reggie told me, when he first got hold of me, that your aunt was here and that she had already called you. And so, knowing it was going to take me some time to get here and certain that Father Reggie was going to be very busy, as he has been, I told him that I was naming Eulalia here and you and Martha, when you got here, as my personal representatives until I could get here."

"But why!"

The bishop and Lady Fairgrief exchanged a puzzled glance. Seeing which, Miss Worthing took a big breath and exhaled it with a prayer for patience.

"The police are already here," she explained carefully. "They will have—probably already have had—experts, scientists and such, and investigative officers, probably several of them, on the job. I've worked with them before."

"When they were wrong," said the bishop.

"But only because they didn't have all the data."

"A lack they did nothing to amend."

"What are you talking about?" asked Lady Fairgrief.

"A case I had several years ago," said Miss Worthing. "Before you came back to Jolliston."

"Was that the time you got shot?" asked her ladyship.

"It was," said Dr. Fisher. "But never mind that now. One can only hope such won't enter into this case . . ."

"One can only hope," murmured Miss Worthing.

". . . but you have an obligation here. As do I."

And a sudden note of sobriety sounded in the bishop's voice, to which Miss Worthing's only response was a kind of noncommittal grunt.

"I am hoping," said the bishop, "that this will be an open-and-shut case."

"Who wouldn't?" said Miss Worthing. "On the other hand, you don't sound at all sanguine."

Even in the gloom the bishop's expression could be seen. "I am, of course, as much in the dark as anyone else. But in spite of what people may say about me, I do know what's been happening in this parish over the last few years."

"Those were just petty squabbles," protested Miss Worthing.

Lady Fairgrief snorted. "Some of them weren't so petty, in my opinion."

"Nor in mine," said the bishop.

"Enough for murder?"

This time the bishop took a moment before replying. Several times it seemed he was on the verge of speaking and then thought better of it. Finally he sighed: "Yes. Yes, I do, God help me. I can think of three things that might have generated sufficient depth of feeling to reach such a point."

Neither Miss Worthing nor Lady Fairgrief said anything.

"Nor are they," continued his lordship, "problems with which you—as responsible members of this parish—are unaware."

The two women exchanged a glance.

"I can think of one that might qualify," said Lady Fairgrief. "That is if it wasn't just a lunatic lark."

"Oh?" said Miss Worthing. "What was that?"

"That witchcraft business. Last winter."

"Yes," agreed the bishop evenly. "That was one of the things I was thinking of."

"Ye-e-ss," conceded Miss Worthing carefully. "That business never was cleared up satisfactorily."

"Matilda," said the bishop gently, "it was never cleared up at all."

"But, you'll pardon me, it seems . . ."

"What? Unlikely? As unlikely as trying to murder a priest as he says Mass?"

"Seems to me"—Lady Fairgrief put her oar in—"precisely the kind of thing such people might try."

"Oh, very well," said Miss Worthing. "Let's pass on that one for a minute. What else? You did say *three* things."

"Yes, I did," said the bishop, "although the second is perhaps, *perhaps*, a bit more intangible."

"What's that?"

"The ongoing political situation in this parish."

"Dr. Fisher!"

"No, hear me out. I know that ordinarily we like to think that such things are inexpressibly petty . . ."

"And so they are," said Miss Worthing stoutly.

". . . but I was listening to you two talking for a moment before I made my presence known."

"Yes?"

"And don't you think it's a little strange—I certainly do—that neither you nor your aunt seem to find it all that surprising that, first of all, someone might want to kill Leo Cantrell and, secondly, want to do it so badly that, being thwarted at the first go, he/she/it would try it again as soon as possible?"

"Bless my soul!" exclaimed Lady Fairgrief. "I didn't even think about that."

"No," said Miss Worthing thoughtfully, "I didn't either. Nevertheless"—she rallied—"just supposing the sordid political ructions of the Church of All Saints were the *reason* for this mess, the *reason* these crimes were committed, can't you see that that means that, probably before we can even begin to make any sense out of whatever *physical* evidence there might be, we're going to have to figure out the *nexus*, the reason why *now*! Why, at this particular juncture does it all eventuate in murder?"

"Of course. And so there was," said Dr. Fisher. "Which brings me to the third reason I can believe there's murder being done at All Saints. I spoke, albeit briefly, with Father Reggie, and he gave it as his opinion that in all likelihood all of this had to do with the play."

3 After rather a long moment of—at least on Miss
   Worthing's part—somewhat bemused silence, she
said, "The play, Bishop?"

While, at the same time, Lady Fairgrief said, "The *play!*"

The bishop sighed.

"I know. It sounds absurd. But Reggie is convinced it's
the case. Then, too . . ."

"Yes?" prompted Miss Worthing after his lordship's voice
had trailed off.

"There's no reason not to tell you. Last night, late, Leo
Cantrell called to tell me he had canceled the play and dis-
banded the company."

"Did he?" asked Miss Worthing. "By what authority?"

"His own. As rector."

"Can he do that?" asked Lady Fairgrief.

"Probably not. Although a great deal will depend on the
church's corporate bylaws."

"And?" Again Miss Worthing prompted.

"I don't know anything more. I haven't had time to do
much more than learn the bare facts. It was while I was
getting those that Father Reggie expressed his opinion that
the play was at the root of all this."

"That's even less to go on than the witchcraft business."

"It is and it isn't. At least we know who was involved with
the play," said the bishop, and then added cheerily: "So tell
me. How do we remedy the situation, Matilda?"

"Yes, indeed, Matilda," said Lady Fairgrief. "Tell us what
to do."

"Okay, folks," said Miss Worthing, rather grimly. "It is
definitely time to get cracking. First of all, you, Aunt Eulalia."

"Yes?" said Lady Fairgrief eagerly.

"What I think you should do is have Maude—when she
gets back—take you down to the gym and give Martha a
hand in checking around."

"Oh!" said her ladyship, the eagerness skimmed clear off her voice.

"Something wrong?"

"The gymnasium smells of chlorine and sweating adolescents. That's precisely why I chose to wait for the bishop and you out here."

"Nevertheless, it is where they are keeping all the witnesses to this—happening. And while no doubt Martha will be busy, you're even better at ferreting out, shall we say, odd things."

"So kind of you to say so."

At that very moment Maude emerged into the light of the west colonnade, a steaming Styrofoam cup in hand, and peering into the garth called. "My lady? Are you still there?"

"Yes, Maude."

Lady Fairgrief received the tea gratefully and issued the order to be taken to the gym.

Maude, it appeared, was seriously prepared to object to this.

"Please, Maude," said Miss Worthing. "It shouldn't be for much longer and—well, we do need my aunt's—talents."

Lady Fairgrief nodded regally, which rather unexpectedly prompted a slow, ever-so-sly look to creep across Maude's broad countenance.

"D'you mean the way she snoops so well?"

Her ladyship glared.

"Maude, you will propel me to the gymnasium at once!"

"Oh, well. As you wish, my lady," said Maude obediently, and, still chortling massively to herself, she hauled the chair up into the cloister and pushed it off.

"And me, Matilda?" asked the bishop.

"You and I are going to have a little talk with Father Reggie."

"Yes," agreed the bishop dryly. "They will be waiting for us."

"They?"

"Oh, yes. Father Reggie is upstairs with the sheriff and the D.A."

"Ren d'Arcy did say something about that. They're *waiting*?"

The bishop nodded. "For you."

"For me!"

"I told you. You and your aunt are my official representatives in this matter."

"And they agreed?"

"Oh, yes."

"Why?"

"As to that, I'm not altogether sure. It might be because they're as much at sea as we are."

"Humph! Even if they are stumped—which would hardly be unprecedented—they'd never welcome me in a zillion years."

"Nevertheless, Matilda . . ." said the bishop with a smile.

"Okay, okay. I'll believe it when I see it. Besides, if they are going to cooperate, far be it from me to complain. But there is something I think we need you to do."

"And what might that be?"

"For a while, at least, you have to be the one to take charge here."

"I?"

"Yes. Not only do you have the authority, but you know so much more than I do."

"Matilda, you know as much as I do. You're an active member of this parish and—"

"I am," interrupted Miss Worthing, "but that's nonsense. I know and you know that there are many, many things in any parish that few or no lay people are ever going to be privy to, no matter how active they might be. Besides, lately," she added wryly, "I haven't been active at all."

"Oh, very well," said Dr. Fisher after a moment. "I do see your point."

"Okay, then let's get to it."

4 A short time later, Miss Worthing and the bishop paused on a landing of the stairs to get their breath. "I don't know how you people in the Valley stand this kind of weather," observed the bishop.

"We don't," said Miss Worthing. "It's unusual for us, too." She turned to begin climbing again.

"Matilda."

"Yes, Bishop."

"I've been thinking. Until we shed a little light on what's been going on around here, I want you to keep your wits about you."

"Good heavens, Dr. Fisher, what a very murky order!"

"Nevertheless, I mean it. Remember what you said— about finding the nexus before we'll be able to make any sense of whatever evidence might be uncovered."

"Yes."

"Well, that certainly is not the way that either our esteemed district attorney or the sheriff is given to thinking."

"I know."

"And furthermore, in spite of all my efforts to the contrary, this mess is bound to wind up all over the papers and TV. And that means there's going to be a lot of pressure on to find *someone*—even, I fear, anyone—to take the blame. Now, I wouldn't like to think that Sam and George are going to be too blatant about going for the most expedient solution, but . . ."

He left it there.

In reply Miss Worthing nodded grimly and began once more to climb the stairs to the second floor of the church hall.

The upper floors of the parish hall had once upon a time been the quite palatial residence of the rector. In the fifties, however, it was finally acknowledged that such a vast white elephant was impossible to a servantless generation. Since then each priest of the Church of All Saints had been provided with a nice, modern, suburban villa as a perquisite of his job, and the second floor had been dedicated to clergy offices, the parish library, and the choir rooms and office. The third floor had similarly been given over to storage of all those ecclesiastical oddments that no church is without and that are never, ever thrown away—broken furniture, discarded liturgical books, worn-out vestments, even (as Father Reggie discovered one day lurking in a darksome corner) an unnerving "Icon of God" of uncertain provenance.

Finally, on the roof, in the southeast corner thereof, was the tiny apartment of the resident caretaker.

Standing rigidly at attention outside the door of the parish counsel room, her eyes carefully fixed on the opposite wall, was a deputy sheriff.

"They have a guard posted?" Miss Worthing whispered to the bishop.

"Apparently. Most interesting. They certainly didn't have one when I left to go find you. Excuse me," said the bishop aloud to the deputy. "Father Reggie *is* in there, isn't he?"

"Yes, sir."

The bishop made to open the door. At once, the young deputy raucously cleared her throat and put a hand out toward the doorknob.

"What's this?" said the bishop.

"Sorry but the sheriff said no one was to go in."

"Nonsense!" said the bishop, reaching once more for the doorknob."

"Wait a minute, Bishop," said Miss Worthing. "Teresa?"

"Yes, ma'am?"

"Does that mean that George and Sam aren't in there?"

"Yes, ma'am. They said they'd be back in a while but—"

"But Father Reggie *is* in there?"

"Yes, ma'am."

"Well, Dr. Fisher and I do need—rather badly—to talk to him."

"Sam said . . ." the young woman began, and then flushed slightly.

"Sam said he wanted to be here when we talked to Father Reggie. Right?"

The deputy nodded.

"That's nonsense," said the bishop.

"Indeed it is," agreed Miss Worthing.

"Maybe so, ma'am, but—"

She was interrupted as the door suddenly opened and the round and—at the moment—white, wan, and infinitely weary face of Father Reggie peered out from within.

Under normal circumstances the Reverend Mr. Reginald Tinsdale was a fairly good-looking man, even though first youth had flown and his straight, brown hair was thinning like the tonsure of a medieval Benedictine. As though in compensation, he sported large and, somewhat untidy, bandit's mustaches. Any raffish effect, however, was completely spoiled by the large horn-rimmed spectacles that covered his rather soft brown eyes.

He was not a tall man, only five six or so, and was in the unfortunate position of being a sedentary bachelor who enjoyed his own cooking. And his beer. He accounted it, therefore, one of the mercies of life that, most of the time, he was required to wear a cassock, while for those times when a cassock was inappropriate, he had dozens of large sweaters his devoted mother, back in Boston, indefatigably knitted for him.

This evening, of course, with its searing heat and even more searing events and emotions, cassock or sweater had been out of the question, and he looked like a pudgy, superannuated college student or an off-duty waiter in a pair of black clerical trousers and a white dress shirt open at the collar.

Father Reggie, in the opinion of many, had been a bachelor far too long. He had only recently passed his fortieth birthday, but he had already, it seemed, settled into determined middle age.

He had been one of the foremost scholars of his year and had, furthermore, passed through the seminary in record time. He refused, however, to countenance being addressed as Dr. Tinsdale—perhaps because he was not unaware that there was a good deal about him of the finicking and old-maidish don.

Fortunately, the latter tendency was more than adequately offset by his possessing one of the more mordant senses of humor in Christendom and a gift for truly trenchant observation on the whole of the human comedy.

At the moment, however, he was not laughing.

"I was just wondering if I could go down the hall for a minute," he said rather plaintively.

This time the poor deputy's confusion and embarrassment were plain to behold.

"Oh, of course he can, Teresa," said Miss Worthing with a twinkle. "You can escort him as far as the door while Dr. Fisher and I have a seat in there and wait for Sam and George."

"That was rather neatly done, Matilda," said the bishop once they were inside the chamber. "And what was all that about?"

"Suspicions, Bishop. Suspicions."

"Of Father Reggie?"

"Of everyone."

"But . . ."

"It's perfectly natural, Bishop, given the system. It may not be right, but it's what we have to live with—have had to ever since there were policemen."

"What do you mean?"

"Everyone is guilty of everything until proved innocent."

"In clean contravention of the Constitution?"

"Bishop, given the fudging of the separation of church and state you're getting away with here, I don't think . . ."

"Never mind that. *This* is intolerable."

"Perhaps it is. But until we're prepared to pay the cops a bit better, we're going to have to live with that kind of primitive mentality."

"Fabulous forensics and dolts on the force?"

"That's about the size of it."

"Disgraceful."

Out in the hall, through the open door, they heard Father Reggie's voice: "Well, then, come in and wait for them with us. But I am going to talk to my bishop."

And apparently without waiting for an answer, Father Reggie bustled into the room, the deputy following after, looking abashed but holding her tongue.

"Where *are* Sam and George?" asked Miss Worthing.

Father Reggie began to speak even before he was seated. He actually looked a little better, as though the sight of the bishop in tandem with Miss Worthing had somehow refreshed his spirit.

"They said they couldn't wait for you two and that they both had things to attend to. Which, I have to admit, was no surprise. Rather a lot of things to do, I should think."

"I'm sure," said Miss Worthing. "Did they say they'd be back?"

"Oh, they'll be back. They aren't through with me, not by a long shot."

"No, and neither are we."

"Oh? Oh, well, I guess I was expecting that."

"Oh, come now, Reggie," said the bishop. "You must have known we'd be getting into this."

"I know. At least knowing you two, I know."

"Very well, then. Father Reggie, the play."

"Yes, ma'am. As I told Dr. Fisher, I'm sure that the play lies at the root of this madness."

"You do keep saying that," observed the bishop, who sat back and took a deep breath. "D'you know, I keep hearing all this talk about the play. But I really don't know all that much about it. How 'bout you?" he asked Miss Worthing.

"Other than that it was poor Father Hughie's idea to get up a theater company and that our resident caretaker wrote the thing, not much. I do remember that there were definitely what you would call mixed feelings about the whole project when the vote came up at the annual parish meeting whether or not to vote start-up funds for it."

"Mixed feelings, indeed," said Father Reggie. "I've never seen such a disgraceful exhibition of bad manners in my life."

"Ah, me," said the bishop. "Doesn't that sound just like the Church of All Saints."

"Never mind, Bishop," admonished Miss Worthing. "Father Reggie! The play!"

CHAPTER THREE

1 "First of all," began Father Reggie, "the play is called
Death of a Heretic."

"Yes, I know," said the bishop, adding dryly, "and I still
think it's rather a peculiar title."

"Do you think so?" said Father Reggie, surprised. "That's
funny. It's nothing more than just a description of what it's
about."

The play was, in essence, a political statement about the
nature and state of the Church. And it achieved its purpose
by telling the story, somewhat fictionalized and very definitely romanticized, of the last days on earth of that dark and
difficult figure, Gottschalk of Orbaix, the ninth-century here-
siarch who troubled the counsels of heaven and, rather more
importantly, the great by preaching throughout France and
Italy the doctrine of double predestination—which is to say,
predestination not only to heaven but to hell.

All this really means is that if, at the beginning of His
creation, Almighty God ordained that when your earthly
time came you would be saved, saved you would be regardless of whatever you might have done in life. Con-
versely, according to this doctrine (and it was this that
caused Holy Mother Church to ring for brandy), if He or-

dained that you would be damned, damned, reprobate, and unregenerate you would be and there were no means of mercy in heaven or on earth to succor you.

Half a millennium later, John Calvin, John Knox, Ulrich Zwingli, and their cronies would preach the very same unlovely doctrine and establish themselves as ruling theocrats in Geneva, Amsterdam, Edinburgh, and other grim fortresses across northwestern Europe. For it was there, in the towns, with their exemptions from feudal duties, that an emergent and gorgeously self-satisfied bourgeoisie found such a dogma to be appealing, convinced, as they were, that those upon whom they preyed were born to it and that their own commercial success on earth simply had to be an indication of prominent status in the Kingdom of Heaven. . . .

In the ninth century, when there was no bourgeoisie to speak of and what middle class there was survived by groveling sycophancy to the military aristocracy, Holy Church was utterly unprepared to let things get along so far. Straightaway, She summoned John Scotus Erigena, that brilliant if somewhat erratic theologian, urgently to refute Gottschalk and his horrible doctrine, which he did most successfully, in a highly publicized and public debate.

Whereupon, as things so often did in those uncouth times, things got rather Gothic. In fact, they got downright ugly.

The Church, resolving that this man "obstinate and damned" (*"Gothescalcus pertinacissimus damnatus est"*) must never be allowed to disseminate his appalling doctrine again, forced him, after torture, to burn his own manuscript *manibus suis*—with his own hands. And after that, as if it were not enough, he was taken into close custody and confinement and held for the rest of his life until he died, unrepentant, unshriven, and excommunicate in an obscure monastery in fee to Hincmar, archbishop of the royal see of Rheims.

Not a very pretty story, nor, at first blush, the likeliest material for a play. Nevertheless, it was the considered opinion of everyone involved in the production that the playwright had constructed his opus, on the whole, rather well, and that the audience was almost certain to find it enthralling, edifying, and—perhaps most surprisingly of all—entertaining.

2 When Father Reggie had finished his little exposition, for rather a moment Miss Worthing could find little to do but boggle at the man.

"And you're telling us that this—this academic exercise is at the root of our troubles?"

"It is not just an academic exercise," said Father Reggie rather testily. "It's a damned good play. And I never meant to imply that it lies at the 'root' of this mess. But let me tell you . . ."

"Yes?"

". . . you have no idea how high feelings are running in the parish."

"Because of Dr. Cantrell's canceling—or trying to cancel—the play?"

"Yes! I'm telling you—I know that's the reason someone tried to kill him today. Twice."

"I'm afraid we're going to have to look at this very, very carefully, Reggie," said the bishop soberly.

And all four of the people in the room were uncomfortably surprised to hear the level, urbane voice of the district attorney say almost jovially, "I'll say we will. I only hope we're invited to the party. Hello, everyone. Bishop. Miss Worthing."

"George. Sam." Miss Worthing nodded to the district attorney and the sheriff, who was quietly but forcefully dressing down his red-faced deputy. "Go easy on her, Sam. We just wanted to find out where you were in all this."

"Out!" said Sam to the deputy. "And close the door behind you."

George Lorris, the district attorney had already sauntered around the table to take a seat on the long side opposite the bishop and Miss Worthing, who sat with their backs to the door. Father Reggie sat in isolation at the foot of the table, and presently Sam Marshall, the sheriff of Jolliston County, stalked around the table and sat next to Lorris. Sam was one of those big-bodied, bearish individuals of enormous physical strength and presence. Over time, however, he seemed to have gone completely to pot, with a gigantic beer belly and pale eyes peering out from rolls of fat, with smooth-shaven dewlaps sagging under his chin. But his khaki uniforms were always crisply starched and creased, and he was as strong as ever and as quick on his feet. He was, moreover, a very good man, and if his education had been less than first-rate and if he still spoke with a touch of the Cracker in his speech, his mind was shrewd and, if not especially analytical, remarkably good at cutting through irrelevancy. He had been reelected time and again for more than twenty years, and if there were occasional grumbles, they had never been enough to unseat him.

George Lorris, too, had been reelected many times over. At practically every election his wife would harass him about returning to private practice, but always their friends and neighbors would go to work on her and, presently, George would be running again. Of medium height, sandy coloring, conventional good looks, he appeared in no way a formidable individual—which for a prosecuting attorney can be useful; defense attorneys tended to discount him, which was invariably a mistake. He was also far more the politician than was Sam, which, combined with his legal training, sometimes hampered him with a concomitant lack of any genuine moral insight. But his intelligence was almost as sharp as Sam's and was, furthermore, far more analytical—which meant that, between the two of them, they ordinarily made quite a good investigative team.

"So did you find out what we had?" inquired George affably.

"If we did, I'd have to say, not much," ventured Miss Worthing.

"You're so right," he commented and looked at Father Reggie. "What have you been telling them?"

"Just what I've been telling you."

"About the play?"

Father Reggie nodded.

"Do tell me, Dr. Fisher," said George, "what do you think?"

"I?" asked the bishop. "Why, we—Matilda and I—haven't formed an opinion yet."

"Why not?" demanded Sam. "If what Father Reggie here's been telling us is true, seems your parishioners here got pretty het up over this here play."

"That's as may be," said the bishop coolly. "There are, however, other things that, perhaps, we should acknowledge and consider lest we risk getting too far ahead of ourselves."

Both Sam and the district attorney looked irritated but interested at this announcement. Miss Worthing, thoughtfully taking notes, felt a surge of admiration for the bishop: This was taking charge very effectively indeed.

Father Reggie, meanwhile, was regarding his superior with a faintly puzzled expression.

"Other things, Bishop?"

"What other things?" asked Sam.

For a moment his lordship made no reply as he weighed his words. Then, very gently, he said: "I make no claims to special knowledge. But I cannot help but feel that, at the moment, we're leaving something out of the equation—such as it is."

"What is it?" insisted the D.A.

"Black magic."

This time the silence seemed to stretch on forever. Father Reggie frankly gaped at the bishop, while Sam screwed up his face as though he hadn't heard properly. The D.A. wore an expression of cool skepticism bordering on disdain.

"Black magic, Dr. Fisher?" he said.

The bishop waved a hand impatiently. "Oh, black magic, demonolatry, witchcraft—call it what you will."

"Here?" said the sheriff. "In Jolliston?"

Instead of answering Sam's question, the bishop looked to Father Reggie.

"Would you care to respond, Father?"

But that good clerk was still agog.

"My lord," he said softly, and no one ever knew which of his superiors he was addressing, "I never thought of that."

"No," said the bishop. "I wondered if you had."

"I've been so wrapped up in the play."

"Just so."

"Are you trying to tell us," said Sam, "that you folks here at the All Saints have had problems with cultists?"

"It would be nice," said the bishop, "to think we are immune from such filth. But, alas, even here. Well, Father?"

"It was last winter," said Father Reggie. "When it was raining so hard. Do you remember?"

"How could anyone forget?" said Sam. "Had more cases of domestic violence in those two weeks than we usually have all year. Folks just bored out of their skulls keeping indoors and trying to stay dry."

"Some people weren't so bored," said Father Reggie.

3   In fact, the unrelenting rains may very well have been the reason for their incursion into the sacred precincts. February second, it had been—Candlemas, the great fire festival between the solstice and the equinox, and a day set apart thousands of years before the Roman legions marched north. Father Reggie knew very well that various groups, magniloquently styling themselves *wicca*—the old Anglo-Saxon word for the Wise and the word from which our "witch" derives—had readopted the ancient custom of fire and prayer on that night. And (it being, after all, a pluralist

society) he accepted it, even if privately considering it a twee outré.

But he also knew something else about the history of such things; that when the Inquisition—that foulest of institutions—tried to stamp out what was really nothing more than the preliterate shamanism of Western Europe, the old religion had merely gone underground where, demeaned, degraded, defeated, and despised, it had adopted an altogether unsavory overcast of Christian dress. And the innocent religion of meadows, growing things, fire festivals, and animism had been utterly perverted, and the Horned God, Robin Goodfellow, the deity of luck in the hunt to a populace that lived by the hunt, had been transmogrified into the Christian Devil—and Satanism was abroad in the land.

That week in February it had been Father Reggie's turn to preach, and late that Thursday night, alone at home, working on his sermon, he realized he had left a whole sheaf of notes in his office at the church. Wide-awake and impatient to finish, he had driven to the church, in spite of the blinding rain, and let himself in to fetch the notes.

Then, standing in the darkness of the upstairs corridor, there had come upon him a feeling of profound malaise, that all was not as it should be. Too experienced in the quiddities of human nature not to take cognizance of such "lights," he cast about mentally, as it were, for the reason for this disquiet.

And stepping out into the cloister, he had seen a light flicker briefly in the small window of the sacristy that opened onto the cloister.

There was someone in the church.

Cautiously, his mind racing, he let himself into the back of the nave by the cloister door, cursing both at the way the door creaked as well as at himself for being a bloody fool. A priest in the Bay Area had, not all that long before, done what he was doing now and had been found—in several pieces—the next day. And there, in the darkness in the vast overarching emptiness of space that was the nave, it was easy to imagine . . .

And then there was no more need to imagine. First had come the muffled sound of chanting in that stupid dog-Latin common among cultists and lawyers. After that, however, came a sound that was infinitely more horrible and that, in spite of all common sense, galvanized him to a ferocity of which he had not known himself capable: A dog whimpered and then, goaded by something, screamed. And Father Reggie went into action.

In a transport of sheer righteous anger, he did that for which he was later officially reprimanded. Dashing to the corner of the rood screen, against which it stood, he seized the bishop's staff and, hefting it in his hands, nodded appreciatively. The solid oaken staff with the gold head and silver shoe was eminently satisfactory and, without more ado, he charged into the sacristy.

Things got considerably more confused thereafter.

The small number of people there gathered scattered in a high and vocal panic, no doubt laboring under the illusion that Father Reggie was some wrathful demon their puling obscenities had conjured.

In any case, with the army of perverts well and truly routed, he was able to untie the dog. It was probably some homeless stray and, when no one came forward to claim it, it had become his own boon companion, though a more foolish animal it would be hard to imagine. Even there, at the very scene of its torture, as soon as he had soothed it and loosed its bonds, it had proceeded to lick his hand and then follow him about as he assessed the damage, telephoned the sheriff's department, and, finally, called the rector and the bishop for instructions.

And early the next day the parishioners of the Church of All Saints who happened to be about were astonished to see the bishop arrive and, assisted by his chaplain, the three resident priests, and a tiny congregation of members of the parish council, solemnly reconsecrate the church. . . .

4 "Wait a minute!" said Sam. "How come I never knew any of this? A break-in, all that stuff happening?"

Father Reggie turned to the sheriff and sternly said, "Well, it wasn't for lack of trying, you know."

"Whaddya mean?"

"We called at least a dozen times."

"And?"

"'Was anything of value taken?' No! 'Anyone get hurt?' No! 'Well, then, I'm sorry, there's not much we can do.'"

This time it was Sam's turn to be a mite embarrassed.

"Well, fact is, there isn't much . . ."

"You might have helped us find out who they were."

"You never found out?" said Sam.

"No," said Father Reggie. "And furthermore . . ."

"Excuse me, Father," said Lorris, interrupting. "You said you and the bishop here reconsecrated the church."

"Yes."

"Well, pardon me—and I don't mean to try to teach you your business—but was that strictly necessary?"

Father Reggie was not the only one to looked shocked.

"All I'm trying to say," Lorris explained, "is can you be sure this incident *was* that kind of thing and not"—he shrugged—"some kids fooling around?"

"But what difference . . ." the bishop began only to be overridden by Father Reggie.

"First of all, Mr. Lorris, I don't give a flying—hoot if they were kids, adults, or dotty seniors. That kind of thing is never just fooling around. And last time I looked, breaking and entering was still a crime."

"Hey, now calm down," said Lorris, embarrassed. "It's just . . ."

"What it's *just* is that you and too damned many other people like you think that kids and their high jinks—and in particular the bratlings of those rich folks you soak for campaign funds every four years . . ."

"Now, just . . ."

". . . and you all think that money and youth can excuse behavior that is nothing less than criminal, immoral, and in this case, downright blasphemous."

"Now see here . . ."

"And I don't give a damn if they were serious or not. There was a pentacle drawn on the floor with a circle inscribed within it, which was where the dog was tied up with a slash in his shoulder and a blood-stained athame . . ."

"A what?"

"A ritual dagger lying on the floor next to the dog. There were big, fat, black candles in the points of the pentacle and chalked around the circle—in Hebrew—was the Tetragrammaton. And with all *that*? Goddamn right we reconsecrated."

"You didn't tell all this to the sheriff's office, surely," said Lorris, clearly impressed.

"No. What would be the point?"

"Well, damn it all," Sam barked, "there is a point. Christ, Father, you said just now you knew about that priest down in Santa Clara County."

"Santa Clara is two hundred miles away and notorious for that kind of thing."

"Reggie!" said the bishop, calling him to order. "Sam happens to be right. There has been altogether too much of all that sort of thing happening all over Northern California in recent years. Good heavens, even I didn't know about—all those ritual objects. What did you do with them all?"

"I mopped the floors and threw the candles and the athame into the garbage and patched the dog up with the first aid kit till I could get him to a vet."

"Jeez, I wish you hadn't done all that," said Sam.

"Well, so do I," said Father Reggie. "Now. But how was I

supposed to know you people were interested in that kind of garbage if you go all hush-hush about it?"

"Okay," said Sam. "I guess you got a point there. So what happened after that?"

"Nothing. When it became clear no one was going to come and dust for prints, or anything"—Father Reggie shrugged—"by then the rain had been pouring into the sacristy all day and all night and all day again. So we just had it fixed and—forgot it."

"Well, perhaps not exactly forgot it," murmured the bishop.

While the others pursued this conversation, George Lorris had remained silent, his glance resting on Miss Worthing, who sat, looking at no one, doodling on her steno pad.

Presently, sensing that intense regard, she looked up.

"You don't buy it, George?"

"In what sense?" he countered. "Of course," he went on immediately, "I am aware of the almost subterranean growth of that kind of thing all over the country. As Sam indicated, any person involved in law enforcement has to be. Do I believe it?"

"I'm not sure that that's altogether relevant," said Miss Worthing.

"Of course, it isn't," said the bishop impatiently. "The point I'm simply trying to make is that we had this happen and now we have a priest attacked at the altar."

"Miss Worthing," said the D.A., "you're thinking out loud again."

"Thanks, George," she said with a small chuckle. "As for my answer: Maybe."

"Maybe what?"

"Maybe we should keep it in mind. It is a possibility."

"But what do you think?"

"I don't think anything. I'm remaining agnostic."

"Excellent procedural method," commented the bishop with a grin.

"Very well, then," conceded Lorris, "I suppose you are

right; it does have to be kept in mind. So what do you suggest we do now?"

"Oh, just a moment," said the bishop. "I'm not through yet."

"What?" Sam all but bellowed.

"Now, don't you get your dander up, Sam Marshall," said the bishop, still somewhat impatiently. "All I simply wish to point out is that so far no one has been willing to deal with the main problem in this church."

"That would lead to somebody bumping a priest off?" asked Sam.

"A rather more crudely expressed version of the very same question Matilda here asked me a little while ago," said the bishop austerely. "And my answer is still, unfortunately, yes. I refer, of course, to politics."

"Meaning?" asked the D.A.

"Neither of you are members of this church, are you? Well, then, neither of you is likely to know about the problems that have beset this parish for a long, long time. . . ."

"But I do!" said Father Reggie, the expression on his face suspiciously like one of anger. "And believe me, Dr. Fisher, if I weren't so aware of those damned political problems, I wouldn't be so damned certain that the whole business of the play will give us the answer we need."

For a moment after this outburst no one said anything. His lordship, however, looked decidedly annoyed and seemed about to speak sharply.

It was Miss Worthing who brought it all to a halt; things had gone quite far enough. "Bishop," she said, "stop. We have to start somewhere, and Father Reggie's hypothesis that it was the play strikes me as as good a place as any in which, at least, to start."

"Hear, hear," muttered Lorris, while Marshall allowed himself a rather more vulgar expression of agreement.

And the bishop sighed and asked, "So what do we do now?"

"Well, it's a delicate situation, now, isn't it?" said Lorris, and added carefully, "That's why we thought we'd leave it up to you."

And across the breadth of the table, Miss Worthing and Lorris exchanged a glance that rapidly turned into a knowing little smile on her face and a somewhat abashed expression on his.

"Sam and I already talked about this," he answered the bishop, though manfully his eyes never left Miss Worthing.

"And?" asked Dr. Fisher.

"Well, you see, Bishop, Sam and I are, of course, the official investigators in Jolliston. But—" He and Sam exchanged a quick look, following which in a burst of most unlawyerly candor Lorris pointed out, "We're both elected officials."

And at once Miss Worthing laughed aloud, saying, "I thought as much!" The bishop looked puzzled, and Father Reggie looked shocked.

"You obviously understand, Miss Worthing," said the bishop.

"I certainly do," said Miss Worthing with considerable spirit, and then glared censoriously across the table, "and a more cynical plan I've never heard of. I wondered why you two were being so bend-over-backward helpful to the bishop and me. However"—again she snorted, piqued by the paradoxical nature of the situation—"since your timidity comports with what the bishop wants, I'll go along with it."

"With what!" demanded the bishop.

"Father Reggie," said Miss Worthing, "do you have a list of the cast and crew of the play."

"Yes, I do."

Father Reggie handed it to the bishop, who in turn handed it to Miss Worthing, who read it and leaned with it in hand toward the bishop. "See here," she said, jabbing a finger at the list. "Look at these names: Robinson, Yates, Cartwright, Miller, Watanabe, Pirelli—some of the richest, most powerful families in Jolliston County."

This time it was the bishop's turn to look upon the legal officials with a knowing look. Somewhat disconcerted, but bold as brass, said officials merely returned the look levelly as Miss Worthing continued: "So, naturally, if I take on the investigation and manage, thereby, either to offend half the people in the Valley or fall flat on my face, these two will be off the hook."

"It's not only that, Miss Worthing," said Lorris.

"Oh?"

"No, of course not." There was a touch of dull rose in Lorris's cheeks as he continued. "Well, it isn't," he insisted yet again. "The fact is you've not only had some experience in these matters, but you also happen to be one of them."

Upon receipt of which syntactical curiosity, Miss Worthing could only look blankly at the man.

"Miss Worthing"—Sam came to the rescue—"what George means is that you know all those folks. Like he says, you're one of 'em. You're a member of the parish. Hell, you were even born here."

"All of which is true and all of which is irrelevant," said Miss Worthing. "Or would be, as I said, if it didn't work for what I want myself. Very well," she said. "Dr. Fisher here has appointed me his personal representative, and that fits into you two political animals' game plan. So one good turn deserves another. We're going to do this my way."

"Fine," said Lorris, "but which way is that?"

"Father Reggie," she addressed that long-suffering clerk, "of the folks involved in the play, can you name, oh, two, or three, let's say, whom you would consider to be the most observant and"—she shrugged—"the least likely actually to have committed murder to achieve his or her ends?"

Lorris and Sam frowned suspiciously, while Father Reggie looked considerably taken aback.

"That's a terribly unfair thing to ask," he protested.

"I know," said Miss Worthing evenly. "Nevertheless, I'm asking."

Father Reggie shook his head distractedly, sighed once or twice, and finally said: "I could answer better if I knew what you had in mind."

"It's very simple," said Miss Worthing. "We're going to get them up here and take them over, what?—the last week or so, and see what comes out in the wash."

"And if one of them was involved? Directly involved?" said Lorris.

"That's why we'll have 'em up here together. If one is lying, another will catch it. I would like a shorthand reporter, too. Maybe Martha won't mind."

"If you want a reporter, we'll get you a reporter, but I've never heard of a deposition *en banc* before," said Lorris.

"Well, you live and learn, don't you?" said Miss Worthing. "Even lawyers." She didn't even try to resist the dig.

Marshall chortled as the district attorney colored, and the bishop addressed his fellow priest. "Well, Reggie?"

The latter was chewing on a thumbnail. Eventually he broke off that activity and gestured openhanded. "Well, I think I know who would be best. But . . ."

"But you just can't swear that they weren't involved," suggested Miss Worthing.

Father Reggie nodded and muttered, "Even though I'd like to."

"But it's okay," said Miss Worthing gently. "I assure you there will be adequate safeguards."

"I guess I'll have to take your word for it, won't I?" said Father Reggie. He sighed again and ventured, "Okay, so how about Elspeth Robinson for one?"

"Excellent choice," agreed Miss Worthing. "Elspeth's an observing lass. Anyone else?"

After a moment of nail nibbling Father Reggie shook his head.

"The only other person I can come up with decisively is Belinda Sue Morgan."

"Ah, yes," said the bishop. "The learned Miss—soon to be—Dr. Morgan."

"Yes," said Father Reggie, "she's very bright," and then added as a complete non sequitur: "Actually, she and I are engaged to be married."

"Are you now?" said Miss Worthing. "Congratulations! How nice for you," she added, not missing for a second the regard of the other three men in the room refocusing on Father Reggie with a respect not untinged with envy—Jolliston was not, after all, so large a town that anyone as spectacular as the spectacular Miss Morgan could possibly go unremarked.

5 It was in that interval of awed silence greeting Father Reggie's announcement that a knock sounded on the door of the chamber.

"Come in," barked Marshall, frowning.

The door opened and a round, flushed face peered within.

"Whaddya you want!" growled Marshall.

"I know you said not to disturb you, Sheriff," said the face, "but we thought you ought to know."

"What?" said Marshall.

"They were able to save the kid and the old guy at the hospital."

And there wasn't a person in the room who, in spite of that good and welcome news, did not zero in immediately on the way in which that news had been communicated.

"And Father Hughie?" asked the bishop.

The deputy shook his head. "I'm sorry, Bishop; they tried. But he died a few minutes after getting to the hospital."

The bishop, Father Reggie, and Miss Worthing each blessed himself almost by reflex, as the bishop uttered a heartfelt, "And now, through the mercy of God, may the soul of our dear faithful departed Father Hugh Barnes rest in peace."

"Amen," said the others, with Lorris and Marshall a moment later.

And for a moment no one really knew what to say or do. For Miss Worthing—as for Lorris and Marshall—a sort of shifting of mental gears was taking place, recognizing that, to a great degree, when one is pursuing one who has attempted murder, it is qualitatively different from pursuing one who has actually done it.

Then, too, the bishop and Father Reggie, as well as Miss Worthing, were all having a broad spectrum of reactions, emotional and rational, to the fact of poor Father Hughie's death, and that death by, apparently, malicious intent. Even if, it appeared, malicious intent by inadvertence.

The bishop, on his part, was aware of the loss of a spiritual son. A less than perfect one, perhaps, but a son—a man he himself had ordained to the priesthood and set upon the path at the Church of All Saints.

Father Reggie was remembering a young, earnest, and not very bright colleague with whom he had been able, nevertheless, to put a great many of the things in motion that had gone so far to revivify the parish.

And Miss Worthing, in spite of her own pangs of personal grief—and for her, like so many others, Father Hughie had commanded an instinctual parental response—suddenly thought of a datum which, remarkably enough, had not yet been addressed.

"What killed him?" she asked of Lorris. "What was it?"

"Chlorine," said Lorris.

"Chlorine?"

"Near enough as makes no never mind. Yes, chlorine, fundamentally, It was that stuff they clean the pool with."

Miss Worthing digested this intelligence for a moment, clearly somewhat nonplussed by it. Then she scowled. "All right. I think I can understand how a priest at the altar might drink a chalice thus doctored. If you've ever inadvertently drunk a bit of wine that's gone off, you'll know what I mean. But once the chalice was actually consecrated at the Mass, the priest, in spite of the noxious smell and taste . . ." She waved a hand and left it unfinished. "But I understand Dr. Cantrell drank poisoned tea!"

Slowly, as though it pained him, Lorris nodded. "It wasn't pool chemical in Dr. Cantrell's tea."

"What was it?"

"Essentially arsenic. We think, preliminarily, that it might have been some kind of commercial ant powder."

Father Reggie's mouth gaped.

"Yes?" Lorris whipped out.

"Ant poison?"

"Father Reggie"—Miss Worthing also was on it like a shot—"there is something about ant poison?"

The priest nodded eagerly and began to speak.

"No! Please!" Miss Worthing cut him short. "We will wait till the others are with us."

Lorris made a disgusted sound, and Sam was actually angry.

"Don't do that, boys," said Miss Worthing minatorily. "I know what I'm doing."

"I sure hope so, Mattie," said the sheriff, in his frustration lapsing from the formality of the proceedings thus far. "We got us a murder one now. And you know and I know and so does everyone else in this room know that this whole mess is gonna hit the TV and newspapers any minute now. Specially now that Hughie Barnes is dead. So go ahead. Do your thing. But we gotta find us a murderer. Quick."

The bishop and Miss Worthing exchanged a glance, their previous conversation about expedience still fresh in their minds.

As though in response to that look, Dr. Fisher pushed his chair back and stood up. "Very well, then, I will take your request for Mrs. Robinson and Miss Morgan to the gym. And leave you all to it. I am not as young as I was and must get some rest. Ren and I will take services in the morning," he said to Father Reggie. "You do what you must here." He sighed. "I guess I'll also have to see Fiona, too, poor wretch. May I also intercede for the others, those innocents stuck in the gym?"

"They may not be so innocent," said Sam.

"Indeed they may not," said Miss Worthing, and asked the lawmen, "Does anyone else know about the poisons, who got what, and the disparity between them?"

"No," replied Lorris. "We just got word a little while ago ourselves."

"Excellent," said Miss Worthing. "Please, Father Reggie, Bishop, all of you. Don't talk about it. Let's hold it for now. Okay?"

Everyone agreed, and the bishop repeated, "So what of the people in the gym? Are you going to keep them cooped up during the whole of your deposition *à trois?*"

Sam looked at Lorris, who shrugged.

"Let 'em go with the usual warning," suggested Lorris.

Sam nodded and stood up, and, followed out of the room by the sheriff, Dr. Fisher left. Father Reggie lay his head down on the table on crossed arms.

After a moment a thought occurred to Miss Worthing. She cast a quick glance at the top of Father Reggie's head, pulled her notebook toward her, opened it to a fresh page, and wrote on it: "George: The tea? Who made it? Was it poisoned in the pot? In the cup?"

She tore out the leaf, folded it, and passed it to Lorris with a speaking glance at the dozing priest.

Lorris read the note and, taking a gold pen from his breast pocket, scribbled a reply, refolded the paper, and handed it back.

From what we've gathered so far, Mrs. Cantrell put the tea into the pot. But Julian Richards, the resident caretaker, brewed it and took it up to the study where Mrs. Cantrell had already gone ahead. Mrs. C. said she was waiting for the kettle to boil when Richards came by and asked if he could help.

As to the poison, it wasn't in either the pot or the cup. The whole bag of Cantrell's personal tea supply was laced with the stuff.

Raising her eyes from this missive, Miss Worthing glanced at Lorris, who was watching her expressionlessly. She mimed a whistle and tucked the sheet back into her notebook. And she and the district attorney settled without further communication to await what was to come.

CHAPTER FOUR

1 Meanwhile, in the gymnasium, Lady Fairgrief had taken up a position in that circle in the geometric center of the floor in which innumerable basketball games had begun. It was merely the more effectively—explained her ladyship to Miss Shaw—to command a ready view of everyone present and thus be in a position to note anything suspicious anyone might get up to. Nevertheless, the sight had a certain incongruity that tickled Miss Shaw's funny bone as she herself went about her own assignment.

Which was proving rather more difficult than she had anticipated.

As the evening wore on, and the temperature climbed higher and higher, and the heat generated by a hundred or so human bodies continued to accumulate in the already stifling confines, almost no one seemed other than subdued, dispirited, nursing a soft drink or beer perhaps, or nibbling listlessly at a sandwich. Certainly they were in no mood to answer what seemed to them irrelevant questions.

Two deputies stood guard at the street door of the gym. At the opposite end of the gym, at the door that led down to the locker rooms and pool, stood another. The latter's zealous refusal, at first, to allow anyone downstairs had nearly led to wholesale revolt. Until, that is, Miss Shaw had, not unkindly, suggested that the deputy could easily take note of the names of those descending to the facilities and then tick their names off when they returned. Order was restored, and the grateful detainees responded less grudgingly to Miss Shaw's questions.

Fiona MacLaren, not too surprisingly, sat apart and remote from her fellow creatures. Attempts had been made to sit with her and offer whatever solace can be offered in such a delicate situation, however she had gently but firmly rebuffed all such attempts.

Miss Shaw herself had been rather busy. Drifting, in what seemed an aimless fashion, about the gym, she visited first one and then another group of persons or this or that isolated individual until she felt reasonably confident that she had spoken to all of them.

Elspeth, Mrs. Robinson, and Miss Belinda Sue Morgan had kept themselves occupied with the business of distributing the food the deli had delivered, both of them unaware of the impending summons to witness.

Also alone and isolate, both by preference and the common consent of those present, was Millie Cantrell. She had taken up a position in the bleachers about ten feet from and slightly above the refreshment table where Mrs. Robinson and Belinda Sue presided, and there she sat, her face controlled but shut, head bowed as, over and over again, she told the beads of a rather beautiful gold and garnet rosary.

The fact was, however, that her very presence in the gym had excited considerable, if discreet, comment: Why (it was asked) was she not at the hospital at her husband's bedside? On the other hand, to be sure, she and Elspeth Robinson were well known to have a deep and close personal friendship. Was it all that unlikely that Millie had come back to the Church of All Saints in order to be propped up a bit by that unfailing tower of strength?

Mrs. Cantrell—Millie, to just about everyone except her husband—was a fine-looking woman, though definitely mature. Her hair was still the color of burnished copper, though with streaks of white directly over her temples, and she wore it rather short and brushed back. Furthermore, she had been blessed, as redheads so frequently are, with skin of poured alabaster, which only around the eyes and mouth showed the effects of time and her particular mode of living. She was of only medium height and fine-boned. And though she had not lived in the south for forty-five years, her voice still retained a measure of that drawling softness that made it such a pleasure to listen to her.

She was Cantrell's second wife, as he was her second husband and the father of her three girls—all of them grown now and, if not exactly estranged from their father, distant both in mind and space. She herself was a woman of unsparing common sense, the result of twenty-five years of being assistant choir master and teaching some thirty to thirty-five piano students a week.

Now, Dr. Cantrell was not exactly underpaid for his services to the Church. Nevertheless, a simple calculation would inform anyone nosy enough to perform it that Millie's labors must have contributed handsomely to the exchequer of the Cantrell family. Yet, every year when Cantrell's "month" fell due, it was always, "Dr. Cantrell has decided to go to . . ." It might be the Holy Land, it might be the South Seas, it might be the Arctic, it might even be the Soviet Union—but it was always, "Dr. Cantrell has decided. . . ."

In spite of her really admirable loyalty to her husband, Mrs. Cantrell had remained remarkably free, over the years, of those party politics that are an inevitable concomitant of any human institution, even one of divine origin. She had good and close friends on both sides of most issues and was held in the deepest regard of all.

Her own interview with Miss Shaw had been terse in the extreme.

"No, I didn't 'notice' anything, Martha. How could I? I was tending my unhappy and distressed husband in his study."

"Oh, really? What was he distressed about?"

"Oh, come, Martha," said Mrs. Cantrell irritably. "Probably anyone here can tell you, and if you don't mind, I'd rather be alone."

Miss Shaw backed off and, seeing Clyde Cartwright, the president of the parish council, returning from a trip below, she scuttled over to him before he had a chance to rejoin the little circle of cronies with whom he had been sitting and playing an endless game of penny-ante poker.

"Clyde," she hailed him.

"What is it now, Martha!"

"Now, just have patience with me, Clyde. Millie just told me her husband was 'unhappy and distressed' this afternoon."

"Yes?"

"Was that why he canceled saying Mass?"

"I couldn't say for sure, but I would imagine so."

"This was before he was poisoned."

"Yes, Martha, that seems fairly obvious."

"Now, Clyde, don't be difficult. All I want to know is if you know what had so distressed him."

He goggled at her.

"Do you mean you don't know?"

"No. I don't, or I wouldn't be asking."

The man's cronies were calling more and more insistently for him to return so they could get on with their game.

"Look," he said to Miss Shaw, "there's any number of folks here who can tell you—graphically—what it was all about. But, basically, the parish council voted him down for trying to stop the play."

"So the play is going on? After all?"

"Yes, it is. Now, if you'll please pardon me, Martha."

And that was that. And pretty much all Miss Shaw was able to gather.

Indeed, other than her inventory, as it were, of the folks present and accounted for in the gymnasium, Miss Shaw's labors had been, for the most part, singularly unrewarding.

Furthermore, in looking back over such notes as she had been able to jot down, one would find that an appreciable amount of historical revisionism was already at work, as is so frequently the case with human beings. At least half those present had, by now, been ready to swear that they *knew* that *something* was wrong at *least* as early as the offertory of the Mass; of *course*, they had seen Father Hughie flinch aside at the mixing of the chalice; Father Hughie's aura had even been tinged with black—this last from a gentleman who published "New Age" volumes through a vanity press. . . .

Miss Shaw paused briefly in her peregrinations to wonder what she ought to do next: continue this pointless exercise, buttonhole someone about this parish council meeting (When had they met? They usually met on Monday nights, not Saturday afternoons), or rejoin Matilda, wherever she might be.

At that moment, the outer door of the gym opened.

Immediately the buzz of conversation within damped down a bit as the assembled craned to see what might be happening. Another deputy entered and began at once to talk to those two already on the door. Whereupon, seeing that it was just another lawman, most people returned to those activities with which they were wiling away their captivity.

Miss Shaw, however, noticed that, upon hearing whatever news had been brought, the eyebrows of one of the regular guards shot heavenward, while his comrade-in-arms uttered a brief and all but inaudible whistle.

And without even having been conscious of crossing the floor, Miss Shaw heard herself demand of the news bearer, "Okay, Darryl, what's going on?"

The three deputies looked mutely at one another.

"I don't know, Miss Shaw," one of them temporized.

"Nonsense, Fred. I'm here as a personal rep of the bishop. And if you don't believe me—"

The deputy addressed as Darryl nodded and interrupted, "Miss Worthing was up there with the sheriff and the D.A."

"Up where?" asked Miss Shaw.

"In the parish council room."

"Thank you. Well?"

"Father Hughie is dead, ma'am," said Darryl. "They just couldn't save him."

Instinctively, Miss Shaw blessed herself.

"And the others?" she asked.

"Oh, they're gonna be okay."

She sighed and turned back to regard the crowd, her mind in something of a whirl. Fortunately, most of those there in the gym seemed wholly uninterested in the little tableau that had just occurred at the outer doors. One, however, had not missed a thing: Lady Fairgrief was glaring malignantly at her and gesturing with sharp little hand flappings that Miss Shaw was to come over and inform her ladyship of developments. At once!

Obediently Miss Shaw ambled to the parked wheelchair and unburdened herself of the distressing news.

What she did not see—as did neither Lady Fairgrief nor Maude, both of them being much too interested in the latest intelligence to be paying any attention—was someone creeping up upon them.

For another person had seen that hasty, reflexive blessing of Miss Shaw's and had known upon the instant what it meant. She crept toward the group in the center of the gym. She was not sneaking. Not really. She was just uncertain of her reception. Her rubber-soled shoes did the rest, and Fiona MacLaren was thus almost upon them when she heard the words she had been waiting with dread to hear all evening: Father Hughie, her fiancé, was dead.

Her reaction was spontaneous, instantaneous, and very, very loud.

"Oh, God, no!" she wailed at the top of her lungs, setting the rafters to ring, startling the three women in conference nearly out of their skins—and announced for all the world to hear: "Hughie's dead!"

Maude, reacting with characteristic professional aplomb (and charity), went to Fiona. In that labor, also characteristically, Belinda Sue Morgan immediately joined. Together they helped the distraught woman to a seat.

Under the circumstances, Miss Shaw felt that a general announcement might very well be in order. "People!" she shrilled out in her best Sunday soprano. "Please, people, may I have your attention a moment?"

Avid for information, not only did they give her their complete attention, but came crowding around as well.

She gave out the bad news they had already heard and the good news they had not and then had to make it quite clear, upon the spate of questions that followed, that she had no further information to impart but would be happy to do so when she herself knew anything more.

Clucking among themselves like agitated chickens, everyone returned to his or her own pursuits, leaving Miss Shaw wishing she did have some clearer idea of what exactly was going on. . . . And felt a tugging on her skirt. She looked down to see her ladyship handing up to her a silver vinaigrette and gesturing toward the still faltering Fiona.

Miss Shaw could not help but gawp at so antiquated an implement. But, "Take it to Maude," commanded Lady Fairgrief, "for Fiona." And added, in reply to that look of astonishment, "I keep it with me out of habit more than anything else. But they are useful things to have around on occasion."

A few minutes later, under the influence of soothing words and ammonium carbonate, Fiona had calmed somewhat, and Miss Shaw felt she should return to Lady Fairgrief's side while the old woman's nurse was still thus occupied.

And was met with the urgent command: "Martha! Get down to the locker room. Now!"

"Whatever for?"

"Because a few moments ago Millie Cantrell ran out of here weeping like Rachel for all her children, closely pursued by Elspeth Robinson."

"So?"

"Martha," said her ladyship furiously, "she's just received word that her husband is going to be all right. And still she runs out of here weeping!"

Miss Shaw prepared to balk.

"Martha!" said her ladyship in her most menacing tone.

Miss Shaw went.

2   At virtually the same moment that Miss Shaw went out one door of the gymnasium—the door leading to the stairway down to the various facilities below the gymnasium and church hall—the bishop and Father d'Arcy came into the gym from without, followed by yet another deputy. The latter quickly gathered up Belinda Sue Morgan and called out, "Mrs. Robinson?"

Miss Shaw heard that call as she began to descend the stairs and heard the deputy guarding the door call back, "She's downstairs!"

Quickly Miss Shaw nipped back through the door and told the deputy there that she would notify Mrs. Robinson and that, furthermore, for the moment, no one else was to be allowed downstairs.

The latter caution she took having no wish to be seen or interrupted at this chore Lady Fairgrief had set her. In spite of the old woman's reasoning, reasoning by no means convincing (given Miss Shaw's sturdily held opinion that her ladyship was more than a little dotty), she was not altogether certain that she was not just being a thoroughgoing voyeur. To a person of Miss Shaw's generation and background, to penetrate into the rigid conventions of a public restroom with intent to spy was torture.

And yet, reluctantly, she had to admit that her antic ladyship was, nevertheless, possessed of a genuine intuitive gift for spotting anomalies, sometimes of the first import, in situations like the present one. The several cases on which Lady Fairgrief had already worked with Miss Worthing and herself had demonstrated that quite amply.

Like many large persons, Miss Shaw had the ability to move surprisingly lightly on her feet. And she did so now. For at the foot of the stairs, which descended into the corridor leading in the one direction to the pool and in the other to the locker rooms, she realized that something odd was definitely afoot.

Whatever time had done to Miss Shaw's charms, it had been kind to her senses. She had no need for glasses except for the closest work, and her hearing was quite as acute as ever it had been. On the other hand, she would have had to have been deaf not to hear the weeping coming from the women's locker room—or not to realize that the voice so audibly wailing was that of Millie Cantrell.

Of course it might mean nothing more than that, hearing of Father Hughie's death and immediately assuming that Dr. Cantrell, too, had died, the poor woman had not waited to hear the rest of the news before bolting from the crowded gymnasium in abandoned grief.

Perhaps.

But Miss Shaw had been for far too long a parishioner of the Church of All Saints and, as such, she had witnessed the interactions of Millie and her husband for several decades now. While Miss Shaw had no reason to doubt that—at least in some regard—Millie loved her husband, she rather doubted it was the kind of love about which heroic romances might be penned.

Nor, indeed, could it be ignored that Millie had returned

from the hospital *before* she was even certain (it seemed) of her husband's fate.

These speculative thoughts flickered through her head as she moved forward. And as she did so, the spasmodic utterances of Mrs. Cantrell and the murmured solaces of Mrs. Robinson began to become clearer.

"He'll never know now."

That seemed to be the endlessly repeated burden of Millie's plaint.

"Now he'll never know. And I wanted so much to tell him someday. I wanted so much to be able to tell him. But somehow the time never seemed right for it. It was never the appropriate time, and now there's no more time. I never had time to tell him!"

And Mrs. Robinson's voice murmured, "He'll know now, Millie. Whatever else we may believe, believe that now."

"I know. I do. Oh, God, that's all I can hope now. He died saying Mass, and what better way is there for a priest to die? But, oh, God, Elspeth, I loved him so and was so proud of him, and now I'll never, ever get to talk with him and tell him."

Now all of this, needless to say, while uncomfortable-making in the extreme to overhear, was highly intriguing. All but unconsciously, Miss Shaw moved forward some more. She was between one of the rows of benches bolted to the concrete floor and its accompanying bank of lockers. Immediately, as she inched forward, her right foot came down in a most awkward way upon an athletic shoe one of the "little beasts on the basketball team" (as she would style it later) had left lying around. And unable to do anything else, she fell—hard—against the row of metal lockers.

The resulting bang was really quite amazingly loud.

Naturally, both voices ceased instantly like a radio shut off. Miss Shaw righted herself and, scowling with supremest irritation, checked herself out lest any damage had been done her person. Righteously minatory came Mrs. Robinson's voice, "Who's there?"—accompanied by the sound of very determined footsteps, following which Mrs. Robinson herself appeared around the row of lockers to confront the agitated but determined Miss Shaw.

"Martha!" said Mrs. Robinson in great and none too pleased surprise. "What on earth are you doing here?" And then immediately added, "And what do you mean, sneaking up on us like that?"

"I'm sure I'm sorry, Elspeth," said Miss Shaw, "but as I'm quite sure you know by now, I am on assignment. And judging from what little I did hear—and you'll just have to pardon me if it looks like I was spying—"

"Of course it looks like spying. What else could you call it?"

"Never mind!" snapped Miss Shaw right back. "I know it's awful. Nevertheless, I think you and Millie have rather a lot of explaining to do."

3   As soon as she perceived that Miss Shaw had vanished into the depths, Maude returned to hover over her ladyship, who appeared to be wrapped in thought.

"A penny for them, my lady."

"Hmm? What? Oh, well, very well. You can help here. Do you see that gentleman over there?"

"Which one? Jack Cartwright or Alan Brown?"

"Brown."

"Yes, my lady, what about him?"

"Bring him over."

"You want to talk to Alan Brown?"

"Yes, I do."

"My lady, are you feeling all right?"

"Of course, I am. Why do you ask?"

"Well, you have made it rather plain on occasion that you haven't much use for him."

"Probably have. Nor have I had any reason to change my

mind. But I think I should talk to him. So just bring him. And do hurry. It looks as if his lordship is going to spring everyone out of here."

"Very good, my lady."

Alan Brown was not a conspicuously masculine sort of fellow. He was dressed to a fault, well-preserved, with a face virtually unlined though it was well known he was in his late sixties, with a luxuriously full head of superbly styled and tended blond hair that had fooled no one for a second. His eyes were blue and wide with an expression that some had called childlike, others vague—while still others employed adjectives considerably less kind.

Mr. Brown was the fellow who earlier had informed Miss Shaw, in a voice throbbing with emotion, that he had perceived a tinge of black invading poor Father Hughie's aura—an announcement that had been received by Miss Shaw at precisely its real worth.

Lady Fairgrief, however, had been thinking.

"Alan!" she barked as the man came tripping toward her.

"Yes, dear lady. Your good maid said you wished to speak to me."

"Wish is wrong. Need is right. Now, see here, Alan. You are probably the stupidest man it's ever been my misfortune to know. . . ."

"Dear lady!" said Mr. Brown with a petulant droop.

"But the fact is you know things—well, at least in a certain area."

"I assume you mean the occult?"

Her ladyship nodded.

"Well, yes, I am, even if I do say so myself, quite an expert in it. More specifically in all those wonderful things pertaining to the New Age."

"Whatever that might mean," grumbled her ladyship. "But never mind. Now, see here—oh, do stop posing as though you should be wearing a green carnation. I need to know something."

"Very well. What is it?"

"Witchcraft."

"Ah!" said Brown, raising both hands in a gesture of ecstasy. "The *wicca*. Such dear, dear friends. Although, naturally as a Christian, I cannot entirely approve of their revival of the Great Mother cult. Still, all of them such good, good people, so earnest and so kind and so very, very reverent about our dear Mother Earth . . ."

Her ladyship sighed.

"Alan!"

"Yes, dear lady."

"Shut up."

It is to the unfortunate Mr. Brown's credit that he didn't immediately smack her ladyship. Instead, he frowned and said, in an altogether different tone of voice: "So, okay, then why don't you just tell me what the hell it is you want?"

"Well, I emphatically do not mean friendly little covens of naked twinkies all prancing about half frozen one minute and sizzling their—ahem—being sizzled the next when they jump over their bonfires. Not this time, Alan. I'm talking the real stuff. Devil worshipers."

For a moment Mr. Brown said nothing, his eyes seeming to rove casually over the crowd in the gym. But as smoothly as it was done, her ladyship did not by any means miss the way the man's face had gone shut and expressionless, his eyes veiled and wary.

"They do exist," insisted Lady Fairgrief. "We know that."

"Perhaps they do," conceded Mr. Brown. "But it's right outside my bailiwick."

"Oh?"

"Damn skippy, it is," said Mr. Brown, his voice soft and emphatic. "Look! I play around with this stuff because it's fun. I enjoy the business of writing about it, and who knows?—there may actually be something to it. But I am not getting involved with those people. No way."

"But you know who they are?"

"No," came the instant reply, and her ladyship knew that

there were no means, at least none legally available, to get the man to change his tune.

Nevertheless, she had, it seemed, piqued his curiosity. "Why?" he asked. "Why do you want to tangle with—them?"

"I should think it would be fairly obvious, don't you?"

"No, I don't. What do you mean?"

"A priest? Killed? And while saying Mass? Surely . . ."

"Tchah. You've been seeing too many horror movies."

"Have I? But there's so much of that stuff going around. Some of it is innocent enough, I daresay. Some of it . . ." She left it there. "But if someone or group of someones are playing with hellfire, if you want my opinion, it does rather fit in—well, with a lot of other things I've heard about."

For a moment Mr. Brown said nothing.

"What other things?"

"People—experimenting for, shall we say, less than the most religious of reasons."

"What do you mean?"

"Well, let's just say I heard there was a—a coven of older people who have found a pleasant and piquant way to get a number of younger folks together and . . ." Rather elaborately, she shrugged.

"Humph!"

"Oh, don't snort it away, Alan."

"I wasn't. I was just wondering how you manage to hear all the bilge."

"I keep my ear to the deck; the bilge is usually right underneath."

"Okay, then how come—"

"Oh, come, Alan. People might talk about something like that. After all, there's no more harm to it than a little sexual titillation. I speak as a woman of the world now, not as a Christian, you understand. But the other kind of thing? No, Alan, they don't talk about that and you know it."

"Perhaps not to you, they don't."

"So you have heard something!"

"No, I haven't. But—well, they do kind of trust me. At least they have in the past. To a minor extent. I think," he explained wryly, "they see me as a not very bright visiting anthropologist. But for now, if you want my advice, just shut up about it."

"Alan, we have to . . ."

"I'm telling you, leave it alone. Let me see what I can find out."

"Very well. Yes. Okay. That's fair enough."

The man turned to rejoin the group that had gathered around Father d'Arcy and the bishop who was quietly addressing the assembled.

Then he turned back.

"Oh! And one more thing, Lady Fairgrief."

"Yes."

"I think you're barking up the wrong tree altogether."

"Why?"

The man smiled. It was not a particularly pleasant smile. "Because the time's all wrong." And when she just looked blankly at him, he added: "Work it out for yourself."

Without a word of explanation, he left her.

4   When, presently, Miss Shaw, Elspeth Robinson, and Millie Cantrell reemerged into the gym from the lower regions (thus greatly relieving the deputy on the door, who had begun to get seriously agitated at their continuing absence), they were greeted by a completely unexpected sight: The gymnasium was all but deserted. Only the deputies remained on their several doors, and in the center of the floor, chatting with Lady Fairgrief and Maude, were the bishop and Father d'Arcy.

Almost at once the bishop looked up and caught sight of the returning trio, all three of whom, in spite of the raw emotions of the previous minutes, had schooled their faces to a decent blankness.

"There you are!" he said, advancing upon them.

The trio came to a halt, waiting upon the bishop and rather wondering what had been happening in their absence.

Coming up to them, Dr. Fisher spoke first to Mrs. Robinson. "Elspeth, you're wanted upstairs in the parish council room."

"A meeting?" asked Mrs. Robinson in surprise.

"After a manner of speaking," replied the bishop. "Matilda asked that you be there."

"Who all is up there?" asked Miss Shaw.

"The sheriff and George Lorris, Matilda, of course, Father Reggie and, by now, Belinda Sue Morgan."

"I wonder if they need me," said Miss Shaw, knowing at last what was happening upstairs.

"Matilda did say something about wanting a reporter," said the bishop vaguely.

Miss Shaw frowned, clicked her tongue, and grumbled, "Sometimes I wonder why I bothered to retire!"—and turning to Mrs. Cantrell, asked, "Are you okay?"

Mrs. Cantrell nodded. "I'm all right now. Thank you, Elspeth—and you, too, Martha. Dr. Fisher, are you and Father d'Arcy . . ."

"Lady Fairgrief has made arrangements for us. I think it would be much better if you just went home and got some sleep. Thank God Leo is going to pull through!"

"Yes," said Mrs. Cantrell in a curious tone of voice. "Thank God."

And without another word, she walked to the door and out, leaving Miss Shaw and Mrs. Robinson to stare after her and exchange a covert glance between them.

"Elspeth?" gently urged the bishop.

And coming to, Mrs. Robinson excused herself and followed Mrs. Cantrell out the door.

When she had gone, the bishop promptly waxed efficient. "And now you, Martha!"

"I know, I know," she sighed. "Let me get my notebook."

Instead, the bishop chuckled. "Come along, Martha," he said, and led the way back to Lady Fairgrief's side.

"Martha," said her ladyship peremptorily, "take the bishop home—and Father d'Arcy."

"I beg your pardon." Miss Shaw blinked. "But I thought I was supposed to . . ."

"Matilda is perfectly capable of taking notes herself," said Lady Fairgrief. "The bishop needs someplace to stay the night, and you and Matilda have heaps of room. He's going to have to take service in the morning, and it's damn near nine o'clock and none of us have had our suppers."

Which, of course, was precisely the kind of appeal to which Miss Shaw was never insensitive. There may be thousands of excellent court reporters in this wicked and litigious world, but there was only one cook with the talents of Martha Shaw. Accordingly, and with nary a twinge of conscience, Miss Shaw promptly led the procession outside, leaving the gymnasium, finally, to the deputies.

Steaks from the freezer, she reflected, zapped in the microwave, and then broiled under the gas while potatoes replaced the steaks in the microwave for quick baking. Surely there was sour cream in the fridge and God knows there was an abundance of chives in the backyard, so even if there was no sour cream, she could whomp something up out of yogurt. Then there was that lovely '78 cabernet sauvignon they'd been saving for a suitable occasion. And finally, there was all that crumpet batter working away in the oven. And after all, Mattie would also be wanting something to eat when she got home—at whatever ungodly hour that might be. . . .

5 Somewhat earlier, upstairs in the parish hall building, Miss Belinda Sue Morgan had knocked discreetly at the door of the parish council chamber.

Afterward Miss Worthing realized she had no memory whatever of the knock on the door. In fact, all she was aware of was Lorris's voice, sounding as if it were only fitfully emerging from a labyrinth of sound baffles.

At first she had not even realized what George had said. Until, abruptly, it penetrated.

"Come in!"

It was finally beginning.

Nevertheless, it was still rather a struggle to open her eyes and sit up, in spite of the fact that, as the bleak light of the overhead incandescent bulbs once more began leaking into her consciousness, she felt thoroughly disgusted with herself: falling asleep in the middle of the investigation! What next? And after those three mugs full of strong tea she had already put away not an hour before!

But what was this? The smell of coffee?

As the world finally pulled into focus, she looked up to see Belinda Sue Morgan, a cardboard tray of paper coffee cups in hand, walking around the table handing cups of steaming coffee into grateful hands.

Father Reggie certainly looked perkier with the advent of his fiancée as he sipped the scalding stuff. Lorris, too, had unbent a bit, thanking Ms. Morgan for her thoughtfulness—sentiments the expression of which Miss Worthing hastened to share.

The other man, sitting at the end of the table opposite Father Reggie, had obviously come in while Miss Worthing dozed. Before him on the table sat a stenotype machine along with several spare rolls of tape beside it. He had obviously taken the somnolent interval to pass out legal pads and disposable pens along the length of the table.

Good, thought Miss Worthing to herself, now I can concentrate on questions and not have to take notes. But what on earth has happened to Martha?

The reporter, too, had taken a container of coffee and seemed as content as the others to ogle Ms. Morgan.

Meanwhile, under the idle chitchat, Miss Worthing

watched—and rather enjoyed—the effect Ms. Morgan was having on the men in the room, and reviewed what was known of her:

Belinda Sue Morgan had appeared at the Church of All Saints the previous spring. She was, incongruously, working on her doctorate in theology at Berkeley, and had fetched up in Jolliston through a somewhat complicated chain of family ties—her father was a prosperous mushroom farmer in Pennsylvania and she boarded here in the Jolliston Valley with some remote cousin by marriage while she finished her unlikely education.

Actually, there was nothing at all unlikely or incongruous about it, and Miss Worthing instantly chided herself for thinking of it that way.

And yet, she thought, everyone did think of it that way.

For Belinda Sue Morgan was, simply stated, one of the most beautiful women whom Miss Worthing, and many another parishioner of the Church of All Saints, for that matter, had ever clapped eyes on.

She was, first of all, that most luscious of beauties, the dark blonde. Her hair, the color of ripened wheat, was in startling contrast to dark brown eyes and skin the color of honey. She wore that hair in what for most women would have been an inconvenient length, brushed back and parted in the middle, its only "do" a natural and perfect wave. As for her features, there was not the remotest hint of the pretty about her. Rather her regular, well-shaped features, in near perfect relation one to the other, could have served Praxiteles as the model of Pallas Athena; when she was sixty, happy woman, she would only be even handsomer than she was now at twenty-seven. She was a fairly tall woman and well-proportioned withal, although by some genetic twist she had been bequeathed a *poitrine* of luxurious proportions. Miss Worthing, having seen Martha Shaw both blest and cursed with a noble prow, wondered privately if, perhaps in middle life, the woman might not be encumbered by said secondary female sexual characteristic. In the meantime, however, it was quite plain that Ms. Morgan was by no means above enjoying the sensation she so obviously and regularly caused.

And Ms. Morgan had also taken a part in the play: She had been cast in the role of the *Spiritus Mundi*—the Spirit of the World. And Miss Worthing recalled very well that when word of this had gone out some weeks before, there had been those in the parish who had expressed themselves completely unsurprised that Ms. Morgan would play such a role, the hussy. But most folks in the parish, bless 'em, just ignored these wizened souls, recognizing their spite for what it was, a crabbed hatred of all that was young and beautiful.

Having finished distributing coffee to the four people present, Ms. Morgan took one for herself and flowed into the seat on Father Reggie's immediate left, which put her on the same side of the table as Lorris. Her right hand and Father Reggie's left were at once inextricably intertwined as, very softly, they spoke together—so softly that Miss Worthing, sipping her own coffee and trying to look as uninterested as possible, couldn't hear a word.

And as she covertly watched the two of them, the priest and the beauty, out of the corner of her eye, she wondered if she had been the only one wise to Ms. Morgan.

For Miss Worthing had known for months, as though it had been shouted from the housetops, that, Ph.D. in theology notwithstanding, when Belinda Sue Morgan went to assume her crown in heaven, she would account it tarnished for all eternity if she did not go to assume it as Mrs. Reginald Tinsdale.

It had been, moreover, an ambition with which Miss Worthing, Miss Shaw, and half a dozen others in the parish were in complete accord. Father Reggie was, thank God, a normal, red-blooded male—if a bit of an auntie on occasion. In Miss Worthing's none too humble opinion it was high time he desisted from foolishness, married, and settled down. And if Ms. Morgan wanted to be the one, well, then wasn't Father Reggie an extraordinarily lucky man?

Oh, well, she thought with a quick glance at Lorris and the reporter, who were both trying very hard, if none too successfully, not to keep staring at Ms. Morgan; if Belinda Sue and Father Reggie have already progressed to the stage of a secret language . . .

And she found that on the whole she was delighted that, when this mess was over, Father Reggie would no longer be a bachelor.

Unless—the horrid thought intruded—unless Ms. Morgan . . .

Well, it was, for all Miss Worthing knew at the moment, a possibility.

Patience, she told herself; patience.

And presently the door opened again and the sheriff ushered Elspeth Robinson into the room, also carrying a carton of coffee cups.

She looked from the tray in her hands to those cups already on the table and laughed richly.

"I see Belinda Sue's already beat me to the draw."

"Come in, Elspeth," said Miss Worthing. "Come in. Don't worry; we'll very likely need it before the end of the evening."

And this arrival—at least as far as Miss Worthing was concerned—was very welcome indeed.

For this was that Elspeth, Mrs. Robinson, who once upon a time had been Elspeth Boyd whom all the world had admired and loved in *Puritan's Good-Bye, Beyond the East, Comfort Forever, Joy and Jillian,* and any number of other seemingly ephemeral "women's movies," films which, as the years had passed, became more and more recognized as the delightful little masterworks they were.

She was still a vital and handsome woman, being probably no more than sixty or so. Her figure had filled out some with age, but her jet-black hair was now rather beautifully streaked with white, and she had down cold the professional actress's ability to use makeup to seem as if she weren't using any—and looked, consequently, at least fifteen years younger than she really was.

She had raised a rather sizable brood of children, and, together with her late and much lamented husband had run one of the larger and certainly one of the more successful winery operations in the Valley. She could be imperious, daunting, and more than a little overbearing. She could even, on occasion, be accused of arrogant disregard for the wishes of others. But the simple fact was that she was one of those (mercifully) rare people who can cheerfully shove others along in the absolute conviction that what they want is the right thing because they are right; what they desire usually is the right thing.

It was, of course, a charism, a pure gift of grace, and Mrs. Robinson tried very hard—under the firm direction of both her confessor and her own considerable common sense—not to let it get out of hand, as charisms can so easily get.

It was, however, another gift that had Miss Worthing eager to have her present: She was an enormously accomplished actress. And Miss Worthing was very well aware that one simply does not get to be a first-class mummer unless one has a certain rather acute, off-the-cuff psychological insight into the stuff that makes people tick.

Mrs. Robinson frowned and set her tray of coffee cups down on the table.

"The bishop—and Sam, here—said there was a—a meeting?"

"After a manner of speaking," replied Miss Worthing.

"Elspeth." Father Reggie spoke up. "I'm afraid I got you into this."

"Into what?"

Miss Worthing explained for the benefit of Ms. Morgan and Mrs. Robinson.

"Elspeth, I'm afraid we're all pretty much at sea in all this."

"Yes?"

"Well, I asked Father Reggie here who among you—specifically from among you people involved in the play—who would be the most cogent, coherent, and observant witnesses."

Suddenly Mrs. Robinson sat down, her face stricken. It was probably just by accident, but the chair she had chosen to collapse into was the chair immediately to the right of Father Reggie.

In a way, it looked a trifle absurd. There were the three deponents at one end of the table and down here, the whole length of the room and the broad swath of the table away, the three deposers and the reporter.

"It *was* the play!" Mrs. Robinson whispered, half to herself.

"We don't really know that, Elspeth," said Miss Worthing. "There are—other things it just might be."

"But you do think it is the play?" said Ms. Morgan.

"She said to the bishop," Father Reggie explained, gesturing toward Miss Worthing, "that the play would probably be as good a place as any to start."

"So what do you want from us?" asked Ms. Morgan.

"I want you to go back in your minds to whenever you think this mess might have begun. Then, from each of you, I want as clear a picture of events as you can draw. It's just routine, really."

Ms. Morgan seemed rather amused.

"But what if I should be the guilty party? I could throw you off the scent easily."

"Could you?" asked Miss Worthing.

"Don't even joke about that!" Father Reggie had whirled to say to his fiancée.

"It's okay, Reggie. I won't. But to answer you"—she addressed Miss Worthing—"yes, I think I could."

"I don't. You're a remarkably intelligent young woman, Belinda Sue, but you're going to have to be more than that to get around having every statement you make here checked out both by Mrs. Robinson and Father Reggie, but eventually by everyone else who was involved as well."

"Checkmate," said Ms. Morgan with a mocking smile and a bow, as somewhat irritably Miss Worthing checked her watch.

It was just on nine o'clock.

"Please, I'd like us to get started." Miss Worthing looked at Ms. Morgan.

"Fine with me," said she.

"Let's do it," said Father Reggie impatiently, prizing the lid off another cup of coffee.

"Elspeth?" said Miss Worthing, and then, more forcefully: "Elspeth!"

Mrs. Robinson came to with a start. "Oh! Sorry! Yes, Matilda?"

"We ready to begin?"

"But what's to begin?" said Mrs. Robinson in an unexpectedly bitter tone of voice. "All three of us"—she gestured toward Father Reggie and Ms. Morgan—"know perfectly that it's all my fault that Father Hughie is dead."

CHAPTER FIVE

1 It took a moment or two for the full import of that announcement to penetrate.

Whereupon Sam, who had been slouching in his chair, toying with a pencil, and perhaps not paying particular attention, came upright and alert in a big hurry. George's eyebrows rose nearly to his hairline and, turning, he gestured sharply to the reporter, telling him it was time for him to start taking notes *now*!

Miss Worthing, though at least as taken aback with surprise as were the lawmen, contented herself with saying, mildly enough, "I don't suppose you'd care to clarify that remarkable statement, Elspeth?"

"Of course, I will," began Mrs. Robinson.

Before she could say anything more, however, Father Reggie barked: "Elspeth, don't be ridiculous!"

And hard on his heels, as it were, Belinda Sue said, "It had nothing to do with that, Mrs. Robinson!"

"Nonsense, you two!" rejoined Mrs. Robinson with spirit. "You know perfectly well that—"

"No, Elspeth!" insisted Father Reggie. "If anything, what you did turned out to be good for the company."

"It certainly did," said Belinda Sue. "It was all Dr. Cantrell's doing."

"That's where the problem was," said Father Reggie.

"Yes, but don't you realize," said Mrs. Robinson, "that if I hadn't been so foolish—"

"I hate to interrupt this no doubt fascinating conversation"—Miss Worthing raised her voice and interrupted— "but you do realize, I hope, that you three are the only ones who have the remotest idea of what you're talking about."

Father Reggie and Belinda Sue exchanged a glance that could only be called covert. Seeing which, Mrs. Robinson smiled—albeit a trifle bleakly—and said: "Sorry, Matilda. But, you see—even if these two won't see it—I'm afraid it really all began with something I did that I now realize was very, very foolish."

"And what was that?" said Miss Worthing. "And perhaps even more important: When was that?"

Father Reggie spoke up, his tone almost truculent. "Elspeth, let me! It would be far better if we put this whole thing into its proper context."

"Precisely," said Miss Worthing. "So what are you people talking about?"

The three deponents all exchanged glances.

"Problem?" asked Miss Worthing.

"Where do we begin?" asked Belinda Sue.

"Just begin."

"Very well," said Mrs. Robinson. "If I am correct—and I'm convinced of it—it all began on Wednesday evening. At rehearsal. Four days ago."

"It seems like forever," observed Belinda Sue.

"I know," agreed Father Reggie ruefully.

"So what happened!" demanded Miss Worthing.

"It was supposed to be the first complete run-through of the play," said Mrs. Robinson.

"And it was about as close to being a total disaster as I've ever witnessed," said Father Reggie.

"Me, too," said Mrs. Robinson grimly. "And, believe me, I thought I had seen it all. . . ."

2 Finally, after some six weeks of more or less intense labor, the entire cast and crew were forgathered in the parish hall of the Church of All Saints.
A first run-through is always a delicate moment in the production of anything theatrical—play, operetta, opera, musical comedy, whatever. During previous days and weeks, the necessary if often tedious preliminary work will, it is to be hoped, have been done. The director, having communicated with the scenery designer and the set decorator, will have "blocked" the actors into their movements onstage, worked out any problems of characterization and relationship, mediated in the inevitable jockeying for stage position, and arbitrated between the actors and the playwright over niceties of speech and diction.

Then comes the great day when the first run-through rehearsal is called. And the actors are admonished, under threat of severe injury, to have all their lines and movements completely memorized, for there is at that point a great deal of important work still to be done; honing characterizations, beefing up or toning down individual performances, smoothing out awkward sequences either of movement or of picturization—in short, the fine tuning without which no work of art deserves the name.

That first run-through also marks a very special turning point in the production. If one be of bilious temperament, the experience may induce near suicidal despair. If of sanguine temperament, one sees, however, that, in spite of the appalling amount of work still to be done, much has already been accomplished, and it can't *really* be all that difficult to whip it into shape!

Or can it?

Unfortunately, the greater number of those working on *Death of a Heretic* were of the sanguine sort. Which was probably inevitable. In spite of the remarkable collection of genuinely talented people they had managed to assemble, it was still an amateur production.

Now amateurs are a lovable lot, submitting themselves to grinding hard work for nothing more than the love of it—in French, after all, *amateur* means *lover*. Lacking the professional eye, however, amateurs—in the English sense—are too often too easily satisfied and, as a result, the audience may be severely tried by the amateur's incapacity to perceive just how bad things might actually be.

What made it even worse on that Wednesday night, August twenty-second, was that someone—and afterward no one really could remember who it was—decided in the fullness of his or her wisdom that the run-through, the first run-through, really ought to be something in the nature of a celebration. The suggestion was accordingly made and bruited about with considerable enthusiasm that a potluck supper should be provided. This, in itself, was not such a bad idea. The cast and crew would thus be provided a decent dinner instead of the usual burger or sandwich most of them made do with on rehearsal nights.

But this was California. And along with all the excellent food everyone brought, a large galvanized aluminum tub—a very large tub—of iced beer, wine, and wine coolers had also been provided.

And even though they were still only working with ordinary incandescent lights, the heat in the church hall was fierce. It was like prancing around in an oven, and had been that way for weeks. Not unnaturally, in that debilitating heat, frequent repairs were made to the tub.

Meanwhile, backstage at stage left, Father Reggie stood at the small stand-up desk he was using as his stage manager's table, a half-empty iced beer at his elbow with an unopened one right behind it. And even as he took frequent swigs of that refreshing beverage, he wondered at the wisdom of having had it available at all. No one in either cast or crew had been so ill-bred as to get squiffy with it; indeed, there had been any number of people who had been sensibly content with soft drinks or coffee. But he had no doubt at all that Alcohol Would Be Mentioned.

Along with a great deal else. Of that no one could doubt for a second.

His attention alternated, in a stupor of disbelief, between the script before him on his desk and the Wilderness of Sin into which the stage had been converted wherein actors wandered, like Israel lost in the desert, and almost all of them in a state of aphasia, their tongues cleaving to the roofs of their mouths. . . .

And poor Father Reggie had spent an inordinate amount of time scuttling about, prompt book in hand, attempting to rescue lost souls from aimless peregrinations. It was in the all-too-brief intervals of this helpful activity that the good father became gradually aware of the distinctly ominous pall that had settled over the darkened auditorium.

Out in the "house," a half dozen rows of those dismal folding chairs every church in America has a supply of had been set up in anticipation of opening night—now but some three short weeks away. In the meantime they were dedicated to less worthy ends as those members of crew and cast, not needed at that moment onstage, sat and watched disaster unfold.

Three people in particular held Father Reggie's rapt interest.

First in order, both of dignity and outrage, was the large, well-fleshed fellow in the center of the first row of seats upon whose raddled and incarnadined countenance was fixed a scowl of unspeakable ferocity. In front of him a folding table had been set up upon which was a small but powerful tensor lamp, a number of pens, and an eight-and-a-half-by-fourteen canary legal pad.

This was Mr. Neil Bonewarden, the reluctant director of the play.

Once upon a time Mr. Bonewarden had been a more than usually rufous strawberry blond. With the passage of time, however, he had gone, as such redheads often do, the dullish color ginger gets on being exposed to the air. But if his hair had dulled, the same could not be said of his complexion. The ruddy color of yore had been replaced with that of a less than ripe Santa Rosa plum—bespeaking volumes about his general temperament and his blood pressure—and he was only just this side of corpulent. His eyes were the blue of the true Celt (in spite of that Saxon name, the man was actually of Welsh–Irish extraction), which, contrasting with that florid complexion, gave them an aggressive intensity. His voice, finally, was a well-trained, orotund, and, frankly, rather fruity baritone of which he was inordinately proud.

In daily life Mr. Bonewarden was the organist and choir master of the Church of All Saints, a position he filled with learning and accomplished skill. Nevertheless, once upon a time Mr. Bonewarden had struggled for a number of years to become, not a church organist, but a director of opera. Unfortunately, opera is a field that has never been overfond of brash young Americans, and in those days, even less so. Still, for several remarkable and happy summers, he worked at his chosen profession at one or another of those opera festivals which, unaccountably, spring up here and there in odd coigns of the Rocky Mountains.

But no door opened to him. No matter how brilliantly he may have done, say, *Lady MacBeth of Mtiensk* in Picketwar, Montana, the establishment companies remained unimpressed—precisely because it had been in Picketwar and not Culo di Cane, Italy.

Not having any kind of private fortune on which to "fall back," Neil had found the necessity to make a living going from concern to urgency, and finally he had accepted a temporary post at a small church in Sacramento, where he stayed for five years. From there he moved to a larger and more "important" parish in San Francisco, whence, after eight more years, he came to Jolliston. Where he had been ever since.

He was not by any means an aggressively masculine sort of fellow, which, in a smallish community, can give rise to certain difficulties. He had managed, however, to keep his life apart from the Church cloaked in impenetrable privacy. Even if it was known that the man's consumption of vodka was at just about a liter a day. But again, his demonstrated discretion kept that consumption from being a problem to anyone—except, of course, Neil Bonewarden. He managed, after all, not only to fulfill his obligations to the Church of All Saints with the highest competence, but also managed to give some fourteen or fifteen voice lessons a week. Accordingly, the powers that be for the most part left him alone—which suited him admirably.

Then, at the beginning of summer, had come the—as far as he was concerned—lunacy about the play.

Even when rumors began to reach him that the instigators of that madness had been having no luck in finding a director, still he held his peace: Surely there had to be someone in Jolliston to play main lunatic!

And, of course, there was. In the abstract there were any number who thought it would be a hoot to direct a play. Such things, however, cannot be conducted on an abstract plane; few, as it transpired, had the skill; fewer still could get along with the playwright. At which point someone recalled the nature of Neil's early experience and a delegation of those concerned had come to his house, pleading with him to please, *Please* undertake the job!

In the end he consented. To be sure, it was a good play; it was even a beautiful play. It was just too tempting to pass up. Even now—even now, after all these years, was it really too late? Really?

Then, as is the way of such things, had come the reality—the reality staring him in the face right now.

Of course, there was no way for Father Reggie to know

what was actually going through the man's mind. But Neil had long since balled up the piece of paper on which he had been writing, thrown his pen down, snapped off the tensor lamp, and was sitting, arms folded, glaring up at the farce upon the stage.

3 "I didn't know that about Neil," said Miss Worthing, making a note. "Did he really want to be a director?"
"He's mentioned it," said Father Reggie.
"Oh?" She looked up.
It was again fairly obvious that Father Reggie was uncomfortable.
"Well, naturally, it was on his résumé."
"But that was years before you got here," observed Miss Worthing. "Or does," she asked after a moment's thoughtful silence, "he maunder about it when he's drinking?"
"Now, don't get me wrong," protested Father Reggie. "Neil's not a sloppy drunk or anything. . . ."
"We know," said Miss Worthing gently. "But—as you say—he drinks. And—well, people—it is not unknown for folks with a failed ambition to"—she gestured—"maunder. Does Neil maunder?"
"Yes," said Father Reggie dully. "He does."
"He feels that he never got the right breaks," said Belinda Sue.
"He says that when he's drinking," said Mrs. Robinson crisply. "Sober, he has more sense than that."
"Sense, Elspeth?" queried Miss Worthing.
"Of course. Breaks come—to anyone who tries hard enough long enough. Anyone in show business can tell you that. But when they come, you'd better be prepared for them or eventually they do stop coming. For Neil"—she shrugged—"I gather they stopped coming."
"How sad," said Belinda Sue.

"But I do assure you that Neil," concluded Mrs. Robinson firmly, "Neil sober, that is, has no illusions about it."

"Interesting," observed the district attorney, making a note.

"Yes, it is," said Miss Worthing with a frown. "But do go on. You said there were three people upon whom you were focusing that night, Father."

"When I wasn't busy."

"We got that," growled Sam. "So who else was you worried about?"

Father Reggie looked about to bridle at the man's truculent tone.

"Never mind, Father," ordered Miss Worthing. "He's right. Who else had you concerned? And—again, at least as importantly, why?"

"The other two who had good reason to be angry," said Father Reggie.

"And they were?" asked Miss Worthing.

"Julian Richards."

"Ah, yes. Our playwright," said Miss Worthing.

"Yes," said Father Reggie.

"He the guy what wrote this play?" said Sam.

"He's our author," said Father Reggie. "Yes."

"I thought he was your caretaker," said George.

"He is," said Father Reggie, puzzled. "But what does that have to do with anything?"

"Isn't it kind of strange," asked the D.A., "to put on a play written by your janitor?"

The three deponents and Miss Worthing turned a look of pure astonishment upon the district attorney.

Mrs. Robinson, lighting a cigarette, paused in the act of waving out the match, observed with a very sharp edge to her voice, "George dear. You're thinking like a tiresome lawyer again. Not everyone, you know, went to a trade school like you did." She exhaled through her nostrils and added, "He works for us as a caretaker. But that is just a job, George. Julian is a published poet, a first-class writer, and a genuine Christian gentleman, if," she conceded, "a bit odd on occasion."

Sam snorted, and George wasn't buying it, either.

"Tell me," said Miss Worthing. "What do you two have against Julian?"

"I've had dozens of complaints 'bout him," said Sam.

"What on earth for?" asked Belinda Sue.

"Walking around talking to himself," said George. "And don't you think . . . What are you all laughing about?"

"We told you," said Father Reggie, greatly amused. "He's a poet."

The D.A., too, looked blank.

Mrs. Robinson explained: "Apparently, our suburban populace has never observed a poet wandering around working out his verse. I must tell him to come out and wander in my vineyards when the fit is on him. Nevertheless, I do assure you, it's done all the time. In fact, I gather it's done that way for the most part. Of course it's peculiar," she said, observing the others' expressions; "I'm not going to quibble with that. Julian is peculiar. Harmless. But peculiar . . ."

4 . . . though of a type that has hardly been rare in the history of art—at least in the history of art since the rise of Romanticism. For Richards was, in the full pride of consciousness, Artist, with a sublime disregard for craft, communication—or even beauty—wherever it interfered with the Expression of Himself.

He had published over the previous years a handful of slim volumes with a frightfully significant small press in San Francisco. And Father Reggie, in heroic earnest of his friendship with Julian, had actually purchased and (moreover) read the entire corpus.

It had yielded little in the way of meaning, and Father had been rather reminded of descriptions that early explorers had penned of Bottomless Ocean—of miasmal abysses steeped in impenetrable gloom, whence, like grotesque pelagic beasts, images briefly emerged into the light only to be swallowed up again, leaving behind impressions of a disquieting nature. . . .

5 "So how did this guy wind up your janitor?" George interrupted.

Everyone in the room but him and Sam were laughing, but all he could see was that time was a-wasting. He certainly was not expecting the response it got.

"God damn it, Lorris!" Father Reggie suddenly raged. "Will you knock that off! He isn't our janitor, he's our caretaker. And furthermore, there's a goddamned good reason he is, too."

6 . . . For what income there was from these volumes had been far too exiguous to provide anything beyond the most inadequate of livings. When, therefore, Richards began to brood upon his *magnum opus*, which was to emerge as *Death of a Heretic*, he was looking around for one of those jobs that can be done with a minimal outlay of energy and also allow him time in which to write.

Thus it was that he had come to the Church of All Saints to become the church's resident caretaker. The job, however, quickly became more than had been intended. Certainly more than he was paid for. It was as though in pursuing his chores around the complex—and they had not been many or onerous—Julian found a vocation of sorts.

In no time he was not only caretaker, but handyman, brass polisher, pool man, and gardener as well. And emergency acolyte, cheerfully substituting for whoever didn't show up to serve Mass. In fact, he was very devout. And if his manner was gruff and sometimes downright rude, the members of the parish took his real measure when, in addition to everything else he did, he began coaching the "special" swimming team, the one comprised of the variously handicapped children of the parish.

And so, in spite of a somewhat standoffish personality, he had become very popular around the Church of All Saints.

He was, not too surprisingly, a scruffy-looking individual. Though of scrupulous personal cleanliness, his hair was an untidy and flyaway mid-back-length hank of thin brown hair, and his beard had manifestly not felt razor or scissors in a long time. His coloring was of the indeterminate type; depending on available light, he might appear blond or brunet or even a coppery auburn. And he dressed for the most part in blue jeans and T-shirts—tie-dyed T-shirts, of all things—looking like nothing so much as a hippie who had wandered in out of time.

It was also unfortunate that Julian was more poet than playwright. To be sure, the nature of drama, even poetic drama, had forced him to an unwonted clarity in *Death of a Heretic*. But over the rehearsal period, time and again, he had shown himself even more than usually inflexible about those inevitable requests from actors for some reshaping of their lines. Some had reasoned with him, others cajoled, and still others had raged. But all had been unsuccessful. The man believed his verses sacrosanct; the play would be done his way or not done at all. An attitude that had not been easily borne. Julian, however, remained adamant.

And that was very likely the reason the man was sitting on the edge of his chair—he was seated at the extreme left of the front row of seats in the auditorium—muttering audibly against all those onstage who had been so insufferable as not to have his verses letter-perfect. . . .

The woman sitting next to Julian, and to whom these volleys of vituperation were addressed, herself never said a word. Occasionally she smiled. Other times she frowned and raised her eyes briefly to the stage before dropping them once again to her beautifully manicured hands, which never once ceased from crocheting some small lacy thing in white silk.

For this was Miss Bonita Harris, Richards's solemn betrothed. And a woman in more complete contrast to Richards it would have been difficult to find. Where he was tall, rangy, and thin, she was tiny and pleasantly zaftig; where he was scruffy and ill-kempt, she was stylishly, even elegantly dressed—exquisitely finished from her coiffure and expert makeup to the shoes on her feet.

So well done was the package, in fact, that it took a moment to realize that Bonnie was not perhaps the most handsome of women, being possessed of rather thickish lips and a generosity of nose not found in any canon of beauty. Her eyes, however, and her glossy brown hair were her best features, and she was wise enough to make the most of them.

She was the owner/manager of a small but growing chain of boutiques. Father Reggie had had occasion recently to visit the original one in Mission Square in Jolliston and had come away more than a little impressed. The pile of the carpet was inches deep, the lights dim, the music, too, and in the resultant soft, even religious, hush, cool-voiced women fleeced the faithful for goods and services at remarkable prices.

7 "Hey, are you talking about The Lace Place?" asked George.

Father Reggie and the other deponents nodded.

"You know it?" asked Miss Worthing.

"Of course I do," said George.

"Me too," said Sam. "Leastways my wife's credit cards do."

Miss Worthing, eyeing the expression on Lorris's face, said, "George? Got something you want to say? To us?"

After a moment the almost sullen reply came: "She contributed to my campaign fund."

"Well," said Father Reggie, attempting lightness, "she does get around. I can't say I'm terribly surprised. . . ."

8 . . . For Miss Harris was, not too surprisingly, rich and daily growing more so. It had, in fact, been she who had brought Julian Richards and the Church of All Saints together to their mutual benefit—a fact upon which she still rather prided herself.

Nor had anyone been in the least interested in squelching that pride. For a number of reasons.

First, there was the practical fact that she, from the first, had been a generous contributor to the financial well-being of the parish. A successful businesswoman, she, at least, had been under no illusion that the church somehow survives on honeydew, manna, vague goodwill, or vaguer hopes.

At least as important, however, had been her willingness—nay, her eagerness—to undertake the tedious, unending and expensive business of repairs to those tears, strains and wear spots endemic to vestments, hangings, altar cloths, what-have-you.

Previously these had been handled by some commercial "shop" in the Midwest somewhere. But the expense and the six-month turnaround had preyed on everyone's nerves for years, culminating in a particularly disastrous occasion when, on the Feast of the Assumption, the blue cope was holed by an unconscious and ruinous encounter between the officiating priest and a votive candle. It would have to be sent away for reweaving. Which would take six months. Meanwhile, the Nativity of the Mother of God was only three weeks away. Do we buy a new one? Loud protests about spending too much money. Tableau!

And there was Miss Harris quietly asking if they would like her to do it.

It seems she had actually gone into her business through an abiding love of all the fiber arts. But as is so often the case, the business end had overwhelmed the creative side, and in her joy in attending to the fabric stuffs of the Church of All Saints a solution had been found pleasing everyone.

That she could speak at least as plainly as her fiancé, Father Reggie knew very well. But as he watched her placidly thread over, hook, thread over, hook, he could only hope that the calm she radiated would somehow defuse and tranquilize Julian.

His own prayer was a bit confused. Mostly it was that Bonnie just calm Richards down. He also prayed that Bonnie herself be not too disgusted. For Miss Harris had been appointed, naturally enough, costume director of the play. Furthermore, she had also volunteered to design and build the requisite costumes, and all at her own expense—a munificent gift the fledgling company could ill afford to jeopardize by its corporate and individual inadequacies.

These scatty ruminations, however, were interrupted.

"No, Hughie, that's not right!" a singularly unmusical voice honked from the apron of the stage. "Gee, Hughie! When ya gonna get it right?"

Thus spake the Reverend Dr. Fiona MacLaren as she addressed, as well she might, her own fiancé, the Reverend Mr. Hugh Barnes, who was doing his level best to confuse everyone onstage by his utter incapacity to delineate his character, namely that of Hincmar, Archbishop of Rheims, into whose keeping the unfortunate Gottschalk had been given.

Fiona was sitting on the edge of the stage, her own prompt book open in front of her as, in spite of the heat in the hall, she knitted furiously at some indeterminate garment in searingly scarlet acrylic yarn. She had been knitting at that, whatever it was, since practically the first day of rehearsal.

For Miss MacLaren had actually volunteered for the ungrateful post of assistant director. It was, therefore, she who had industriously written down all the pearl drops of wisdom as they fell from the lips of the director, and it was now her unhappy chore to prompt the captious memories of the actors careering about the stage.

Fortunately for everyone, however, that career was abruptly terminated. Indeed, Father Reggie had been wondering for quite some time just how long Neil would let this farce continue. Poor Father Hughie was like some Dantesque figure wandering about between hell and purgatory, not quite sure of what or where he was supposed to be or even what he was.

And one person like that in a scene can wreak near-endless havoc. Misread lines, misfed cues, never being quite where one is supposed to be—all of which will have a devastating effect on one's fellow actors, especially if they are just as insecure.

"Enough!" bellowed Neil, clearly at the limit of never-abundant patience.

The effect was not unlike that of a bolt of lightning. One held oneself in readiness for thunder to follow.

Neil, however, contented himself with a long silence during which you could all but hear the man count to twenty.

"We will leave this scene for now," he finally growled. "Next scene, ladies and gentlemen."

And all over the house and backstage, everyone immediately relaxed—the next scene was the last scene in the play.

It was also a scene much like the Nurse's scene in *Medea*. In fact, it had been to Greek models that Julian had turned for the climax of his play.

Onto the stage comes a woman, her middle age only just behind her, dressed (come the night) in the rich black serge and purple satin of a ranking abbess.

This woman purports to be some cousin or other of Gottschalk who had known him in the Elysian days of their childhood. She is a purely fictional character, though Julian had admitted the role was loosely based on Walafrid Strabo, the poet/abbot who had remained friendly to the doomed Gottschalk even in his utter defeat.

We learn that she had always had a great regard for her unhappy cousin, has several times visited him in his prison and tried to convince him to recant his dismal heresy, and that, in spite of her own position in the Church, she yet admires his determination. She comes now to tell us of the death of Gottschalk.

Baldly stated like that, it sounds, admittedly, immeasurably dull. And perhaps it might have been had there not been a truly remarkable actress cast in the role. Elspeth Robinson.

9 For a long moment, when Father Reggie stopped speaking, everyone in the room was afflicted with acute self-consciousness.

Mrs. Robinson herself had gone very still, looking down at her hands folded together on the table.

Presently Miss Worthing asked: "It's perhaps an inopportune moment, Elspeth, but, I'm sorry, it did seem rather soon after Barney's death for you to get involved in—all that, you know."

"Yes," said Mrs. Robinson, barely above a whisper. "I expect it did rather seem like that."

10 Though perhaps a bit pushy on Miss Worthing's part, the question was not an unnatural one.

The fact was Mrs. Robinson's thirty-year marriage to Barney Robinson *had* completely terminated her film career. Indeed, until poor Barney's death, she had never planned on acting again.

But her great friend, Millie Cantrell, had unrelentingly gone to work on her to convince her that she simply had to read for the play—Mrs. Cantrell knowing full well that the part of the Lady Abbess had actually been written for her.

Reluctant at first, Mrs. Robinson had read the play, seen not only what a very good play it was, but that the part was the kind of role of which an actress, any actress, dreams. She had accepted the part and, by means of that alchemy peculiar to great artists, she had begun transforming her deep and bitter grief for the newly departed Barney into a performance that was a wonder and a joy to see.

And she was also, still, the consummate professional.

Letter-perfect with her words, her movements were deft and assured, having taken the blocking given her by Neil and, again by the magic of superb acting, made it uniquely her own. Her voice sang with perfectly controlled emotion in the hot, still air of the hall, and in the house her colleagues were thrilled into that greatest of compliments, complete silence, silence unbroken but for the sounds of discreet weeping as she reached the coda of the piece:

> *And so to that great final mystery,*
> *Unafraid and confident of love*
> *He's gone—and I alone remain to fear*
> *The work that men have done this day. . . .*

And finally it was over. And Father Reggie was conscious, first and foremost, of sheer, unalloyed relief.

But he was also in a stupor of admiration for Elspeth. What a great, what a superb performance!

Unfortunately, he was also aware that if her performance had moved him like that, what, O Fairest Lord, had it done to the others out there in the hall?

He had known this group far too intimately over the last few weeks not to realize what kind of effect Mrs. Robinson's, alas, unique achievement would have on the rest of the cast and crew.

"A-a-and curtain!" sang out Neil as Elspeth slowly glided toward stage left.

There was a sudden rush as those two lads, whose job curtain pulling was supposed to be, leaped from their chairs and clattered up the side stairs to the stage.

"Don't bother!" came a thunderous bellow from Neil.

At once, like children released from class on the last day of term, the assembled began to murmur among themselves. And even from the edge of the stage, where he stood along with Mrs. Robinson and Fiona MacLaren, Father Reggie could hear a self-congratulatory note begin to emerge from the susurrus.

And sure enough, a voice soared over the rest, "Well, that wasn't so bad, was it? I think we're doing just fine."

"Oh, no!" breathed Mrs. Robinson beside Father Reggie, as Neil swung his bulk around to bark at the unfortunate speaker: "Oh, you do, do you? Well, let me tell you, young lady, if that's what you're thinking, then you're just not thinking at all."

The young woman thus addressed, a rather flighty teenager in the Chorus of Women, turned beet-colored.

Neil, however, took no further notice and, raising his voice, addressed the entire company: "I want all of you, every last one of you, up here on the edge of the stage. And I want it now!"

"Oh, dear," said Mrs. Robinson, "I was afraid this was going to happen."

CHAPTER SIX

1 "Well, you know, folks," said the sheriff, sitting back and rubbing his chin, "I suppose all this is kinda interestin', but so far I can't see anything coulda led to violence."

"Of course not," snapped Mrs. Robinson irritably. "But Matilda here said she wanted to know everything precisely as it happened."

"So I do," said Miss Worthing.

"But unless you people understand the situation in which we found ourselves—and then how my idiocy compounded it . . ."

"And what the result was," Father Reggie finished for her. "If," he emphasized, "we're—she—is right."

"Besides," commented the D.A. thoughtfully, "I'm getting some idea of people who, frankly, I don't know all that well."

"Yes, there is that, too," said Miss Worthing. "Very well, people, please proceed."

2 In what was, considering that crowd, a relatively short time, the cast and crew were lined up on the edge of the stage like birds on a telephone wire, ready for whatever potshooting Neil had in mind. The more foolish among them, incredibly enough, were still all quivering eagerness for the glowing praise they remained certain would follow.

The rest watched, in mingled curiosity and dread, as Neil regarded the line in silence, his usually full vermilion lips a grim empurpled line, until only two bird-witted young things still prated. And presently it penetrated even their feather pates that they alone were chattering.

And so silence was restored.

The only sounds now were of the occasional car passing by outside the front doors of the hall, which had been left open in hope they would admit any passing breeze, the wheezings of an asthmatic fan at the midpoint of the hall, and the stirrings of thirty-odd souls restless with heat and apprehension.

Seeing that finally he had their full attention, Neil nodded once curtly. "Good," said he. "Now see that you stay that way."

He turned his head to look at Julian Richards. The playwright and his fiancée had remained in their chairs at the extreme edge of things, she still placidly crocheting away, Julian staring straight in front of him chewing his mustaches.

"Julian!" Neil's bellow summoned the playwright from whatever realm of poetic frenzy wherein he wandered. The man's furious brown eyes, regaining focus, turned to meet those of the director.

"What?" he demanded sullenly.

"Come here," said Neil. "I want to talk to you."

"Yeah?" said Julian, unfolding his limbs and rising. "Good! 'Cause I wanna talk to you."

And everyone watched as, turning on his heel, the director waddled halfway to the back of the hall and turned again to await the arrival at his side of the more slowly shambling playwright. Even Bonnie Harris turned in her seat to watch the intense little colloquy that proceeded between Neil and Julian.

No one, however, could hear what passed between them in little bursts of furious whispering, until, after a number of interchanges, Neil said something to Julian softly but very intently. To which everyone heard the reply. Julian barked, "No!"

And Neil, exerting his well-known and detested capacity for overbearance, leaned on Julian. Heavily.

"Believe me, it's the right thing," they heard.

After which, Julian sighed and, with the greatest reluctance, nodded agreement.

They heard Neil's clipped "Thank you!"—and again the director made a curiously balletic turn and led the way back toward the flock of sparrows on the stage's apron.

Behind him, however, Julian had not entirely had his say. "You'd better be right, you know," he addressed Neil's retreating back. "If you're not, everyone'll be s.o.l."

"I'm aware of that," rejoined Neil without even turning his head.

He came to a halt in front of the assemblage and eyed them, arms akimbo.

"And I'll bet you were all just itching to know what we were talking about. Weren't you?" Neil barked at the company, and then answered his own question. "Of course you were. Well, I won't keep you in suspense. We've made a decision. We've had to make a decision. And it wasn't exactly hard to make, either. Because this will simply not do!"

He paused to let his final bellow reverberate around the hall while he drew breath through wide-flared nostrils and went on somewhat more gently. "Now I know that because of the weather we've been having the harvest is coming in early. I know that, and, believe me, I sympathize. For those of you, that is, who have to devote your time to it. Nevertheless, the fact remains that this will simply not do. . . ."

3 "Pardon me for interrupting," said Miss Worthing, "but this touches on something that's been puzzling me for some time."

"What's that, Miss Worthing?" asked Father Reggie.

"Why in the world did you people decide to do a play in early September when there's a *harvest* coming in?"

"It's a fair question, Matilda," said Mrs. Robinson wearily. "And believe me, I wish we'd chosen some other time. As it is, I'm spending at least eight hours a day in the winery before I even get here for rehearsal."

"So why . . ."

"Just hold your horses, Matilda," said Mrs. Robinson impatiently. "First of all, no one dreamed the harvest would be coming in a whole month early. We thought we'd be over and done with the play by harvest."

"And then there are all the students, like me," said Belinda Sue. "*And* Jack Cartwright—and at least half the chorus members. We also thought it would all be over by term time. And we wanted to be involved, you know."

She and Father exchanged an affectionate glance as he added, "And, finally, we wanted to get the company up and running. That was poor Hughie's doing. He wanted us to proceed as quickly as possible not only to demonstrate to the parish that we could do it, but, also, I think, as *bona fides* to Julian, who, I suspect, couldn't quite believe it was really going to happen until we actually went into production."

"So you could say we decided time was of the essence," said Mrs. Robinson wryly. "And then got hoist on our own petard."

"Too bad," murmured Miss Worthing.

"I know," said Father Reggie bitterly. "And maybe if everyone hadn't been so damned tired and on edge . . ."

He gestured elaborately and helplessly.

"Yes," said Miss Worthing briskly. "But never mind what might have been. What happened next?"

"Well, we certainly found out what Julian and Neil had decided," said Belinda Sue.

4 "And so," Neil went on, "we've had to make our decision. Or at least," he added more honestly, "I've made a decision and Julian has agreed with me. People, we have a rehearsal on Friday night. Two days from now. And if"— you could hear that he was speaking through clenched teeth—"on Friday night this thing is not one hundred percent—no, two hundred percent—better—and I mean lines learned, blocking memorized, and all the rest of it—we are going to cancel the show."

The outcry was immediate and very, very loud. Amid the hubbub, Father Reggie turned to look at Mrs. Robinson—to whom the news could hardly have been surprising—and was considerably taken aback to see that she had gone white with dismay.

Neil, meanwhile, once more waited for the noise to lessen, whereupon he railed: "Come on! What else can we do? We're supposed to open in three weeks. Three weeks, ladies and gentlemen. And if you couldn't see what a total shambles this thing was tonight, well, okay." He picked up his legal pad and flipped through twenty or thirty pages heavily overwritten with notes. "I'll be more than happy to tell you what was wrong."

And from the side where, once again, he had retaken his place, came Julian's reedy baritone, "And so will I."

"Yes, Julian," said Neil somewhat impatiently, "you'll have your chance."

Whereupon, out of the assemblage, Jack Cartwright spoke up in a light, rather well-produced tenor voice that had been intended by its Creator to be pleasant and sweet but that seemed always to issue forth with an unfortunate note of petulance in it. "What's the point of notes, Neil, if you're just gonna cancel anyway?"

Neil's eyes narrowed as he focused on the speaker. "Apparently you didn't hear what I said. Not that I'm surprised. You're good at not hearing what you don't want to hear. Aren't you?"

Jack wasn't the only member of the company to begin stirring restively.

"What I *said* was that if things don't improve, *then* we'll cancel. There are still two days before we make that final decision. And if God found a mere six days adequate for the creation of the whole goddamn universe, you lot can learn your goddamn lines and blocking in two!"

But even Neil seemed to find that last outburst a bit much. Using his sheaf of notes as an improvised fan, he observed in a normal conversational voice, "My God, it's hot in here."

"So have a beer, Neil," someone suggested; "it's good and cold."

Immediately Neil's flailings with the yellow sheets ceased abruptly. "Is it?" he inquired. "I'm surprised there's any left. The way all of you have been swilling all—"

"Oh, come off it, Neil," said Jack, cutting him off. "Nobody's been drinking that much."

"Oh? I was rather hoping that this—this exhibition could be blamed on alcohol. But apparently I'm not to be allowed even that bit of grace."

Father Reggie began fervently to wish that either the man would get on with it or dismiss them.

"Neil!" he said sharply. "Never mind that now. Give us the notes or let us go."

Neil sighed theatrically and nodded. "You're right, of course. Sorry. However, I have a request to make of you— you, that is, and Mrs. Robinson and Miss Morgan." He bowed to those two members of the company as he named them. "There is no reason for you three to listen to any of this. Your work is exemplary. In a better-ordered universe I'd let you go. But I'd like to ask you to make some iced tea and bring it out to us. The cold will be welcome and the caffeine just might make our minds more alert."

The three fortunates eased themselves from the edge of the stage and moved obediently toward the oblong of darkness at the entry to the kitchen, all three of them aware of the intense scrutiny—and envy—of their fellows left behind.

5   Father Reggie made it first and, darting within, snapped on the light as the other two also reached it and slipped inside.

Neil waited until they were out of sight and then, in a voice of tightly controlled fury, began.

The three in the kitchen, of course, paused to listen to the savage diatribe plainly audible through the doorless entryway of the kitchen.

Finally, however, Mrs. Robinson gave a little snort of mirthless laughter at some particularly virulent turn of phrase and, moving across the kitchen, seized two of the gallon-sized kettles on the stove and began filling them at the sink. The other two, hearing the sound of running water, started and looked around guiltily. "What can we do, Mrs. Robinson?" asked Ms. Morgan.

"You can stand right there and listen," replied Mrs. Robinson, "and let me know if anything productive comes out of this." She slammed the filled kettles onto the stove and turned the gas on high underneath them.

The other two nodded and turned their attention back to the outpouring of vitriol as first Neil, and then Julian, and both of them antiphonally, dressed the company down severally and corporately in no uncertain terms. It was, in its own way, quite a spectacular performance, and even though Father Reggie was becoming ever more acutely aware that something was bothering Mrs. Robinson, he was still fascinated by the *tableau vivant* without.

Meanwhile, Mrs. Robinson began to collect the impedimenta required to make a quantity of iced tea in a hurry.

She herself could hear the substance of Neil's and Julian's harangue as plainly as the pair in the doorway. And for the most part, she could not have agreed more with what was being said. Nevertheless, she had a low opinion of a director, or anyone in a position of power, who wields sarcasm and bitchery as weapons to get a desired result. In her opinion it was seldom necessary; it was usually imprudent; it was always ill-bred.

These meditations, however, were interrupted as the two in the doorway turned together to see Mrs. Robinson patiently stirring tea bags and lemon wedges into a large bowl of boiling water.

"Oh, Mrs. Robinson," said Miss Morgan contritely, trotting around the large central table toward her. "You've done all the work."

"What's to do making iced tea?" asked Mrs. Robinson, and then added in rather a drier tone of voice, "Besides, you and Father Reggie can help with the ice trays. Lord!" she muttered half to herself, still stirring the tea to cool it more quickly, "I have got to get some decent ice trays for this kitchen. Maybe we should just get an ice machine."

"The kids would love it," said Father Reggie. "They're always kvetching about the ice supply."

"One can hardly blame them," said Miss Morgan in a dry voice as she opened the standup freezer and began passing ice trays to Father Reggie.

The ice trays she handed out had been manufactured sometime around the end of the Second World War, unyielding mechanical devices in slab aluminum. The Sisterhood had accumulated these inconvenient antiques at about that time in the late forties when refrigeration was becoming more a necessity than a luxury. The faithful had dutifully presented their old trays to various rummage sales. Since—not too surprisingly—they had never sold, the Sisterhood, with admirable frugality, had pressed them into service. It had been, however, at a cost of temper and general irritation, which had given more than one otherwise virtuous matron pause when preparing for the sacraments, and those ominous words, "sins both voluntary and involuntary," were brought to mind. . . .

Such, at least, was the tale Father Reggie told Miss Morgan upon her inquiry, "Where on earth did you find these things?"

He had no idea if the tale was true, though knowing something of rummage sales and sisterhoods, he didn't doubt he was correct in the larger sense.

"Am I not right?" he asked Mrs. Robinson who, in spite of her placid performance of the tasks in hand, was still obviously in the grip of some inner struggle.

She responded gamely enough, however. "It's all quite true," she said, squeezing yet more lemons and dropping the rinds into the cooling tea. "Hand me down the sugar, Father Reggie," she commanded, pointing to a shelf of canisters. "No, not that one. Yes, that one. The Sisterhood," she went on, "has several times thought about getting new ice trays, but it has not, hitherto, had a very high priority. Thank you, Father. Now, please put it back, would you? And—my goodness, what's that?"

6 Out in the hall a real shouting match had erupted. Father Reggie nipped to the door, closely followed by Miss Morgan—and Mrs. Robinson, too, this time—where they watched the unfolding contretemps.

The time had apparently come to give Jack Cartwright his "notes." An herculean task that, thought Father Reggie privately and sourly.

Jack was a good actor. Quite a very good actor. After Mrs. Robinson herself and Stringer Yates, who was playing Gottschalk, he was unquestionably the best actor in the cast. Unfortunately, he was also that most difficult creature in the whole of theatrical life, that thing feloniously styled a "method actor"—feloniously, because, as has been justly observed, poor old Konstantin Stanislavsky would probably spin in his grave at the twaddle perpetrated in his name.

Jack, it must be said in his defense, was young, twenty-one or twenty-two at most. Strikingly handsome, the nephew and ward of his stinking-rich old uncle Clyde Cartwright (one of the larger growers in the Valley and president of the parish council), he was a student of "drama" at Jolliston State College and a man who made no pretensions about either his ambitions or his opinion of his own ability.

Trouble had begun to brew early on between Jack and Neil. Neil had directed Jack into a scene in a manner to which Jack objected. Nothing had been said at the time, for such is not the way of actors like Jack. Instead, he bided his time till the next rehearsal and then did the scene precisely the way he had wanted to do it in the first place. Not unreasonably, Neil objected. Words were exchanged which, on Jack's part, reached fever pitch until he came out with that classic demand of the "method" actor: "What's my motivation?"

In response to which Neil rejoined with the equally classic response—and in a deadly earnest voice pregnant with menace, "Keeping the part!"

Jack retired in impotent fury. And obeyed. For the most part.

If, however, his relations with the director were cantankerous, they were as a thing of sweetness and light compared to his interactions with the playwright.

As has been noted, Julian was far more poet than he was playwright, and considered the alteration of a participle a treachery in comparison to which that of Benedict Arnold was but a suburban intrigue. Jack, on the other hand, in common with most of the adherents of his peculiar school of acting, considered a script but a bare bones outline upon which the "genius" of the actor was at liberty to improvise, rephrase, paraphrase, and, generally speaking, "improve."

It was, so to speak, an unstoppable force meeting an immovable object, and the resulting explosions, like the one occurring at that very moment, were loud, contentious, and bitter to an uncommon degree.

Father Reggie heard Mrs. Robinson behind him sigh and turn back to the table. Belinda Sue must also have sensed something. She scowled rather fiercely at Father Reggie and jerked her head toward the table where Mrs. Robinson had begun to wrestle with the ice trays single-handedly. Father Reggie nodded wordlessly, and he and Miss Morgan returned to their proper tasks. He reached down to take the tray with which Mrs. Robinson was laboring and was surprised to feel a drop of warm moisture fall from her onto his hand.

For a moment he was nothing more than slightly embarrassed, thinking it a drop of sweat fallen from her brow. Then he realized that the reason she had her head bowed was because she had actually shed a tear.

"Elspeth," he said forthrightly, the time for pussyfooting clearly over, "what's wrong?"

She was just not a weeping kind of woman. Even during the hellish days following her husband's death, it had been a rare thing for her to be seen weeping.

She sniffed and relinquished the ice tray and looked up to see Belinda Sue being practical and holding out a handkerchief. She chuckled and accepted the handkerchief. "Thank you," she said, and put it to good use before saying, rather cryptically, "I've been a vain and foolish old woman."

Belinda Sue and Father Reggie could only stare at each other blankly.

"What do you mean?" demanded Father Reggie.

The three of them went on breaking ice cubes free and tossing them into the bowl of tea. The crack and shatter of the cubes from the parent trays helped to cover the somewhat eyes-downcast and embarrassed falterings of Mrs. Robinson attempting to articulate her dilemma. Finally she sighed and, shrugging her shoulders, seized a tea towel with which she wiped her hands.

"It's really very simple and it's very, very stupid," she said. "But after Millie Cantrell persuaded me to read for the play (and really, you know, it didn't take a whole lot of persuading) and I got the part, well . . . Perhaps I can explain it by saying that Millie and Edgar, my youngest son, have been trying to get me to go back to work."

"Acting?" asked Belinda Sue.

Mrs. Robinson nodded. "But it's not all that easy. It's been nearly thirty years since I made a film, other than the odd TV thing here and there, and the people who make movies are the kind who think last year is ancient history. Most of 'em think I died years ago. And all of them will want to know if I haven't lost it, or some such nonsense."

Father Reggie nodded, trying to look encouraging. The noise in the hall had diminished to a dull and inchoate kind of murmuring, and he wondered if that savage note session was drawing to a close. But Mrs. Robinson was coming to the crux of her problem. "Fortunately, I kept up some, not many, but some of my ties to the industry, people who had been good friends as well as colleagues."

"And?" prompted Belinda Sue.

Again Mrs. Robinson sighed. "Well, when I got cast, and I knew what kind of a job I could do with that part, I invited some old friends up for the weekend of the opening. I didn't tell them what I was up to. But I knew that once they were here, they'd want to come to the play to see me, and I particularly wanted them to do so, because, frankly, I think this play would make a fine film, and I want to do the same part in a movie."

"Whom did you invite, Elspeth?" asked Father Reggie, with a pit of the deepest dismay opening just above his solar plexus.

She told them. The names in and of themselves meant nothing whatsoever and after a moment, then, perceiving this utterly blank reception of her bombshell, Mrs. Robinson smiled rather tightly and explained, "They are, my dears, respectively, my former agent, a director, and one of the top independent producers in all of—"

"Mrs. Robinson!" The voice from the doorway made all three jump and turn.

Jack Cartwright stood in the doorway, his face appreciably more flushed than usual.

"Yes, Jack?" said Mrs. Robinson, that superb actress, tranquilly.

"Neil wondered if the tea was ready yet. He said to tell you he had a few more general announcements and the schedule. . . ."

"We'll be right out," said Mrs. Robinson.

Jack vanished from the doorway.

In silence Father Reggie hefted the bowl of iced tea, while Mrs. Robinson fetched out a long roll of Styrofoam cups.

"And now it only remains to be seen," said Belinda Sue, "whether Jack was flushed like that because of his fight with Neil and Julian or because he heard what you were saying."

"That, my dear," said Mrs. Robinson dryly, "is a mystery that will be solved soon enough. If he heard me, it will be all over the cast by tomorrow midday, the Church of All Saints by tomorrow evening, and all of Jolliston by Friday night."

And, turning, she sailed from the room ahead of them.

CHAPTER SEVEN

1 "Very well, Elspeth," said Miss Worthing; "this invitation of yours. This is the foolishness of which you spoke and that you contend led to—all this?"

"I do," affirmed Mrs. Robinson. "Oh, now, don't get me wrong. If it caused anything, it was only because everyone else's foolishness compounded mine own."

"And just what do you mean by that, Mrs. Robinson?" asked the D.A.

"Just what I said," replied Mrs. Robinson tartly. "I think everyone went nuts."

"Well, now," said Belinda Sue, "I think I have to dispute that."

"Oh?" said Mrs. Robinson.

"Yes," said Belinda Sue. "Oh, I think they may have been very foolish in what they were all thinking. But you do have to admit that the *result* was all to the good."

"Like murder?" asked Mrs. Robinson sarcastically. "Father Hughie's murder?"

"I'm sorry, Mrs. Robinson," said Belinda Sue. "I don't know what led to Father Hughie's murder, or, rather, the attempt—attempts—on Dr. Cantrell's life. That's what we're here to find out about, isn't it? But, personally, I don't think for one minute that your—indiscretion was all *that* important."

"Excuse me," interrupted Miss Worthing. "We're getting ahead of ourselves again. What was the result you spoke of just now?"

"I found out"—Belinda Sue twinkled at Father Reggie— "when I got back from Berkeley on Thursday afternoon. After I had called Mrs. Robinson . . ."

"What for?" asked Miss Worthing.

Belinda Sue held up a hand. "I'll get to that."

"Hmph!" grunted Father Reggie. "She just came along to disturb my peace of mind!"

"Did it, too," said Belinda Sue smugly.

2   That Thursday afternoon, miraculously, Father Reggie had an hour with no appointments, no meetings, or anything else. It seemed appropriate, therefore—given the day so far—to begin making notes on a sermon on the sin of gossip.

He was engaged in this virtuous activity when, at the same time, the telephone rang, yet again, and his office door opened and Belinda Sue Morgan walked in—which had its usual effect on Father Reggie of complete discombobulation. Perceiving which, Belinda Sue waved without a hint of the knowing smile to which she was fully entitled at the telephone still ringing on the desk.

Coming to, Father Reggie picked up the phone and had the interesting experience of hearing the normally exquisitely possessed Bonnie Harris speaking breathlessly and excitedly.

"Oh, good, you're in!" she began.

"What I can do for you, Bonnie?" he asked, knowing with existential certainty that she, too, was going to seek confirmation of the rumors.

Bonnie, however, had progressed beyond the need to know to realms of the purest theological faith.

"I finished the costumes!"

"You did?" he said. "But what if . . ."

About to say, "But what if the play is canceled?"—upon maturer reflection, it seemed an impolitic thing to say to the playwright's fiancée, prudence being, after all, a virtue. But Miss Harris was clearly too full of her own news to hear the unfinished suggestion. And, in a rather atypical fashion, she proceeded at some length to talk about slaving away over a hot sewing machine to finish and could Father Reggie—if he wouldn't mind *too* dreadfully—get someone to come get them? She couldn't leave the shop and, really, they should get to the church to have a chance to hang before Friday's rehearsal.

"I mean I know that no *professional* actor needs a costume," she gushed, "but they *aren't* professional, are they? At least not most of them." She actually giggled. "And maybe having their costumes will encourage them. Don't you think so?"

"I'll see what I can do," said Father Reggie when he finally could get a word in edgewise.

Belinda Sue, when this conversation was reported to her, started laughing.

But Father Reggie could only shake his head, muttering, "I don't know what's gotten into this parish."

"Oh, really?" asked Belinda Sue. "Do you mean Bonnie isn't the only one het up?"

"My God!" said Father Reggie fervently. "Even Neil was in here . . ."

"On a Thursday? Neil?"

Thursday evenings were immemorially sacred to choir rehearsal, which meant no one ever, *ever* saw Neil as he prepared to forty well-intentioned but, for the most part, musically illiterate souls through the music chosen for the week.

"More than that," said Father Reggie dryly. "He *canceled* choir rehearsal."

"What?"

"Yep. Said at least half the choir said they couldn't come anyway."

"Now that is interesting," observed Belinda Sue.

Father Reggie frowned. "And furthermore, you're the second person that's said *that*."

"Oh?"

"Yeah. Mrs. Robinson copped very much the same attitude."

"Oh, good," said Belinda Sue, suddenly distracted. "You've talked to her? Did she tell you what we've got planned?"

"What?"

"I'm taking you to dinner this evening."

Not being altogether an idiot, Father Reggie responded gamely: "Why, thank you, ma'am. Such kindness to an aging priest . . ."

"Aging priest, indeed," said Ms. Morgan. "Anyway, I've invited Elspeth, too. She said to come by her place for an aperitif."

"Good." He perked up. "Maybe she'll give us some of that dynamite vermouth she brews up in the backyard. But no, to answer your original question, she didn't say anything to me about dinner. You must have talked to her after I did."

"When was that?"

"Right after I spoke to Neil."

"And just what *did* he want?"

"He came nosing around just a little bit too casually."

"So what did you tell him?"

"I told him the truth. My God, by the time Jack got through babbling, we were apparently going to be visited by a plenary council of every major director, producer, agent, and screenwriter in lower California."

"That's *Southern* California, Father." Belinda Sue grinned.

"Hmph! Same thing," rejoined Father Reggie austerely. "What did that boy do? Run out of the kitchen last night, yelling, 'The movies are coming! The movies are coming!'"

Ms. Morgan chuckled appreciatively.

But Father Reggie was anything but amused by what he considered a shocking display of provincialism on the part of his normally levelheaded parishioners and failed to see what was so funny.

"Dear Father Reggie"—Belinda Sue smiled indulgently upon him—"you're being an old maid."

"I'm being nothing of the kind," said Father Reggie, turning bright red.

"Yes, you are, and it's very silly. Of *course* they're all agog. Why shouldn't they be? They were all raised—just as you and I were—on movies and TV. Ever watched a crowd of people around a TV? They're mesmerized by the thing. Even if they're not really watching it and the sound is turned off, their eyes still keep getting drawn to the screen.

"And, of course, the unfortunate thing is all they see is a slick, finished product. So between that and all the PR hoopla, everybody imagines life as a movie star or director or producer must be just *so* glamorous!"

"You sound like you know something about it."

"I do," she said. "I once thought I might like to be an actress. Even made a movie. Don't worry, you never heard of it; it died an early and wholly justified demise. It's too much hard work for me."

"But you're getting a Ph.D. In theology!" protested Father Reggie. "That's not easy. I know."

"Yes," said Belinda Sue crisply. "And when I'm fifty, I'll still be able to do theology and, furthermore, I'm just vain enough to think I have something—well, let's not say original (What a horrible thought! Can't even *imagine* what kind of critter an 'original' theologian would be!)—but I can do something to add to the work everyone in the Church is supposed to be doing. But that has nothing to do with our current *social* concern," she concluded with a grin.

"Well, I still think it's disgraceful," said Father Reggie, though even as he said it, he knew perfectly well he sounded like a stubborn old fussbudget.

He sighed and stood up.

"But none of this is getting us anywhere. I'd better get down there and pick up those costumes."

"No!" said Belinda Sue firmly, standing up also. "I'll do it. You've got quite enough to do without running errands all over creation in this heat."

"I am the stage manager," said Father Reggie, adding in avuncular tones: "Besides, my dear Miss Morgan, what else do you suppose a priest's life consists of if not running errands of one sort or another for his parishioners? Besides, don't you have any work of your own to do?"

"Just check some references in Augustine. And believe me, even luxuriating in his gorgeous Latin can't make up for having to wallow about in that nasty little crypto-Manichean mind. We'll go together. Many hands make light work."

They strolled companionably down the corridor together—and came to an astonished halt just outside Father Hughie's office.

The door was ajar and from within came Father Hughie's flat voice reciting, over and over again, the words of his speeches from the play. And when he stumbled, there came the proper words buzzed back at him as Fiona McLaren prompted him.

Afterward, neither Father Reggie nor Miss Morgan could say just why the thought of that unlikely pair being excited by the advent of movie moguldom should have struck them as funny. The fact remains that, after that first astonished glance at one another, the two of them literally fled down the corridor, down the stairs, and out the front door, fetching up on the sidewalk in front of the church hall, holding onto each other and rocking with laughter.

3   Gradually the sun beating down upon them stilled their shouts and order was restored—particularly after old Miss Morrison came down the steps of the church and eyed them with a glance carefully devoid of expression. At which point it occurred to both of them that for a priest to be seen clutching a beautiful young woman, to whom he was not married, and laughing like a maniac was distinctly open to misinterpretation.

Which, of course, set them off again.

When, presently, they were in Father Reggie's venerable Buick with the air conditioning wheezing away—and they had calmed somewhat—Belinda Sue asked, "So do you think Neil and Julian'll decide to cancel tomorrow night?"

"I really couldn't say," said Father Reggie, before adding, rather thoughtfully, "though, frankly, I doubt it. Especially now. There'd probably be a riot. In fact, I wouldn't be a bit surprised if everyone has their lines letter-perfect tomorrow night. And their blocking."

"That's what I've been thinking ever since I began hearing the rumors. What *was* Neil's reaction, incidentally?"

Father Reggie frowned and said, "I'm not sure about this, but it seemed to me that he was pretty elated."

"Well," said Belinda Sue after a moment, "let's hope you are right. Let's hope so. Although I wonder if even Fiona can get Father Hughie . . ."

"I know," said Father Reggie grimly. "And let's all pray she gets some results. Honestly, sometimes Hughie is an absolute disgrace."

Miss Morgan looked over at him. "I take it you do not refer solely to his interpretation of the wretched Hincmar."

"In this instance I do," replied Father Reggie. "Do you mean you don't know?"

"Don't know what? You know, I wish you folks would remember I've only been here for five months."

"Is that all?"

Belinda Sue clicked her tongue. "Yes. But never mind that. What are you talking about?"

"It was Father Hughie who persuaded us to start a theater company."

"Father Hughie!"

"The same. Now, don't be that way. He's done quite a good deal for All Saints."

"Okay, so what happened?"

"It was after Julian moved in. Upstairs, on the roof. Bonnie, you know, practically commandeered the job for him, so I suppose none of us should have been surprised when she all but moved in as well, leaving her nice little condo out on Protrero as storage for whatever wouldn't fit up there."

"Ooh!" said Belinda Sue appreciatively. "And just how did that go down?"

"Well," said Father Reggie, "most of us felt it was none of our business. They were solemnly betrothed, after all, and what with the theology of matrimony being considerably plastic . . ."

"Never mind the theology of matrimony! Gimme the dirt!"

"There wasn't any! At least, not at first. Julian was already proving to be a real diamond in the rough, so most folks just ignored the whole situation. However, as always—"

"Yes," interrupted Belinda Sue with another gurgle of laughter. "There are always—kind friends."

"To be sure. Anyway, someone eventually blabbed to Dr. Cantrell and, though I did my level best to try to persuade him otherwise, he said he was going up to put a stop to what he was pleased to call 'fornication under the very roof of the church.'"

"Or *on* the roof as the case might be."

"Hmph!" said Father Reggie. "Anyway, off he charged and after a minute I thought I had better go up, too, even if it did mean getting my head chewed off."

"Why? Was Cantrell angry with you?"

"No, not at all. Or at least no more than usual. No, I was

worried about Julian. Because Julian—quite rightly, I believe—thought and thinks that, when he is at home, even if it *is* right up on the roof of the church hall, he shouldn't have to be disturbed. By anyone."

"Very proper."

"Yes, well, apparently . . . Now, mind you, all of this was before I got up there—I've had to piece this together from bits here and there that various parties to the drama have dropped now and again—before the elevator had even creaked to a halt, and you know how noisy it is, Julian was already furious. So just as Cantrell gets all set to pound authoritatively on the door, Julian yanks it open and stands there fuming. Stark naked. And so, for that matter, is Bonnie, though she, at least, had the sense to grab a bed sheet.

"I got up, by the stairs, about five minutes later and both Julian and Bonnie were giving him hell. Julian from his outraged sense of territory, and Bonnie because, it seems, Dr. Cantrell had just referred to her as 'this *girl*'—mind you—'with whom you are living in sin.'"

"My word!" said Belinda Sue.

"Cantrell was looking rather like a boiled fig, and I, my dear, turned lily-livered coward, turned right around and fled down the stairs. And ran straight into Father Hughie. Who, once more proving that old adage about fools rushing in where angels fear to tread, found out from me what was happening and before anyone could stop him or even imagine what he was going to do, twittered off 'to do something.'"

"And?"

"And he found Bonnie, quite decently clad, frying onions, Cantrell nowhere to be seen, and Julian placidly at work at his typewriter."

"He didn't fly at Father Hughie?"

"No. He'd taken Hughie's measure early on and treated him"—Father Reggie sighed—"as most of us do, with that somewhat exasperated respect that one has for a not very competent boob."

"So what happened then?"

"Well, it seems Father Hughie came in all atwitter, wouldn't take no for an answer, and was, in fact, far more distressed about the whole business than were either Bonnie or Julian, so Julian went to fetch him a slug of brandy to calm him down, and I'll be damned if Hughie doesn't pick up and start reading Julian's manuscript."

"Oh, my God!"

"Which was, for Julian, the last straw, and although Bonnie says he restrained himself admirably, he was clearly fuming. Hughie, of course, saw nothing, grabbed the brandy, belted it back, and took off like a blue streak about how brilliant it all was and it was positively a miracle, an answer to his most fervent prayers, because he'd been thinking for *months* that what All Saints really needed was a theater group. It was the *only* thing missing from our roster of activities! And, by God! Here we had a genuine God-sent playwright living in our very midst!"

Father Reggie broke off his accurate if not very kind imitation of his fellow priest.

"And Julian agreed?"

For a moment or two longer Father Reggie continued to drive in silence.

"Well, you know," he finally said, "I've known a playwright or two in my time. I don't have the foggiest idea about how difficult it is to write a play, and don't particularly want to find out. But a really astonishing number of them do, for all that, get written. And most of them are never performed. And you do have to admit that whatever else might be true of Father Hughie, he does get things done.

"It must have been a powerful temptation to Julian. I'm sure that like any would-be playwright he must have thought about production. And despaired.

"So apparently, when Father Hughie made his suggestion, all he did was laugh and point out that it was moderately likely that he wasn't even going to have a job. Father

Hughie said, 'Don't be silly,' and went right on making plans for a drama group."

"Which patently were eventually made manifest," said Belinda Sue, "but surely Dr. Cantrell. . . ."

"Oh, he tried. To get Julian fired, that is. But there were enough people like Elspeth—and me, for that matter—who told him not to be such an old stuffed shirt."

"That wouldn't have stopped *him*."

"No, of course not. But the church's lawyer gave his opinion that if they terminated Julian for doing something in his own home, there might be a cause of action. And you know what chicken shits churches are about lawsuits."

"So the play went on."

"Yes, and Dr. Cantrell and Julian hate each other like poison."

Upon which depressing note Father Reggie pulled his aging car to a halt in front of Bonnie's shop, and any further elucidation of the unofficial history of the Church of All Saints was temporarily put on hold. . . .

4 Besides, the costumes were absolutely splendid. One by one and with attentive care they carried them from the workshop in the back of Bonnie's shop, where she had built them, to the car. Gorgeous things: sumptuous and heavy tabards, gowns, and robes in velvet and satin and brocade.

Finally Belinda Sue was unable to refrain from comment on the rich stuffs of which they had been made.

"Bonnie," she said, with awe, "they're the most stunning things I've ever seen. But they must have cost you the earth!"

"Oh, they did!" averred the practical Miss Harris with a smile, "but I assure you it'll all come back."

"How's that?" asked Father Reggie, laying yet another sheet of tissue paper over a velvet tabard so that the satin dress Belinda Sue carried could be laid down.

"Well, first of all—and most obviously—as a very nice tax deduction. And secondly"—she lowered her voice and looked around as though she were fearful of being over-heard—"I've only just been getting into *designing* clothes. In fact, I've been thinking of adding a special line in all my shops. And I suspect, or at least I hope, that when the women in the audience see these and 'designs and execution by Bonnie Harris' in the programs—well, word will get out."

Finally her excitement could no longer be contained. She clasped her hands together and exulted, "I can't *wait* to see them on the stage tomorrow night! And I know they'll help the actors. This play has got to work!"

And then, unexpectedly, she confessed ingenuously, "Julian said he won't marry me till his income at least matches mine."

Father Reggie and Belinda Sue sedulously avoided each other's eye as Bonnie went on wistfully: "So if those movie folks really are coming, and there's even the remotest chance they'll buy the property, I want this to be the best damned show they ever saw."

Belinda Sue and Father Reggie duly sympathized with her, complimented her on her business acumen, and, mur-muring their adieux, clambered back into the car and drove off. They had driven halfway to the church in a musing si-lence when, seemingly out of left field, Belinda Sue said, "I think we had better pray for a quick break in the heat."

"Why?"

"Because, considering the stress that's already on us, I don't think I'm looking forward to a rehearsal while we're all dressed up in clothes—and cloth—designed to be worn in Northern Europe in the Little Ice Age. Not in California. Not with a heat wave on."

5 Later that evening, after dinner, Mrs. Robinson invited them all back to her place again.

"Some more vermouth?" asked Belinda Sue.

"Something even better."

And presently, in the living room of the Robinson house, with its front window framing a vista of rolling vineyards rising to the eastern hills and the deepening sky above, Mrs. Robinson brought out liqueur glasses and a bottle with a faintly greenish liquid within.

Mischievously Father Reggie asked, "Experimenting again, Elspeth?"

"Um-hmm." Mrs. Robinson nodded with a glint in her eye and poured out small shots. "It's something Barney and I were working on. You know the herbal wine Mattie Worthing and Martha Shaw make?"

Father Reggie nodded and began to look interested. Miss Morgan, on the other hand, looked blank.

"It's some concoction," explained Mrs. Robinson, "that Mattie and Martha have been serving at their Christmas open house for years now."

"And ever since I've been here," said Father Reggie, "every vintner in five counties has tried every trick in the book to find out how they do it."

He tasted the brew.

"No," said Mrs. Robinson, answering his unspoken question as he savored the stuff, "that's *not* it. What that is is pure serendipity. Barney and I were trying to duplicate their formula when this happened. At first we were just going to toss it. Then I had the idea of adding some honey and waiting a bit."

"It's fabulous," said Belinda Sue, taking another sip of the liqueur.

"I'll be with you in a moment," said Mrs. Robinson, turning to leave the room. "Coffee will be ready."

A pleasant and easy silence descended on the room.

After a moment Father Reggie said, "I wonder if Barney got to taste it."

Mrs. Robinson chose that very moment to return. "Yes, he did," she answered the question placidly. "Practically his last words of advice were to make it and market it. Pity he never got to taste it after it was barreled awhile as well. This is the first decanting. I wanted your opinion. You like it?"

"It's glorious, Elspeth. I think it would definitely sell!"

Father Reggie looked to Belinda Sue for corroboration.

That young woman, however, was staring sightlessly into her glass.

Mrs. Robinson poured coffee, picked up her own pony glass, sat on the sofa next to Belinda Sue, and said, "All right, young lady. Out with it."

Miss Morgan looked up. "I beg your pardon."

"You've had something on your mind all evening," said Mrs. Robinson. "Now we've talked about the play and the various ways all our good parishioners are reacting to my foolishness, so it isn't that. So why don't you just tell us."

Belinda Sue laughed. "Well, as a matter of fact, I did almost ask Father Reggie about it this afternoon. And it is something that's been bothering me. Maybe the two of you, together—"

"What's up, Belinda Sue?" asked Father Reggie, and then, pointing to the bottle of liqueur, asked Mrs. Robinson, "May I?"

"Help yourselves!" replied Mrs. Robinson. "Just be careful. I don't have the foggiest what the alcohol content is yet. Other, that is, than high."

"That could just be the ginger root in it," said Miss Morgan, holding her glass out to Father Reggie to refill.

Mrs. Robinson was genuinely surprised by that one.

"You *are* an observing wench," she said admiringly, holding out her own pony to be filled.

"Yes, I am," averred Belinda Sue. "And that's why I can't quite understand . . ."

"Yes?"

"Pardon me," she said, and looked directly at the older woman, "but what *is* a priest like Father Hughie Barnes doing at a church like All Saints?"

For rather a long moment neither Mrs. Robinson nor Father Reggie said anything. Mrs. Robinson busied herself with cream and sugar in her coffee while Father Reggie sought counsel in the swirling depths of his liqueur glass.

"Oh, come on, you two," snapped Belinda Sue. "It can't be all that bad."

"Can't it?" said Mrs. Robinson dryly.

"Father Reggie?"

"I'm sorry, Belinda Sue. It was not one of our finest hours."

"So I gather," said Belinda Sue.

Presently, after a moment more of silence, Mrs. Robinson said, "It has to do with the rector."

"Dr. Cantrell?"

Mrs. Robinson nodded. "Tell me, Belinda Sue, what do you think of him?"

"He's a dreary old poop," said Ms. Morgan coolly.

Father Reggie made a faint sound of protest.

"No, Father Reggie," said Mrs. Robinson. "I asked."

"When I first came here," said Belinda Sue, "I was surprised by two things: First of all, that a man like Father Hughie should be attached to a parish like this in any capacity. And second—well, I thought they only made priests like Cantrell in bad Hollywood romances."

"My dear," said Mrs. Robinson, "you're much too young to realize that, not all that long ago—or at least what seems not all that long ago to me—priests like Dr. Cantrell were the rule rather than the exception."

"You see," Father Reggie picked up the unpleasant tale, "when Cantrell was a young man, the clergy was—well, a *profession*. Like lawyering or doctoring or schoolmastering. It was something a *gentleman*," he explained sarcastically, "went into. And, by the standards of the time, he was very good."

"Yes, he was," said Mrs. Robinson. "He was learned, a good administrator, and an extraordinary preacher."

"By the standards of the day?" asked Belinda Sue.

"By the standards of the day," replied Mrs. Robinson.

"His preaching always sounds like so much well-practiced cant," said the younger woman.

"Be kind, dear. Leo Cantrell's life has not been an altogether happy one."

"Him?"

"Him!"

"You see," said Father Reggie, "the Church has changed in the last fifty years. That kind of vocation among the clergy is not only no longer encouraged, but even the laity has changed. There was a time, that even I remember, when folks went to church because it was the thing to do. Belief had nothing to do with it. It was nothing more than a particularly respectable way to be entertained."

"And be like those 'who to church repair, not for the doctrine but the music there,'" Miss Morgan quoted cynically.

"That, too," said Mrs. Robinson. "A sermon, after all, is a bastard form of the theater."

"For theatrical personalities," said Miss Morgan repressively.

"Which, you have to admit, Dr. Cantrell certainly is," said Father Reggie.

"Okay. But you still haven't said how Father Hughie fits into this."

"Well, you see, my dear," said Mrs. Robinson, "Leo wants—wanted to be a bishop."

"And in what he would no doubt call 'his day,' it would probably have just been a matter of time," said Father Reggie. "But bishops just don't get chosen in the old way anymore. Oh, there are, to be sure, dozens of 'em who are little more than political functionaries. But for the most part they're men committed to the faith."

"And Leo Cantrell," said Mrs. Robinson, "as far as I know,

hasn't been seriously considered as a candidate for higher office for at least the last twenty years or so."

"And?" said Miss Morgan.

"We had an opening for an assistant priest," said Father Reggie.

"Before Father Hughie?"

Mrs. Robinson nodded.

"And Dr. Cantrell found us a candidate," said Father Reggie.

"Who was he?"

Mrs. Robinson said a name.

Miss Morgan sat back and looked wide-eyed from one to the other. "*That* family?"

Priest and older woman nodded.

"You know him?" asked Father Reggie.

Miss Morgan shook her head. "Not personally. But, of course, I know the family. They've been bishops and deans and whatnot all the way back to the Revolution."

"I know," said Mrs. Robinson. "Well, unfortunately, this particular sprig of ancient lineage that Leo brought forth turned out to be a man not unlike himself."

"Nothing would surprise me less," said Miss Morgan. "I know—knew one of them, a bishop back East. He's dead now, but I wasn't exactly wild about him either."

She said his name.

"That was our candidate's uncle," said Father Reggie. "Which—God, I'm being bitchy again."

"No, you're not, Father Reggie," said Mrs. Robinson. "You're right, what you were about to say. Two of the man's uncles were bishops and his father was the dean of a pretty important cathedral."

"So you think," said Belinda Sue, "that Dr. Cantrell hoped that his chance of getting a bishopric would improve by getting this—person at All Saints. . . ."

"Not think, dear," said Mrs. Robinson; "know."

"What happened?"

———————————————————————————— 147

"We rejected him," reported Mrs. Robinson placidly. "Those of us who take our responsibilities as parish council members *talked* with the parishioners. And most of 'em were of the opinion that one Cantrell was one too many."

"Very good," said Belinda Sue, "but you still haven't said who proposed Father Hughie."

"Leo," said Mrs. Robinson. "I—I wouldn't *want* to say it was for revenge, but . . ."

"But he had to be elected, too," said Belinda Sue.

"Yes," said Father Reggie. "But he came in, preached an indifferent good sermon, he was awkward, shy, and pleasing if a bit thick. But he is, these days, I need hardly remind you, not the only one like that in the ranks of the clergy."

"And there was a certain amount of fence mending to be done with Leo," said Mrs. Robinson.

"God!" said Miss Morgan with deep feeling. "I hate politics."

The other two sighed and nodded agreement.

"Actually," said Mrs. Robinson after a moment, "I like Hughie Barnes. And, for a number of reasons, I'm very glad that he's with us."

"He does have his points," agreed Father Reggie.

And almost reluctantly, Ms. Morgan, too, gave her assent. "Yes, that's true—though they're sometimes hard to decipher. Of course, as you pointed out this afternoon, he does manage somehow to get things done."

"And, furthermore," said Father Reggie, rather forgetting himself, "if it's got to be a tossup between a hypocritical old fart like Cantrell and a wimp like Hughie, at least Hughie's faith, sentimental and adolescent though it be, is solid as a rock."

At which point, Belinda Sue gurgled that rich laugh of hers and, leaning forward, picked up the bottle to refill all their glasses, saying as she did so, "On which note, my dears, let's all have another shot of venom—and try to forget all about Jesus saying anything whatever about judging one's neighbors."

CHAPTER EIGHT

1 Fridays were supposed to be Father Reggie's day off. That Friday was anything but. First of all, it was the Feast of St. Bartholomew, which meant he had to say two of the regular holy day Masses in the morning. Then, of course, that evening was rehearsal. That all-important, decisive rehearsal.

So between Mass and rehearsal, clean contrary to his usual practice, he spent the day at home, puttering about the house, playing with his moronic dog, and, generally speaking, avoiding the outdoors at all costs and keeping the air conditioner turned to full blast. At first, the latter bothered him; he was, he realized, being selfish, wasteful, and unecological. And after taking Demon for a brief walk, he also didn't care.

Indeed, as the day progressed, any thought of budging from his comfortably cool house grew increasingly antipathetic. Finally, at three or so, he stretched out on the couch with a book he had read at least half a dozen times already and, in spite of his fidgets, fell asleep . . .

. . . and woke up feeling greatly refreshed, the house feeling almost cold, and the idiot Demon sound asleep and chasing rabbits. It even looked cooler, he decided (more hopefully than rationally) as he looked out a window into the westering light. Maybe, he thought prayerfully, just maybe the heat wave had broken.

He put on a jacket, turned down the laboring air conditioner, opened the front door, and walked into a solid wall of heat. There was not a breath of air stirring anywhere, and overhead not a cloud marred the sky. The smells suffusing the air were more than a little disagreeable—a night-blooming tree growing in his front yard was vigorously exuding wave after wave of pungent, oversweet scent with a rather sickening hint of underlying corruption, which combined with the dust already in the air to lend a distinctly charnel smell to the night.

Filled with apprehension as he remembered Belinda Sue's words about the costumes, he got into his car and headed across town.

When, later, notes were compared, everyone confessed to surprise that, confronted that Friday night by the costumes, there had *not* been wholesale rebellion in the ranks. Instead, everyone actually donned those heavy, enveloping vestments with positive delight.

But within minutes sweat was pouring off all of them—with a single exception—and presently tempers grew markedly short.

More than once over the course of the evening, rehearsal was brought to a halt as someone or other flew at someone else for some trivial reason.

The hall was, if anything, even more dismal than it had been the previous Wednesday. The heat was bad enough, muggy and close. But the smells added a distinctly unhealthy aura. The regular Friday seniors' luncheon and bingo had been held earlier that afternoon and, judging from the lingering aroma, they had dined on mutton fat and sago. And as if that weren't horrid enough, the swimming pool in the basement had been freshly scoured and chlorined in anticipation of the use it received every Saturday, and the chemical effluvia rising from below was enough to turn even a cast-iron stomach queasy.

And in spite of it all, rehearsal was a minor miracle.

Subsequently there were any number prepared to take credit for the extraordinary turnaround: Neil was sure his impromptu and savage harangue had done the trick. Bonnie was equally certain that it had been the timely production of her costumes. And any number of actors averred it had been their own eleventh-hour work that so inspired their fellows.

But in point of fact, everyone knew what had, in reality, brought about this quasi-miraculous sea change. And it had nothing to do with Bonnie's costumes, lovely though they were, or Neil's familiar snarling, or any actor doing work he should have done weeks before. Everyone knew—though not a single word was said—that the sole reason for the extraordinary turnabout was the giddily anticipated arrival of a small knot of cinemagnates.

The actors were all but letter-perfect in their lines; they moved about the stage with grace and security; and even characterizations that had flopped about looking as though they would never jell had begun to set nicely and, for perhaps the first time, the extraordinary power of Julian's poetic drama was made manifest.

After the first act Neil, rather nonplussed, looked at the virtually blank sheet of paper in front of him and called a twenty-minute break.

It was more than welcome.

Like things possessed, people whipped their costumes off and stood holding them away from them like hateful objects while they panted and prayed that the wet patches on the clothing they had worn under the costumes were not as obvious as they suspected them to be.

Whereupon Bonnie rose with a little cry of distress, which had the effect of bringing Neil to his wits. "All right, you dingalings," he shouted, "you're doing a good job. But that is no reason to abuse those costumes. Hang 'em up if you're not wearing 'em!"

Father Reggie, relieved of his duties in the smothering aromatic oven of the backstage regions, bore down upon the vat of iced tea Elspeth Robinson had made before anyone arrived—an inspired stroke on her part.

Elspeth, magnificent in snow-white wimple under a black velvet habit trimmed with purple satin, was slowly and with evident relief absorbing glass after glass of her own brew as Father Reggie came up to refresh himself.

"Great idea, Elspeth!" he said, before practically pouring the first glass into himself. "I can't believe we're actually managing to do this in this heat."

A rich baritone chuckle sounded behind him, followed by, "You should just be thankful you don't have to wear one of those costumes."

2   It was Stringer Yates, the man essaying the role of the unfortunate Gottschalk. He had stripped off his Benedictine robe and was in twill trousers, a sweat-stained T-shirt, and his monastic sandals.

"I may not have to wear a costume," replied Father Reggie, refilling his glass, "but I have to stand back there in that black hole of Calcutta smelling the blasted swimming pool. Enough to make you sick."

Stringer laughed and, also refilling his glass, eyed Mrs. Robinson. "My God, Elspeth! Why don't you get out of that thing?"

Mrs. Robinson snorted and held her glass toward Father Reggie, who plied the dipper and refilled it.

"Thank you, Father Reggie," she said, and then, with a smile, added to Stringer, "I would like to, but unlike yourself, I don't think I should be strutting around the place in my scanties."

"Why not, Elspeth? You did it in *A King's Fancy.*"

"Sweet of you to remember, Stringer, but you will also kindly recall that I was twenty-three at the time."

"Still look good to me, Elspeth."

"Humph," said that good woman, not unpleased. "I must tell Maria you said that."

"Why not? She thinks the same."

"But speaking of telling things, Stringer, I've been wanting to tell you: I think you're doing a really wonderful job with Gottschalk. Really wonderful. It's as good, maybe even better, than anything you did—well, in the old days."

Mr. Yates looked considerably surprised.

"You didn't know I'd seen you?" asked Mrs. Robinson.

"I didn't know anybody remembered."

"I remember. You can be very proud of yourself for this performance."

"What are you folks talking about?" said Father Reggie.

Mrs. Robinson looked a trifle uncertain, seeing which Mr. Yates smiled a somewhat rueful smile and came to the rescue.

"Elspeth's being kind again," he said as one man will to another.

Father Reggie nodded. "She does that," he observed.

"I know," said Stringer with a grateful glance at the somewhat disconcerted Mrs. Robinson. "She was telling me in her own kind way that she remembers when I was a leading actor off Broadway."

"Really, Stringer?" said Father Reggie. "Gee, I didn't know you were an actor. I mean, it's clear from your work here you've had experience, but—"

"He was one of the most brilliant of a whole crop of young actors just coming up," Mrs. Robinson cut in.

"Wow!" said Stringer. "Nice to hear that from the great Elspeth Boyd."

"So what happened, Stringer?" asked Father Reggie.

Mrs. Robinson looked slightly scandalized at the direct

question. Mr. Yates, however, had no apparent reluctance to speak.

"The bottle," said Stringer simply. "Fell into it and wondered if I was ever going to get out of it again. Wasn't even sure I wanted to get out. Lost everything and no one would touch me for a part with a ten-foot pole. Can't say I blame 'em. That was when my Uncle Heinrich—he was actually a distant cousin—asked me to come out here and help with the vines. He and Maria—"

"Your wife!" interrupted Father Reggie.

"Yeah," nodded Mr. Yates. "Yeah. She was his daughter. The two of 'em dried me out, got me working my butt off in the fields, and"—he shrugged—"the rest, as they say, is history."

"I was so pleased when you and Maria fell in love and got married," said Mrs. Robinson. "It seemed like a fairy tale come to life."

"For me too," agreed Mr. Yates. "Maria's quite a gal, too. She was the one who wanted me to read for the play. Said 'idt vass dime,'" he parodied his wife's German accent, and laughed. "And she was right. It is nice to be acting again. Never thought I'd get such a juicy part, though. That was nice, too. But I'll tell you, I'm about beat, what with the white harvest and all. Aren't you, Elspeth?"

She laughed and shook her head. "Fortunately, I'm just in the winery these days. I'm too old for all that roistering about in the fields. I hire people to do that now."

Stringer sighed. "Yeah, well. Wish I could afford to do that." Then he laughed and said, "But you wouldn't believe how Maria took on when I told her Neil had threatened to cancel the show. Said I had to devote every spare minute to learning my stuff."

"Well, I'm glad she did it," said Mrs. Robinson, and repeated her earlier remark, "You're doing very well indeed."

"Thanks, Elspeth," said Yates, yet again filling his iced tea glass. "Let's just hope we can make something out of it."

Upon which distinctly ambiguous note, work was resumed.

3   And onstage the tormented Gottschalk, trapped in his
    cell, paces to and fro, haunted by the specter of the
theologian who trounced him in debate. "Go away," he
shouts; "you're dead. You were killed by your students in
Paris. . . ."

But the specter of Erigena persists, dragging him once
more into the debate, the pointless debate of a deranged
man who can think of nothing but endlessly to say to himself, "This is what I *should* have said."

And the Spirit of the World, flitting around the figures of
the two men onstage—Jack as the specter of Erigena and
Stringer as Gottschalk, both of them endlessly debating a
dead issue—made, by her very presence, the simple query
whether either man had been motivated by love of truth, or
whether, just possibly, it had been for the glamour and
power pertaining to one triumphant in these matters.

The scene segues into another, where Gottschalk asks his
cousin, the Lady Abbess, still a specter in his own mind, if
he had done the right thing. From this, the *Spiritus Mundi*
is excluded, for it is a scene wherein Gottschalk reaches
down into the troubled depths of his own mind in search of
the honesty he has thought himself to be pursuing all along.

Belinda Sue came and stood next to Father Reggie to wait
for her next entrance. Of all the characters in the play, Bonnie Harris had chosen only the Spirit of the World not to be
swathed in bolts of cloth. Indeed, her costume was one constructed of that most evanescent of stuffs, sheer muslin,
while the garments themselves were of the most attenuated
nature, all of which, it might be added, set off Ms. Morgan's
appreciable charms to devastating advantage.

And she loved it. Not only for the fact that she alone in the cast was relatively cool, but she was enjoying with great satisfaction the effect she was having upon poor Father Reggie's equanimity of mind.

And they watched raptly together the unfolding of the drama on the stage. The scene had been wrenching enough previously when only Mrs. Robinson had been really "into" it. Now that Stringer had settled down, learned his lines and blocking, and had let the character itself develop out of the peculiar alchemy of the actor's craft, they began to realize that this was truly a remarkable piece of theater.

It was, at that point, that Father Reggie's life was forever changed. He leaned his head toward Miss Morgan and whispered, "It's fabulous, isn't it?"

She turned to look at him . . .

. . . And by the end of the scene, some ten minutes later, they were finally, satisfactorily, engaged.

It was, in a way, ironic that it should have been Father Hughie who was the first to find out. He came upon them as he rounded the various stage draperies preparatory to making his entrance, shadowed, according to the script, by the *Spiritus Mundi*. It was altogether characteristic that, instead of retreating discreetly, his embarrassment at finding his fellow priest with an extraordinarily beautiful woman wrapped around him made him stumble, nearly fall, and, generally speaking, make a great deal of noise.

Neither that fellow priest nor that beautiful woman were anything but too happy at the outcome of events to be in the least distressed by the falling in of Father Hughie. In fact, they rushed to rescue him before he pulled down the leaders he clutched in desperation and generally chivied him back to equanimity.

"It's okay, Hughie," said Father Reggie, slapping his colleague on the back, "we're engaged."

As usual, Father Hughie gaped for the moment or two it took for this intelligence to penetrate. Whereupon he began volubly to congratulate them.

Out in front, a stentorian, "Quiet backstage!" issued from Neil.

"We have to celebrate," said the unrepentant Father Hughie.

"We'll do that later," said Belinda Sue. "Right now you get out there and knock the socks off 'em. We've finally got a play."

"Not for me, "sighed Father Hughie. "It's not working."

"So what's wrong, Hughie?" asked Father Reggie.

"Well, I mean, I got the words and I got the blocking—Fiona finally drilled it all into me. But I can't get him."

"Who?" asked Belinda Sue.

"Hincmar. He's such a nasty man. I mean, I just can't get him. I mean, what kind of a man would act like that? I mean, it's so unchristian."

"Hughie," said Father Reggie censoriously, "surely you have dealt with people in the past whom you've considered unchristian."

"Sure. Lots of 'em. What's that got to do with it?"

"Oh, ye pigs and little fishes of the Lord!" exclaimed Father Reggie, and was promptly silenced both by Belinda Sue and a look of wounded uncertainty from Father Hughie.

"Nevertheless, Reggie does have a point, Father Hughie," said Belinda Sue, taking the younger priest's hand in her own. "That's the way actors work. They think of someone they've known, someone who might act the way you're trying to work it, or even dig out some kind of motivation in yourself that might have perhaps wanted you to act that way."

"Ye-e-s," said Father Hughie doubtfully. "I think I see what you mean. Do you think that if I—well, imitated someone that I think is as nasty as Hincmar, it would work?"

"That's what they tell me acting is all about, Hughie," said Father Reggie, wondering if this thirty-second exposition of acting technique would do anything at all for his dim colleague.

"I'm going to go over there and think about this," said Father Hughie, his face still twisted into a puzzled frown. "I think I know what you mean. I don't know—" He cut himself off. "I—I can think of something that might work. Thank you, guys. And congratulations."

He trundled off around the heavy black leader, and for the duration of the present scene they could hear him occasionally muttering to himself.

"What do you think he has in mind?" said Father Reggie, torn between a laudable desire to continue making love to his new fiancée and enormous curiosity.

"I'm sure we'll find out," said Belinda Sue practically.

"I'm not sure we did the right thing."

"Why not?"

"What if he chooses as a model someone everyone knows? I wouldn't put it past him."

Belinda Sue shrugged. "We'll find out. Though frankly," she said, not unkindly, "one suspects that that poor man could think he was doing an absolutely faithful takeoff of someone and no one on earth would recognize it. Sorry." She shook her head. "I'm being bitchy again. It is one of my major faults, you know."

"Mine, too," said the fond Father Reggie.

"I know, it's what attracted me to you."

The next several minutes and the rest of the scene passed in pleasant pursuits, and before they were quite aware of what was happening, once again Father Hughie was with them, this time in a blaze of excitement.

"Thank you, you guys," he twittered at them. "That was a wonderful suggestion. I think I got it. Yeah, yeah, yeah. I really think I got it. You ready, Belinda Sue?"

"Ready as I'm gonna be, Hughie," she said, kissing Father Reggie lightly on the end of his nose. "Let's hit it."

Doing various interesting things with her incompletely clad body, the Spirit of the World led the unbending archbishop Hincmar to face the unrepentant Gottschalk for their final scene together.

Backstage, Father Reggie watched with a new eagerness, curious as to what a half-minute pep talk and ten minutes of brooding might have effected on the hitherto ineffectual performance of his fellow curate.

The scene is not a quick one to develop. As is so often the case in real life as well as on stage or screen, when two enemies passionately devoted to their enduring enmity meet, there is almost invariably a preliminary period of purely social sparring. And in the case of two purported Christians, each convinced the other is intent on the utter perversion of the faith, those preliminaries can be, and frequently are, conducted in a spirit of tolerance and charity that makes the loathing and hatred they really feel for one another that much more horrific. It is, of course, disgustingly hypocritical—but it sure makes awfully good theater.

Which was why, probably, they were a good five or ten minutes into the scene before Father Reggie understood completely what was happening out there. He was not unaware that, several times, Belinda Sue cast a quick glance in his direction. Later he discovered that she had realized almost at once what was happening. But then she could see Father Hughie's face and hand gestures, and Father Reggie could not.

At about the same time that he was beginning, and that reluctantly, to credit the evidence of his own senses, he grew aware of a rustling murmur among those other members of the cast and crew who were also watching.

And still he could not believe that Father Hughie would have the nerve to do it. Because the man of whom Father Hughie was doing an absolutely faithful imitation—a man upon whom indeed the character of Hincmar might very well have been modeled—was the Reverend Dr. Leopold Cantrell, Rector of the Church of All Saints.

4 And as if on cue, at the very back of the hall, a chair crashed loudly to the floor and a voice bellowed, "And that will be just about enough! This abomination will cease at once! Lights! Put some lights on in this hall! Now!"

No one moved, too stunned to do anything. For there was not a soul in the room who didn't recognize Dr. Cantrell's voice.

Onstage Mrs. Robinson, in the wings opposite Father Reggie, jerked her head up to stare across the stage at him. On the stage Belinda Sue did the same, while Stringer Yates stared angrily into the darkened hall. Father Hughie just gaped.

It was Neil who terminated the frozen tableau. Leaping from his seat, he whirled to face the darkened house. "Who's there?" he demanded. "What is the meaning of this?"

"What is the meaning of this, Mr. Bonewarden? What is the meaning of this?"

Dr. Cantrell came striding forward into the light. "I think I am the one who should be asking that question. Lights!" he bellowed again. "Lights, I say."

"Lights, Mr. Madiera," barked Neil, but Mr. Madiera was nowhere to be found, and Father Reggie and Father Hughie made a concerted dash to the control panel.

"So this is what's been going on behind my back!" Cantrell orated, striding down the hall toward the stage. "How could any of you, responsible members of this church and community, allow yourselves to be duped into sponsoring, and in the very fellowship hall of the church, something like this?"

It was magnificent. The Reverend Dr. Leopold James Cantrell, M.A. Oxon., and D.D. Harvard, was a man to draw the eye in any crowd. His name, Leo, was singularly apt; he was a lion of a man, six foot and broad-shouldered, with a figure remarkable for a man in his mid-sixties. His head was a leonine mane of the purest white, and his handsome, clean-shaven features were large and regular, though his complexion was so choleric his blue eyes seemed at times almost turquoise.

As Mrs. Robinson and Father Reggie had indicated the evening before, Cantrell was a man who had spent fully two-thirds of his life being thwarted and never once understanding why. He had seen curates and even two or three assistant priests go on to deaneries, canonries, four bishoprics, and even the headmastership of a very upper-crust school in the East. While for him, nothing. Not even a suffraganship somewhere.

Some years before, it had been noticed that Cantrell had taken to wearing a ring, on his middle finger, of a sapphire set in massy gold. No one said much of anything; they merely pitied.

When, however, he appeared one morning wearing a gold cross and chain, it was felt that the man had gone too far. And so, later that night, a phone call had come from the bishop. The gold cross was seen no more, and Cantrell was much, much older.

It was not even that he changed all that much; he just became more prickly, slightly more irascible. His fierce blue eyes flashed fire whenever he got on the subject of one of his particular bugaboos—which were, in fact, the standard shibboleths, all of which have been railed about since McKinley was President and which, very likely, were deplored in Ur of the Chaldees.

For all that, he really wasn't looked on as such a very bad fellow, for all his irritating posturing. Members of his own generation, after all, were pretty much used to his type. Besides, there was also a sizable party in the parish of fellow travelers who thought and spoke much as he did. . . .

Abruptly the lights came on, illuminating the scene at the foot of the stage with the harsh, ugly, fluorescent lighting of the hall as Neil and Cantrell faced each other angrily, while actors, technicians, playwright, and interested parties began to cluster around, fanning themselves with scripts and loose bits of costumes.

"I'm sure I don't know what you mean," said Neil, cold as ice.

"Oh, don't you?" demanded Cantrell. "Well, then, I shall tell you." He jabbed an angry finger at the stage. "I can only thank Almighty God that I decided to look in after my Bible class. And to think I almost let Millicent persuade me not to look in! Did any of you seriously think that I would be fooled, just sit back and allow this rubbish, this lunacy, this—this *communist* propaganda—"

"Oh, for God's sake!" expostulated Jack Cartwright, hearing Cantrell's old familiar song.

"Yes, you disgraceful child!" Cantrell rounded on him. "It is precisely for *God's* sake that I—"

"Oh? Can you be sure about that?" and Father Reggie wasn't the only to cringe as the buzz-saw tones of Fiona MacLaren interrupted angrily. "Was it for God's sake, Dr. Cantrell? Or was it really just because Hughie was doing such a great imitation of you?"

"I'm sure I never noticed anything of the kind," averred Cantrell austerely—causing cynical snorts to erupt all around—as he turned to confront his accuser.

When he did so, his fury redoubled.

"You!" He jabbed a finger. "And what are you doing here?"

"She is my assistant director," rejoined Neil, his voice rising above the angry murmurs of the crowd.

"How many times do I have to tell you—how many times do I have to tell you all—that I will *not* have a woman priest in my church!"

And the chorus began rising both in wrath and in volume.

But this time it was Belinda Sue Morgan's voice that rose clearly and angrily above the ruckus. "Your church, Dr. Cantrell? Why, my goodness! And all this time I thought it was the Church of Jesus Christ!"

Father Reggie was, to put it mildly, startled. And then perceived immediately it had been precisely the right thing to say. At once the angry mutterings began to turn to laughter—laughter directed at the one person in the room who could not abide being laughed at.

Father Reggie glanced quickly at Julian, who alone of the company stood outside the angry circle around the combatants, plainly holding himself in check, his hands held rigidly at his sides, clenching and unclenching his fists. But at that juncture Bonnie Harris chose to enter the fray.

"What the hell are you talking about?" she demanded furiously of Cantrell. "What's wrong with the play?"

"I would hardly expect anyone of your dubious moral character to understand," said Cantrell in would-be crushing tones.

Which was altogether too much for Julian, who pushed through the crowd and snarled directly into Cantrell's face, "At least she's *got* a character, you senescent horror, instead of some loose collection of hypocritical pomposities."

Loud and general agreement was so instantaneous that Cantrell was forced to take a step backward.

It was Neil who shouted everyone down.

"That's enough! Everybody! That's enough! Quiet!"

And when, presently, some semblance of order was restored, Neil turned to Dr. Cantrell and, in a voice dripping irony as a serpent's fangs drip venom, said, "Thank you, Dr. Cantrell, for sharing your opinion with us. It is, no doubt, unfortunate, but we don't happen to agree with you. So, if you don't mind, why don't you just butt out so we can finish—"

"You don't understand, do you?" said Cantrell. "You *are* finished. As of right now. This loathsome—play is canceled!"

"What!" demanded Julian.

With the ghost of a cruel smile playing around the corners of his mouth, Cantrell purred, "I wouldn't expect you to understand plain English. So I shall repeat: This play will not be produced here. Not in this church. Not ever!"

"Dr. Cantrell!" Mrs. Robinson spoke from the apron of the stage, the added three feet and her abbatial robes making her a towering figure of dignity. "You overstep your authority."

"Oh, I do, do I?"

"Yes, you do. You cannot act unilaterally here. We have already spent parish money on this, money that was duly budgeted and approved by the parish council. To stop it now, it will have to go before the parish council."

"And the bishop," reminded Father Reggie.

Which reminder rather depressed the already sinking spirits of the company. The bishop, a busy and practical prelate, had made it his almost universal practice throughout the diocese to back up parish council decisions. Which meant Cantrell would probably have his way; the man's party was currently controlling.

Small wonder, then, that Cantrell smiled in a not very attractive way and acceded, "Very well, then; by all means, the parish council."

"Where I will certainly not support you," said Mrs. Robinson.

"Nor will I, Dr. Cantrell," said Father Reggie.

"Nor I," said Neil, though his own seat on the counsel was, strictly speaking, a nonvoting one.

"And you can bet your fat ass my Uncle Clyde won't either!" vowed Jack Cartwright offensively.

At which point, to everyone's utter astonishment, Father Hughie, looking as though his knees had turned to water, said weakly, "Nor will I, Dr. Cantrell."

Cantrell turned to look up at poor Father Hughie on the stage and in a voice cool and direct said, "We'll just see about that, Hughie," before turning to confront the entire company. "We'll just all have to wait and see, won't we? But as of now and on my authority as rector, this is finished!"

And without another word he shouldered his way through the crowd, strode toward the open front door of the church hall, barking, "Come, Millicent," to his wife, still sitting rigid and horrified at the back of the hall.

5   And reaction settled visibly over the company, that kind of shocked aftermath of battle that leaves one wondering, what next?

For most, this dreary reaction was compounded by a sudden feeling of distasteful silliness: Here they were, responsible members of the community, all got up in heavy, stifling, and gaudy costumes on the hottest night of the year. Those costumes began to come off one by one, signaling that there was no savor left in the proceedings that had begun so miraculously.

And seeing it, those who had perceived that the fight was not over but only beginning were roused to fury.

"What are you doing?" demanded Neil. "We have—"

"Aw, hang it up, Neil," said Jack bitterly, pulling off his tabard.

There were murmurs of agreement.

"I think Jack is right," said Stringer Yates, removing his own Benedictine habit. He spoke more calmly than Jack had done, but the man was clearly in the grip of powerful emotion.

"He's won. The son of a bitch has won."

It was the voice of one who has been well and truly shocked. It actually took a moment for everyone to identify the source of those unwontedly gentle words to be Julian, who stood as one transfixed.

"The bastard has won. And, by God, he knows it. And so do you." His eyes seemed to regain their focus as he glanced from one member of the company to another, his expression one of unfathomable contempt. "He's got you cowed like he's got the whole damn parish cowed, and all you can do is bow and scrape and mutter, 'Yes, Dr. Cantrell.'"

"Goddamn it, Julian, that's not fair!" yelled Jack.

"Fair?" demanded Julian. "What the hell is fair? Do you think *he'll* fight fair? Do you, Father Hughie?"

He rounded on that unfortunate priest, who could only redden and shake his head.

"Do you?" Julian demanded of Mrs. Robinson.

"No," said she calmly, "but he is going to have a hell of a fight on his hands, nevertheless. And maybe"—she stepped forward, as though to bring all those looking up at her further into the field of her presence—"we can win."

"Right," said Stringer Yates, next to her. "That's why we've got to plan."

"Stringer is right," said Neil, picking up the conciliatory tone. "We *can* win this thing if we plan it properly. What do you think, Father Reggie?"

"I think that before we talk anymore, we should get out of costume—providing"—he looked down at Neil—"we aren't going to rehearse anymore tonight."

Neil shrugged and scowled. "Why bother?" he asked rhetorically. "Frankly, right now I think it would be far more useful to have a good planning session. Shall we all meet at Cippolla's, as planned, in, say, twenty minutes?"

There were murmurs of assent.

"You're a bunch of fools. You know that, don't you?" Once again it was Julian. "Go! Go on! Go swill your beer and gobble—like the bunch of turkeys you all are. He's won, I tell you."

He turned to leave.

"Oh, come on, Julian," urged his fiancée. "Come on! We need to plan. Besides"—Bonnie tried to lighten things a bit—"I'm hungry."

No one was prepared, least of all Bonnie, for the sudden eruption of savagery as Julian abruptly whirled around and yelled at her, "Go, then! Go with them. You don't think I need you, do you?" And without more ado, he strode off toward the elevator, leaving an embarrassed company staring at his departing back and his fiancée staggered.

Immediately Belinda Sue and Mrs. Robinson were at her side.

In the event, however, the solace was rebuffed.

"I'm okay," said Bonnie. "It's just the play. It means so much to him. Too much. Three days ago he was already—" She broke off and, shaking her head, uttered a little laugh and turned to the others. "Thank you," she said simply, and looked around the company. "What's everybody standing around for? Come on! Hang those rags up and let's get some planning done."

CHAPTER NINE

1   Several hours and many gray hairs later, Father Reggie and Neil Bonewarden drove back to the church, each man rapt in his own thoughts.

Presently, however, Neil stirred and, glancing across at Father Reggie, grunted and growled, "Thank you, Father."

So intent had Father Reggie been on his own thoughts that he was actually startled.

"You're more than welcome. Least I could do."

"Shouldn't drink that much. Hope Romero doesn't forget to drive my car to my house after he shuts up."

"I'm sure this isn't the first time Romero's had to have one of his staff drive a customer's car home," observed Father Reggie. "Not the way he pours drinks. Besides if he does forget, I'm sure Millie Cantrell wouldn't mind picking you up in the morning."

In response Neil merely grunted again. Nor had Father Reggie anything further to say. It was as though the mere mention of the Cantrell name recast a pall of gloom.

"What a gaudy night," said Neil quietly but with intense feeling.

And Father Reggie could only nod grimly.

Soon, however, they pulled into the clergy parking lot at the Church of All Saints.

"We're here," announced Father Reggie, looking over at Neil, whose head was nodding loosely. "Neil," he said gently, "why don't you just let me drive you home?"

Neil snapped to.

"No," he said. "No, I've been doing this a long time now. Get this crap out of the way Friday night, and I get to sleep in another hour on Saturday morning." He snapped the car door open. "And I'm going to need that hour tomorrow."

"Okay, Neil," said Father Reggie, settling back. "I'll wait for you here."

"Thanks," murmured Neil and, turning, went around the church hall and vanished.

Father Reggie sighed and wished that he had thought to bring a book with him. Jolliston's only classical music station had long since gone off the air, and Father Reggie was indifferent to rock and actively loathed jazz, which ruled out the only two other audible stations. Which was too bad. It threw him back on his own resources. And while an empty hour was usually a welcome time during which to meditate, at that moment Father Reggie's prayer was, by any criterion, not very successful as his attention kept escaping from its proper focus, going back, again and again, to the disagreeable developments at Cippolla's Pizzeria.

2   Romero himself had greeted them. "I have set up the back room for you." He beamed at them.

"And for this mercy, O Lord, we do thank thee," Father Reggie heard Belinda Sue mutter, half to herself.

He shot a look at her.

"Aren't *you* grateful"—she grinned and took his arm as they walked into the large and private dining room—"that we're not going to have this discussion in one of the public areas?"

"You've got a point," he muttered back at her; "it would be a trifle unseemly."

But at first no one actually said much about anything, total concentration being given to consumption of pizza and pitcher after pitcher of beer.

And drinks.

Quite a number ignored the pitchers of foaming beer and the carafes of lambent local wine and kept the waitress rather busier than she would have liked, running back and forth to the bar for whiskey and sodas, gin and tonics, old-fashioneds, rye and gingers. . . .

And in the blessed chill of the air-conditioned restaurant, everyone forgot that for three and a half hours that evening they had sweltered in the church hall as in a Turkish bath and that most of them had serious fluid imbalances.

Drinks were gulped. Clarity of diction failed. Clarity of thought next. And presently, observing the intense conversation at Neil's table, most stood up, belched, and assuming something was being done, departed to drive home, committing themselves to the mercies of God and the California Highway Patrol.

Seated at a large round table in the center of the room were Neil, Father Reggie, Belinda Sue, Mrs. Robinson, Bonnie Harris, Jack Cartwright, and, surprisingly, Stringer Yates. Father Reggie would have liked to have seen Father Hughie and Fiona. But the latter pair had slipped from the church hall and vanished. Which was hardly surprising. Tepid, hesitant, and timid thought it had been, for the first time in recorded history Father Hughie had defied Dr. Cantrell. He was probably at home immersed in a sweat of guilt, wondering whether he would still have a job on the morrow.

Whereupon, realizing that these reflections were anything but charitable, Father Reggie turned his mind back to the present conversation.

As for everyone else in the room, the service of large pizzas and pitchers of beer had put a temporary end to the preliminary conversations that had taken place over cocktails. Both Mrs. Robinson and Father Reggie had exchanged a glance of some concern when Stringer Yates had spoken quietly to the cocktail waitress. Especially when she returned and placed a chimney glass in front of the man.

"Ginger ale," mouthed Mrs. Robinson across the table to Father Reggie, after peering for a closer look as discreetly as possible.

They relaxed, therefore, as Yates downed it and rapidly asked for another.

And everyone dived in.

Belinda Sue, retrieving a string of drooping mozzarella with a catlike lick of the tongue, chuckled and observed after swigging half a mugful of beer, "There's nothing like sweat and strong emotion for an appetite."

"I know," said Elspeth, eating her own pizza with knife and fork. "You read and hear about people who are too angry or too excited to eat. But all it ever does to me is send visions of steaks and baked potatoes through my head."

"And it was strong emotion," said Neil, tossing back his third vodka and tonic.

It was the opening of the sluice gate.

Bonnie Harris and Jack Cartwright exchanged an excited, conspiratorial glance and leaned forward.

"Father Reggie!" said Jack.

"Mrs. Robinson!" said Bonnie at the same time.

They stopped, exchanged another glance, and laughed nervously. Bonnie hefted the pitcher of beer, filled her glass, and nodded encouragingly at Jack.

"Father Reggie, Mrs. Robinson"—Jack held his own glass out to be filled—"Bonnie and I were talking on the way over here—thanks, Bonnie." He retook his glass and poured half of it down his throat. "Could he really cancel us out?"

"I don't *think* he has the authority," responded Mrs. Robinson. "It is a matter for the parish council. . . ."

"Yes, Elspeth, that's true," said Father Reggie, "but canonically he is the rector and that gives him some pretty heavy duty power."

"I'm aware of that, Father," said Mrs. Robinson. "But he is also, legally, an employee of a California corporation."

"And employees can be fired!" said Jack jubilantly.

"It's not that simple," said Neil.

"I'll say," said Father Reggie, amused and pleased that Jack, that most willful of actors, and Bonnie, so protective of the playwright, should have made common cause.

It was Neil who proved practical. These days never without pad and pen, he wrote down a list of the members of the parish council and for the next twenty minutes or so they discussed who was likely to vote with whom. When they were done, it looked possible. But grim.

"One or two votes either way will do it. Or us," said Neil.

The others nodded somberly.

"Can we do anything?" asked Jack.

"I don't know," began Father Reggie, but he was interrupted by Mrs. Robinson laying a hand on his.

"Wait," said she. "Maybe there is." She seemed excited. "Your Uncle Clyde is president of the council," she said to Jack Cartwright, repeating what everyone already knew. She turned to Father Reggie, her eyes aglitter. "Do you see?"

And Father Reggie saw. His own face lit up. His brow shot upward.

"Well, yes! Of course! But it's awfully underhanded, isn't it?"

"Of course it is. But so has Leo been," rejoined Mrs. Robinson. "Several times," she added dryly.

"Would you two mind telling us what you're talking about?" said Neil.

Mrs. Robinson nodded to Father Reggie.

"It's very simple," said the good father. "Clyde Cartwright is president of the council and that gives him the right to call an emergency meeting of that council, should he feel the need. I think what Elspeth is saying"—he looked at her as he said it and was rewarded by a slow smile spreading across her handsome face as she nodded encouragement—"is that you, Jack, should get your uncle to precipitate matters—that is, if you're sure he'll support us."

Jack smiled rather impishly and said to Mrs. Robinson, "You know he will. He may not think much of my being an actor—wants me to take over the vineyard from him," he explained to the others, "but he thinks even less of Cantrell."

"So he calls a meeting," said Neil. "What then?"

"All we need is a quorum on the council. Have Clyde call the meeting for tomorrow afternoon and I'll bet you anything that there will be at least a third of the council who won't be able to make the meeting."

"You're right," said Neil with a broad grin, knocking back yet another vodka and tonic. "But it is underhanded."

"There is one problem with it," said Jack practically.

"What's that?" asked Neil.

"What if the quorum that attends are all Cantrell's people?"

And thus do houses of cards flutter down after rising to dizzying heights.

For, of course, Jack was right. Regardless of who precipitated this fight in the only forum where it could properly be fought—in the parish council—there were no guarantees as to who would win when the final votes were tallied.

"Maybe we should just leave it to the regular Monday meeting," suggested Jack. "That would give us time to politic."

"Maybe that's not such a bad idea," said Father Reggie.

"On the other hand," said Mrs. Robinson, "the longer we give Leo, the more time he'll have to work on people like Helen Spinner—who, as you may recall, sees 'communists' under every bed in Christendom."

"She'd like nothing better than to find one under her own," muttered Neil, winning a somewhat frosty smile from Mrs. Robinson.

"To be sure. But she isn't the only one. There's that utter nit, Harvey Nash."

At which point the conversation—the useful conversation—effectively came to an abrupt end as they were all startled by Stringer Yates suddenly giving a great twitch, raising his head, which had been bowed over his glass of "ginger ale," and peering around owlishly at them all, a would-be cynical smile on his face. "You can fix Harvey Nash's wagon real good. Him and that triple asshole Mike McFarland—fix 'em real good."

"Oh, dear," said Belinda Sue in a small voice meant to be heard by Father Reggie alone. "Stringer's drunk."

Unfortunately, with that captious capacity of the alcoholic to perceive things others probably would not, Stringer heard. And sniggered.

"Goddamn right!" he shouted, and then, mostly to himself, "God! Maria's gonna be pissed. But the hell with it." He lurched to his feet, that last bellow having drawn every eye in the room to him. "I'll tell you how we'll fix their hash. There's three or four of the biggest contributors in the parish in this play. There's you, Elspeth. Bonnie! You too, Belinda Sue!" He glared at each of the three and ignored the bright pink each of them turned and added, "And there's me and Maria. And your Uncle Clyde, too, for that matter." He whirled around to face Jack. "We'll just tell 'em that we'll withhold . . ."

That abrupt turnabout to face Jack, however, had been extremely injudicious. The man halted abruptly, swallowed once, twice, said, "Oh, shit!" in a very small voice, and fell face forward into Jack's hastily put-up arms.

The younger man lowered the somnolent form into a chair, looking acutely (and pointlessly) embarrassed as he did so. When he was through, however, he turned to regard Father Reggie.

"What about it?" he asked. "Could we do that, Father Reggie? Threaten to withhold our contributions to the parish?"

And it was Father Reggie's turn to be embarrassed. "I—I can't answer that, Jack."

"But I can," said Mrs. Robinson. "We can't."

"Why not?" demanded Jack.

"Because we just can't do that," repeated Mrs. Robinson tautologically.

"But why?"

"Because it's blackmail," said Belinda Sue succinctly. "I know we all get confused sometimes, but let us please remember we are talking about the Church. If Dr. Cantrell seems to wish to remake the Church in his own image, do you want us to fall into the same—"

As she hesitated over a sufficiently incisive word, Neil offered, "Sin?"

Belinda Sue smiled. "Well, yes, though perhaps a bit judgmental. Let's just say folly."

A vexed little snort emerged from Bonnie Harris. "I don't care. I know you're right," she said to Belinda Sue, "but someone has got to do something about Cantrell. I love the Church of All Saints, and I, for one, refuse to allow that disgusting old bastard to continue dragging it down."

"Easy, Bonnie," said Mrs. Robinson.

"I'm sorry," said Bonnie, running a hand against her cheek and nodding. "You're right." She gave a little laugh. "No need to get shrill. But never mind anything else, for the moment. Who is going to call Maria Yates?"

"Bravo, Bonnie," said Belinda Sue. "Practical as always."

"Maybe so," said Bonnie, "but I sure don't want to be the one to do it."

"I'll do it," said Mrs. Robinson, standing up. "She and I get along okay," and she left to find a telephone.

"Then you're the only one," muttered Jack when he was certain Mrs. Robinson could no longer hear.

"Maria's okay," said Neil a trifle absently. "Once you get to know her. Should we try to get some black coffee into him?" He gestured to the slouched form of Yates.

"It won't do any good," said Belinda Sue. "And he'll be easier to handle this way."

Mrs. Robinson rejoined them, pink of face, with a brandy

balloon with half an inch of spirits in it. Father Reggie's eyebrows shot up, seeing which she snorted and neatly tossed the drink back.

"I'm not a nervous type," she said, "but even I can't face what's coming without a little buffer."

And, indeed, there was really nothing to do but to order another round of drinks. Mrs. Robinson had, as usual, been a sensible soul, and all—all—knew what was coming.

3   A small woman appeared in the doorway of the private dining room. Her straight brown hair was fading to gray, and she wore a pair of steel-framed granny glasses that only emphasized the thyroidal bulge of her dark brown eyes. Her face was a square, rather ferocious affair. Nevertheless, it was obvious that, had she cared to make the effort, she would have been more than a little striking. But worry was deeply etched upon her face, and she carried herself with the overintense, jerky movements of clockwork wound too tightly. And her voice, when she found it, was not pleasant.

"What did you do to my husband!" shrieked that Maria, Mrs. Yates, in dread of whom went half the populace of the Jolliston Valley and whom the other half dearly, if with a generous measure of tolerance, loved. Nor was her first outburst at all uncharacteristic. As is so often the way of these things, her love of her husband and family was at one and the same time the woman's glory and her besetting sin.

That shriek, however, had two effects on either side of the doorway in which Mrs. Yates stood. Without, poor Romero appeared, a look of pained distress replacing his normal unctuous expression. Within, Father Reggie rose to his duty.

"Maria," he said, attempting to stem the flow. "Maria!" He took her hand, whereupon she glared at him. "You! How could you? To take my husband to a bar. When you know . . ."

Romero's hand went to his heart on hearing his beloved and chichi establishment thus dismissed as a "bar."

"It's okay, Romero," said Father Reggie, gently urging Mrs. Yates into the room. He turned to close the double doors to the outer dining room, then turned back, put an arm around Mrs. Yates's shoulders, and led her gently toward the table. Under the weight of his arm he could feel her whole body trembling as she approached the floodgates.

"Hush now," soothed Father Reggie, handing her one of the spare handkerchiefs with which any good priest keeps himself supplied. He explained briefly and quietly what had happened.

"He is such a good actor," said Mrs. Yates. "And he wants—*ach*, it does not matter. I—I must get him home. An alcohol rub used to help with—the mornings. . . . Oh, Mother of God, what if he starts all over again? What will I do? What will the children do?"

And then the emotional fit was over, and she planted her feet, shook her head, and stood as tall as her five-foot-four-inches would allow her. She clicked open her purse and thrust Father Reggie's handkerchief within. "I will launder and iron it tomorrow morning," she said. Then, advancing on the table, she touched her husband's drink-raddled face with a gesture of infinite solicitude, sighed, and turned with a questioning look to the others.

At once Belinda Sue and Mrs. Robinson were beside her.

"We'll help you, Maria."

"Thank you, Elspeth. Miss Morgan, you are kind. You are all really kind. I know that." Again her eyes filled, but angrily she shook her head. "Miss Harris," she said, "you must thank Mr. Julian for his lovely play for me. Assure him my husband will be well again by the time of the next rehearsal. And there will be a next rehearsal, Mr. Bonewarden," she said, seeing him about to speak. "I guarantee that." She glanced at Jack. "It is late. Young men need their sleep. Go home and wake your uncle. Tell him I shall be calling him as soon as I have this lump in bed. I don't know what we can do, but together we *can* do it. This I know."

And, surprisingly, it was Bonnie who burst out almost angrily, "You betcha, Maria. You betcha. I don't know about anyone else, but I'm sick of Cantrell's hypocrisy and arrogance. And never mind what it's doing to the church, look at what it's doing to our people." She gestured at Stringer, and everyone knew she was worried about her fiancé as well. "That old bastard leaves nothing but destruction in his wake. We'd all be a lot better off if the son of a bitch just died."

"Or if someone had the nerve to kill him," said Mrs. Yates with quiet passion. "Come here, Father," she directed, "take his legs. You, Jack, take his arms."

And the little procession hauled the man through the main dining room, which immediately hushed, except for a few snickers instantly silenced by a glaring Maria.

4 When Maria and her cargo had driven off, with Mrs. Robinson following in her own car, Belinda Sue and Father Reggie stood together in the still-hot night. Above them the stars shone steadily and the moon rode majestically across a completely clear sky.

The two regarded each other for a moment before Father Reggie put his arms out and Belinda Sue was nestled in them. But too much had happened, too many emotions had roiled their usually so-placid lives, and after a moment Belinda Sue raised her head from Father Reggie's shoulder, brushed his cheek with her lips, and said, "I'll call you in the morning," and was gone.

Back inside, he found Neil brooding over another vodka and tonic. He looked up when Father Reggie approached. "Can you give me a lift?"

"But your car . . ." began Father Reggie, and then understood. "Oh! Yes, of course."

"I already spoke to Romero; he'll have one of the boys drop it at my house." He breathed out lustily and looked puzzled. "You know, I do drink a lot, Father. But Stringer got zonked out on three, maybe four highballs."

"It takes him that way," said Father Reggie laconically. "You ready?"

"Yeah," said Neil, and rose, none too steadily, to his feet. Suddenly he smiled, "Oh, well, I may be a fat and middle-aged soak, but, oh, Lord, how grateful I am that my inhibitions run deeper than that. Oh, Christ!"

"What's wrong?"

Neil looked sheepish. "I have to go back to the church."

"Why, Neil?" sighed Father Reggie.

"I have to set up for junior choir practice tomorrow."

"Tonight?"

Neil nodded. "It does make it easier."

And Father Reggie, acutely aware that there were less than eight hours altogether until he had to say the seven-thirty Mass could only sigh once more, and agree. . . .

5 "Father Reggie! Father Reggie!" a voice whispered furiously into his left ear, while a strong-fingered hand gripped his left shoulder, shaking gently but firmly.

"Huh?" asked Father Reggie, coming to.

"I said," Neil repeated urgently, "there's someone in the church."

"Course there is. Julian's in—"

"Father Reggie, it's one o'clock in the morning. Julian's in bed and the alarm wasn't set."

That brought Father Reggie awake. Fast.

"Not set?"

"Or turned on," said Neil ominously.

"Oh, hell," said Father Reggie with feeling. "Where are they?"

"In the sacristy."

And in the sodium glare of the standard lamps in the parking lot, the priest and organist could only stare at each other.

"You don't suppose . . ." began Father Reggie.

"I don't know," said Neil. "All I know is that I was up in the choir loft when I heard something clink in the sacristy and a voice begin singing—chanting."

"Chanting?" said Father Reggie, feeling very cold inside. Neil nodded.

"Yeah. Gregorian. Possibly Znameny."

"Never mind what kind of chant it was," snapped Father Reggie. "Didn't you notice if the alarm was off?"

"No. Why should I? I just went through the combination. I didn't notice whether the light was on."

"Damn!" said Father Reggie. "It's probably just Julian setting up for tomorrow."

But even as he said it, he did not believe it. He was feeling a distinctly unpleasant sense of *déjà vu*, and the hollow sensation he had in the pit of his stomach had nothing whatever to do with too much beer, pizza, and emotions.

"Could they be back?" asked Neil, voicing Father Reggie's own thoughts.

"Well, I guess we'll just have to find out. Won't we?"

"We could call the sheriff."

"Maybe," temporized Father Reggie.

The idea had its virtues, certainly. But for several reasons he had no great wish to call the cops. First, unlikely though it might seem, it could be Julian. And there they would be with egg all over their faces for having called the sheriff on their own caretaker. And then there was the fact that, if Julian *had* neglected the alarms, it would only add fuel to Dr. Cantrell's fire, and Father Reggie wanted Julian's position to come out of this mess intact. Finally, Neil was with him, so, unlike the last time, he would not have to tackle the obscenity alone.

He followed Neil back into the cloister.

The garth, open to the sky and surrounded on all sides by colonnades, was a deep well in which the heat was mitigated slightly by the tinkling water of the fountain in the center of the garden. Moonlight glinted off the shivering water in the basin. And, just as it had the previous February, a light flickered in the sacristy window.

Once again the door into the north aisle of the nave creaked as they opened it, and as they crept up the aisle, the same furtive mutterings could be heard issuing from the sacristy ahead. This time, however, Neil was a solid and comforting presence behind him. Even if—in spite of the sobriety which appeared to have been shocked into him—he was probably still a bit unsteady on his pins.

Indeed, as it turned out, rather more unsteady than either expected.

Suddenly the noise within ceased and a particularly nasty laugh sounded, low and unspeakably evil, and Father Reggie came to an abrupt halt.

And Neil just plowed right into him and then, in an effort to regain his balance, bounced directly into one of the icons hanging on the wall, which rattled and banged, sending up loud and reverberant echoes.

Whereupon the whole thing disintegrated into low comedy.

A figure appeared bracketed in the lighted doorway ahead, a frightening figure hulking in the doorway and scaring the bejabbers out of both men until a familiar voice called out aggressively, "Who's there!"—only it was more like, "Hoozh dare!"

For, of course, it was Julian, and he was very, very drunk.

Neil was furious and began to rant: "What are you still doing here! What are you up to? You jerk! We almost called the cops on you."

Father Reggie tried to bring Neil to heel, but the combination of events and booze and raw emotions had worn the choirmaster to a frazzle and, while it was clearly nothing more than displacement activity, it was still impossible to stop him.

Until Julian turned on his heel and simply vanished inside the sacristy, leaving Neil addressing the air.

Which, if anything, made Neil even more apoplectic. He waddled to the door of the sacristy, bellowing. "How dare you turn your back on me! I'm speaking to you."

"You may be speaking to me, Neil," said Julian with immense dignity, "but I do not have to listen to your bullshit. You wouldn't listen to what I wanted, so why should I listen to you now?"

Neil swelled up, and it was time for Father Reggie to intervene. Which he did. Loudly. And no doubt rather more angrily than was entirely necessary.

"That's enough! Stop it. Both of you. At once!" Both men turned astonished eyes on him. "Both of you get a grip. Isn't it bad enough, the situation being what it is, without you two tangling assholes over nothing? Neil, you yourself admitted you've had too much. And as for you, Julian, you're drunk, too."

"I'm very drunk" assented that worthy.

"So what are you doing here?"

"Preparing for tomorrow," replied Julian, and then chortled as if at a private joke.

"Why now?"

"Gonna have a hangover in the morning." He peered at them. "Where's Bonnie?"

"Where do you think she is?" said Father Reggie. "She went home."

"This is home."

"After the way you spoke to her?"

"I better call her," Julian muttered, vaguely looking about. "Just got to finish—" He hauled up from the floor of a cabinet one of the gallon jugs in which the altar sherry came. "Oops," he giggled, "I finished that one."

"Never *mind*, Julian!" said Father Reggie. "I have Mass in the morning; I can do it."

"No. You might use the wrong jug."

"What difference does it make?"

"It makes a difference," the man suddenly shouted, stunning both Father Reggie and Neil. "I'm sorry," he said almost immediately. "No need for that. Quite unpardonable." He picked up another jug, clasping it to his bosom. "I came down to pray." That seemed to strike him as funny. "I wonder if that old bastard knows that even *communists* can pray?" He caught himself up short and looked at the other two as though he were seeing them for the first time clearly.

"I'm sorry. I—I didn't mean to hurt you or scare you. I came down here to pray and had a little glass of wine when I came in to set up, and it tasted so good. And now I've yelled at you and I have to pray for more forgiveness. I'm always praying for forgiveness. You guys better just go on. I'll just finish up here and—and . . ."

"Set the alarm, Julian," said Father Reggie.

"Right. Set the alarm."

Neil snorted, but Father Reggie just tugged him by the sleeve and led him out.

"Come on, Neil," whispered Father Reggie when, halfway back down the aisle, Neil protested. "Leave him be; he's hurting."

"Yeah," said Neil. Then he chuckled as he followed Father Reggie once again into the cloister. "And after half a jug of altar wine he's gonna hurt even more in the morning."

The very thought made Father Reggie wince.

He made it home, having dropped Neil off with a very desultory, "Good night."

He let himself back into the cool air of his house and stood for a moment to congeal, before giving a hug to a somnolent Demon. He would have liked nothing more than to run to his bedroom and dive headlong into bed, but a slow plod was all he could manage. His devotions consisted of blessing himself, a brief moment of standing mutely, hands raised toward the heavens, before uttering a heartfelt, "God help us all!"—and falling to the mattress into welcome oblivion. . . .

CHAPTER TEN

1 Ordinarily Father Reggie liked to arrive at church at least a half hour before his Mass was to begin, and so allow himself adequate time for decent preparation.

That Saturday it just wasn't possible. Instead all he could allow himself was a five-minute stretch in the cloister garth. But the sun was already brutally hot, and the scent of dying vegetation mingling with the pall of dust rising from his feet made him sneeze. So muttering appropriate if inchoate formulas, he let himself into the sacristy by the cloister door and began donning vestments.

He was just finishing when he heard, behind him, someone come in and pause.

He turned to confront a very different Julian Richards from the man he had last seen at one in the morning. From red eyes to shuffling feet and trembling hands, it was clear that the man had a ferocious hangover. Before Father Reggie could say anything, however, Julian asked rather meekly.

"Can I serve your Mass this morning?"

"Of course, Julian; glad to have you," said Father Reggie, before asking: "Is it bad?"

Which actually brought a smile to the man's haggard face.

"I've had worse," he said.

"Okay! Ready?"

"Oh, yeah. But, Father?"

"Well?"

"How many hosts did you put on the paten?"

"Four or five. Why?"

"You'll need more than that," said Julian.

"Oh, really?" Father Reggie frowned. "Well, if we need any more, we'll just get them from the tabernacle ciborium. It's late."

He gestured and, obeying, Julian turned, pulled the rope on the bell of the sacristy door, and led the way out. They paused together in front of the high altar, together bowed to the Presence, and proceeded thence into the Lady Chapel.

Afterward Father Reggie would try to untangle the rather complicated chain of reactions he experienced when he entered the chapel.

First and foremost, of course, was the delight of a priest seeing the normally sparse early attendance replaced by a crowd nearly filling the chapel.

Almost immediately, however, that was followed by darker suspicions about just what might have brought them there. The more so when he realized that most of those present were members of the All Saints Players.

Of course, almost all of them did have other responsibilities around the church. But it had hitherto not exactly been unheard of them to perform those responsibilities without perceiving any urgent necessity to attend the Mass that began the day at seven-thirty.

Belinda Sue Morgan and Elspeth Robinson were there— but then Mrs. Robinson was always there on a Saturday morning. Saturday was that day each week when the Sisterhood did all the prep for Sunday. Bonnie Harris was there, too, but the same could be said of her as of Mrs. Robinson.

Belinda Sue, on the other hand, he knew perfectly well was supposed to be on her way to the University library at Berkeley.

Furthermore, it was distinctly odd to see Jack Cartwright

there. Of all people! He did coach the boys' basketball team and the water polo teams, but seven-thirty was awfully early in the morning for that indolent youth.

And the entire Yates clan was there. But again, Maria coached the girls' swimming team—and helped the Sisterhood out however she could while Stringer and his older boys trained the very aggressive soccer team All Saints fielded every autumn. But the Yateses were always protesting their poverty and the consequent need to grab every available moment for their farm chores. They normally attended, *en famille,* the Family Mass on Sundays and accounted themselves adequately blessed thereby.

Father Hughie and Fiona stood toward the back, becking and nodding and blessing themselves. But they often showed up together for early Mass before heading off to do—whatsoever it was they did with their days.

Directly in front of them Neil Bonewarden had his face covered by his hands as he squatted, sitting half on the kneeler and half on the pew seat. Obviously, he had not availed himself of that extra hour to sleep in—and whatever he had had to drink last night was still manifest in the vivid magenta of his ears and neck and that part of his face not covered by his praying hands.

Meanwhile, in a front pew—and here Father Reggie nearly dropped the chalice—sat Dr. Cantrell and his wife.

Now that was unusual. It was true that Millie, in her capacity as assistant choirmaster, would have to be present at junior choir rehearsal. And it was Dr. Cantrell's turn to preach. But it was also his normal practice to say a private Mass at home with Millie in attendance, and then drive in later to use the parish library facilities while Millie helped pound notes into prepubescent ears.

Clearly, it was going to be a very interesting day.

Indeed, all Father Reggie could think, as he turned toward the altar, was: You'd think we were going to war—before dismissing the thought as unworthy at such a moment.

But then, as he raised his hands to begin, the wisp of a thought flickered across his mind: They *were* going to war!

"Glory to the holy, consubstantial, and life-creating Trinity," he intoned, and consigned them all to the bodiless powers of heaven.

2 Afterward, as Father Reggie muttered his Thanksgiving prayers in the vestry, he began to grow increasingly aware of Julian puttering about to no good purpose. Finally, somewhat irritated, he said, "Julian, why don't you go get yourself a cup of coffee."

Julian snorted, not unappreciatively. "Sorry. Just wondering: Are you hearing confessions this afternoon?"

"Yes, I am. At four. Just like it said in the bulletin."

"Okay," said the other laconically. "See you then."

He turned to go.

"We could do it now."

Julian shook his head. "No, thanks. I need to prepare a bit."

Father Reggie nodded. "Okay. Just come in when you're ready."

Julian again nodded and was gone.

Almost immediately, before Father even had time to close the vestment drawers, there came a tentative knock on the lintel of the sacristy doorway.

"Yes?" he called out, and turned to see a sheepish-looking Stringer Yates standing in the doorway, mauling his baseball cap in his nervous hands.

"What's up, Stringer?" he asked, trying to sound as cheerful as possible.

Whereupon, as he expected, after a moment of hemming and hawing, Stringer muttered his apologies for his behavior the night before. "And I was just wondering," he added somewhat hesitantly.

"Yes?"

"Are you going to be hearing confessions this afternoon?"

Father Reggie chuckled.

"Yes. Yes I am."

"Something funny, Father Reggie?" asked Yates rather stiffly.

"No, Stringer, not at all. It's just there's already been one request for that today. And I think there's gonna be more," he added in a conspiratorial whisper.

Stringer grimaced and nodded. "Yeah. I'd be surprised if there weren't."

Father Reggie made the same offer he had made Julian and, like Julian, Stringer said, "No. Thanks. I need to prepare."

"Okay," said Father Reggie, "let's go get some coffee and see what's cookin'."

This time Stringer's grin was amused.

"Yeah!" he said enthusiastically. "Let's go find out what everyone's saying about the play."

When, however, they strolled into the church hall, they discovered that, for one very simple reason, no one was discussing the play at all.

3 Standing in the center of the group, absorbing coffee and pastry and chatting with the greatest bonhomie, was Dr. Cantrell. And everyone else, too. And all of them behaving with perfect punctilio.

"And aren't we just being so-o-o-o good!" a voice whispered in his ear.

"Yes," he said with a chuckle, "you are."

"You'd think," said Belinda Sue wryly, "that a group of people who are, by and large, excellent actors could manage this better."

It was apt, if rather unkind. Those members of the All

Saints Players present were behaving with a self-conscious self-effacement that was almost completely unbelievable.

Only Julian stood on the edge of the group, Julian and Bonnie, both of them eyeing the social scene with ill-concealed distaste. Mrs. Robinson, moving around, with placid mien, pouring coffee into emptied cups, stopped and murmured something to them, after which they seemed to take themselves in hand; at least they both stopped scowling so.

As Father Reggie watched, Mrs. Robinson's glance darted out to meet his own, and an eyebrow elevated marginally.

The most interesting performance perhaps—and it was a performance—was that of Cantrell himself. Standing near him was his wife, chatting animatedly with Neil Bonewarden. But even Millie periodically eyed her husband with a quick, speculative look. Neil, on the other hand, was simply doing his level best to ignore Cantrell.

It was all remarkably unpleasant.

Presently Cantrell, in an access of strained goodwill, laughed at some inconsequential witticism by one of the Yates children and, finishing his coffee with a theatrical flourish, turned to Mrs. Robinson. "Well, Elspeth, it's time to get to work."

In response to which just about everyone breathed a none-too-covert sigh of relief.

"But I think," Cantrell continued, "I won't have any more coffee. How about some tea?"

"Tea, Dr. Cantrell?" Mrs. Robinson said. "A tea bag?"

"Why, no, Elspeth," said Cantrell. "Let's have some of my private stock," he said and stalked toward the kitchen. "I'd like you all to try it."

A frown flicked across Millie's face while Mrs. Robinson replied, blandly enough, to several inquiries that it was indeed a wonderful tea.

"I'm missing something," whispered Belinda Sue. "What are they talking about?"

It was clear to her that Father Reggie had also been surprised by the turn of events.

"Well!" demanded Belinda Sue.

"Oh, it's special all right," responded Father Reggie *sotto voce*. I believe they pay something like three hundred bucks a pound for it—and the Sacred Tea is not often shared, I need hardly add."

Belinda Sue found this piquant.

"Don't you think it's rather a hoot that our good rector, who does go on and on so about drugs, should have such a very expensive habit himself?"

As they spoke, the business in the kitchen was going forward. It being Saturday, there was an ample supply of water already on the boil on the back of the stove, and the marvelous tea was brewed. Furthermore, in their eager curiosity to try it, a good measure of self-consciousness had evaporated.

"But what is this?" asked Cantrell, taking down another, almost identical brown paper bag from the cabinet. "More tea?"

To his and everyone else's surprise, Mrs. Robinson rather peremptorily plucked the bag from his hand. "Be careful with that!" she snapped.

"Well, I'm sure I'm sorry," said Cantrell icily.

"No, Dr. Cantrell, I'm sorry. Forgive me," said Mrs. Robinson. "It's just—"

"But what is it?"

"Poison?"

"Poison!"

Mrs. Robinson nodded.

"But what is it doing there?"

"I'm sorry. It was careless of me. We have trouble with ants."

"Who doesn't," called out someone.

"Excuse me, Elspeth," Dr. Cantrell pursued, "I don't presume to teach you your business, but don't you think it dangerous to keep that stuff not only in a food cabinet, but in a fairly ambiguous packet?"

"Yes," Mrs. Robinson agreed reluctantly. "Of course, you're right. Julian, when you get a chance, would you put this back with the rest of it? In the shed?"

Julian took the bag and said, "I'll go do it right now."

By the time he had returned, tea was brewed. Dr. Cantrell peered into the glass pot and presently pronounced it ready. And it was a pretty sight. Whole green leaves had unfurled under the action of hot water and floated lazily about on convection currents within the pot. From the liquor, of a deep golden color, came a heady perfume that teased the nose pleasantly.

"That's very good," said Father Hughie. "What is it?"

"My dear?" said Cantrell.

With something of an effort, Millie Cantrell, holding her own cup of the brew, said, "It's an oolong. Which means they only partially ferment it before drying it. I don't think they ferment it more than two or three days. It's a whole-leaf tea, too."

"Where do you get it?"

"In San Francisco. We first had it in Taipei. And Leo loved it so much he badgered a merchant in Chinatown to start carrying it."

"Well, I can't say I'm surprised to hear that," a loud voice spoke from the doorway of the kitchen.

As though on cue, all those clustered in the kitchen turned to face the doorway in which stood Clyde Cartwright, Jack's uncle, sometime guardian, president of the parish council, and, probably, Dr. Cantrell's single most vocal critic in the parish.

Cartwright was an elderly widower, both of whose sons had been killed in Vietnam. He was a big man with that rangy yet solid muscularity common among men who wrest their living from the soil. The vintner, however, is an unusual kind of farmer. Dependent, like any farmer, on the infinite variations in sunlight and rain, the caprice of the California water authorities, and the depredations of mists and blights, bugs and scales, when—finally and against all odds—his crop is brought in, crushed, and the first fermentation begins, his life thereafter is an exercise in patience.

And in Cartwright a half century of patience had produced

a man of deep attentiveness. By no means an educated man, he was yet a man whose wells of silence had become fountains of a profound, practical, and, above all, charitable wisdom. He did not condemn Cantrell. He was far too deeply into the mystery of agape to do anything so silly. But he did not have a great deal of regard for him, and frankly despised some of the things he had said and done. He had also come to a place of clarity in his own life from which he could see what Cantrell apparently could not—that it is existentially possible for others to differ from one in good faith. Therefore, while he had his own (usually reserved) opinions about the tack upon which the parish of All Saints was heading into the wings of change blowing through the Church and the world at large, he was able to see plainly and to concede that the results had so far not exactly been unimpressive.

There was also the fact that in this particular battle shaping, there was the hardly negligible datum of Jack's involvement, and while it would be excessive to say Mr. Cartwright had spoiled his nephew and ward, he had come over the years to dote upon him rather thoroughly. . . .

And now, like two characters in a nineteenth-century melodrama, Cartwright and Cantrell faced each other across the breadth of the kitchen—and their convictions—and spoke with that deadly courtesy utilized on such occasions.

"Mr. Cartwright," said Cantrell, ignoring the dig in the other's opening remark, "how nice to see you. I would have thought you would be busy amid the vines today. Tea?"

"I'm sure my foreman is glad to be rid of me. For the day. And thank you, a cup of the famous tea would be welcome."

"Here you are," said Cantrell, pouring a cup and handing it to Cartwright. "Were you looking for me?"

"As a matter of fact, yes."

"Shall we go to my office?"

"It might be better."

"After you."

The two men left—and a positive babel of comment shot up.

4 Presently, when order was restored, Jack was heard telling all and sundry that, yes, when he had left the house, his uncle had already been on the phone trying to get a quorum of the council to meet that afternoon.

"Great!" observed Father Reggie to Julian and Bonnie, who, in the drifting currents of the crowd, had fetched up next to him and Belinda Sue.

It was Millie Cantrell who threw a dampish towel over everyone.

"I'm sorry. Maybe I shouldn't say anything . . ." she began.

Now, no one who begins a sentence like that must *ever* be allowed to get away with it. And so, presently, it came out: Of course, Dr. Cantrell knew that a gathering of forces was likely. He had, accordingly, telephoned his own troops.

Then came the additional shocker; it was not just the play; Dr. Cantrell wanted to have Julian dismissed as well.

"We've been through all this before, Millie," said Mrs. Robinson.

"I know, but"—Millie shrugged and turned to Julian—"he really does dislike you, you know."

"That is not exactly surprising news, Millie," said Julian. "Actually, I think *hate* would be more accurate than *dislike*."

He said it bravely enough, but it was, nevertheless, a bitter pill.

"Damn it all, people! I know you said last night," said Bonnie to Mrs. Robinson in a fervor of indignation, "that whatever happens we can't stoop to blackmail, but I tell you that I, for one, will cease *all* further contributions of any kind if that—I'm sorry, Millie—that *man* gets his way."

"Bonnie . . ." began Julian.

"No! I'm tired of all this. You try so hard to help make a parish work, and some asshole with a dog collar on thinks that with a flick of his finger he can wreck it all. Well, I won't stand for it! I won't!" Her voice rang out, pregnant with tears of frustration. Everyone, rather embarrassed, muttered the appropriate mouthings, and, determinedly getting hold of herself, she dashed away the tears starting in her eyes and said, "I'm sorry. I'll be up in the church. The red cope needs mending," and she swept up her carryall wherewith she conveyed the tools of her craft and was gone.

"Who speaks of blackmail?" demanded Maria Yates. "It is not blackmail. If a leader acts irresponsibly, the people who employ him *must* object. Even if he is a priest."

And surrounded by her brood, she, too, went off.

Millie and Neil departed to conduct the junior choir rehearsal, and presently, ever so faintly, the sound of the organ came dimly penetrating into the kitchen as Millie or Neil tried over first one and then another passage of whatever anthem the junior choristers would carol at the nine o'clock Family Mass on the morrow.

"I'll be in the library," muttered Belinda Sue. And feeling Father Reggie's eye on her, she gurgled and said, "Yes, I am supposed to be in Berkeley. But today I work in our own parish library—and await developments."

And she, too, went, leaving only Stringer, Jack, Mrs. Robinson, and Father Reggie, who could only shake their heads and disperse to their own waiting chores and duties.

5 At one, however, he was surprised in his perambulations from table to table at the seniors' luncheon by a smiling Miss Belinda Sue Morgan, who promptly ordered, "Come along, Father; it's lunchtime," and without more ado led him off to his office where, spread on a cloth on his desk, was a most fetching little luncheon of toast, boiled eggs, caviar, and that *pâté de campagne* a wonderful little shop next to the Mission downtown prepared on its premises and stored until the brandy and truffles with which it had been made reached just the right stage of mellowness. And further provided with this austere little luncheon was a bottle of

a singularly *brut* champagne, one sip of which was enough to tell Father Reggie that he was, in fact, a great deal hungrier than he had suspected.

When, presently, the first edges of hunger had been blunted, Father Reggie sat back—a toast point upon which a negligent spoonful of caviar had been overturned in one hand, and in the other a glass of champagne—looked over the delightful spread, frowned at Miss Morgan, and said, almost accusingly, "You must be rich!"

"Actually," said Miss Morgan, "strictly speaking, I'm not. But honesty compels me to add: Though I'm not, Daddy's rolling. It's one of the more disgraceful facts of life in these United States that the only way a twenty-seven-year-old woman could possibly be studying for her Ph.D. in theology would be to have some mad rich relative footing the bill."

"Oh? Is Daddy mad?"

"No. Merely a bit quirky around the edges. And he does so dote on his defenseless little girl."

"Lord!" breathed Father Reggie. "If you're defenseless, I'd like to see armed-to-the-teeth."

"How rude!"

"Not really. Just a backhanded compliment."

"The only place for backhanded anything is in tennis."

And both of them chuckling happily, they returned their attention to the absorption of food and drink and lapsed into that kind of companionable silence that is the best sign of all that a first-rate relationship is on the bloom.

It was only when the mantel clock struck two, and up above them the great boom of the tower clock bell gave the same warning, that Father Reggie sighed and stood up.

"I'm becoming too much a creature of habit," he said, stifling a yawn.

"Oh?"

He nodded. "I got in the habit over the last few months of going down to the pool for a few laps on a Saturday afternoon when the place is finally deserted. And now I want my swim and I have to go to that damn meeting."

"You shouldn't swim so soon after eating anyway," said Belinda Sue, and asked, "Don't the other adults swarm to take advantage of such an unusual state of affairs in the pool?"

Father Reggie chuckled. "They would if we let 'em, which we don't. If we don't lock the doors and keep 'em locked, and turn off the pump and let the pool settle, the whole place smells like a swimming pool. Even the church."

"It's not an unpleasant smell."

"I don't think so either, but enough people complained that the parish council decided it had to be that way."

"Hmph! How is it any worse than those damned piroshki the Sisterhood makes on Sunday mornings? There you are, wafted on the wings of angels to realms ineffable—and all you can smell is boiling fat. It's all too disquieting a reminder," she concluded darkly, "of what, anthropologically speaking, Communion really is."

"Now, cut that out!" protested Father Reggie, laughing, and suddenly, unable to stifle this time, yawned and stretched his arms to the ceiling. "Oh, Lord! I better get us a cup of coffee."

"Tidily?" asked Miss Morgan.

"A little. And I want my head to be clear."

"Oh," said Miss Morgan in a much more sober tone of voice. She, too, stood up. "You sit down. You've done enough. All I've done upstairs today"—she smiled—"well, I was supposed to be verifying Greek quotations. However . . . But I'll tell you when I get back."

She ducked out the door and was back almost immediately, bearing a thermos jug and a couple of the heavy clay mugs with which the church had provided itself somewhere around 1947 and which had survived all the punishment the ensuing years had been able to throw at them.

"So tell me what happened in the library," said Father Reggie, sipping the strong dark acid that was all the church's urn seemed capable of making.

"Well, as you know, I was supposed to go to Berkeley

today. But there was no way I was going to leave Jolliston until I knew what was going on. And our library is reasonably adequate in these regards. Not," she added dryly, "that I got a whole helluva lot of work done."

"Oh?"

"Well, I don't know if you're aware of it, Father, but the compound is packed with people. Virtually everyone who has anything to do with the play—cast, crew, you name it—they're all here. Word's out. Interesting thing is that there's an awful lot of people who showed up who have nothing whatever to do with the play but are here because—" She broke off and took a moment to try to order her distracted thoughts. "Let's just say that this may be the straw that breaks the camel's back. The camel in this instance being the congregation at large. In fact, I think Dr. Cantrell may very well have precipitated something he is going to regret dearly."

"Tell me what happened, Belinda."

"I guess," she said wryly, "it's because of my sympathetic mug. But an awful lot of people stopped by to talk to me in the library. Including Clyde Cartwright, whom I barely know."

Father Reggie snorted.

"What's so funny?"

"It's not that he doesn't know you, my dear; it's that Jack would like to know you a lot better."

"Oh, pshaw," said Miss Morgan. "He's not a bad-looking boy. But that's what he is. And one suspects that's all he will ever be."

"Don't let Clyde hear you say that."

"Oh, I suspect that Clyde knows more than you might expect. I don't think he has any illusions about Jack. But he does love him. And I gather that Clyde has no use whatever for Dr. Cantrell."

"That, my dear, is putting it mildly."

"I know. Anyway, Clyde has the idea that this play will do something for Jack's career."

"The funny thing is that if Elspeth goes through with her little bit of skulduggery, it very well might."

This time it was Belinda Sue's turn to snort.

"You don't agree?"

"Not at all," she replied. "It's a question of economics. Just suppose her friends do arrange for a package to produce this thing, an outcome more than a little unlikely. Do you seriously suppose that, even if the money men let them cast a back-from-the-dead movie queen of the fifties in a major part, they'd then go on to fill up the cast with inexperienced unknowns? Come on! No matter how good they are, it's just foolishness to encourage that kind of thinking."

"No doubt, you're right," said Father Reggie, knocking back the last of his coffee and standing up. "But I, for one, am going to leave the poor darlings' illusions intact."

"That could be—a mistake."

"Maybe. But if you want my opinion, though it be the most romantic kind of nonsense in the world, it's done the play nothing but good, and put a goodish amount of backbone into our good parishioners as well. And I'll tell you frankly. It may be a pretty Mickey Mouse reason to bring the whole business of Cantrell to a crisis, but I'm glad that it has finally come. Maybe now . . . But no. No. I mustn't say such things. I have to learn to leave it in the hands of the Holy Spirit."

"Much better," said Belinda Sue.

6   The parish council of the Church of All Saints was
     called to order at precisely two-thirty that afternoon
by the presiding officer, namely Clyde Cartwright.

And then, for three-quarters of an hour, the council assembled in judgment was regaled by the less than edifying spectacle as first Cantrell and then Cartwright each gave his viewpoint. Cantrell spoke eloquently and to the point. And his reasoned and (inevitably) pompous presentation was followed by a rather more emotional appeal by Cartwright.

It was unfortunate that, in his urgency, Cartwright should have reminded the parish council of their Christian duty in virtually the same breath he spoke of Dr. Cantrell's personality—and in such a way as to imply the two were mutually exclusive.

Whereupon, at precisely three-fifteen by the bell of the great church clock, logic went out the window as Dr. Cantrell and Mr. Cartwright got into a heavy-duty slinging match, right there in front of God and everybody.

Thinking with no little exasperation that this would never do, Father Reggie, in a transport of righteous anger, stood up and bellowed in a parade-ground voice, "Stop this at once—" and received grateful looks from almost everybody else on the council. Except, of course, the two combatants.

Cartwright had the good grace to be embarrassed. Cantrell, that impregnable ego, merely gobbled at Father Reggie, his incarnadined wattles quivering with indignation that a junior priest should have spoken so to him.

Father Reggie, however, was beyond concern for egos. He told them both summarily to sit down and, if they couldn't behave like Christian gentlemen, to shut up. Whereupon angrily (and angry with himself for being angry), he summarized the points at issue, informing them, as he did so, that he himself happened to agree with Clyde Cartwright that it was, in fact, their Christian duty to allow the play to go forward.

Could he remind them that many members of the parish community—generous members of the parish community—had enthusiastically devoted long and hard effort to it? That gadding about an altar in gaudy replicas of Roman dress clothes was not the only way in which to serve Almighty God? And if they *did* agree that the play could *not* go forward, could they live with it on their conscience that each of them who so voted would have contributed substantively to the ultimate decay of All Saints parish into a moribund, slightly precious, and wholly ludicrous nineteenth-century relic?

In spite of Father Reggie's impassioned little plea, it was fairly obvious the governing body of the parish of the Church of All Saints, Inc., had already been effectively polarized into whatever position they would take when it was put to the vote.

And for Father Reggie it was increasingly important that it be brought to that vote as quickly as possible. The clock was relentlessly turning toward four o'clock, at which time, vote or no vote, Father Reggie would have to be in his confessional in the church. Nor would it have surprised him to discover that Cantrell's party was deliberately putting off the tally until there was one vote less among the opposition.

When, along about twenty till the hour, he had looked at his watch for the second time in as many minutes, it occurred to Neil Bonewarden what the problem was. His own position on the council, being strictly an advisory and *ex officio* one, he leaned across the table and muttered something to Mrs. Robinson, who looked startled, looked at her own watch, and then, rather grimly, set her jaw, nodded, and rapped on the table for attention.

"I move for a vote," she said.

Cartwright promptly seconded.

And so it began.

What made it worse, too, was that the various members of the council seemed to feel compelled to preface their votes with a few words on the subject, thus effectively raising the tension in the room to an unspeakable degree.

The vote, as expected, went strictly according to party lines. Father Reggie, Mrs. Robinson, Mr. Cartwright, Mr. Chalk, the teacher, and Mrs. Blank, the social worker, voting for the play, with Dr. Cantrell, the church lawyer, the church accountant, the housewife, and the college administrator voting against it.

So in the end, there was one single vote remaining to be cast by one single, rather weak-minded person who throughout had sat, eyes downcast, his hands clasped before him on the table, which could not hide the fact that they trembled. And, as everyone had feared, the outcome hinged on the vote of Father Hughie Barnes. They were weak shoulders to be carrying such a burden, and he was, moreover, a creature of Cantrell's own devising. The collective shoulders of the pro-play party slumped in dejection as they waited. And waited. And waited.

"The Reverend Mr. Hugh Barnes," the recording secretary of the council prompted for the third time.

"Are you abstaining?" demanded Cantrell.

Father Hughie shook his head.

"Is that no, you're not abstaining, or no, the play will not go on?" Cantrell continued to taunt.

All of a sudden, ever so slightly, Father Hughie straightened, even though his face was still hidden by the fall of his hair as he gazed downward at his hands on the table in front of him.

Everyone could see the flaming red of his ears. Most, however, probably thought that it was nothing more than the man's usual acute self-consciousness. But it was, as it transpired, more than that.

And it was at that moment that, for the first time, Father Reggie began to believe that a miracle was about to occur.

For, after a seemingly interminable time, Father Hughie looked up and said, in a not very strong voice, "No, I'm not abstaining. And no, it does not mean I am voting against the play. I tried to tell you last night, Dr. Cantrell, I cannot support you in this. I am voting yes, the play must go on."

It took several seconds really for the shock to fully set in. And it was shock. No question about it. After all, only once before had Cantrell been successfully frustrated. In their astonishment and chagrin, Cantrell's supporters looked back and forth among themselves with varying degrees of glowering dissatisfaction, muttering foolishly (as even they knew) about a recount.

Those who had supported the continued production of the

play flashed broad if somewhat surprised and disbelieving grins among themselves. Father Reggie was perhaps the only one who watched his fellow clergymen.

It was quite clear, at least to Father Reggie, that just as on the previous occasion, so in this one, Dr. Cantrell was shocked and disbelieving. The glance with which Cantrell continued to skewer the uncomfortable Father Hughie was one of gimlet intensity and of great and implacable fury. It was up to Father Reggie to break the tableau. Indeed, he had no choice.

He stood up and, turning to the recording secretary, said, "I'm sorry. I have to go hear confessions. I move to adjourn."

"Seconded," said someone, and in a confusion of voices and roiling emotions. Father Reggie departed for the church.

But he didn't get very far. Lurking outside the council room door were a dozen or so interested souls all standing about, waiting to discover the outcome of the meeting. It reminded him of one of those scenes in old movies where doors are opened and immediately a gabbling crowd of reporters descends upon those emerging.

"Excuse me, please," he said, trying to push through.

"What happened, Father Reggie? What happened! Come on, tell us. Who won?"

"We did," he said. "But you'll have to get the details from someone else. I'm going to be late. I've got to get down to the church."

"Let him through," yelled someone. "Yeah, come on, Father Reggie."

"We really won?"

He nodded, still in rather a grim mood. He was only too aware it was almost certain to lead to further ructions in the days ahead. . . .

7 Father Reggie slipped into his office in order to change into a lighter-weight cassock, and found his fiancée seated at his desk patiently scribbling in a three-ring notebook open before her. Abandoning whatever gem of wisdom she was garnering from the tone of distinctly nineteenth-century provenance lying open beside the notebook, she looked up and smiled.

"You look a good deal less like David after slaying Goliath than the Apostle Paul sneaking out of Damascus. I hope you don't mind my working in here. But I decided nobody would think to come tell me the upshot in the library. Besides, I thought you would rather I were here than in that crowd that was gathering outside the council chamber—"

"Even though," said Father Reggie with mock severity as he went to his closet, "you're just as curious as anybody else."

"Well, of course, I am. What did you think?"

He sighed and gave her a précis of events.

She nodded. "Oh, dear."

"I know," said Father Reggie. "I know." He paused as he opened the door and looked back over his shoulder. "I'll see you at Evensong?"

"Oh, yes," she replied. "I think we have a great deal to be thankful for this day. Don't you?"

"Yes," he admitted, and left her once more ponderously opening that ponderous volume.

He glanced once more at his watch. He was already a minute late. He dashed down the stairs, unwilling to wait for the elevator cage to creak its way to that floor—and was accosted, in the cloister garth, by a distrait-appearing Bonnie Harris.

"Do you have a moment, Father?" she stood up and called.

"Actually, I don't," said Father Reggie, feeling harassed. "I'm supposed to be in the confessional. Now."

She nodded, looking very unhappy, and sank back down.

Whereupon Father Reggie decided those waiting for penance could bear the weight of their sins another few minutes.

He sat down next to her.

"It's Julian, isn't it?"

She nodded. "He hasn't spoken to me all day. I don't think he's spoken to anyone since this morning."

"Well, Bonnie, you have to consider Julian's personality and how important all of this is to him."

"To have had it turned into a circus?" she demanded bitterly.

Father Reggie nodded.

"Even that. After all, not only does his play mean a lot to him," he continued, "but I suspect that the Church of All Saints means a great deal to him as well—in spite of Dr. Cantrell."

"Yes. Everyone is saying that he did everything today he was supposed to do."

A bit of information at which Father Reggie chuckled. "Supposed to do! The only thing that Julian is supposed to do around this place is be a night watchman. Which he does admirably. But you and I both know that it's like he's found himself here."

"I know. I've been thinking rather a lot lately that maybe—maybe Julian ought to be a priest. I mean, I make enough money. . . ."

The confusions of the average lay person about what it takes to be a priest are not to be resolved in a five-minute conference.

"Listen, I really do have to get into that blasted box," said Father Reggie, standing up. "But there is one thing you can do, you know."

She looked up, a world of infinite trust in her face. "What else do you think I've been doing all day, every day for the last weeks? Unfortunately, since yesterday, the only answer I keep coming up with is not an especially Christian one."

And though Father Reggie would have loved to have

plumbed the meaning of that last gnomic utterance, he just simply didn't have the time.

He went into the church, where there was a line-up beside his confessional, some people pointedly checking their watches. He muttered an apology, ducked into the confessional, kissed and donned the purple stole, and for the time being, at least, lay aside all earthly cares.

CHAPTER ELEVEN

1 Father Reggie's first inkling that something had gone
awry was at approximately eight minutes to six.
He was still in the confessional and furthermore, expected
to remain there till well after the beginning of Mass at six-
fifteen.

Somewhat earlier, at twenty minutes to the hour, he had
looked at his watch, observing gratefully that he had only
five minutes left—and had heard the unmistakable sound of
someone crawling into the box on the other side of the grille.
Sliding back the window and giving the usual blessing, he
was rewarded with the words: "Bless me, Father, for I have
sinned; it's been fifteen years since my last confession. . . ."

Now, to inquire after particulars in such a situation is unutterably feckless. Father, therefore, gradually and patiently
took the fellow through the Decalogue, asking pertinent
questions. Unfortunately, in spite of the necessarily perfunctory nature of this procedure, it still takes rather a time.

And presently he realized that Evensong still hadn't begun. Puzzled, he glanced at his watch, trying to keep his
attention focused on the spate of trivia pouring into his ear
from the other side of the grille. But it was already five-fifty-
two. What was wrong?

As though in response to his mental query, he heard the sound of the congregation rustling to its feet, and he settled back to give his attention more fully to his reluctant penitent. And then he heard that which brought him up short in utter astonishment.

For chanting the beginning words of the service was the unmistakable rancid voice of Fiona MacLaren.

Fiona? he thought. Serving? Fiona MacLaren serving at the Church of All Saints?

What could possibly have happened that something so truly radical could come about during the previous two hours while he had been cooped up in his little booth?

And there was absolutely nothing he could do about finding out.

Well, actually, he realized after a moment's thought, there was.

"Just a moment!" He interrupted the nervous mutter from the grille and in his sternest voice admonished: "Now, see here. I'm going to give you absolution. I want you to go to Communion, and you are to go to Mass every day for a week. Spend at least twenty minutes every night examining your conscience and then come back next week—at a reasonable hour."

"But I haven't finished."

"Yes, you have. You've obviously repented. Forget your sins now and follow St. Ignatius's advice and practice a bit of gentle amnesia about them and let God take care of the bookkeeping. Now say the Our Father while I give you absolution."

And forty seconds later, Father Reggie burst forth from his confessional even before the penitent within had had time to pull himself together and leave.

And sure enough, there was Fiona, in cassock, surplice, and stole, reading vespers.

From his standpoint at the back of the church it was difficult to tell who was in the congregation. Which didn't prevent him from casting wildly about trying to see if there was *anyone* present who could explain this phenomenon.

Then, through the open door into the cloister, he suddenly realized that, sitting on the lip of the fountain in the center of the garth, was none other than Millie Cantrell, along with Dr. Cantrell, who was supposed to be taking the service going on right now.

And both of them were looking very strange indeed.

Father Reggie scuttled out into the cloister and on down into the garth.

"What's going on?" he asked solicitously.

"I—I couldn't help myself," Cantrell gasped out, his complexion waxy.

He was mopping his face with a handkerchief which he appeared to have soaked in the fountain. Nor had he been particularly careful with it; his clothing was appreciably stained here and there with dark blots of moisture; even his shoes looked as though they had been immersed.

Abruptly he stood up. "Millie, I'm going upstairs and lie down. Would you please bring me a cup of tea? I'm sure that will help."

"Of course, dear," said Millie, rising also. "I'll be up in just a moment."

He staggered off.

"He looks terrible," said Father Reggie.

"Yes, he does," said Millie.

"Is he ill?"

"What did you expect? He isn't used," she pointed out grimly, "to being crossed."

"Let alone successfully," added Father Reggie.

Mrs. Cantrell inclined her head without comment.

"Who is—" began Father Reggie, and then stopped. "Father Hughie's saying Mass?"

Mrs. Cantrell nodded again. "Dr. Cantrell asked him if he would, as soon as he knew he wasn't well enough to say it himself. I knew he was seriously ill when Father Hughie asked if Fiona could say Evensong, and he agreed." She stood up. "Excuse me now. I had best go make Leo some tea."

A sudden rather horrible thought occurred to Father Reggie. "Oh, my God," he swore. "Does this mean Father Hughie's going to improvise a sermon?"

For some reason Mrs. Cantrell took umbrage at the tone in Father Reggie's voice.

"I imagine he'll have to. Leo may be scheduled to preach this weekend, but I cannot see how he could possibly preach tonight—and Father Hughie is perfectly capable of preaching a sermon in his stead."

Rebuked, Father Reggie nodded meekly, turned and went back into the church, walked up the side aisle until he found the person he most wanted to see—and slipped into the pew and knelt down next to her.

"I can see there have been developments," said Belinda Sue quietly.

"You could say," said Father Reggie inadequately, and turned his attention to the service.

And approximately a third of the way through Fiona's already hasty recitation of the office, above them in the tower the great bell bonged out the Angelus. . . .

2   "Yes, thank you," said Miss Worthing. "I already got from my aunt what happened next, during Mass. How about you boys?" she asked the D.A. and the sheriff.

Both nodded.

"We've already got half a dozen eyewitness reports of what came down," said Lorris.

"Okay," sighed Miss Worthing, grateful it was finally over. "Thank you all very much."

Father Reggie looked ready to drop, and Belinda Sue and Mrs. Robinson looked not much better off.

It had certainly been an interesting narrative. At first, slow and hesitant, then, as the three had gotten into it, the tale had taken on a rhythm, a life of its own, as it were, each filling in what the others had left out. It had even seemed that the two lawmen, Miss Worthing, and the reporter might just as well not have been in the room, so intent were the three on each other.

And by the end of it, Miss Worthing felt she had a reasonably accurate idea of what had taken place at the Church of All Saints during the previous few days.

Not that—as far as she could see at the moment—it helped all that much.

"Yes, thank you," Lorris was saying. "And thank you, Miss Worthing," he added, observing wryly, "Good idea. Have to keep it in mind."

Miss Worthing nodded almost absently, flipping through the notes she had made.

"So if we are to credit," she finally said, "that someone would actually try to murder Dr. Cantrell for trying to cancel the play, where does that put us?"

"I'm sorry, Matilda," said Mrs. Robinson with a helpless little gesture. "Perhaps, on the face of it, it does look ridiculous. To any normal person it would be. But I can speak with some authority when I say that actors—particularly ambitious actors—are not the most rational of human beings."

"But, first of all, most of these people are not professional actors. And second, as Miss Morgan indicated—and several days ago, apparently—that it was all too absurd," protested Miss Worthing, "that even were Elspeth's friends able to cut a deal to get the movie made for her—"

"Of course it's absurd," Father Reggie snapped, a hand slapping the table for added emphasis. "But are you going to sit there and tell us that things—murders included—don't happen because of absurd reasons?"

"Of course not," said Miss Worthing calmly. "I dislike having to do so, but, of course, I can concede that people can be that stupid."

Ignoring the glares from the deponents, she again glanced down at her notes, irritably aware as she did so that across the table the two lawmen were huddled together muttering indistinctly to each other.

She sighed and began ticking off names. "Very well, people. If we do accept the thesis that it was passionate regard for the play that was a primary motive and allowing also for people who knew the church well enough to have known where—the necessary was kept and have access thereto, we have, by my count: One, Julian Richards; two, Bonnie Harris; three, Stringer Yates; four, Jack Cartwright; and"—she looked up, eyed the quartet, and added in a level voice, "five, Neil Bonewarden, and six—Elspeth Robinson."

Mrs. Robinson sighed wearily and nodded. "Yes, I suppose that's only fair," she conceded. "But—well, I gather you aren't going to tell us what kind of poison was used, are you?"

Miss Worthing merely shook her head before continuing. "And then we have to add those who are emotionally tied to someone involved."

"Such as?" asked Belinda Sue.

"Well, Maria Yates, for instance."

"She was very upset about Stringer's—breakout," said Father Reggie. "And she definitely blamed it on Cantrell."

"Yes, and knowing Maria, I can just imagine what she was like," said Miss Worthing. "But furthermore, she apparently actually said"—she flipped pages—"'. . . or if someone had the nerve to kill him.' Meaning Dr. Cantrell, I presume."

Father Reggie nodded. "Yes," he said reluctantly, "yes, she did say it." He brightened. "But neither Stringer nor Maria was there at Mass this evening. I know they were waiting around till the decision was made in the parish council, and I know also that Stringer went to confession this afternoon, but I didn't see him or Maria or any of the kids at Mass."

"Neither did I," said Mrs. Robinson.

"In fact," said Belinda Sue, "I saw them drive off."

"But why should that make a difference?" asked Miss Worthing. "In fact, the altar wine and Dr. Cantrell's tea may well have been doctored much earlier in the day as a kind of one-two punch. Besides," she sighed, "if the real poisoner *wasn't* there, it could explain why what was set up for Dr. Cantrell was left for poor Father Hughie."

"You have a point. Is there anyone else on your little list?" asked Father Reggie.

"Oh, yes," Miss Worthing said thoughtfully. "There's Clyde Cartwright."

"Clyde Cartwright!" protested Mrs. Robinson. "But that's ridiculous, Matilda. The most upstanding man! A true Christian! And much too good a man to have done anything—"

"Yes, and he's spoiled his nephew rotten," Miss Worthing pointed out severely.

"That's putting it much too strongly, Matilda," said Mrs. Robinson.

"Is it?" demanded Miss Worthing. "Doesn't it strike any of you as even a little peculiar that, after being the leading member of the anti-Cantrell faction in the parish for donkeys' years, it was only in this essentially trivial business that he should suddenly rouse himself to rally the troops and exercise an authority he's had all along?"

No one had anything to say.

"Besides, you mustn't get all in a dither, people," Miss Worthing went on tranquilly. "We're still just talking avenues of inquiry."

"Do you have enough?" asked Father Reggie, almost, if not quite, sarcastically.

"Well, no, actually. No, I'm afraid we can't, we daren't stop there. We also have to ask ourselves, what if?"

"What if what?" asked Father Reggie.

"What if, in this ferment of emotions, someone rather more politically motivated used it as a cover, so to speak, and—"

"Implying?" demanded Father Reggie.

"That I think we have to add three more names to our preliminary little list."

Belinda Sue gave Miss Worthing a thoughtful look and said, supremely disingenuously, "Dear me! Why, I do believe she means you and me, Reggie."

"What!"

"Oh, will you keep your shirt on," said Miss Worthing. "I told you; we're still just counting possibilities. And yes," she said to Belinda Sue, "you're right. At such a preliminary juncture, of course you and Father Reggie have to be included. But you're forgetting someone else."

"Who?"

"Fiona."

"Oh, now really!" protested Father Reggie. "Do you actually think Fiona could have possibly killed Father Hughie? Or let him drink a poisoned chalice if . . ."

And, rather abruptly, Father Reggie's voice trailed off.

"She is a complicated woman," he concluded lamely. "I *can* see how— Excuse me," he said to the two lawmen, an edge to his voice. "Sam! George! If you two aren't interested in any of this, then why . . ."

"Actually, Father," said Lorris, pulling back from his whispered colloquy with Sam, "I don't think we are."

"What?" said Miss Worthing.

The others just gaped.

"Aw, come on, folks," said Sam. "Y'all're just messin' things up. There ain't no need for all this complication." He stood up and clearly intended to dismiss them. "Thanks for all your help."

"Just like that?" asked Miss Worthing in deepest suspicion. "What do you think you're doing?"

"Come on, Mattie," repeated Sam. "It's about as plain as the . . ." He took himself firmly in hand. "If what you folks say is true, there's only one person coulda done it. Mrs. Robinson," he asked, "that ant powder you was keeping in the kitchen—who put it back in the shed?"

"Julian, of course."

"Yep. And who was in the sacristy last night, fiddlin' with the wine jugs? Even said something 'bout using the wrong one?"

"Julian," said Father Reggie.

"And who," interjected Lorris, "was more 'passionately' concerned about the play than perhaps anyone else?"

"Julian again," answered Belinda Sue. "But you don't . . ."

"Listen!" said Sam, and counted the points off on his fingers. "He's caretaker, pool man, handyman, and part-time gardener. He has complete access to every part of the whole damn church complex, including the shed where you folks store all them damn chemicals . . ."

"Sam!" Lorris and Miss Worthing shouted simultaneously.

Marshall ignored them and simply continued, ". . . and he hated Cantrell even before the old bastard tried to step in and stop the play."

After the long moment of silence that greeted this summation, Lorris, observing Miss Worthing looking very angry indeed, asked, "Something bothering you?"

"Of course, there is," she snapped back at him. "I'll concede that such a scenario is attractive. Even that, on the face of it, Julian looks very much like he might be our pigeon. But, damn it all, you can't arrest a man on evidence like that without looking at the whole picture. What if someone else did it all, knowing that it *would* look like Julian had done it? How's that for a for-instance?"

Sam just stubbornly shook his head. "And I'm tellin' you, you're probably just complicatin' things."

"So what now?" asked Mrs. Robinson, looking very distressed.

"Contrary to what you all—including you, Miss Worthing—are thinking," said Lorris, "we have no plans at the moment to *arrest* Julian. . . ."

"No," said Miss Worthing sourly, "you're just going to take him in 'for questioning.'"

"That's right," replied Lorris coolly. "And now, if you'll

excuse us, we have to get on upstairs. You folks can go home. We'll have to get signed affidavits from each of you, by the way, but that's all for now."

And in a surprisingly short time only the three deponents and Miss Worthing remained in the council chamber, looking at each other with helpless disbelief at the sudden and radical turn of events.

There remained a good deal more Miss Worthing would have loved to ask about. But it took no particular insight on her part to see there was no way she was going to be able to ask anything at that precise juncture. Everyone, and not least herself, was just too done in.

Wearily Mrs. Robinson rose to her feet and took charge. "Father Reggie, Belinda Sue, go home. You all look half dead."

"But so do you, Elspeth," said Father Reggie.

"Thank you so much. I can't tell you how much I needed to hear that right now."

The ghost of a chuckle went around the group, and Father Reggie hauled himself to his feet.

"You go on, Elspeth. I gotta lock up after everyone's gone. And set the alarms if they've gone up to take Julian in."

"Nonsense," said Mrs. Robinson. "I'll do it. I've done it before. Besides, I have to air out the bishop's vestments anyway, and, believe me, I'd rather do it tonight and have an extra few minutes in bed tomorrow morning."

"Suits me," said Father Reggie, and, yawning, led Belinda Sue out.

"If you don't mind waiting a bit, Matilda," said Mrs. Robinson, "I'll give you a lift home."

There was no response.

"Matilda?"

Miss Worthing came to with a start. "Oh! Sorry. What did you say?"

"I said," repeated Mrs. Robinson with a patient smile, "that if you don't mind waiting, I'll drop you at your house."

"No, I don't mind waiting. As tired as I am now, a few

more minutes aren't going to make any difference. I had planned to have Sam drop me off, but I don't want to see that man's big mug right now."

"You're not happy," observed Mrs. Robinson.

"Of course not," snapped Miss Worthing. "How could I be? How could anyone be? Except maybe a small-minded small-town politician!"

Mrs. Robinson smiled wearily. "Well, I can't say I'm exactly pleased about the way things have developed either. But I don't suppose you can talk about it with me."

"Not really, Elspeth. If you don't mind, I'd better talk to Dr. Fisher first."

"Of course. So come along, Matilda. Let's shoo the law out of the buildings and get out of here."

3 When Miss Worthing and Mrs. Robinson descended to street level, however, they discovered, to their relief, that the forces of the law had already left.

"Do you have much to do, Elspeth?" asked Miss Worthing wearily.

Mrs. Robinson chuckled. "Don't worry, Matilda; I'll get through it as quick as I can. I'm just as tired as you are. But to answer your question, not really. Setting up in the church is the only thing that might take more than a few minutes."

And indeed there seemed to be little more to do, as they progressed through the auxiliary buildings, than to make sure certain lights were extinguished and various alarms set.

As they so progressed, however, they were both a little astonished by the amazing amount of yellow plastic ribbon the sheriff's men had left behind, tying off locations.

Outside the doors of the gym and those leading to the parish offices, Mrs. Robinson paused to test the locks and then open and set the alarms, little gray nine-by-six boxes, inside each of which was an alphanumeric keyboard, and a green light and a red. The lights changed from green to red as, quickly, almost absently, Mrs. Robinson keyed in the appropriate letters and numbers and closed and locked the boxes.

After watching this procedure several times, Miss Worthing asked, "Elspeth, how many people know that combination?"

"Well, now, let's see," said Mrs. Robinson, pausing to pinch her lower lip thoughtfully. "There's the clergy, of course. Me, Neil, Millie, the parish secretary, Julian, naturally, and, since she's been living with him up there, I would expect that Bonnie would have to know it, too."

And almost immediately the words were out of Mrs. Robinson's mouth, a look of horror swept across her face. Her mouth gaped open and a hand went to cover it.

"Elspeth! What's the matter?"

"I have grievously sinned—by omission," said Mrs. Robinson, and she turned and hurried into the cloister and into the elevator, Miss Worthing hastening after as best she could.

"Elspeth?"

"Matilda, those two sorry excuses for lawmen left us in the parish room a quarter of an hour ago to go up and arrest Julian—whatever fancy term they use for it—and I never even thought that poor Bonnie will have been there when they came for him."

She slammed the cage door shut as Miss Worthing nipped within, and presently they emerged onto the roof.

In the corner stood the caretaker's apartment, almost a little house perched adventitiously on top of the larger building. Lights were blazing from every window and the door stood open, through which they could hear the sound of a recording of something baroque, fugal, and soothing being played inside.

Mrs. Robinson knocked loudly on the open door.

"Bonnie!" she called. "Are you there?"

"Just a second, please!" came Bonnie's voice. There followed a brief moment during which they heard her apparently speaking to someone on the telephone. "Very well," they heard, "just see to it as quickly as possible. I'll be there as soon as I can." They heard the phone cradled, and not gently, and Bonnie strode purposefully into the room.

"Yes?" she asked, and came to a halt, seeing who it was. "Mrs. Robinson," she said with no emphasis whatever.

"Bonnie, I came up to see if you're all right," said Mrs. Robinson, moving forward anxiously into the tiny foyer.

Bonnie cocked her head and actually smiled—albeit a grim sort of smile—at the form of the question.

"Oh, yes," she finally said. "I'm fine. Now. I'm ashamed to admit that I did rather go to pieces at first. I do that sometimes, you know. But now that I've gotten busy, I'm okay."

"Busy?" asked Mrs. Robinson.

"Well, of course. Calling friends. Here and in San Francisco. We're going to get the best damned son of a bitch of a lawyer I can afford."

"Good for you, Miss Harris," said Miss Worthing.

Bonnie peered around into the gloom to see who had spoken. When she realized who it was, a frown creased her brow. "Oh, it's you, is it?" she said, and asked coldly, "Was it you who put them up to arresting Julian, Miss Worthing?"

"No, it was not," replied Miss Worthing forcefully. After which, honesty forced her to add, "Although you must admit that it does look bad for him."

"Oh?"

Ignoring the frost, Miss Worthing continued, "I'm very sorry, Miss Harris, but it happens to be true. Nevertheless," she replied, "I did tell them that I thought they were being entirely too precipitate."

"Bonnie," asked Mrs. Robinson, "is there anything we can do?"

"No. No, thank you, Mrs. Robinson, not right now. If I do think of anything, I'll be sure to let you know."

"Be sure that you do. Have you enough to eat? Drink?"

"Yes. And thank you for asking."

"And, please, don't be afraid of Matilda here. The bishop would not have appointed her if he didn't trust her, as we all do, completely."

It was during this brief exchange of communal civilities that Miss Worthing suddenly had an idea that was eventually to give her such trouble in the hours ahead. As Elspeth had just indicated, his lordship *had* appointed her his representative during the preliminaries downstairs; surely the good bishop could have no possible objection if she expanded that commission somewhat.

And, in fact, even before the question had formulated itself in her head, she knew perfectly well he would not; he, as did she, wanted the truth of this matter snuffled out. And in this passage of *politesse* here on the moonlit roof of the Church of All Saints, she suddenly saw her way to snuffle. It only remained to be seen if she could manage it before total collapse from fatigue—and whether she would be able to get anyone to cooperate.

Therefore, as Bonnie murmured, "I know," in response to Mrs. Robinson's admonition, Miss Worthing was turning to the latter and instructing, "Elspeth, why don't you get on down to the church and see to those chores you were telling me about?"

And before Mrs. Robinson even had time to reply to this abrupt departure from the game plan, Miss Worthing turned back to Bonnie and said, "Miss Harris, I know it is late and you are overwrought and furthermore have much to do. But would you mind terribly if I asked you a few questions?"

Bonnie frowned, her irritation evident. "I don't—" she began. "I have an awful lot to do."

"So do I, Miss Harris. And while I can appreciate just how you must be feeling right about now, nevertheless, you will not be likely to get hold of your attorneys till morning, at the earliest, and if Julian is not guilty of this murder, don't you think it rather behooves you to cooperate with me?"

"But you think he's guilty. You said so."

"I said no such thing. I merely pointed out that we have to admit that it does look bad for him. Which indeed it does. So if he did not do it, help me now to discover who did."

Mrs. Robinson said gently, "Bonnie, I really do think you should talk to Matilda."

It took a moment, but presently, and with something of a wry smile, Bonnie said, "Oh, all right. And you are right, Miss Worthing; I *haven't* been able to get hold of the lawyer I want for this. Will you come in?"

"And I shall leave you to it," said Mrs. Robinson. "Will you be long, Matilda?"

"I certainly hope not."

"Very well. I expect you'll find me in the sacristy. Come in through the cloister door at the back of the nave."

"I could just come to the sacristy."

"You could," said Mrs. Robinson dryly, "but I'm going to lock it while I'm in there. The last thing I need in the state I'm in is to be going busily about my little chores and have someone, anyone, come through that door and scare the life out of me. This way I'll hear you *before* I jump out of my wits."

Bonnie actually grinned at this little bit of nonsense, and it was good thus to see her mood somewhat lightened. Mrs. Robinson went back to the elevator and slammed the cage door shut as Bonnie led Miss Worthing into the postage-stamp-sized living room of the apartment.

4   The room, though hardly underfurnished, was really quite remarkably tidy. But then she rather supposed it would have to be, with two creative souls sharing such cramped quarters.

"Would you care for anything?" asked Bonnie, gesturing to a chair. "Although," she added with a little grimace, "I'm afraid all we've got is some instant coffee or some brandy."

Briefly Miss Worthing considered brandy and rejected the idea. She needed to keep as alert as possible. There was no way she could take notes in a situation as delicate as this one, and that meant she was going to have to rely on her memory to hold all the salient points.

Instant coffee did not even enter into consideration—in spite of a great longing for vast quantities of caffeine. . . .

"No, thank you, Miss Harris. Although, please, don't let me stop you."

"Call me Bonnie," said the other with a little smile. "And if you don't mind, I will have a little brandy. I think I need it."

Presently they sat, Miss Worthing in an armchair, Bonnie poised, back straight, on the extreme edge of the divan.

Before Miss Worthing could ask a single question, however, Bonnie said, "I'll help all I can, of course. But I don't see how I can be of any help to anyone. I don't know anything. Other than what people have told me. And what Julian told me."

"Oh? And what did Julian tell you?"

"That it was almost certain that he was going to be arrested."

"My goodness! Why did he tell you that?"

"Because Dr. Cantrell had been poisoned."

"But why?"

"Because it was Julian who brought him his tea." She looked directly at Miss Worthing and said, "And also because of all the people here at the Church of All Saints, and of all the people who might have had access to all the—chemicals that are kept here, and of all the people who don't like Dr. Cantrell any more than Julian does, he is the only one who is not particularly rich or particularly powerful.

"And no," Bonnie went on, "that is not wild-eyed socialism. It's just common sense."

"For the most part, Bonnie, I agree with you," replied Miss Worthing and was amused to note that that surprised the younger woman somewhat. "Do you—or Julian—happen to know what poison was used today?"

"No, of course not. How could we?"

"Indeed."

"But, as Julian told me, we've got pool cleansers, water purifiers, bug spray, ant powder, herbicides, rodenticides—you name it. For the garden, vermin, gym, pool, all the things a plant like this is going to need."

"Where were the two of you when you got the news?"

"I was in church. Julian had just been to confession, but he had bell ringing and such to do. And then, as I'm sure you know, he took Dr. Cantrell his tea. I wanted to hear Mass again before I came home. Julian was going to join me as soon as he could."

"Did he?"

Bonnie shook her head. "No. He told me that after he had taken the tea upstairs, he just continued up to begin supper for me."

"When did he learn of what had happened?"

"After Lady Fairgrief told us all to go to the gym, I went up to tell Julian and to fetch him down to wait with the others."

"Why did you do that?"

Bonnie shrugged. "Because I thought it would be best."

"Okay. What about yourself? You spent all day in the church, didn't you?"

"Pretty much so. Except when I came up here to fix some lunch for Julian and me."

"He ate lunch with you?"

Bonnie shook her head. "Julian wasn't around much yesterday. He certainly didn't feel much like eating."

"Anxiety—about the play, I mean? Or just hung over?"

Bonnie looked sharply at her. "You do seem to have been pretty well informed."

"I try," said Miss Worthing tranquilly. "Well?"

"A bit of both, I would imagine. You know, Miss Worthing, before we go any further, I do want to point out that I'm not being this way just out of loyalty to Julian."

"I beg your pardon."

"I think you should know that I *know* that Julian is innocent."

"Oh?"

"Yes. And for one simple reason."

"Which is?"

"He had no motive."

For a moment Miss Worthing could only look blankly at her.

"No motive!"

"That's right."

"But the play? His job?"

Bonnie smiled a tight, little, knowing smile and nodded. "Oh, yes," she said. "Julian does love it here at All Saints. Much better for him than clerking in dreary bookshops on Telegraph Avenue in Berkeley. But does *anyone* imagine Julian would starve if he got canned?"

"No, of course not. But if not his job, then what about the play and this production of it?"

"What about it? You know, everyone seems to forget how devout Julian is. He was perfectly willing to leave it all up to the Holy Ghost and the parish council. Especially considering . . ."

Bonnie's eyes opened wide in shock, and she actually clapped a hand to her mouth.

"Especially considering what, Bonnie?"

"It—it's nothing."

"It can't possibly be nothing if you're having that kind of a reaction."

"I—I promised Julian I wouldn't . . ." She shook her head firmly and said, "Sorry, you'll just have to ask him."

"Thank you, Bonnie. I certainly shall," said Miss Worthing, hoping it wasn't too obvious how irritated she was.

"Anything else?" asked Bonnie.

"Yes. Do you know what Julian did all day yesterday?"

"Only in outline. But even if I knew the details, don't you think you had better ask him that?"

"Yes, I do," said Miss Worthing. "Again, you're quite right. Nevertheless, I can ask you the same question."

"But I told you."

"You were in the church all day?"

"Yes. Except for an hour or so at lunch."

"Did you notice anything?"

"Like what?"

"Specifically, anything out of the ordinary."

Before answering, Bonnie frowned and turned her head aside as though mentally running over her day. "No. Nothing unusual."

"There were people in and out, I would imagine."

"Of course."

"Anyone"—Miss Worthing shrugged—"who didn't—belong?"

Bonnie returned the shrug. "Who's to say? I heard Mrs. Robinson guiding a group of tourists around. She does that when they come by on a Saturday. I imagine any number of people may have come in for a visit, but I'm always up front. The light's better and for some reason people tend to leave you alone if you're up front."

"What about in the sanctuary? Or the sacristy?"

"Don't think that I haven't been trying to think of someone. But no. There wasn't anyone there who didn't have a perfectly legitimate right to be there."

Which, of course, was as Miss Worthing had expected all along to hear. The homicidal maniac wandering in to wreak random havoc had never been, in this case, anything but the remotest of possibilities; besides, the very nature of the crime was indicative of someone who knew the terrain intimately. Still, even to eliminate such a rococo possibility was something.

"And they were?"

Again Bonnie shrugged. "The women of the Sisterhood

were in and out, cleaning and fussing about with linens and vestments and such."

"Clergy?"

"Yes. All of 'em at one time or another. Except Father Reggie, now that I think of it. I didn't see him from Mass in the morning till I spoke with him on his way to hear confessions."

"Father Hughie?"

"Oh, yes. He came in to fetch Fiona."

"Fiona was in the church, too?"

Bonnie nodded and smiled. "Yes. She was up at the lectionary Bible. I don't know what she was doing, but she must have been there for about fifteen minutes."

"What was she doing?"

"I asked her that. She said, and seemed kind of embarrassed to admit it, that she wanted, had always wanted to see what it would feel like to preach a sermon at the Church of All Saints."

"So why didn't she just climb up into the pulpit?"

"I don't know. Failure of nerve, maybe."

"What time would that have been?"

"Probably about five. I was almost done with my mending."

And there was the opening, modest though it might be.

"It really is very kind of you to do all that for the church," said Miss Worthing casually.

Again the younger woman merely shrugged. Which was frustrating. And to herself Miss Worthing said, "All right, then. To hell with delicacy."

Aloud she said, "Tell me, Bonnie: You were the—are the costume director of the play."

Bonnie nodded. "It was how I could help best. I'm no actress."

"But surely you didn't have to donate the costumes yourself. And I'm told they're quite spectacular."

Bonnie actually smiled at the description and admitted, "I think they are. But you're right. Of course I didn't *have* to do it," she went on. "But I can afford it, you know, and it will—would have—I'm almost sure of it—been good for business."

"Ah, yes. Your new line of designer clothes."

And turning her head to look directly at Miss Worthing, Bonnie said, "You're really very good at this, aren't you?"

"What do you mean?"

"Miss Worthing," said Bonnie crisply, "let me save us both some time by telling you that I did not try to kill Dr. Cantrell. Period. Not because I think, as I quite legitimately do think, my costumes for the play would help sales in my stores. Not because I wanted Julian's play to go on, which I do. Not even because the property might be bought by those friends of Mrs. Robinson's for her comeback. Although I would be delighted if it were. But not for any reason did I try to kill Dr. Cantrell."

"Yes, my dear," said Miss Worthing with a chuckle, "put as baldly as all that, perhaps it does sound absurd. But . . ."

"But you had to find out."

"Well, it is my job. At least at the moment. Were you in the sacristy yesterday?"

"Of course. I was there several times. But both times it was in the company of Elspeth because we were going over what needed doing in the way of the fancier kind of repairs that I can only do at the shop. Oh, I suppose I could have gotten in easily enough," she went on to answer Miss Worthing's next question, "but I didn't. No point to it. And I don't know about you, but I was taught you don't go prancing about the sanctuary and sacristy unless you've got an awfully good reason for it. Besides that, I had no way of getting into the shed where all the dangerous stuff is kept, even if I were so inclined. What was it, by the way?"

"Never mind. We're keeping that in reserve for now."

"Okay. I guess I can understand that."

"You say you had no access to the shed?"

"That's right."

"And that's where all the—chemicals are stored."

"That's right. And, for very good cause, under lock and key at all times."

"But surely Julian's keys—"

"Are with him wherever he happens to be. And no, I don't have copies. My position at the Church of All Saints is invidious enough that I hardly think I should be going around like I owned the place, opening doors that ought to be kept locked."

"Very well, what about the alarm combination? Do you know that?"

"What for? It isn't necessary to get up here, and the same is true of the combination as of the keys."

5   It was an interesting point. Though Bonnie's position around the Church of All Saints was not, perhaps, quite as invidious as she seemed to think it was. She was, in fact, a generous donor, and her work with the vestments was even more valuable. Furthermore, she knew it. Her explosion earlier that morning and her subsequent threats to withhold her contributions were sufficient indication the woman knew her worth.

If, however, she was not being entirely candid about her value in parochial life, she had been all candor and openness about the possibility that she herself might have a motive for murder. She had certainly rattled off the three motives she might conceivably have with admirable if less than disarming clarity.

She was, of course, quite right; the train of thought leading from murder to success in a dress shop did indeed appear moderately ludicrous. But people have done worse things for even more ludicrous reasons—an admittedly rather blither-minded dictum which seemed (at least in Miss Worthing's mind) tied up with the idea of anyone trying to murder Leo Cantrell because he wished to cancel the play.

But then, as always, she had to remind herself that murderers are *de facto ipsissima* insane. Reason, while the main prop and stay of investigation, might very well have nothing to do with the motive or motives of the murderer. Which is why the consideration of motive, though sometimes useful, can so often lead into muddy waters.

And I'm right back to square one, she thought.

"Bonnie, I'm sorry, but you brought it up yourself several days ago. You told Father Reggie and Belinda Sue Morgan, didn't you, that Julian had told you he wouldn't marry you till his income matched your own."

"That's right. And he did. He's a very simple man in many ways, Miss Worthing. He's a real male chauvinist, as I'm sure you're aware, and a lot of my so-called friends have said I'm a fool for putting up with him. Except, of course, I love him. And he loves me. But a man, especially a man like that, has got to have his pride."

"Oh, I know what you asked me that for," she said almost wearily. "But frankly, I think that kind of insinuation is at least as absurd as the one about my designs for the costumes. No pun intended. I know it may seem unlikely to you, but I don't care that"—she snapped her fingers—"for what all the cats and bitches in the parish say about my relationship with Julian. As far as he and I are concerned, we are married. One day, in the fullness of time, we will ask the Church's blessing on it; in the meantime, we have God's."

"Nevertheless—"

"No, Miss Worthing, there is no nevertheless about it. I do not care if Julian wishes to go on from poetry to potboil popular novels and gets stinking rich, or chooses—as he very well might—to become a priest in a mission parish, it is my job, as I perceive it, to help him. And that's no one else's business. Believe me, I know—and Julian knows I know—the cost, the personal cost of choosing to make money when your whole being longs just to do the creative work you were born to do."

"Yet money has its uses," said Miss Worthing.

"No one is more aware of that than I," replied Bonnie.

"Very well, Bonnie. I'm sorry if I angered you."

"You didn't. As you said, you're just doing your job. But I do get tired sometimes of defending what is no one's proper business to attack."

Miss Worthing was about to stand up and effectively terminate the interview when she remembered something else, a question that had nagged at her during the earlier narrative downstairs.

"Very well," she repeated. "I'll take your word on all this for now."

"Good of you," said Bonnie with a dry expression that made Miss Worthing smile appreciatively.

"But perhaps you can tell me something, Bonnie. If you will."

"If I can."

"What precisely was Julian's relationship with Father Hughie?"

Bonnie hesitated a fraction of a second before answering, "Well, I will tell you. But again, frankly, I think that's the kind of question you should be asking Julian himself."

"Of course it is," said Miss Worthing, and added in a dry voice, "but if Julian is the kind of man you say he is, would he, could he—would he tell me?"

"*Touché!*" said Bonnie. "Actually, it's very straightforward. Both Julian and I absolutely adored Father Hughie."

"You did!"

"You don't need to sound so surprised," said Bonnie with an attempt at lightness. But her head went down as she stared at her fingernails, and her voice was by no means steady. "We got very close with him during the days when we were still just talking about the play. Even before Julian had finished writing it. Believe it or not, Father Hughie made some excellent suggestions about the structure of the play when it was still in draft." She uttered a little laugh. "He even tried to make some language suggestions. But that Julian quashed right away.

"And Hughie was always so enthusiastic. But he was also so damned—hapless. That was the word Julian used for him. Hapless. And people were always making such fun of him. And he knew it, too. And it hurt. He wasn't unaware of his lacks, you know. And he was so grateful when you did anything for him.

"And Julian's relationship with him was a lot deeper than mine. They were like brothers. Julian honored and respected Hughie's priesthood—was almost in awe of it. But he did love it that, whenever Hughie was in trouble or had a problem, which was, let's face it, most of the time, he would come and talk about it with Julian. He always said Julian was so wise." Tears were trickling down her cheeks, wreaking unsightly damage to her mascara. "Julian was constantly hauling Hughie off to some out-of-the-way watering hole for a heart-to-heart, and I know that Julian was so proud that Hughie wanted him to be his best man when he and Fiona got married, and Julian said he wanted the favor returned when we got married. . . ."

"Why didn't you tell any of this to the sheriff?" asked Miss Worthing gently.

"No," said Bonnie angrily, "and I am not going to! I think we'll just reserve all of it for the defense—if it comes to that. If I tell them, or Julian does, I know them—they'll just pervert it into something horrible."

"They're not as bad as all that, Bonnie," said Miss Worthing.

But Bonnie steadfastly refused to be convinced.

And so, giving it up and finding nothing more to ask, Miss Worthing stood up and prepared to take her departure.

"Okay," said Bonnie, standing up also. "Let me put out the lights and I'll ride down with you."

"But where are you going?"

"San Francisco."

"You know, I really don't think you should do that."

"Why not? Because I'm a suspect?"

"Frankly, yes."

"Don't worry. I should be back by tomorrow afternoon. I'm going because I have a friend who thinks he knows where the lawyer I want for Julian hangs out on weekends. And everyone tells me he's the mean mother I want."

6 A few minutes later, after watching Bonnie's red Porsche tear off down Church Street, Miss Worthing opened the door into the church and entered.

For a moment she halted as the heavy door creaked to behind her. Deep as the gloom had been outside in the cloister, it was darker still in the back of the long nave, and she waited for her eyes to adjust.

It was utterly silent, cooler than outside where the temperature was still in the eighties, dampish, and smelling of sweating stone. And altogether spooky. A large, deserted, and unlit church in the dead of night is not a pleasant place to be, and all the old hooey about ghostly priests appearing appareled in cold blue light to offer silent Masses of reparation comes back to haunt the mind—and suddenly does not seem like quite so much hooey.

As she went up the central aisle, which at least could be faintly made out in the moonlight penetrating the clerestory windows, her heels' tap-tapping, sounding loud and unnatural, echoed faintly back at her from the vaulting above, lost now in impenetrable shadow.

"I'm in the sacristy, Matilda," she heard Mrs. Robinson's cheerful voice call out, thus inserting a welcome note of normalcy into these Gothic meditations.

And momently Miss Worthing climbed the three steps to the ambo where she paused to look about the desecrated sanctuary.

The altar stood completely stripped. Apparently the police scientists had been swift in their ministrations—and so cooperative with the needs of the parish. All the detritus of the so disastrously interrupted Mass had been cleared away, and the bare stones stood ready for the bishop to reconsecrate them in the morning.

It was an odd thing to be investigating a crime like this in precincts so intimately familiar to her over such a very long time. Indeed, part of the problem confronting her was one of perception—how to *see* such familiar things in a new light, or at least a bit more clearly. Nor did the fact that she was so tired make this attempt at clarity of vision one whit easier. The only thing she could see—perhaps the only thing to *be* seen—was a result of the curious fact that until this moment she had never actually been physically present on the ambo of the main altar. She could see that the marble from which the ambo and altar had been constructed must have been of a particularly soft variety. Constant use had worn the surface of the ambo into a series of waves of ridges where, over ninety years, feet and knees had worn grooves and pits and sundry unevennesses.

"Matilda?"

"Coming, Elspeth."

And suddenly hungry for human company and light, she hurried toward the light-filled doorway of the sacristy.

Mrs. Robinson had clearly been busy. Closets stood open, revealing a splendor of vestments and emitting smells of cedar and naphtha to mingle in the close atmosphere with the prevailing odor of stale incense. Mrs. Robinson was in the process of wrestling a rack of heavy brocaded garments over a vent in the floor.

"Here," said Miss Worthing, "let me help."

Together they got it into place and Mrs. Robinson bent to open the vent.

"I'd rather just open a window," she said, tugging at the recalcitrant handle, "but the alarm will go off if so much as a leaf blows in."

The vent opened with a metallic shriek and a gust of stale, earthy-smelling air.

Miss Worthing was about to point out that there hadn't

been enough breeze to blow a leaf two inches for the last two weeks when the thought was startled out of her by the insistent ringing of a telephone.

Immediately she whirled around, wondering where on earth it could be coming from. Mrs. Robinson, however, had already crossed to the wall beside the doorway leading into the church and answered.

"It's for you," she said, handing the phone to Miss Worthing.

"When are you coming home?" she heard Miss Shaw's voice ask.

"In a few minutes, Martha," she replied. "Elspeth Robinson is giving me a lift."

"Oh, good. Then I won't have to come and get you. I'll have something for you to eat when you get here. Ask Elspeth if she's hungry."

Miss Worthing smiled and covered the mouthpiece.

"Martha wants to know if you're hungry."

"What's she got?"

"What've you got, Martha?"

"Crumpets."

"Martha's famous crumpets?" said Mrs. Robinson with a laugh. "You bet I'm hungry."

"We'll be there shortly, Martha," said Miss Worthing, and hung up and looked more closely at the telephone apparatus.

A row of buttons indicated various wires, while at the extreme end of the row was another button with a double-digit number written over it.

"45," it said.

An intercom?

And sure enough, taped to the wall on the side of the cabinet nearest the phone was a piece of paper with parallel columns running down it.

"Are you ready, Matilda?" asked Mrs. Robinson, closing closet and cabinet doors. "I'm done now."

"Just a moment, Elspeth," said Miss Worthing, and turning on the light switch beside the door, peered more closely at the piece of paper.

As she had anticipated, it was a list of the various numbers one might dial in order to reach a specific part of the church. There was the gym, the church hall, the parish office, the offices of various personages; there was the choir loft, the bell-ringing chamber, the locker rooms, and the library.

"When was this installed, Elspeth?" asked Miss Worthing.

"A couple of years ago," said Mrs. Robinson, who had come over to watch her. "Why?"

"Yes," said Miss Worthing thoughtfully, "I do seem vaguely to recall the vote about it. But I can't say I ever noticed the system before."

"Well, we did try to install them in relatively out-of-the-way places," explained Mrs. Robinson, "so the kids wouldn't play with 'em. Why? Is it important?"

"I don't know," said Miss Worthing with a frown. Something tugged at the edges of her mind, but shadowed by fatigue, hunger, and general confusion, it steadfastly refused to come clear. "But for some reason I rather think it might be."

7 The two women left by the cloistral door—that door of the sacristy leading into the cloister. Again Mrs. Robinson paused to set the alarm box to the side of the door, while Miss Worthing went on ahead into the garth and thus out of the deep and strangely depressing shadows of the cloister colonnade.

A moment later Mrs. Robinson caught up with her, and together, wordlessly, the only sound the crunch of their feet on the gravel of the path, they passed through the close-held heat of the garth, up the steps to the west colonnade, and while Mrs. Robinson paused to lock and set the alarm at the nave door, Miss Worthing proceeded down to the sidewalk of Church Street.

"My car's over there," said Mrs. Robinson, gesturing to the lot across the street, and led the way toward the crosswalk where the stoplight now blinked only amber caution to the deserted street.

Out of the cloistral confines, the air seemed to be at least fresher, if not appreciably cooler. But the debilitating heat of the daylight hours had passed, and the air on their faces had the soft texture of silken velvet. Overhead the moon still rode through cloudless skies and, kept awake by its light, a thousand crickets stridulated in the hedgerow surrounding the lot.

When they reached Mrs. Robinson's automobile, the only one left in the lot, Mrs. Robinson looked across the roof at Miss Worthing patiently waiting to clamber in whenever Elspeth got around to opening the door.

"Your silence is most eloquent, Matilda," observed Mrs. Robinson with another one of her soft chuckles.

The older woman's eyebrows rose marginally.

"Is it, Elspeth?" she asked. "I'm just trying to think of what more I've got to ask."

"Well, then, why don't we get in," suggested Mrs. Robinson and gestured. "It's unlocked," she added and pulled her own door open. "If we have to talk further, then at least let's do it in the car."

Presently, then, Mrs. Robinson leaned back against the door as she turned to look at Miss Worthing and observed, not without humor, "I would have thought you'd have had your fill of asking questions."

"I have," replied Miss Worthing. "But it seems fairly clear that, if I don't get on with it, no one else is going to."

"And you think you're going to figure it out?"

"I certainly think I have to try."

"So you don't think Julian is responsible?"

"I didn't say that. But that business upstairs was hardly conclusive."

"So what else do you want to ask me?"

"First of all, Elspeth, and I'm sorry, but I do have to ask, did you—"

"No!" said Mrs. Robinson, interrupting. "What could I possibly gain by trying to kill Leo?"

"The play. As you maintain."

"I concede that I was distressed that, after I'd asked my friends up here, the play might be canceled."

"But you said you hadn't told them yet you were in the play."

"That's true. It was going to be a surprise. But I wanted them to see it."

"But what if it hadn't pulled together? And Neil and Julian did cancel the play?"

"You know, Matilda, I don't know. I didn't even think about that until you asked me the question. Probably sent them the script—eventually.

"But, Matilda"—and suddenly Mrs. Robinson actually seemed to find the idea downright hilarious—"we are leaving something out. At least concerning me and my putative motives. If I were going to try to resurrect my career, do you think, does anyone seriously think that the only way I have to do it is by appearing in some provincial little theater?"

"But you said you wanted them to see you."

"So I do. And in this play. Yes, that's true. Still is. I still think it would make a good film."

"Commercial?"

"Good God, not at all," said Mrs. Robinson dryly. "More like, oh, something like *Murder in the Cathedral.*"

"How appropriate," observed Miss Worthing. "Tell me something else. Just supposing this thing was made into a film, would it be—the same?"

"No," said Mrs. Robinson forthrightly. "And I think, if you want to know my opinion, that Julian knew that very well. He would, as you say, on the off chance a deal was struck, get some recognition, a rather nice sum of money, but he would *not* get to see his great poetic drama immortalized on celluloid."

"So that's something else I have to ask him," muttered Miss Worthing half to herself.

"Anything else for me?"

"A couple of things. You were all over the church and the whole complex yesterday."

"Yes."

"Didn't you see anything—well, I guess I shouldn't say suspicious." Miss Worthing frowned and tried to formulate the question as clearly as she could. "Let's just say out of the ordinary?"

Mrs. Robinson exhaled forcibly and shook her head. "Believe me, Matilda, I've been racking my brain about that. Who wouldn't be? But you know what it's like around here on a Saturday. People here, people there, people everywhere."

"Yes, I know," said Miss Worthing. "That's precisely what I want to know. Who was where? More specifically, who was somewhere where they had no business being? And I would have thought you'd be the perfect person to ask."

"Why?"

"Because you're so very much in charge."

"Perhaps I am," said Mrs. Robinson sarcastically, "but, unlike the Holy Ghost, I am not omnipresent and omniscient."

"Don't get flip, Elspeth," admonished Miss Worthing. "Think."

But Mrs. Robinson, carrying out this command, still could only shake her head yet again.

"No one, Matilda. Sorry I don't remember a single thing out of the ordinary. Other," she added dryly, "than the fact that, because of the upcoming parish council meeting, the place was awash with gossip and speculation."

"What a mess!" observed Miss Worthing in a malignant mutter.

"Yes," said Mrs. Robinson, "I quite agree. Maybe," she

suggested with a little shrug, "it's like that dreary old 'Pur-loined Letter' business—it's something too obvious to have been noticed."

"Oh, God!" swore Miss Worthing, with great feeling. "I don't even want to consider that. Although, God knows, I've got to."

"Anything else?"

"Just this," said Miss Worthing after fetching a deep and near-despairing sigh. "And I really do want you to give your serious consideration to it. Who is there, among all the All Saints Players, idiotic enough really to think that assassinating Leo Cantrell would actually lead to a part in a movie?"

"No one," said Mrs. Robinson without hesitation. "though, frankly, I also have to admit that, at bottom, I really just don't know. That kind of—mind-set, if you will, isn't the kind of thing you're going to latch on to readily. It's like superstition. I mean, I do know actors who really believe all that old business about *Macbeth,* for example. But it's not the kind of thing you find out on casual acquaintance. I think the only sensible thing to do is to talk to all of 'em and form your own judgment about it."

"I expect you're right," said Miss Worthing, and added, "And I'm so damned tired already."

"So get some sleep," suggested Mrs. Robinson. "You're not going to be able to do much till morning anyhow. Then get out there and see what you can find."

"I haven't had a lot of experience with actors, you know," said Miss Worthing.

"Matilda, you're on the board of the opera company."

"Yes, and may I remind you that opera singers, at their worst—" She cut herself off abruptly.

"Yes, that's true," said Mrs. Robinson, interpreting that interrupted remark with no difficulty whatsoever. "Compared with actors, opera singers are monuments of stability."

"So?"

"So I'll tell you what I think."

"Yes?"

"I think you'll find that when the story got out—about my foolishness, that is—people didn't think, not in the sense that you or I might use that word. They just reacted with a purely visceral excitement that had nothing whatever to do with any real expectations. Which, incidentally, in terms of the production, was all to the good."

"So I gather. But what about Jack? What about Stringer?"

"What about them?"

"Weren't they galvanized—"

"Of course, they were. Jack's an ambitious actor, and a very good one besides. And Stringer had—a certain pride to salvage."

"Worth murdering for?"

Mrs. Robinson threw up her hands. "I don't know. I can tell you that I didn't do it. And no doubt they will all say the same. And as I said earlier, to a sane person it would all seem wildly unlikely. Nevertheless, everyone was galvanized, as you say, into getting it together by the news."

"I know," said Miss Worthing sourly.

After another period of silence ensued, Mrs. Robinson asked again, "Anything else?"

"If there is, I can't think of it. Is there anything you can think of that might be important?"

"No," said Mrs. Robinson. "Not a thing."

"Then I guess that's it."

Not without a sigh of relief, Mrs. Robinson leaned forward and began to ease the car out of the lot.

"Then let's get home and both of us have a bite to eat. I'm famished."

And all Miss Worthing could think of on the way home was that, yet again, she was caught in a classic double bind—of needing more data in order to get more data.

CHAPTER TWELVE

1 Whatever Miss Worthing expected to find at home, it was certainly not the assembly into which she and Mrs. Robinson walked.

Seated in the living room were Miss Shaw (the only person reasonably to be expected), Lady Fairgrief, Maude, the bishop, and Father d'Arcy—all of them, in spite of the hour, steadily absorbing tea and buttered crumpets.

Everyone except Father d'Arcy paused in his pursuit of nourishment.

"Don't look so sour, Matilda," said Lady Fairgrief, observing her niece's expression. "We decided we'd all wait up and listen to your report to his lordship. . . . Great heavens, why are you looking so unhappy?"

At which point Miss Worthing did the only rational thing to do. She sat down and laughed till the tears ran down her cheeks, the others, meanwhile, looked on with varying degrees of concern.

It was only Father d'Arcy who acted with any presence of mind. Popping the rest of the muffin on which he was engaged into his mouth, he rose, gracefully ambled over to the drinks cabinet, opened the bucket, filled a largish tumbler with ice cubes, poured over them a good four fingers of bourbon, splashed in about the same amount of ginger ale, stirred it all up, and bore the resulting very strong highball to Miss Worthing.

"Here, Matilda," he said cheerfully. "After the day you've had, the only really satisfactory remedy would be to get roaring drunk."

"Ren," said Miss Worthing, accepting the drink, "if I were thirty years younger, I'd marry you." She drank deeply. "That's the ticket," she said appreciatively, and looked up to see everyone still staring owlishly at her. "And no"—she scowled at them—"I am not hysterical. For God's sake, Elspeth, fix yourself a drink and stop staring at me as though you were wondering whether I'm going to be hauled off to Napa.

"On the other hand, don't fix yourself a drink. You've been just as busy as I have. You sit down and let someone else get one for you. You hear? One of you get Elspeth something. No," she repeated, "I am not hysterical. I am weary nigh unto death, I'm thoroughly disgusted, I'm totally at sea, I'm hungry, and my feet hurt. But I am not hysterical. Although," and again that well-developed sense of the absurd threatened to get out of hand, "you do have to admit that to come home hoping for nothing more than tea, a crumpet, and the solace of one's virtuous bed and find instead . . ." She waved her glass at them. "Skoal!" she said and drank some more.

Mrs. Robinson, meanwhile, gratefully accepting a drink from Father d'Arcy, began, "I don't blame Matilda for being upset. In spite of what she says—"

"Upset!" Miss Worthing slammed her drink down on the occasional table next to her chair and rose, furious, to her feet in a transport of passion. "You betcha I'm upset. Do you know what happened?"

"Yes, Matilda," replied the bishop, carefully wiping butter from his fingers and rising and sauntering to the drinks cabinet. "I left a message on Father Reggie's machine that he was to call me here whenever he got home. So we do know that Julian was arrested and—a little something about why. "Now, I thought I saw some Calvados in there. Ah, there it is." He poured a tot into a balloon glass.

Wearily Miss Worthing sighed and sat down, picking up her drink as she did so. "It's wrong, Bishop. I'm not sure why I think so, but it's all wrong."

"Do you mean Julian's arrest?" asked Lady Fairgrief.

Miss Worthing paused and drank, finishing her glass. Immediately Father d'Arcy, douce man, took it from her for replenishing. Having surrendered it to him, Miss Worthing looked at her aunt and shook her head.

"Aunt Eulalia, I just don't know." She hesitated, aware that everyone was watching her. "Sorry. What can I say? I'm no wizard. I can only rely on evidence. Data. And there isn't any. Not what I would call evidence."

"That's not entirely true," protested Mrs. Robinson.

To which the bishop added, "They did draw a fairly reasonable conclusion."

"Did they?" asked Miss Worthing. "It seems to me they drew an awfully quick one under the circumstances. In fact"—she looked at the bishop—"they drew a damnably expedient one."

"But the evidence?" said Dr. Fisher. "And it is evidence, Matilda."

Miss Worthing drew in a slow, deep breath and blew it all out again.

"Yes, of course, it is. And"—she shook her head—"I'm not even saying Julian *didn't* do it. But"—she glared at Mrs. Robinson—"I did not draw up that list of possible suspects out of frivolity, you know."

"I know that, Matilda," said Mrs. Robinson.

"Oh?" said the bishop, looking up from his contemplation of the swirling spirits in his glass. "*Was* there more than one reasonable—suspect?"

"Oh, yes," said Mrs. Robinson.

And she and Miss Worthing sketched for them the preliminary conclusions they had been drawing together with Father Reggie and Belinda Sue when the lawmen had announced their decision to go off and arrest Julian.

"Maude," said Lady Fairgrief suddenly, her voice commanding. "I, too, will have a Calvados."

Maude frowned and, rather surprisingly, complied without a word, until she returned and handed the old woman a balloon glass holding a generous measure. "Here. You need it."

"Good heavens!" said her ladyship. "Agreement." She sipped the apple brandy appreciatively, equally appreciative of the fact that the others were waiting for her to continue.

"You know, Matilda," she said conversationally, "all of this rather reminds me of that dismal business I told you about at Swaddle Hall in 1913."

"The one where they found the marchioness stabbed to death in the summerhouse?" asked Miss Worthing.

"That's the one. Stabbed through the heart with a sterling silver chopstick, she was," Lady Fairgrief explained darkly to the others. "But the point here is that I was also angry as the devil at the time because there, too, there were a horrible number of people who would not have wept to find the marchioness dead—she was no prize, was Lady Swaddlebourne—and Arthur and I were hampered by a conclusion being drawn much too preliminarily while we were still trying to unravel the tangled threads."

"So what do I do?" asked Miss Worthing.

Her aunt chuckled.

"Get rid of us, and while you're having your bit of supper, talk it over with his lordship here and Father d'Arcy, who, one suspects, will also be full of good advice. It's time for Elspeth, Maude, and me to go. We've done our jobs—incidentally, I've already made my report to his lordship—and we shall only hamper a free exchange. Oh!" she said as she suddenly thought of something else. "Martha! I nearly forgot. What did Millie have to say for herself?"

Miss Shaw looked for a long time at Mrs. Robinson. Seeing which, Lady Fairgrief frowned malignantly and groused, "Oh, very well. Keep it to yourselves. But when this is over . . . I'm too old to wait patiently for dramatic revelations."

When, presently, only Miss Worthing, Miss Shaw, Dr. Fisher, and Father d'Arcy remained, and Miss Worthing had finished her frontal assault on a plate of muffins, crudités, and prosciutto that Miss Shaw had brought in, the bishop said, "Martha, I gather you've got something we should know?"

"I do indeed," said Miss Shaw.

"Is it important?" asked Miss Worthing.

Miss Shaw chortled. "Now, that I couldn't begin to tell you. Besides, you're the one who's supposed to make such determinations. But I can tell you that it certainly was interesting."

"So?" said Miss Worthing.

"So," said Miss Shaw, rather enjoying herself, and addressed Dr. Fisher. "Tell me, Bishop. What do you know about Father Hughie?"

His lordship looked to Father d'Arcy and said, "What? A reasonably good education. On scholarship mostly."

Father d'Arcy nodded as Miss Shaw asked, "His background?"

"An orphan, one gathers."

"Martha!" warned Miss Worthing. "You will desist from this mystification at once!"

Miss Shaw sighed. "Yes, I suppose you are right. It really isn't any fun anyway," she admitted and said, "Father Hughie wasn't an orphan. Not entirely. His father is dead. But his mother, my dears, was none other than our very own Millie Cantrell."

It took a moment for the others to absorb this.

"Well, I did know that she'd been married before," the bishop said after a moment.

That, however, was the only discernible reaction.

Seeing the general blankness, Miss Shaw continued, and

not without a certain measure of indignation. "It seems that Millie was married to a young career officer back in Eisenhower's day. Well, guess who got sent out to 'train' Vietnamese soldiers and who never came back—leaving Millie with a babe in arms?"

"But why did she—as she apparently did—give up the child?" asked the bishop.

"She met Leo," said Miss Shaw as though that were the clearest of explanations.

"So?"

Miss Shaw looked at the bishop almost pityingly. "Bishop, just how do you think Leo Cantrell would react to having another lord of creation in his nest—and that one of which he was not the father?"

"I've often thought," said Father d'Arcy unexpectedly, "that it was fortunate that Leo Cantrell got only girls on Millie."

"Ren!" said the bishop, rather scandalized.

"But he's right," said Miss Shaw. "When she and Leo got serious, she gave Hughie up for adoption. Which, considering that by then he was about two years old, he never was adopted. That poor child! He grew up in various orphanages and foster homes. No wonder he was as indecisive as he was. We should just be thankful he didn't turn into a crook. But maybe that's because Millie tells me she was able to send him money on a fairly regular basis, although—and this is what is so sad—she never did tell him who she was."

"Did she have anything to do with his proposal as our priest?" asked Miss Worthing.

"No," said Miss Shaw. "I asked her that naturally. She was, of course, enormously pleased that he was going to be here. She was the one, incidentally, who paid his 'scholarship' through college and the seminary."

"Well," said the bishop with a nod and an exhalation of air, "that finally explains what the MBC Foundation was."

"Didn't you inquire?" asked Miss Worthing.

"Whatever for?" said the bishop. "There must be thousands of odd little foundations scattered about the world."

"The question, of course," said Father d'Arcy, "is did Leo Cantrell know?"

"You know," said Miss Shaw, "I never did ask that. Sorry."

"It's okay, Martha," said Miss Worthing. "I'll have to talk to Millie tomorrow. And that is one chore to which I do not look forward."

Upon which note, depressing as it was, Miss Worthing said, "But this, I'm afraid, while indeed fascinating, is not really getting us any forwarder."

"And it is getting late," said Father d'Arcy.

"I know," agreed the bishop. "Matilda?"

Miss Worthing was shaking her head and frowning intently. "As I said, I'm not sure—how could I be?—that Julian *isn't* the guilty party."

"But—" supplied the bishop.

For a long, long moment, Miss Worthing did not reply. Finally she shook her head again. "I'm just too tired to think. There's something I'm forgetting. And for the life of me, I just cannot remember what."

"It is time to go to bed," said Miss Shaw, yawning cavernously.

"Lord, yes," said Father d'Arcy, munching a final crumpet. "Martha, your muffins are an occasion for sin such as I have not encountered for years. Bless you, my child. Now, all of you, go to bed! You need data, Matilda, and all of us need sleep."

"I know, Ren," said Miss Worthing. "But I can't help thinking that if I could just remember what I've forgotten, in spite of not having enough data . . ."

"Yes, Matilda?" said the bishop.

"There's danger," she said. "If Julian really didn't do it, Bishop, there's a singularly vicious murderer on the loose out there."

2 For the first several hours after Miss Worthing retired, she slept the sleep of utter exhaustion of body and soul. And mind. Subsequently she could never remember her head touching the pillow before she was out. But she was a strong and healthy woman withal, and once the first careless rapture of deep repairing sleep had passed, a series of vaguely disturbing dreams began to percolate through her mind until, finally, she had that exceedingly disagreeable one in which, try as she urgently might, to get to some (ill-defined) place, she could not find her way, all the while dodging trains and buses and cars careering about her with clearly malicious intent. . . .

And she awoke, refreshed but by no means rested, and noticed that she had not even turned off her bedside lamp before slumber had overtaken her. Raising herself on an elbow, she switched off the light, fell back supine, closed her eyes, and settled herself to return to sleep, listening to the familiar and comforting ticking of her old-fashioned wind-up alarm clock.

And ten minutes later she was still listening, with her eyes wide open, staring sightlessly at the ceiling.

"This will never do," she finally groused irritably and, throwing back the covers, sat up and flicked the light on again. She put her glasses on, looked at the clock (which stood at three-thirty), and groaned.

"What a case!" she muttered to herself and clambered out of bed. Then, jamming her feet into her slippers and throwing her well-worn white terry bathrobe about her, she headed toward the kitchen.

After all, she reflected, there are effective remedies for sleeplessness. A glass of warm milk and honey—with perhaps a dash of whiskey in it, usually a sovereign soporific. And if that didn't do the trick, she could always mix a little tincture of valerian into a bit of lemon and soda. And valerian was only the beginning of the herbal possibilities. . . .

She put on a dressing gown and a fairly sturdy pair of

slippers and presently was bending down to turn on the garden hose at the spigot behind the house. Carrying it by the closed nozzle, she stalked toward the bottom of the garden, where the herb garden breathed pleasant odors into the night and the glazed brick pathways reflected back the light of the moon.

There, she bent over and began to pluck leaves from a plantation of small, low-lying plants and turned the garden hose on low to rinse them off. The smell rose heady to her nostrils, and the water from the hose was cool on her hands, and in the dry, dusty air the scent of the water mingled with the herbs.

It was still unnervingly hot, even now at the coolest time of the day. Too bad her ingrained modesty forced her to be running around in a double thickness of cotton. There were times she wished she and Martha could be more modern and approach their gardening chores—well, in the same spirit as some of their more ebullient neighbors.

And she chuckled aloud as the sudden picture developed in her head of her and Martha waddling about the garden in bikinis. . . .

"Something funny, Matilda?" said the bishop from behind her. "I'm sorry. I didn't mean to startle you so."

And immediately Dr. Fisher began to chuckle, confirming Miss Worthing's impression, once again, that his lordship had a streak of the practical joke-loving schoolboy running through him.

"That's all right," she replied, recovering her composure, and added: "I just had a picture of Martha and me got up— or down as the case might be—gardening in bikinis."

Before he could help himself, the bishop gave a great bark of happy laughter. "Sorry," he said after a moment. "Hardly an unnatural thought in this heat. But what are you doing out here?"

"I thought I'd come get some fresh mint—it settles the stomach, you know. And I need it."

"Well, I'm surprised you didn't sleep till noon, then, instead of coming out to garden in the middle of the night."

"Lord knows I wanted to. But after a bit I just couldn't sleep."

"No," agreed the bishop with a sigh. "Nor could I."

"Worried?"

The bishop's eyebrows twitched.

"Who wouldn't be?" he said. "My intellect is telling me, desist and get some sleep; the police know what they are doing. And then I remember what you said about no really substantive investigation having been undertaken, and my stomach, as you say, tells my intellect to go stuff itself."

After a moment Miss Worthing closed the nozzle of the hose and threw it to the ground.

"Come on, Bishop, let's boil these mint leaves up and top it off with some whiskey and hot milk."

"Excellent prescription," said his lordship, following her up the garden path.

They strolled back to the house and into the kitchen, pausing only to turn off the hose at the spigot.

As they did so, Miss Worthing suddenly snorted mirthlessly. "Another unseemly thought, Matilda?" asked his lordship.

"You could say so," said Miss Worthing. "I was just thinking that it's too bad whoever is responsible didn't just sneak into Leo's study, extract his Saturday night special from his desk drawer, and shoot him. . . ."

"Leo keeps a gun in his office?"

"Bishop," said Miss Worthing, "consider the man. He has, or so Millie once told me, guns squirreled away here and there."

"But why?"

"Why, to protect his person and property—which, I daresay, in his mind includes Millie," said Miss Worthing, hovering over the stove and a saucepan of milk in which mint leaves floated, turning the milk a very peculiar color, "from, the thundering herds of perverts and hardened criminals thronging the bushes of rural Jolliston."

"Humph!" said his lordship. "Although someone does seem to have tried rather determinedly to kill the poor bastard. Oh, well. I'll have to have a talk with him. There are, in case he has either forgotten or never knew, canon laws about priests and firearms. Not," the bishop added with a sigh, "that it will do any good. He doesn't like me very much. But never mind that—why would you wish he'd been shot instead of poisoned?" he asked.

Miss Worthing chuckled and added whiskey to the milk and pulled the pan from the heat and filled two mugs standing ready. "Because then we could have rounded everyone up and done cering or moulage or any of the other tests there are to find out if someone has fired a gun. Or maybe there would even have been fingerprints. As it is—" She shrugged and ran the saucepan under the cold-water tap.

"You know, I do believe this is one of the few times," said the bishop conversationally as Miss Worthing set a steaming mug in front of him, "that I almost regret the strict separation of church and state."

Miss Worthing settled with her own milk across the table and, intrigued, cocked an eyebrow at him. "Why? What would you do?"

"Very simple. I would say that I have no essential difficulty with keeping Julian in the pokey. Not if, as you seem to indicate, he is the most likely candidate." He looked inquiringly at Miss Worthing, who nodded. "But, just in case, it might not be such a bad idea to do a little more investigation."

"Or a lot more," said Miss Worthing.

"Such as?"

Miss Worthing leaned forward and enumerated them on her fingers. "I want to know where everyone was, all day long, there at the Church of All Saints. I want to know what they were doing, why they were doing it, where they were doing it, and if, historically, they have always done it there and in that way and at that time."

"Yes," said the bishop carefully. "I should imagine that would achieve results but, oh, Lord, what a mess that would make."

"I know," agreed Miss Worthing. "Keep a hundred or so of Jolliston's most respectable citizens locked up for—however long it might take, and the news media will descend on us like vultures on a ripe carcass."

"What a revolting image," observed the bishop. "But not, I fear, too strong. Is there no other way?"

Miss Worthing hesitated a moment before replying. "I don't know. I shall do what I can, of course. The problem is that there are just too many people who had too much to gain—always assuming that such an absurd motivation as the possibility of the play being made into a movie can actually count as motivation. . . ."

The bishop sighed and sipped hot milk.

"Delicious," he observed vaguely, and then said, "You're still not wild about that explanation, are you, Matilda?"

Miss Worthing shrugged irritably. "Well, what do you think?"

"That if it is true, then this wonderful renascence at the Church of All Saints is a fraud."

Miss Worthing said nothing.

"Because," his lordship elaborated, "it means that, when all is said and done, one of our members, one of our more active members, and one of my children in God, was so far from an experiential understanding of the faith that he, or she, could commit murder for what is essentially a horribly trivial reason."

"And yet, if not the play, what?" asked Miss Worthing. "What nexus? Why now? What could have precipitated such a determinedly murderous attack on Cantrell if *not* the play?"

The bishop consulted the interior of his cup of milk.

"I wonder sometimes," he said after a moment, "if I shouldn't have taken a stronger stand here."

"About Dr. Cantrell?"

"Among other things. But yes. That primarily. I'm afraid Leo should have been transferred to a parish where the people were a little more in tune with his own—beliefs. And you needn't look like that, Matilda. There are such parishes. I can't say I'm in a great deal of sympathy with them, but this is a pluralist society, after all. And Leo is, in many ways, a good man."

"I know. I know," said Miss Worthing, and took both now empty cups to the sink and rinsed them. "I can't say I'm any sleepier than I was. But I do feel a little clearer in my mind."

"Any solutions?"

"How could there be, Bishop? As far as I can see, there's virtually no data to speak of—much less to be relied on."

"What a depressing thought!" said the bishop, and bidding Miss Worthing pleasant dreams, went off in pursuit of what sleep he could get . . .

. . . and a few moments later was back.

"Matilda, I'm sorry. I clean forgot."

"What?"

"Do you remember what I said earlier about the possibility of—well, what *are* we going to call it? Satanism?"

"It'll do. What about it?"

"Well, it seems your aunt didn't forget it, either."

"What did she do?"

"While she was in the gymnasium it seems she had a conversation with someone. Alan Brown?"

"Oh! Really? And just what did *dear* little Alan have to say?"

3   After the bishop had once more padded off to bed, Miss Worthing sat, nursing her mug, when the grandfather clock in the hall began striking four o'clock.

And still she felt no need to sleep.

Here they were at the beginning of a new day and she hadn't even been able to rest from the previous day's labors. She was not, however, a woman given to self-pity.

"All right," she said, standing up. "If that's the way it's gonna be, let's use it to good advantage."

And fifteen minutes later she was in the car driving eastward, and as the road began to climb, the tidy open vineyards of the Valley floor gave way first to dense chaparral and then to scrubby but equally dense woodland. And presently Miss Worthing noticed that she was coursing a low stone wall overgrown with all manner of creeper, while the verge of the road outside the wall was a carpet of knee-high plants, all of them in vigorous bloom.

She smiled. To most passers-by it would look, no doubt, like a thick and untidy collection of weeds. But as her headlights pricked them out of the darkness, she recognized valerian, feverfew, spearmint, peppermint, rue, savory, sage, and dittany of Crete, all growing jumbled together—it being the strongly held conviction of the party living behind those unusual stone walls that, living thus, the herbs grew more potent to their work.

The walls began rising and presently an archway opened off to the right into which she turned. A gatekeeper's lodge was a picturesque, ivy-covered ruin, and the iron gates stood open, lashed to their posts by several decades of creeper and still yet more ivy.

Miss Worthing went at a snail's pace through the thick woodland she was now driving through. Twice she stopped while first a skunk and then, a little later, a badger loped across the deeply rutted road. And another time her heart was in her mouth as a mule deer bounced once out of the brush, once on the road, and vanished into the brush on the other side.

But soon enough Miss Worthing reached a clearing that held in a bowl of what in daylight she knew would be the greenest grass imaginable, a small stone house set about with split-rail corrals in which dozens of animals of all sorts and conditions dozed as the warm night drew to its close. In an outbuilding an electric light burned, and after stopping the car and getting out, Miss Worthing picked her away across the uneven ground toward the light.

She was halfway there before she remembered her manners and called out, "Hello, Joan Webster!"

Mrs. Webster had lived alone ever since her sot of a husband had finally done the world a favor and had one cocktail too many. And the last thing Miss Worthing needed to do was sneak up on her and frighten her into a heart attack.

In the illuminated barn Miss Worthing found a ripe, rather large woman, bursting with ruddy health, who might have been any age between thirty-five and seventy, busily milking a cow. A number of goats who had apparently already been stripped were busy at their morning rations.

"Come on in, Matilda," said the woman. "I'll only be a minute longer."

"Sorry if I startled you."

"You didn't. I've been expecting you."

Neither said anything more until the cow had been turned loose into her byre with a slap on the rump.

"You were expecting me, Joan?"

"Of course. I heard about what happened—down there."

"You did?"

"Would you and Martha like some butter?"

"Of course, but . . ."

"Come back to the house with me. I have a pound or so all salted and in the well."

She led the way uphill. A house perched just below the wooded crest of the hill. It was formed like a capital E without the middle stroke, and in the middle of the courtyard stood an old-fashioned well—winch, bucket, roof, and all.

The woman leaned over the wellhead and groped about for a minute and came up with a lump four inches or so in diameter and wrapped in snowy white cheesecloth.

"I have coffee on. Come on in."

And a few moments later they were seated at a plain pine table that looked as if it had been adzed, sanded, and nothing more. The coffee was rich and strong, and the cream in it was almost too thick.

"So what did you hear, Joan?"

"I heard that—we might be blamed."

"We?"

"Well, they do call me a witch, don't they?"

"Yes," said Miss Worthing, "they do. Aren't you?"

"I'm no Christian."

Miss Worthing smiled. "That's not quite what I asked."

"I know," said the other with an answering grin.

And after a moment she said, "Alan Brown called me. He was angry and—I think—frightened."

"Did he tell you why?"

"Of course." Mrs. Webster was grinning again. "He said that madcap aunt of yours had been asking questions—and making some pretty shrewd guesses, too."

"So why was Alan frightened?" asked Miss Worthing.

"Hmm," the other grunted and sipped coffee. "I think he worries too much. Although—Matilda, as far as I know you've never made the mistake so many make, that just because we are not Christians, we must, therefore, be evil."

"No," said Miss Worthing. "I've never been, I hope, that idiotic. By that criterion, one would have to consider Buddhists, Hindus, Jews, Jains, and Muslims devil worshipers."

"People do," said Mrs. Webster. "Christians do."

"I know people do," said Miss Worthing. "Whether or not they could accurately be called Christians . . ."

Mrs. Webster's eyes twinkled. "Careful, Matilda. Judging people and all that."

"Yes, I know. But how is this relevant to my mess?"

"People assume that because we don't deny being witches, there has to be some connection with—evil."

"I know there isn't. At least not necessarily."

"But you wonder . . ."

"No, Joan, of course not. Your group isn't going to go about sacrificing priests at high altars any more than you sacrifice babies to the moon. . . ."

"For these kind words . . ."

"But!"

"Oh?"

"You know and I know that there are a couple of—what am I going to call them?—maverick groups running around both the Jolliston and Sacramento areas."

"Maverick groups."

"Yes. Satanists and the like. And the sweetness and beauty of your life here has nothing to do with them. They just might consider blood sacrifices."

"Why do you think I would know anything about them?"

"I don't, necessarily. Well—"

"Yes, Matilda?"

"Listen, what did Alan say to you?"

"He advised me to be as open with you as our rules allow. That it would occur to you to come and see me. Eventually."

"So what can you tell me?"

"I've already thought of that. I can tell you who the various groups in the Delta area are. Some of them I wouldn't want anything to do with, and I can only advise the same for you."

"You'll have to let me decide that."

Mrs. Webster nodded and reached for the coffeepot.

"More coffee?"

"Not right now. But before we get into particulars of these groups—and I gather they're pretty unsavory—"

"Some of them. Most are just plain silly—and some, kind of sexy."

"Oh, yes. Well, I have sort of heard about that. But before we get into particulars, I want to ask you something: Alan said something to my aunt that's stuck in my craw. I can't figure out what he meant."

"What did he say?"

"He said the timing was all wrong. Do you know what he meant?"

For a moment Mrs. Webster just looked blank. Then, slowly, a look of wholesale astonishment swept over her normally placid features as she set the coffeepot down on the deal table, goggled at Miss Worthing, and finally burst out laughing.

Miss Worthing was not amused.

"Joan, get a grip."

"I'm sorry, Matilda. It just never occurred to me. Bless Alan's little heart. And here we're being so horribly serious—and there's absolutely no reason whatever . . ."

4 A few minutes later Miss Worthing was getting into her car ready to drive away.

It had been funny. Except that she felt rather as if the carpet had been jerked out from under her.

Mrs. Webster handed her the packet of butter.

"Thank you, Joan. That's very kind of you. Especially under the circumstances."

Mrs. Webster was still smiling happily.

"It's the least I could do. I'm just glad I could help."

"You have. Even if it's a negative, still at least that's that."

"Don't be strangers, you and Martha," began Mrs. Webster. "You know I always enjoy . . ."

From somewhere in the woods, seemingly very close, a bell began ringing.

"Good heavens," said Miss Worthing. "What's that?"

"My neighbors. The good nuns at San Ysidro. Judging from the bell, it's just about time for their conventual Mass."

"My goodness, it sounds like they're in your backyard."

"I know. Actually, they're about half a mile or so away. It's the shape of the bowl we're in that makes it sound closer, and, actually, I rather like having the bell measuring out my days. . . . Matilda, what's wrong?

A look of great astonishment had broken out on Miss Worthing's face.

"Why, yes!" she said. "Of course. Joan, do you have a telephone?"

"Of course, I do. I'm not that much of a hippie."

5 It is ironic that one of the few folks in Jolliston that Sunday morning who was actually managing to sleep soundly should be one to be rudely awakened by a telephone call. Actually, Father Reggie had been mightily tempted to put the phone on auto-answer the night before. Unfortunately, the bishop had made it quite clear over the preceding years that he would personally discipline any clergyman who did so while he was actually at home.

Nevertheless, in spite of the telephone's insistent ringing and that damn-fool dog Demon yapping his head off as was his invariable habit when the phone rang, it still took Father Reggie a moment to realize the din was not part of a nightmare.

"Hello?" he said eventually and very groggily. "Oh! Miss Worthing. I'm sorry . . . Yes, I was asleep. What? The bell? Oh, that one. Normally. Yes. Whoever's celebrating. Usually. But only if there's anyone there. What? Yes, I guess you're right. Okay. Right. G'night."

He hung up and sank back into his pillows and realized wearily that he might as well get up. He probably couldn't get back to sleep now anyway.

And what had all that been about? What was Miss Worthing up to?

With a touching faith in the experience of professionals, Father Reggie had assumed, in spite of Miss Worthing's perseverations the night before, that Julian probably had been the one to do the assault which had had such a disastrous outcome. It was, no doubt, a depressing thought, but Julian did have the most to lose.

He got up, shambled into a cold shower, and presently whistled up Demon to go for a walk.

As he turned onto the sidewalk in front of his house, a dull light was just beginning to appear at the eastern rim of the Valley, and from everywhere came an excited chattering as awakening birds began questioning the day.

The air felt cooler, but there was still not a cloud in the sky, and it was surely only a matter of an hour or two before it would be as hot as ever.

Demon, as was ever his wont, found every stray scent a source of boundless and bounding wonder, pulling Father Reggie this way and that as he eagerly explored some already quite sufficiently revolting spot.

Then, abruptly, the tug on the leash slackened. The dog stared ahead, testing the air, his normally wildly wagging tail first stilled, fell to half mast, and was finally tucked firmly between his legs, while a low and, for this particular dog, astonishingly menacing growl emerged from the animal's chest.

Groggy as Father Reggie was, such a completely uncharacteristic display on the part of that friendliest of dogs was enough to rouse him thoroughly. What could have caused such a reaction? There was no cat or squirrel or impertinent bird, much less any human soul in sight. No, that wasn't true. There was someone coming, a jogger, judging from the sound of the slap of rubber-clad feet on the pavement.

Then, at the corner, appearing around the screening shrubbery that had hidden his approach from Father Reggie (though not, apparently, his scent from Demon), came Jack Cartwright in shorts, a red moisture-discolored T-shirt, and streaming with sweat from his exertions. He must, thought

Father Reggie, have been at this awhile to have worked himself up like that.

"You're a good piece from home, aren't you, Jack?" called out Father Reggie.

Suddenly Jack seemed to see the man and dog for the first time. He snapped out of a deep abstraction as a hand fell to his waist and clicked off the tape machine he carried there and then pulled the ear plugs from his ears.

"Hi, Father Reggie," he all but yelled, and trotted toward them. And came to an abrupt and startled halt as Demon, howling, lunged to the end of his leash, nearly jerking Father Reggie off his feet.

"What the . . ." began Father Reggie when he caught the sudden drain of color from Jack's face as his eyes widened at the sight of the dog.

"I—I didn't know you had a dog," said Jack.

"I can see that," said Father Reggie, and then, a long-awaited connection meeting in his head, he added shrewdly, "A dog, Jack? Or this dog?"

"I don't know what—what do you mean?"

"I think you know."

For a moment neither man said anything, staring at one another as Demon continued to growl, his lips pulled back from his teeth in a grimace Father Reggie knew—from a perusal of the literature he had felt obliged to undertake when Demon came into his possession—was one not only of threat but of great fear.

"Demon!" said Father Reggie, yanking the chain firmly.

Jack began to back off. "Well, I—I guess I'll see you later, Father."

"Oh, no, you don't."

"Father, I . . ."

"No, Jack. Damn it, I'm your priest. No. Perhaps even more importantly, I am a priest."

"It—it wasn't what you think?"

"Oh? And you know what I'm thinking?"

"Damn it all, Father . . ."

"Yes, damn it all is quite right. What were you and your friends up to? Wait! Wait!" Father Reggie held up a hand and took a deep breath. "Sorry. I must not be angry. But I don't want any bullshit from you either. Jack, for God's sake, we've just had a murder—a priest was killed. And at the altar. Now do you see?"

"Oh, my God!" said Jack as the implication penetrated.

"Yes," said Father Reggie, trying to stay level. "He is your God, Jack. Isn't He?"

"It was nothing, Father."

"Nothing!" barked Father Reggie. "You people broke into the church, you perpetrated God knows what kind of sick ritual, we had to reconsecrate the church, hire a caretaker, and you and your friends were going to kill this dog, and you call that nothing?" He ended on a definitely rising note.

"I didn't know about the dog," protested Jack. "I thought it was all a lark, a joke—that's all they said it would be. A drink and a dance in the buff around a bonfire."

"And then it started raining."

"It just got out of hand."

"I very much doubt that."

"I swear I didn't know what it was going to turn into."

"Oh, Jack," said Father Reggie wearily, "I would like to think that for you that may have been true. But if they had already provided themselves with the dog, don't you see that they all knew what was coming?"

"Yes," replied Jack sullenly. "They were laughing at me when—when I was playing with him." He gestured to the still snarling Demon.

"I don't suppose it ever occurred to you to telephone the police."

"Father, I couldn't. It would have been—I couldn't be a tattletale. . . ." He broke off, flushing deeply, as Father Reggie mouthed the last word in unison with him, a knowing look on his face.

"Well, Jack, I am sorry," said the priest with steel in his

voice, "but I have got to know what happened. You needn't provide names, but I have to know what you people were up to. Was it, as you say, a lark? Or was it something much, much darker. And I have to know the extent of your involvement."

The younger man swallowed audibly.

"Jack," said the priest, "it will be just like confession. I *can't* tell anyone else. Well, except—"

"Except who!"

"I think that I had better have your permission to be able to tell the bishop. And Matilda Worthing."

"But I'm telling you I had nothing to do with that business yesterday. Besides, didn't they arrest Julian?"

"Yes, they did. But"—Father Reggie shrugged and sighed—"there's them as ain't too happy with that particular solution."

"Oh, no!"

"Well, Jack?"

6   At about the same time Father Reggie was weaving sleepily toward a cold shower, Millie Cantrell, after having been awake all night staring upward into the darkness of her marriage chamber, heard the front door of her house open and shut and the familiar tread of her husband step across the foyer into his study. Having a brandy, she thought automatically. And then realized that no, that wasn't likely; not if he was recovering from poison. She sighed and waited to hear him emerge.

And presently she heard him come out of the study, shutting the door behind him, and approach the bedroom they had shared together all those years.

In a trice she turned on her side, her back to "his side" of the bed, and, pulling the bedclothes tightly around her neck, forced herself to close her eyes and to breathe in a slow and even fashion.

She heard him come in and, inconsiderate as ever, flip on the overhead, the light shining pinkly through her closed lids. For a longish time, it seemed he stood there doing nothing. Then, after he turned off the light, she listened to him move off down the passage outside and, almost at once, heard the sound of the shower going with the door of the bathroom open.

For a long while she continued to lie there on her side, her eyes closed, her breathing as regular as she could contrive to make it. And all the while in an agony of apprehension that he would . . .

Soon enough, far too soon as far as she was concerned, she heard the sound of the shower cut off and after a few moments the sound of bare feet padding along the corridor toward the bedroom once again.

And go right past the bedroom door. Another door opened and the next sound was of soft things slapping together. A conscientious housewife, aware of her own domain, she had no difficulty deciphering the sound to mean her husband was at the linen closet. A moment later she heard him pad into one of the guest rooms down the corridor and, a few seconds after that, heard the door click shut. And all was again silent.

For a few minutes longer she lay awake. And then, gradually, finally, her breathing grew deeper, more regular, as she began to relax. Her thoughts were still inchoate, unformed, uncertain. When presently she fell into a light doze, such dreams as she had as she fell into the hypnopompic state, consisted of those scenarios by which it might be possible for a sixty-year-old woman to make her own way in the modern world. . . .

. . . and came awake again, floating up out of a dream of such soul-shattering sorrow it might almost have been a nightmare. A dream of him, the first husband who had fathered Hughie and died before the boy was even born, and the thought and memory of whom she normally kept rigorously suppressed for the sake of her own peace of mind and equilibrium.

And so successful had she been that in the dream she was running after him, calling his name, but he never even turned to look at her, but just continued through the open door ahead that then swung to and clicked loudly upon closing, and there was no way she could get the door open. . . .

And she was awake. And all was deep and utter silence around her, the only sound at all, coming to her through the open window of the bedroom, was the ignition of a car being turned somewhere nearby.

An odd time to be going out, her mind commented, before, resolutely, she put the thought and her sorrow from her and, turning over yet again, tumbled headlong into the slumber of the spent.

CHAPTER THIRTEEN

1 Day had already fully come when Miss Worthing stalked through the automatic doors of Jolliston County Memorial Hospital.

"Excuse me?"

"Huh?"

The sleepy receptionist raised his nodding head.

"Can you tell me what room Dr. Leopold Cantrell is in?"

"Mmmph!" said the man, coming to slightly, and his eyes half-lidded, began flipping cards. And then stopped and shook his head. "Sorry," he said with a sleepy grin. "I forgot. He checked himself out. 'Bout four."

"Did he now? Very well, then, how about Philip Kesterson?"

"Room 502," came the response and, turning, Miss Worthing marched to the elevator and was whisked to the fifth floor, where there ensued a bit of difficulty with the nurse in charge when, presently, Miss Worthing found herself in the appropriate ward.

But Miss Worthing was in no fit mood to be trifled with. She told the woman exactly what she could do with it and ordered her to telephone the sheriff, the bishop, Dr. de Castre, or anyone else whom it might be necessary to consult.

Meanwhile, Miss Worthing would be very pleased to have a seat in the waiting room until results could be obtained—which had better be quickly!

Miss Worthing marched to the door of the waiting room, went in, and was brought up short when she found Clyde Cartwright dozing in one of the chairs.

Almost at once, however, he started awake, though it took a minute for his eyes to focus properly. "Mattie?" he said presently.

"Hello, Clyde," said she, taking a seat.

"What are you doing here?"

"Actually, Clyde, I came to see if Philip was awake and if so, if I could talk to him for a moment."

"Do you know him?"

"Only remotely. I've seen him around church, serving Mass and such. I don't know if he knows me. But I would like to ask him a question or two."

The man sighed. "About the murder?" She nodded. "This has been a real unfortunate episode, Mattie. Real unfortunate."

"So it has," agreed Miss Worthing.

Mr. Cartwright turned his head to look at her, uncertain of her tone of voice.

"Meanwhile, what are you doing here?" asked Miss Worthing.

Mr. Cartwright seemed surprised at the question. "I thought you knew, Matilda."

"Knew what?"

"Philip's father is my foreman."

"Oh. Actually, I suppose I did know it. But that still doesn't explain what you're doing here."

Mr. Cartwright smiled a rather bleak smile.

"Both Marty and Ruth were out with the harvest all day—and you know what that's like. Those poor kids were exhausted."

"Of course they were."

"And then this had to happen. Needless to say, they

wanted to stay here, but I told them I would since I'm not much use in the fields anymore, and I had spent my day at the church instead of breaking my back in the vines like they had. I told 'em to go home and get some sleep."

Miss Worthing looked speculatively at her old friend. "Yes, I did gather that you had spent the day at church."

"Meaning?"

"Do you mind if I ask you a few questions, Clyde?"

"No, I guess not," said Mr. Cartwright with a half smile. "I would have expected you'd get around to asking me a few eventually when I found out you'd been appointed the bishop's temporary chancellor."

"Very funny," said Miss Worthing, and then observed, "Actually, it was very kind of you to stay with Philip."

Mr. Cartwright shrugged wearily. "I try."

"Yes, I know. And I've often wondered if it wasn't that kind streak in you that you try so hard to hide most times"—again Cartwright smiled—"that kept you from confronting Leo Cantrell before this."

After a moment, with his characteristic forthrightness, the man admitted, "I suppose I should have done something before this. But Millie's such a good influence on the parish, even if he's not. And then . . ." His voice trailed off.

"And then," supplied Miss Worthing, "this time Jack was involved."

Mr. Cartwright sighed deeply and said, his head and voice shaking, "Sure haven't done such a good job there, have I?"

"Oh, I don't know about that," said Miss Worthing gently. "Of course, he is a bit of a hothead and . . ." She, too, cut herself off.

"Yes, Matilda?" Cartwright looked up.

She shrugged. "I've heard things."

"So have I."

"But he is young," ventured Miss Worthing.

"Yeah, but, you know, you train a vine when it's young and it grows right always, but you don't get it in time and the thing spreads out all over the place."

In response to which viticultural truism, Miss Worthing laughed and placed a hand on the man's arm to indicate it was kindly meant. "Human beings tend to be a tad more flexible than grapevines, Clyde," she said. "Actually, I think by and large you've done a splendid job with Jack. He is, perhaps, a bit unwise and a bit willful at times, but then"—she twinkled at him—"weren't you, too?"

"Matilda Worthing, fancy you remembering that after all these years!"

"Hey!" said Miss Worthing with a toss of the head. "Don't we always remember when we were young and beautiful and the whole world was our oyster?"

Mr. Cartwright finally chuckled and shook his head. "Thank you, Mattie."

"Think nothing of it. Now, however, I do have some questions."

"Okay, Mattie. Shoot!"

"Excuse me for poking where I shouldn't, but it is fairly obvious that you do love Jack. A lot."

"He's all the family I got left to me, Mattie."

"And this play is very important to him."

The man's expression was suddenly a rather sour one. "Yeah. It sure is."

"You don't like the idea of him being an actor."

"Nope."

"Because you want him to take over for you?"

"It's been in our family for a hundred years," said Cartwright. "I thought I'd like to see it stay there."

"And yet," said Miss Worthing, "you went to bat over the play, even though"—she mentally crossed her fingers as a charm against the fib she was about to tell—"there was a possibility Jack might wind up in the movies because of it."

Mr. Cartwright snorted contemptuously. "Yeah. I heard all that nonsense, too. But I'll tell you, if you'll recall, I thought I was gonna be a rodeo star myself."

"I remember."

"And if I say it who shouldn't, I was as good a rider as Jack is an actor. But my dad never said a word to me. Not one word till the day I hobbled out of the hospital with two broke legs, and there was Dad with the station wagon. And all he said was, 'Gonna come home now?' And I did."

"Okay, Clyde." Miss Worthing laughed at the oft-repeated tale. "So you don't actually discourage Jack's ambitions. I take it, then, that you wouldn't actively encourage them, either."

"I don't know what you mean, but I didn't try to kill Cantrell, if that's what you're going to ask."

Miss Worthing smiled. "Thank you, Clyde. Now I don't have to ask you."

"Besides, didn't they already arrest Julian?"

"Yes, they have," said Miss Worthing, standing up and beginning to pace a bit. "But frankly, there's a flaw in all this, and I'm beginning to think it may be a very serious flaw."

"Can you tell me about it?"

"I'd rather not. Not right away, at least. But I would like to see Philip if I can."

Mr. Cartwright asked simply, "Is it important?"

"I think so, Clyde. Unfortunately, depending on Philip's answers, you and everyone else just might have to answer a hell of a lot more questions from me—or the police—come morning."

Immediately Mr. Cartwright stood up in alarm. "But if they've got the wrong man, Mattie, we gotta find out right away."

"Even if you yourself wind up as a suspect?"

He nodded. "Even then. I didn't do it. I know that."

"I wish I could."

"I know."

"Tell me, Clyde. You're the president of the parish council."

"Yes."

"Do you have a full set of keys to the church?"

"A reasonably full set. Why?"

"Do you have keys to everything?"

"No," said Mr. Cartwright, wearily resuming his seat but looking at Miss Worthing with the ghost of a smile. "The only people who have all the keys are the clergy. Although, now I think about it, Julian must have a full set. And Elspeth, too, I would suspect."

"Do you have a key to the storage shed?"

"No."

"What about the gym?"

"Yes. And to the church hall and to the church itself. But to most of the lesser doors—the closets, storage shed and such like, the pool apparatus—I decided a long time ago that I didn't want those keys."

"Why?"

"Because," Cartwright chuckled, "folks are constantly coming to me and saying that they have just got to get in— wherever. Well, while I know sometimes it seems like we spend money like it was water at the Church of All Saints, the fact is we do try to keep some kind of inventory control. This way, when a member of the Sisterhood, for instance, tells me she needs thus and so, or somebody working one of the lunches says they need access to the food supplies, or the gardener needs to get some stuff, I can tell them that they have to see one of the clergy. It's amazing how often it turns out they didn't really need what they were asking for when they have to go through regular channels."

Miss Worthing also chuckled appreciatively. Presently, however, a silence ensued and Mr. Cartwright stood up. "Let me see if Philip is awake. I'll be right back."

2 A few moments later Cartwright stuck his head through the doorway and indicated Miss Worthing follow him. They went to a room directly across from the nurses' station. The nurse said nothing but glared balefully as Cartwright opened the door and ushered Miss Worthing in.

The young boy lying in the bed, his fingers toying with a rosary, looked at them with large, dark, worrying eyes. His skin was a jaundiced yellow under his tan.

"Philip," said Mr. Cartwright softly, "this is Miss Worthing. You may have seen her around the church."

The boy nodded weakly.

"Hello, Philip," said Miss Worthing, sitting on the edge of the bed and covering the boy's fretting hands with her right hand. "I'm sorry to disturb you—"

"Did Father Hughie die?" the boy interrupted almost accusingly, and then explained in a grieved tone, "Nobody will tell me. Nobody will say anything."

"Yes, Philip," said Miss Worthing, "he died shortly after you and he were brought here to the hospital."

"Was it in the chalice?"

"Yes, Philip. It was."

The boy's eyes closed. "Then I might have died, too."

"I understand it was close."

"I'm sorry Father Hughie is dead," the boy said in a very young voice, turning his head on the pillow toward the wall. "He was always so kind to me. I'm going to be a priest and say a Mass for his soul every day for the rest of my life."

"That's an admirable ambition, Philip. But perhaps you are a bit young to be making such a very large decision. Just pray about it and the Holy Spirit will surely tell you what's right."

"That's what Father Reggie keeps telling me," said Philip with the intolerance of generous youth for niggardly age. "But what did you want to talk to *me* about, Miss Worthing?"

"Philip, when you and Father Hughie were on the way out of the sacristy last evening to offer the six-fifteen Mass, you led the way, didn't you?"

"Of course. The server always goes out of the sacristy ahead of the priest."

"To be sure. Now, Philip, I want you to be very careful

and try to remember exactly. Did you ring the little bell over the sacristy door?"

"No. Of course not. Whenever Mass is offered at the main altar, someone in the bell tower rings the big bell."

"Very good. Now, tell me, Philip. How does the person in the bell tower know that it's time to begin ringing?"

"Well, usually one of us calls up on the intercom and says, 'Okay, it's time.'"

"Okay. Now, last night was it you or Father Hughie who used the intercom to call up to the bell tower?"

"Father Hughie."

"It was?"

"Yeah. He even stayed on the intercom for a few minutes to talk to Julian."

"It was Julian?"

"Well, I guess so. He said, 'Hi, Julian. Hughie.'" The boy nodded.

"Do you remember anything of what was said?"

"Just something about the play. And that they'd won."

"Thank you, Philip," said Miss Worthing with a great sigh. She stood up. "Thank you very much indeed. You can go back to sleep now."

"I haven't been able to sleep," said the boy fretfully.

"Well, you should try. You'll feel a lot better soon if you do."

And a few minutes later, out in the corridor, Mr. Cartwright asked, "Well? Did you find out what you were after, Matilda?"

"Oh, yes," said Miss Worthing. "I certainly did. And I'm afraid it's just blown the whole thing wide open."

3 At four o'clock that morning, as it did every morning at four o'clock, a small alarm clock on the bed table began an insistent shrilling—and was cut off by a sharp little slap of Maria Yates's hand.

Wordlessly, Maria and Stringer rose and donned the clothes left ready the night before on the chairs at either side of the bed. While Mrs. Yates sat at her dressing table and ran a perfunctory brush through her hair, Mr. Yates unscrewed the top of a thermos jug standing on the bureau beside two cups, into each of which he poured a generous measure of the thick, sweet, well-creamed coffee Mrs. Yates made as her final chore before bedtime every night.

Taking his own in one hand and hers in the other, Mr. Yates went to his wife's dressing table and set her cup down in front of her.

She gave him a look of gratitude, picked it up, took a sip, and quietly murmured, "Good morning."

His own coffee finished, her husband put his cup back on the bureau, whence she would retrieve it, and set off for his early-morning chores.

Today, when Stringer finished milking the cows, hauling the cans of fresh milk into the dairy for processing later, and turned to the business of slopping the hogs, he turned into the walled compound wherein the pigs were maintained, an apartment almost too elegant to be termed a sty, and came to a halt in utter astonishment. Leaning over the fence, amiably scratching behind the lop ears of a sizable beast who was swooning in ecstasy at these attentions, was Matilda Worthing.

"Matilda!" he exclaimed, and almost dropped the buckets he was carrying.

Miss Worthing left off her communion with nature and turned to smile at him. The pig, thus robbed of its joy, butted the fence, causing it to shake in an unnerving fashion.

"Hello, Stringer," she called out over the din. "I hope you don't mind my dropping by. I had to pass here on my way over to—well, never mind, and I thought I'd stop to see you. And what is that stuff?"

Stringer was pouring the particularly ripe-smelling fluid contents of the two five-gallon buckets into the trough. The five pigs within found it by no means objectionable and were nosing each other aside in squealing eagerness to get at it. Stringer chuckled. "Whey. We made some cheese yesterday evening." He waved a hand in front of his face. "Whew! It sure got ripe. Even in the dairy."

"Yes, that's right," said Miss Worthing casually. "You folks weren't at church last night."

The man continued to watch the pigs for a moment before turning to look at her. "No," he said, "but we heard."

"Oh?"

He nodded. "Young Darryl Hawks was supposed to come over for supper last night." He referred to the deputy Miss Shaw had steamrolled in the gymnasium the evening before. "He's Maria's godson," he explained.

"So how much do you know?"

He took a deep breath and held it a minute. Then, "I didn't do it, Matilda," he said.

"Thank you, Stringer," she said formally. "I take it then that you do know how it happened?"

Again he nodded and observed, "Seems kinda crazy to me."

"Perhaps so. Stringer?"

"Yes?"

"About the play?"

"Yes?" he repeated.

"What are your feelings about it?"

He shrugged. "A good play. Kinda arty, but it's got a lot of depth to it. Best part I ever had."

"Yes?"

"And even though it sure takes up—took up a lot of time, it was nice to be doing it again."

"Was it?"

"Oh, yeah," he said with another absent nod, and then, quite spontaneously, he grinned. "You know, Matilda, you aren't very subtle sometimes."

She let it go without comment.

"But before you go getting any wild ideas, you oughta know I have no ambition to get back into the theater."

Still she merely looked at him and waited.

"Christ Almighty," he protested, "I wouldn't even know how to begin getting back into it."

"With a good play—and a good part in it."

Stringer snorted. "In Jolliston?"

"With three bigshots from the movies in the audience."

At that he seemed enormously amused.

"What's so funny, Stringer?"

"You know, Matilda, now that I am out of it completely, I can afford to be as wholeheartedly snobbish as ever any theatrical actor could be. I have a little interest in the theater. Who wouldn't with my background? But I don't, repeat, do not have any interest whatever in the movies."

"Even though there might be a lot of money to be made?" she asked.

"And I got six kids and this outfit isn't ever gonna make anyone rich?" he countered.

She nodded in acknowledgement.

"Well, it's true, Matilda. Can't deny it," he admitted, and then added with another grin, "Unless you and Martha would care to make me a millionaire by getting off that recipe for your herbal wine. . . ."

"Stringer! Stick to the point!"

He sobered.

"But don't you see? It doesn't matter." He waved a hand toward the lightening horizon. "This here, these hogs, this land, those grapes out there, that's what matters, Matilda. To me, at least. Now. And furthermore"—he turned to her—"I think you know it."

"Perhaps I do," she murmured, observing to herself that she very much wanted to believe it but that such poetic protestations meant precisely nothing. She changed tactic. "Okay, Stringer, let's move on. You're very faithful to the Church, aren't you?"

"Well, I have good reason to be, don't I? If it hadn't been for Uncle Heinrich, Maria, and God, I'd be dead by now."

"So I understand," she answered, and looked into the sty as though for inspiration. The porkers had finished their treat and were munching on their more usual rations, handsome by swinish standard though it was, with glares at Stringer and grunts of disappointment.

Stringer shoveled a few more pounds of the stuff into the trough, closed the feed bag, and leaned the shovel against a wall.

"Stringer," she said, "you were in and around the locker room and hall most of the morning and early afternoon yesterday, weren't you?"

"Yes."

"Did you see anyone doing anything odd?"

"Matilda, everyone was acting odd yesterday."

"Well, yes, but . . ."

"And second, I was hung over. Badly."

"Yes. I did hear about that. Were you angry?"

"Of course, I was." Suddenly he all but snapped at her. "But for the love of God, Matilda, what kind of sense would it make to kill Cantrell? Sure, one of the first things you do in a situation like that is try to find someone to blame. But surely you must know that one of the points we drunks keep getting pounded into our heads is that it is our responsibility." He frowned and glared at her. "Oh, I know, sure as hell, I gotta be a suspect. I was so mad at Cantrell I was spitting like a rattler with a toothache, and there's a whole lot of folks who heard me doing it. But what kind of Christian would I be if I offed Cantrell 'cause I don't like his politics and he pissed me off so bad I got drunk?"

"A lot of people who call themselves Christians would have done just that, Stringer."

"Yeah, I know," said Stringer almost sullenly. "But I ain't one of 'em."

"Okay. Okay. Let's leave that alone for now. Let me just

ask you this: Did you have any reason to go into the court-yard yesterday?"

"No! I never—" He broke off. "'Scuse me, I was out there."

"When?"

"After lunch."

"That's not very helpful, Stringer," she growled. "When after lunch would be helpful."

"Probably around two." He chuckled at her expression. "I wanted Josh for another practice game, and he was still busy in the kitchen—cleanup chores and whatnot."

"Okay."

"So I gave the kids a hand and took the garbage out."

"And?"

"What?" He shrugged. "Nothing looked any different."

"The shed was locked?"

"It always is. Big Yale padlock bolting the door."

"And you don't have a key."

"Why would I have a key?"

"I'm sure I don't know. I'm just asking. Tell me—"

"Yeah?"

"As I recall there are only two ways into that courtyard."

"Sure. The door into the church hall and the passage between the church and shed. Although, actually . . ."

"Yes?"

"Those are the only two ways to get to the shed. At least that a normal human being would use."

"What do you mean?"

"Well, there is another tunnel from the pool deck in the basement of the gym to the basement of the shed. Has to be so we can get at the workings of the pool if necessary."

"We?"

Stringer laughed at her sudden pounce. "Don't get your dander up, Matilda. Remember, I used to be pool man before Julian took over? A chore I willingly surrendered to Julian. God, I hate the smell of that stuff."

"Interesting," muttered Miss Worthing to herself sourly,

making a mental note and doubly underscoring it in her mind. Just what she needed; another complication. "But at least," she reflected aloud, "the passage gates are kept locked all the time, aren't they?"

He looked at her in some puzzlement. "Matilda, where you been?"

"What do you mean?"

"Two months ago the Fire Department told us to stop locking those gates. What with the garbage being kept in the courtyard and what all we store in the shed, they wanted free access to that area at all times."

"Do you mean those gates are open all the time now?" she almost wailed at him.

"That's right. Some of the old ladies had a good time scaring themselves with dire tales of hoboes who would take to sleeping there once word got out, but Father Reggie put 'em in their place by pointing out that if that was the extent of Christian charity the Church of All Saints was prepared to extend to the homeless, then we shouldn't begrudge them the opportunity to sleep with the garbage cans."

He chuckled reminiscently.

Miss Worthing, however, barely heard him.

It was much the same kind of frustration she had experienced the night before while trying to see things more clearly, or at least with some renewed clarity of vision, in the church before joining Elspeth in the sacristy. She had wanted to go out and take a look at the shed and the courtyard. And would have done so in spite of police tape and such had they been in place (concerning which she had no idea). But Elspeth had already set the alarm, and she herself certainly did not know the combination thereof (or have a key to the box), and any cavalier opening of doors would have led to a wholesale ringing of alarms.

Which might not have been such a bad idea, she reflected sourly now.

And as a result, all along she had been assuming that whoever had sneaked into the shed in order to provide him/herself with sundry chemicals had done so through the courtyard from the church hall. But now . . ."

"So anyone could have gotten into the yard."

"Probably so."

She cast her eyes toward the heavens and sighed a rather distracted sigh.

"Lord! Well, all right. If that's the case. Did you see anyone go in? Into the passage. Anyone? You were out in the playing field, weren't you?"

"Yes, I was. But I can't say that I was exactly paying attention."

"Of course not," said Miss Worthing unreasonably.

"Sorry, Matilda. 'Course, if I'd have known what was going to happen, I'd have paid more attention."

The gentle sarcasm brought her to her senses.

"Okay, Stringer," she smiled at him. "Okay. Don't mind me. I'll leave you to your chores."

"Thanks, Matilda. And if I do think of anything, I'll be sure to let you know." He turned away.

"Okay, then. Where, ah, do you think I might find Maria?"

"She'll be in the kitchen," he answered almost automatically and then pulled up. "What are you thinking about?" he asked sharply. "Maria? What kind of . . ."

"Oh, for God's sake, Stringer, get a grip!" she commanded. "Listen. I don't know if you know it, but the bishop has, in fact, appointed me his representative in this mess. And you know perfectly well that means I have to do some snooping."

"But why you?"

"Well, no one else is going to do it."

"But wasn't . . . surely Sam . . ."

"Sam," responded Miss Worthing grimly, "for no other reason than the most blatant expedience, if you want my candid opinion, discovered a scattering of details last night—and promptly arrested Julian."

The man boggled at her. "Julian?"

"I was on my way over to the jail when I thought I'd stop by and have a word with you and Maria as well."

"But why?"

"Why did they arrest Julian?" He nodded. "Because," said Miss Worthing carefully, "I think that *they* think that, since it was generally perceived to be Julian's big chance (thanks to Elspeth Robinson's bit of nonsense), and when the play was canceled, Julian promptly poisoned the wine for Cantrell's Mass."

"No wonder Darryl wouldn't come across completely last night," said Stringer thoughtfully. "That's just crazy."

"Why do you say that?"

"'Cause Julian's not that stupid. Irritating as hell most times, but not stupid."

"I'm sorry," said Miss Worthing. "I'm not following your reasoning."

Suddenly, Stringer laughed. "Me? I don't know anything. But, Christ Almighty, everybody in God's green earth knew Julian hated Cantrell. And vice versa. I can see Julian shouting at Cantrell. Reading him to filth, definitely. Maybe even beating the old bastard up. But murder him? Christ, he'd be the first one anyone would suspect. And as I said, he's just not that stupid."

"Well, it's an interesting point. Though hardly evidential."

"So you're out looking for evidence?"

"Yes, I am. Doctor Fisher wants me to investigate, so investigating I am."

"Well, all right," he said, his tone actually one of admiration. "I don't know how we can help, but if we can, we have to. As I said, you'll find Maria in the kitchen."

4   And very busy, very hot, very upset, and by no means pleased to see Miss Worthing.

But she was also a creature of habit. So while she banged things about a bit more loudly than was perhaps altogether necessary, she also poured out a large cup of coffee, slamming it down on the table with a jug of fresh cream and a brimming sugar bowl.

"Now sit there," she instructed Miss Worthing, "and don't move."

Sitting at the table to Miss Worthing's right was Joshua Yates, the pair's eldest son, hiding behind the *Sacramento Bee* and working away on a plate of eggs and bacon and potato pancakes with a large coffee mug of his own. The lad, sixteen or seventeen now, lowered the newspaper briefly and grinned over the top of it, "Muti's never really civil to anyone before noon."

"Such a thing to say!" observed Maria, not displeased, as she tossed a roll of pastry over a deep dish filled with what appeared to be stewed raspberries. "You have come about that terrible business at the church, *ja?*"

"Yes, Maria, I have," said Miss Worthing, watching cream swirls in her coffee and little globules of butterfat swimming on the surface.

"I have nothing to tell you," said Maria, proceeding to roll out a further quantity of pastry. "I don't know anything about it." Slam. "I saw nothing." Slam. "But to murder a priest!" Slam. "That is terrible." Slam. "But I don't know anything other than what Darryl." Slam. "Told us last night about it."

Miss Worthing deemed it sensible to wait until Maria had draped the resulting sheet of pastry over the giant pie dish already filled with apples strewn lavishly about with flour, cinnamon, and buttons of butter.

"They arrested Julian," said Miss Worthing.

Immediately, Maria paused in her trimming of pie crust and Joshua emerged from the newspaper.

"But I can tell you that, at least in my mind," continued Miss Worthing, "it's almost certain that Julian didn't do it."

It was Joshua who saw the implication. "Then whoever did it is still running around loose!"

Deliberately, Maria finished trimming pie crust, though not, perhaps, with all her wonted panache, set the dish down, poured herself a cup of coffee, and took a seat opposite Miss Worthing.

The two women stared wordlessly at each other for a moment or two before, very quietly, Maria said: "And who might that be?"

"Unfortunately," replied Miss Worthing, "there are any number of possibilities."

"Joshua," said his mother, "why don't you go see if your father needs any . . ."

"Actually," Miss Worthing interrupted, "if you don't mind—if both of you don't mind—there are some questions I could ask Joshua since he's here."

The boy, frowning, merely nodded. Maria, however, went absolutely still, her pale blue eyes as cold as sea ice. Seeing which, Joshua's own eyes opened wide in alarm.

Miss Worthing, on the other hand, was not impressed.

"Maria," she snapped, "I haven't got time for nonsense. I'm not accusing anyone of anything. And certainly not Joshua! Nor, for that matter, you."

"And my husband?"

"Maria, will you listen to yourself?" groused Miss Worthing. "And if you can't do that, try to hear what I just said: I am not accusing anyone of anything. *But*," she added, "I do have to try and find out what happened at that church yesterday. Is that so upsetting?"

"But why are you doing this? Oh, I know you've done it before, but this time . . ."

Joshua, rather aggressively, joined his own voice to his mother's demand. And, in response, Miss Worthing could only repeat her little speech, which was rapidly becoming a set piece, about tackling what officialdom was unwilling to.

And it did, in some measure, mollify mother and son. But it was beginning to get Miss Worthing's goat in a major way that everytime she tried to ask a few questions, her interlocutor immediately and automatically assumed she had come ready to slip a canvas bag over his or her head and tighten the noose. . . .

"Joshua," she said, after a moment to gather her thoughts—and dampen her irritation a bit—"you were in and around most of the morning and at least part of the afternoon."

"Well, yeah. We all, the family, decided to go to Mass together yesterday morning after—what happened. Then, after coffee, we—the soccer team, that is—we had a scrimmage that lasted till about eleven. That's when I go to help out in the kitchen for lunch. Then, after that, Dad came to get me for another game. We didn't do so good in the morning," he explained.

Miss Worthing nodded. "Good. Now, while you were at the church, did you have any occasion to go into the courtyard?"

"Well, yeah. After lunch. Dad and I took the garbage out. Usually, I do it by myself, but Dad was helping to hustle me along."

"And neither you nor your father had any occasion to visit the courtyard or the shed before or after that?"

"What for?"

"Matilda?" the boy's mother interrupted suddenly with narrowed eyes. "Why don't you just ask the obvious question?"

"Thank you, Maria. I will!" snapped Miss Worthing. "Although I hardly think it will be the question *you* seem to be expecting."

Maria's eyes bugged slightly as Miss Worthing turned back to the boy and, resuming her reasonable, inquiring tone, asked: "All right, Joshua. You yourself did not go out in the courtyard alone yesterday. But you work in the kitchen for seniors lunch."

"Yes."

"Doing?"

"I'm a waiter."

"So you would be placed well enough to be able to notice if people were going in and out of the hall. Particularly into the courtyard. Or even later, when you were out on the soccer field, whether they were going in and out of the alleyway to the courtyard."

This turn in the conversation *had* been unexpected; his mother visibly relaxed, though Joshua merely nodded and said, "Yeah. I guess so. So?"

"So whom *did* you see going in or out?"

Joshua frowned again, his eyes going slightly out of focus as he slowly searched his memory.

"No one," he finally said. "Not that I would have noticed. I was kinda busy."

"Damn!" said Miss Worthing suddenly, balling a fist and thumping the table. "I was afraid you'd say that."

She sat back, clicked her tongue, sighed, and nodded, concluding the interview. "Thank you, Joshua."

"You're welcome," he said out of habit and continued sitting there irresolute, frowning and clearly puzzled.

"Joshua," said Maria, "go see if your father needs any help."

"But, Mother—"

"It's okay, Joshua."

He went.

"So *are* you getting anywhere?" asked Maria when her son had gone. "That didn't seem very helpful to me. Or am I missing something?"

"Oh, it was helpful, Maria," said Miss Worthing grimly. "But only negatively. Only negatively."

"Okay, so what do you want to ask of me?"

Miss Worthing smiled rather wanly and asked, "First of all, Maria, since we've been friends a long time, I'd like you to do me a favor."

"Of course. What?"

"Don't get hysterical."

The only response was a snort of what might very well have been amusement.

"Okay, Matilda," said Maria dryly. "I'll try. What do you want to know?"

"You made some pretty strong statements about Dr. Cantrell over the last few days."

"Oh, yes."

"Including one, if memory serves me, that someone ought to have the strength of purpose to kill him."

"Oh, yes. And I meant it."

"Maria!" admonished Miss Worthing irritably.

"Matilda, please!" she waved away the older woman's irritation. "I say things, yes. And who does not? I was distraught. Who would not have been? That old man angered my husband so much that, for the first time in years, he drank." It was interesting to note that she was still trembling with passion about that. "Did you know that our four youngest children never saw Stringer drunk before? Imagine! That's how long it's been. And then"—she gestured helplessly. "But, of course, you're right; that is no excuse for— what I said. I was angry. And I still am."

"Well, obviously, Maria, someone else was, too. The reason I brought up that irresponsible outburst of yours at Cippola's was not because you're a suspect or anything so melodramatic. But you do shoot your mouth off, my dear."

"Yes, I do," conceded Maria, not in the least penitent.

"Yes, well, you needn't be quite that proud of it. Still, it may yet have been useful. Now, I'm sure no one came galloping up to you to announce that they were a fellow traveler and would cheerfully take on the task of felling Cantrell. . . . Or, at least, I can't imagine that happening!"

"No, Matilda," replied Maria in a very dry tone. "Nothing quite so easy, I'm afraid."

"One can always hope," said Miss Worthing with a glance heavenward. "Okay, so what I want to know, my dear, is if anyone, anyone at all, whether by the most casual word, or a shared covert glance, or even a particularly smug expression, may have"—she shrugged—"tried to do the same thing, that is, communicate to you somehow that they, too, were all in favor of it."

"Matilda," answered Maria reasonably, "everyone agreed with me."

"Oh, God!"

"All I know is that I didn't do it . . ."

"I never thought you had, Maria . . ."

". . . because if I were going to kill a man, I would not poison him."

And she spoke with profound contempt.

"Wouldn't you?" asked Miss Worthing, piqued.

"Of course not! I would shoot him. Perhaps. Or maybe I would club him to death. *Ja.* Now that would be most satisfactory. But poison? Never! Poison is such a coward's way, a *cowardly* method."

And, although she was careful to keep it carefully hidden, Miss Worthing had to admit this brief, unelicited trope on the morally correct way to commit murder was not without humor. But, she had been telling the truth to Maria—even if Maria didn't quite perhaps believe her. In spite of that wayward tongue of hers and her patent obsession with her family, Maria never had been much of a suspect in this dismal muddle! And for the eminently practical reason that, historically, whenever she was at the church, Maria was always surrounded by a small cloud of her numerous younger children. Nor had it been any different earlier that day. One of the few facts checked and verified. And one of the rare negatives that had yielded practical results. She may putatively—very putatively—have had a motive, but access to the known means and the opportunity for implementing skulduggery were ruled clean out.

Indeed, while she was completely aware that such an attitude and approach was intellectually reprehensible, Miss Worthing's instincts were beginning to tell her loudly and very clearly that *everyone* she had been speaking to *was* as baffled as was she. Which meant, of course, correlatively, that they were as innocent—at least of this particular sin—as newborn lambs.

"And the wickedness of it," Maria was enlarging upon her prior remarks: "To poison the chalice that way!"

"Yes," said Miss Worthing absently; "it does rather terrify one to think of such a deliberate blasphemy."

"Ach!" Maria waved the suggestion away. "There was sacrilege, yes. But what is truly horrible in this case is that there was almost certain to be a *child* involved, whoever was serving. And there was, too. Darryl told us. Philip is all right?"

"Yes, Maria. He's going to be fine."

"Thank God for that," said Maria softly, blessing herself, before demanding: "And will you please tell me what kind of a monster would kill a child to get at Cantrell?"

"I'd love to be able to tell you, Maria, but I just don't know," said Miss Worthing. "It is a good point, though."

As indeed it was. Because it was all but impossible for her to imagine, among all the folks she knew in the Jolliston Valley, a single one capable of such callous disregard of the presence of a child, the acolyte serving, in the necessary equation the murderer would have had to construct. Yes, it *was* a good point. Even a very good one. Unfortunately, it was also yet another negative one. . . .

"All I can do," Miss Worthing went on, "is to try and find out who, if anyone, was seen going into the storage shed. But so far all I know is who had the keys—and I have no idea if anyone else went into the courtyard. . . ."

"Poor Matilda," interrupted Maria, shaking her head and regarding Miss Worthing with a kind of perverse satisfaction.

"What do you mean?" demanded Miss Worthing.

"Anyone could have gotten into that shed, Matilda. Once they were in the courtyard. Didn't you know that?"

"How? What are you talking about?"

"The keys. Elspeth Robinson leaves them in the kitchen. On a hook. All day long. Every Saturday."

"What? Why? What for?"

"She says she doesn't want to have to be bothered over trifles."

CHAPTER FOURTEEN

1 There are more difficult things in this world to do
than get into your average county jail at five o'clock on
a Sunday morning in order to talk to the prime suspect in a
first-degree murder case when you have absolutely no official standing in the case. But there aren't many.

Fortunately, in Jolliston, Miss Worthing was known. And
respected. Though it is true that, among the sheriff's deputies, that respect had a certain ambiguous quality to it.

It stemmed largely from the part she had played in the
deplorable business, some years before, of the bodies buried
in the riverbank. That had also been the kind of case which,
under normal circumstances, she would not have touched
with a ten-foot pole. But she had been impaneled as a jury
member in what she had frankly considered a kangaroo
court. Almost single-handedly she had managed a hung jury,
the consequent declaration of a mistrial, whereupon she had
gone at it.

In that instance, too, she had come head to head with Sam
and George, proved in the end to have been right in her
conclusion, and been shot in the leg in the process. . . .

And the story had, among the sheriff's posse, grown in the
telling until it had become something of the stuff of legend.

For all that, when the automatic doors of the Jolliston jail whooshed open in front of her, she didn't expect it was going to be easy.

And it wasn't. From the sleepy deputy manning the front desk, the situation passed over to a superior officer. The latter knew all about the bishop having appointed Miss Worthing as his representative. Indeed, that appointment had been the subject of considerable speculation since the events of the evening before. Nevertheless, surely Miss Worthing was aware that the prisoner was probably still asleep. And furthermore, couldn't it all wait till Monday? Or at least till a later hour?

And, very calmly, Miss Worthing said, "Very well. I'll just call Sam at home and see what he has to say. . . ."

Ten minutes later she was in the visiting room waiting for Julian to be brought in.

And, ever so wearily, she wondered if any of this was doing any good. God knows that so far all she had really managed to do was to lend utter confusion to battle fatigue.

Little more had come of her conversation with Maria. Like all the others, Maria had flatly denied having had anything to do with trying to kill Cantrell. Neither had she seen anything.

Of course, all these bald negatives weren't worth the powder to blow 'em all to hell. But so far she had now talked to five of the people involved (not counting the review last evening with Father Reggie, Belinda Sue, and Elspeth Robinson), and no one, not one, had seen anything.

And in a case like this, with people popping up and in and out all over the place, that was, in and of itself, a datum of no mean significance. Even if a negative datum.

But then, she reflected sourly, rather a lot of the data she was getting was negative: The fact of the gate being kept open; the business of Elspeth's keys.

And hadn't Elspeth been more than a little disingenuous about a number of things? Not the least of which was never quite managing to mention Millie's relationship to Father Hughie.

It was probably just as well that, at that point in these ruminations, on the other side of the glass partition dividing the room, a door in the middle of the wall opened and Julian, preceded by a sleepy-looking deputy, came in. The deputy took up a position inside the door, staring blandly into space, while Julian, after a moment of looking about, proceeded to the carrel opposite Miss Worthing and sat down.

Miss Worthing picked up the phone and put it to her ear—and then for a moment wasn't altogether sure Julian was going to pick up his end. Presently, however—and she could almost hear the sigh of resignation—he, too, picked up the phone. He still hadn't met her eye to eye.

"Julian?"

Still he sat, head bowed, the picture of sullen resentment.

"Julian!"

Slowly he raised his head.

"What!"

"Well, first of all," she instructed simply, "you might stop acting like a child who isn't getting its way."

At once Julian's head snapped up, his eyes flashing.

"Good," she commented and observed: "It does no one nearly as much harm as it does you."

"Okay! Okay!" Finally he spoke. "What do you want?"

"First of all, to tell you that this"—she gestured around—"was not my idea."

He began to speak, but she held up a hand.

"Now just hold on a minute. Because you should also know that I have come to tell you that I am almost convinced that you are perfectly innocent."

"Almost?" said Julian.

Miss Worthing allowed herself a smile, a bit grim perhaps, but a smile nevertheless, and as briefly as could be managed she recapitulated her conversations with Philip Kesterson and Bonnie Harris.

When, presently, she was finished, she waited, watching, as he sat once again with his head bowed.

"Well, Julian?" she said. "Were they right?"

Eventually he muttered, "Yes."

She leaned forward. "Okay. Now, Julian, don't get into a tizzy, but I have to ask: Did you try to kill Dr. Cantrell?"

"I thought you said you were convinced I was innocent."

"My dear fellow," said Miss Worthing, "as you yourself noticed, I said 'almost.' And I do have to ask, if only for the courtesy of battle—did you kill or try to kill Leo Cantrell?"

And looking her square in the eyes, Julian replied, "No."

"You didn't put anything into the wine?"

"No."

"Or into the tea?"

"No."

"You just took tea to Dr. Cantrell's study?"

"I poured the water into the pot when it boiled and took the tray up to Millie. Yes."

"Okay," she said—and filed the bald denial away as she had done with all the others. "How did you come to be in a position to be there to help Millie?"

"When Hughie called me to tell me to ring, he told me Dr. Cantrell had taken sick. So when I came down from the bell tower I asked someone if they had seen—well, either Cantrell or Millie."

"Whom did you ask?"

"One of the ushers—I think it was Billy McClure. He said Cantrell had gone to his study to lie down."

"Did he tell you Millie was in the kitchen?"

"No." He shook his head and actually chuckled a bit. "But in spite of how I feel about him, I figured if the old bastard wasn't feeling well, he might like a cup of his tea. And when I got downstairs, there was Millie already with the kettle on."

"So you actually went to make that tea out of the goodness of your heart," observed Miss Worthing.

"Yeah," said Julian bitterly, "and now look where it's gotten me."

"Don't ever regret charitable actions, Julian," she admonished. "No matter what the consequences might appear to be. But forgive me, I shouldn't sermonize, because there's no time."

"Yeah? I got all the time in the world."

"Well, I don't, and furthermore, if you don't mind, there are some other questions that need asking."

"Such as?"

"Julian, surely you can see that much rests here on who had access to the shed."

"Of course."

"Were you out there yesterday?"

"What for? No. No, that's not true," he suddenly interrupted himself. "Yes, I was. I went out to put some ant powder back."

"Where did you put it?"

"Back in the canister it came from."

"And the bag it was in?"

Suddenly, genuinely amused, it appeared, Julian smiled. "So you knew I'd been out there."

"Never mind. What did you do with the bag?"

"I threw it in the trash."

"Which was where?"

"In the dumpster."

"In the courtyard?"

"Yes."

"And you relocked the shed?"

"Of course."

"And never went back?"

"No."

"But of course you were busy in there on Friday."

"Well, yes, I was. I hauled a gallon of the pool stuff down to the shed basement and dumped it into the system."

"You didn't hold any out?"

He frowned. "Depends on what you mean."

"I beg your pardon."

"When I checked the pH of the water, I found I only needed to use half of it on Friday. I put what was needed into the system and left the rest of it in the shed basement, figuring I'd need the rest of it by Tuesday at the latest."

"You didn't take any out with you?"

"No, damn it. What would I take any of that—stuff out for?"

"At that point? Heaven knows," said Miss Worthing. "You didn't know then that Dr. Cantrell was going to cancel the play."

"Not that it would have made any difference," Julian muttered half to himself.

"I beg your pardon."

In tones of world-weary cynicism, Julian sneered suddenly, "No, none of you people would think to ask me, would you?"

"Ask you what?"

"Every blessed one of you has assumed all along that I would cheerfully commit murder, and that several times over, if necessary to get my play produced."

"That has been the general impression," ceded Miss Worthing.

"Well, I'm not so sure I should tell you now."

"Why not?"

"Reserving my defense," he all but snarled.

"Julian," she said angrily, "that's the second time someone's said that to me." She didn't say that the other had been Bonnie. "And I won't have it. I'm not here to convict anyone . . ."

"So you say."

". . . but I am here to try to find out what really happened."

"Why?"

"Because the bishop asked me to. Because you're in jail,

and from everything I've been able to learn thus far, you are here most unjustly. Did you dream of getting your play made into a movie?"

"Dream? Oh, yes, I dreamed. Who doesn't? Did I think it would happen? No, I didn't. Because I am not that big a damned fool, damned fool though generally I've been. Christ, I didn't even want the play to go on!"

The immediate response to that last statement was, on Julian's part, a kind of shocked surprise that he had blurted out what he had not meant to say, and was fully prepared to resent Miss Worthing for somehow having elicited it from him.

For her part, it took rather a few moments for the import of what Julian had said to fully penetrate.

Clarification, needless to say, was instantly demanded.

But for Julian, war weary and fully prepared to take personal umbrage if the sun should go out, the interview was over, and he stood up and loudly so informed the guard.

A short time later, when she had returned to the public areas of the jail, Miss Worthing made a beeline for the nearest public telephone, fed in a quarter, and hastily dialed a number. The phone at the other end rang maybe three times before a voice barked, "Hello!"

"George? Matilda. I've found out a few things that I think you ought to know," she began. . . .

. . . And in a very brief time indeed, turned away, very angry indeed. In quick succession she had telephoned both of them, and neither Sam nor George had expressed anything but the most academic interest in her findings (such as they were, so far), considerably less than that for her opinions, no matter how strongly they may have been expressed, and none whatever for doing anything until the morrow and normal business hours.

Very well, she thought to herself with an increasing grim determination of purpose, she would pursue her own investigation and in her own way. Ready to drop though she was. It was her duty, damn it all, and she would do it.

Stuffed thus with virtue, she nipped back to the telephone and, after checking the directory, dialed yet another number.

This time there was no answer at all. And after the phone had rung again and again, Miss Worthing hung up and retrieved her quarter, wondering where on earth Fiona Mac-Laren could be at—she checked her watch—five-fifteen in the morning.

2 On the way home Miss Worthing concentrated intently upon the necessity of getting herself there, all too aware that she had long since reached a degree of fatigue that just might affect her driving in such a way as to excite a certain amount of interest among those deputies on traffic patrol.

It was, in fact, her only thought at the moment, other than wondering what to say when she got home and Miss Shaw realized she'd been out half the night driving. Miss Shaw's freely expressed opinion of Miss Worthing's abilities behind the wheel could not be lower—with some justification, if the truth were known. It was getting on for five-thirty, she had had maybe three hours' sleep in the last twenty-four, and that after a day filled with more physical activity, emotional anxiety, and intellectual cudgeling than was normally her portion for a month.

Thus it was that, when she came to negotiate the rather intricate set of maneuvers that would take her home to Jasmine Avenue, and discovered that that high shrubbery still blocked the view of oncoming traffic at the stop sign at Ayala and Tyler, her temper was not sweetened. Fulminating against a mentality so indifferent to the public weal, she realized after a moment that the homeowner she was thus consigning to outer darkness was none other than Neil Bonewarden.

"A perfect opportunity to kill two birds with one irritation," she muttered to herself and, instead of sailing out onto Ayala, praying the while she would not get broadsided, she backed up Tyler and thence into Neil's driveway.

The day had long since dawned, but other than a few especially determined birds twittering the occasional and, on the whole, self-conscious obligatory territorial calls, everything was still and silent, the already remarkably warm air promising no break in the heat wave.

Earthquake weather, she thought as she crossed the lawn to the front door, and blessed herself rapidly as a kind of *absit omen*, trying, and not all that successfully, to remind herself that the myth that earthquakes occurred on hot, still days was nothing more than a folk tale surviving from the '06 quake—which had happened on just such a morning as this.

Upon arriving at Neil's front door, she gave a genteel little dab at the button and heard faintly from within the melodious bonging of a chime.

After a reasonable interval she dabbed again.

Still nothing.

Whereupon, a rather flinty expression settled upon her features, and this time, when she rang, it was no little dab; she put her finger to the button and pushed with a ready will.

Within the chime bonged again and again and, as if that were not enough, she balled her left fist and added a rhythmic pounding on the door.

Later she would wonder where she had gotten the nerve to act in such a way. In spite of the frustrations she had been experiencing, it seemed hardly fair to take it out on Neil's— condition.

"Except, of course," she would observe sometime later, "it's a good thing for Neil I did."

And while Mr. Bonewarden would, eventually, concede the point, at the time all he could do, under the pain of the tenpenny nail piercing his forehead and the black rage resulting therefrom, was to throw open the door and treat whoever it was to a masterful exhibition of sulfurous language.

Now, while it is certainly true that Matilda Worthing is very much a lady, in an almost forgotten meaning of that much-abused word, she is also a person with few pretenses. Which probably explains what happened next.

There was, after all, nary a word yelled at her which she had not heard before. Nevertheless, she was really quite taken with the sheer inventiveness with which Neil managed to put them all together in novel combinations, until, at one particularly vivid turn of phrase, she erupted into helpless laughter, while even Neil had a (weak) grin on his face— even if the tenpenny nail piercing his forehead still throbbed in a cruel and unforgiving way.

"Sorry," he managed eventually to get out.

"Well, I wasn't exactly being the greatest neighbor in the world getting you up that way," conceded Miss Worthing, wiping away the last tears of laughter.

Neil snorted. "If you hadn't, you'd never have gotten me up."

He glanced at his wrist and frowned not to see his watch.

"It's five-thirty," Miss Worthing interpreted that glance.

He sighed. "Then I'm glad you did get me up. Want some coffee?"

She didn't especially. But it would provide opportunity for questions. And Neil, unless she missed her guess, dealt in strong espresso on—such mornings.

"Okay, Neil," she said and followed him inside.

"I really am sorry about all that," he said again as he waddled, an ellipse in mauve silk, ahead of her through rooms still dark with drawn curtains. "It's something of an automatic response when people come calling and I'm not expecting them."

"It's quite all right," she soothed as they entered the kitchen.

It was a bright room and an immaculately clean one, except for a half-eaten pizza on a counter in front of a portable TV, and an empty glass and ditto bottle of vodka.

Rather embarrassed, it seemed, Neil swept all this away, explaining as he did so that he had been hungry when he got home the night before and had then followed his meal up with a few "martinis."

And it struck Miss Worthing that, one day soon, she was going to have to have a talk with Stringer about beginning the necessary process of getting Neil dried out. Today, however, there were more pressing, if just as Christian, obligations upon her.

She had been right. Neil shoveled finely ground coffee into the basket of an ancient espresso maker, set it on the stove, and turned the gas up to volcanic. In no time the central spigot began erupting coffee, Neil slammed the lid shut, and after sundry noises that sounded as though the thing were in imminent danger of explosion, he poured out two sizable cups of thick black coffee, which turned out to taste astonishingly good.

Neil set hers in front of her and, seizing the device, proceeded to wash it out at the sink and refill it.

"I'm sorry I'm so out of it," he apologized yet a third time. "I'll be better after coffee. What's happening with you?"

She sighed. "A good deal of confusion," she answered.

"Yeah, well, I can't say I'm surprised to hear it."

"Neil, I was just over at the county jail."

"Yes?"

"I went to see Julian."

"And how is he taking it?"

"About as you would expect him to."

Neil made a sour face. "As bad as that?"

"I tried," she said, spreading her hands, "not that it did any good. Except—" She shrugged and drank coffee.

Neil looked up from his. "Yes?"

"I think I surprised him into saying something he didn't want me to know."

"Something incriminating?"

"Quite the contrary, I think."

"What was it?"

"He said something about wanting to cancel the production of the play."

For a moment Neil said nothing. It was fairly clear the cobwebs still had not been altogether swept away from inside his skull, although apparently the nail had been drawn from between his eyes.

Just then the espresso pot began its industrial noises again and he got up to attend to it. When he came back, he held it out to her.

"No more for me, thanks."

He nodded, with evident relief, and filled his own cup.

"I did try to tell them last night. But no one would listen."

"I'm listening," she said.

He nodded. "Okay, Matilda. Get ready. That was exactly right. On Wednesday night of last week Julian decided he wanted to withdraw the play from production. In short, cancel it right out."

She took a deep breath, started to speak, hesitated, and frowned.

"I think I must be missing something. I had the distinct impression that it was you who decided to threaten to cancel the play as a means of getting the cast to shape up."

"That's absolutely correct. It was my idea."

"I was right," said Miss Worthing, addressing the ceiling. "I am missing something."

Neil chuckled and said, "Not really. You see, I suggested to Julian that night that we threaten to cancel the play as a"—he shrugged—"bit of gamesmanship."

"Okay."

"But when I suggested it to Julian, he rather rattled my cage by just saying, no, that wasn't good enough. He wanted the play pulled. Right then."

"So when everyone says you were leaning on Julian . . ."

Neil nodded. "Oh, yes, I was leaning on him. And Julian,

let me remind you, is not the easiest person in the world to lean on."

"Even for you?"

"Even for me."

"So what you're telling me is that Julian actually wanted to cancel, whereas you wanted simply to threaten it with no actual plans to do so."

"That's right. After all the work that had gone into it, why should we just up and cancel? And even if Julian couldn't see it, I could see that we had the potential of a first-class production. I don't think Julian's had a lot of theatrical experience and, let's face it, the play is a kind of literary exercise."

"All right. Fine. But if all this is true, why was Julian so upset when Cantrell finally did try to cancel the play if it so comported with his own desires?"

"I think that's fairly easy to answer. First, because it was Father Hughie's pet project. And you do know how close those two are—were . . ."

"I do now," murmured Miss Worthing.

". . . and second, because it was Cantrell who tried to cancel it."

For a moment Miss Worthing stared straight in front of her, her eyes by no means focused, and then abruptly uttered a short little bark of laughter and applied herself to finishing her coffee stew.

Neil looked at her rather strangely as he refilled his own cup.

She shook her head, but it was meant to signify confusion rather than an unwillingness to share.

"I am more than ever," she said, "convinced that Julian is the victim of a frame-up."

"But who?" said Neil, plainly bewildered. "I mean we're talking a real nasty mind behind this one, Matilda, whoever it is. Not only to try, twice, to kill Cantrell, but apparently to hell with any innocents who happened to get in the way as well."

He looked up to see her eyeing him speculatively.

"Don't look at me like that!" he commanded. "I didn't do anything."

"I didn't say you had," she said evenly. "Nevertheless—"

"What? Nevertheless, I had a motive?"

"Well? Did you?"

He exhaled, drank coffee, and said, apparently in all honesty, "I don't know. Maybe I did. I do know that, when I heard what Elspeth Robinson was up to, my feet got awfully itchy. I've done a really good job on this play, Matilda."

"So I've heard."

"Yeah?" He seemed pleased to hear it. "And maybe I had a little revival of post-adolescent fantasies. Yeah. I'll grant you that. There I was. Suddenly I saw myself designing and directing *Turandot* at, say, the San Francisco Opera." He held his hands up to frame the grandiose picture he was seeing. "But in reality?" His hands fell. "I'm fifty-three years old, I'm an obese lush, and I still manage to make a living in music—and hold onto one of the most prestigious jobs in the country. Maybe I did have a motive. Maybe."

"Okay," said Miss Worthing gently. "Okay. Never mind that for now. But, Neil"—she shifted the focus—"what did you do yesterday? You were at Mass in the morning."

"Yes, I was. I know, fairly unusual to see the old booze hound at seven-thirty Mass on a Saturday morning. But I was awake and worrying and—felt in need of whatever solace I could find."

"And after that?"

"Well, Millie and I had junior choir rehearsal till eleven-thirty."

"And?"

"I went up to my office."

"Did you go to lunch?"

"Not at the church. I went to—down the street."

"Alone?"

"No, as it turns out. I picked Millie up at her house and she went with me."

"Millie?"

"She hadn't been feeling any too chipper that morning, and then I heard she'd canceled her lessons."

"How did you find that out?"

Neil made a face. "Oh, you know. One of the bitchier of the stage mothers in Millie's little stable called to kvetch at me. I don't know what they think I can do, but they all do it—on those rare occasions Millie does cancel. Not that they get much mileage out of me. So I called her and said come along and have a sandwich and a beer. I have to admit she seemed pleased to be along."

"What was wrong?"

"She said she was getting a cold."

"Did you take her home after lunch?"

"I was going to, but she said she wanted to stop at the church and tell her husband they were going to have to go out for dinner because she didn't feel like cooking."

"Millie said that?"

Neil nodded. "I know. That's when I figured she must be really feeling low. She said she'd either walk home or take a taxi."

"Do you know if she did?"

"Well, I gather she didn't. I mean not only because she was there when Cantrell was poisoned in his study, but she came up to see me at five-thirty to ask if I wanted the night off and she'd take the six-fifteen."

"Which, clearly, you declined."

"Well, yeah. I told her that if she wasn't feeling well to go home and get some rest. All I had to do at that service was four hymns, a communion, a pre- and postlude, and that I'd rather have her—hell, I'd need her at nine-thirty in the morning a helluva lot more that at Saturday six-fifteen. But speaking of church"—he glanced at the clock—"I do have to get ready. I should be there by seven at the latest this morning."

Miss Worthing nodded. "Yes. The bishop said he'll reconsecrate just before the seven-thirty."

"Oh, me," said Neil with a self-deprecating little sigh, "all this and now a pontifical liturgy as well. What a life we organ grinders do live!"

3 The man parked his car in its usual slot and walked toward the Church of All Saints through the steadily brightening day. He climbed the steps from Church Street into the cloister, crossed the garth and, pausing at the cloistral door into the sacristy, withdrew a set of keys from his pocket, inserted one into the small gray box beside the door, opened it, dialed the appropriate code, withdrew his key without looking further at the device, fished another key from the bunch, and opened the door.

Inside all was in readiness for morning.

He went through the sacristy door into the church and paced slowly around the desecrated altar, scrubbed and bare and stripped, ready for reconsecration later that morning.

Presently, however, he came to a halt, his back to the nave, hands on hips, as incongruously he began to laugh, softly at first, a low, rumbling chuckle that quickly built to a near maniacal howling.

Whereupon a voice spoke, echoing down the great length of the immense nave: "It isn't funny, you know."

He whirled around.

Standing in the choir loft, looking down at him, was Fiona MacLaren.

"What are you doing here?"

"I came to talk to you."

"How did you know I'd be here?"

"Let's just say a little bird told me you would have to come here."

"What do you mean?"

"To make sure you covered your ass."

"What?"

"I saw you. Yesterday."

"You've seen me many times."

"Oh, no. I mean, specifically, I saw you yesterday."

"So?"

"So I saw what you did."

"And what did I do?"

"I saw you come out of the pool."

"My dear young lady, what difference does it make if you did? There are people in and out of the pool all day long."

"That's not true!" she shouted, setting the echoes once more to ringing. Then, taking herself in hand, she returned to the same tone of almost coy badinage with which she had begun. "Perhaps you're right. Perhaps it makes no difference. Still"—she leaned on the balcony of the choir loft— "don't you think the police might be interested?"

"Why should they? They've already arrested Julian, haven't they?"

"But Julian didn't do it."

"And we're to take this on faith? On your word?"

"No. Because after you came out of the pool, you went up to the church and into the sacristy. And then I heard the sound of jugs—wine jugs, I presume—moving around."

"What did you do? Follow me?"

"Yes."

"Why?"

"Oh, come on! Anyone would wonder what you could be up to."

"So what did you see me do with the jugs?"

"Actually, I didn't see you do anything with them. If I had been in the line of sight, you would have seen me. Don't you think, though, that the sheriff just might find all of this an interesting coincidence?"

After a moment he said, "I see. What do you want?"

"I should think that would be obvious."

"I must be getting dim," said the man. "It's not so obvious to me."

"Don't give me that," said Fiona menacingly. "Hughie's dead."

"I know."

"Which means that All Saints has an opening for an assistant priest."

"You have got to be joking."

"I'm not."

Another long moment of silence ensued. Finally the man said, "Oh, very well. Come down here and we'll talk. I can't very well have you blackmailing me the length of the nave."

"I'll be right down," said Fiona.

CHAPTER FIFTEEN

1 By the time Miss Worthing finally arrived home, full day had broken in all its tropic glory—or whatever. Weary and more than a little disgusted, she was also experiencing the liveliest apprehensions: It was quite bad enough that she should be getting, and from everyone, such a negligible amount of data. Far worse was the almost complete lack of any *positive* data. Moreover, there was the added complication that, as things currently stood, there was simply no way to tell whether those whom she had interviewed thus far—for *whatever* reasons they might have—were holding out on her.

Not that the latter factor really mattered all that much. She had perforce already made up her mind as to the next course to pursue. And the little voice at the back of her head was saying over and over, "Scandal! Scandal!"—and was getting louder and louder.

Now this might seem rather a silly reaction. Surely the murder of one priest, the attempted murder of another, and the adventitious poisoning of an altar boy were doings already sufficiently scandalous for anyone.

And so, of course, they were. But so far the whole unlovely mess had been managed rather well, and not a squeak had alerted those media for which such a sordid crime would be jam indeed.

If, however, the investigation went to the stage Miss Worthing was reluctantly coming to contemplate (and saw no way of avoiding)—namely a general roundup of everyone, no matter how remotely involved, and the tedious elaboration of minutiae—the whole thing was going to bust wide open. As the bishop had predicted. And it would almost certainly be quite remarkably ugly.

She parked the car in front and stalked around to the back, hoping to get in without being seen.

Such, however, proved impossible. Seated at the kitchen table, keeping the bishop and Father d'Arcy company, were Father Reggie and Belinda Sue, while Miss Shaw poured tea, offered around a platter of well-buttered slabs of her homemade whole-wheat raisin bread, which had been toasted a lovely golden brown, and glared at Miss Worthing, all at the same time.

"About time!" muttered Miss Shaw. "Why didn't you wake me up to drive?"

Blithely ignoring her, Miss Worthing took in the scene with a somewhat lopsided smile and observed, "One does get such interesting insights into the behavior of the clergy when they're staying with one."

"Actually," said the bishop, completely unruffled, "it was Miss Morgan here who persuaded me to change the practice of many years."

Miss Morgan recited her personal creed on the necessity of some small measure of sustenance on the part of ecclesiastic professionals and concluded, "Especially in a situation like this one, with everyone emotionally and physically exhausted. I hardly think the Holy Ghost is going to object too wildly to a cup of tea with a spoonful of sugar in it and a slice of toast. And today," she added grimly, "they're going to need those carbohydrates."

"And cholesterol," said Father d'Arcy, dabbing at his buttery lips with his napkin. "Actually, I think it was her expressed belief that the lowness of our blood sugar is the reason for the dullness of our sermons that was far the more telling point with his lordship."

"His lordship does not preach dull sermons," said Miss Worthing.

"Kind of you to say so, Matilda," said his lordship, looking not the least contrite as he bit into yet another slice of toast, "but I really must set a good example to my clergy."

"Humph," muttered Miss Worthing, sitting down and joining in with a hearty appetite.

And almost immediately something of a self-conscious silence fell over the assembled group that might have gone on for any amount of time when the bishop, washing his toast down with a half cup of tea, sat back, wiped his hands, cast the napkin onto the table, sighed with contentment, and, looking at her somewhat askance, asked, "Well? Good hunting, Matilda?"

For a moment Miss Worthing said nothing as she, too, finished her tea. "No," she said presently and succinctly. "Except, perhaps, for one thing."

And at once several said eagerly together, "Yes?"

"I am now near dead certain that Julian was in no way responsible for anything yesterday."

"Okay," said the bishop. "And proof?"

"Well, it is," admitted Miss Worthing, "at the moment pretty much intangible. Nevertheless, I personally consider it conclusive. The only trouble is—"

Again there was a chorus of "Yes?"

Whereupon maturer reflection prevailed. Miss Worthing shook her head and stood up. "Sorry, folks," she said with a smile. "I know you'd all like to know what's happening, and I should rather like to tell you. But"—she looked at the bishop—"I think I had better report to his lordship privately."

Scattered sighs greeted this announcement—and grumbles from Miss Shaw, who was, after all, definitely feeling left out of things—in spite of a general consensus that Miss Worthing was acting only properly. . . .

And so, a short time later, in the living room, Miss Worthing provided his lordship with a reasonably detailed précis of her journeyings that morning.

"Which means?" asked Dr. Fisher when she had finished.

"Two things, I'm afraid. First, that whoever did this was either a great deal cleverer than your average murderer or a lot luckier. Either way, it leads directly to point two: It is going to take a lot more in the way of resources than I have available to me to snuffle this thing out. In fact, as I suspected all along, the police are going to have to handle it."

"I don't know, Matilda. I haven't exactly been entranced with the way they've worked so far."

"No more have I. But as we discussed last night, I just don't see any way that I can prevent the kind of investigation in which everyone—everyone—who was at the Church of All Saints from Friday night through Saturday evening is going to have to be interrogated, in detail, and then the whole shebang collated. And, Bishop, I just can't do that."

"And indeed I couldn't ask you to," said the bishop and sighed. "Very well," he said after he had taken a moment to digest the unpleasant morsel. "Have you communicated this to Sam and George?"

"I tried," she replied wearily, and told him of her attempts to get the sheriff or the district attorney moving on it earlier that morning after she had talked to Julian.

"Oh, really?" said his lordship, and rising from his seat on the edge of the sofa, he sauntered to the telephone and plucked it up.

His several conversations, once connected to the appropriate parties, were crisp, brief, and to the point. And when a few minutes later he hung up for the last time, he turned to see Miss Worthing regarding him with a clear renewal of respect for the episcopate in her eyes.

"There now," said Dr. Fisher comfortably, and resumed his seat, "that's settled. They've agreed to bring Julian along with themselves to an assembly at the church directly after the pontifical liturgy at eleven is over. Is that amenable to you, Matilda?"

"Quite," said Miss Worthing faintly.

"At which time all the parties necessary will be summoned and any further questioning, by whomever, will be conducted, during which time whatever might be needed in the way of court reporters, word processors, and computers will, I am quite sure, be made available."

Grateful, pleased, and enormously relieved, Miss Worthing could only lean back, sigh, and say, "Thank you, Bishop."

Even, however, as her shoulders lifted with what she hoped was the removal of their monstrous burden, his lordship spoke further. "And now, Matilda, even though, as I just said, I know I have no earthly right to ask it of you, nevertheless I would still like you to keep on as my minister without portfolio, so to speak."

"Oh, Bishop!"

"Yes, I know, horrible for you. But those two, Sam and George, made what you are now apparently convinced was a serious error in judgment last night. If you don't mind, I should rather like to see to it that no other member of my flock is pounced upon for no other reason than that those two might wish to clap someone in irons simply in order to have done with the whole bloody business."

Not too surprisingly, perhaps, Miss Worthing could only stare straight in front of her with hopeless longing for the sweet-smelling crispness of sun-dried bed sheets.

"I know," repeated the bishop gently, "it is an awful thing to ask. But I wouldn't do it, you know, unless I thought it was necessary."

Put thusly, what else could she do? She straightened her shoulders, sat up, and nodded. "Very well, Bishop, I'll do whatever I can."

2 "Bishop!"

Dr. Fisher and Miss Worthing, rather startled by the interruption, turned simultaneously. Standing in the archway to the dining room was Father Reggie, looking diffident but determined.

"I thought I told you to stay in the kitchen," said the bishop.

"You did, Bishop. But I have to be getting to church soon, and there is something I simply have to tell you."

"Come in, Father Reggie," said Miss Worthing. "And have a seat, for goodness' sake. You look like you're about ready to drop."

"I am tired," admitted Father Reggie. "But I'll be all right—once this madness is behind us."

"You have something to tell me?" asked the bishop, sounding somewhat irritated. "What's on your mind?"

"I had rather an interesting experience this morning while I was walking my dog," began Father Reggie, and proceeded to tell them of his earlier adventure, concluding, "So my own belief is that, for the most part, it probably was a lark. But from one or two things that Jack let drop—probably without knowing he was doing it—that's the way they recruit, by playing it for a lark, there is a hard-core group who are seriously into it."

The bishop was, as might be expected, enormously relieved finally to have an explanation for the unpleasant goings-on the previous winter. Combined with relief, however, was a certain righteous fury that such a sect would so cavalierly invade the sacred purlieus of the Church of All Saints.

"Okay, Reggie. And thank you. No, of course I don't blame Jack—although it's a pity that a man his age hasn't learned to think more clearly. Or choose friends with better manners. But never mind that. I suppose in a pluralist society one must sometimes turn the other cheek with something of a vengeance. Unfortunately, I rather doubt these—

people share those democratic principles. Henceforth, therefore, you will appoint a person, man or woman, of known piety to be the last to go to communion at any Mass, and he or she will make certain that when communion is distributed, it is swallowed. Do I make myself clear?"

"Yes, Bishop."

"For the rest of it, we'll rely for now on the efficient alarm system you people have installed."

"Yes, Bishop."

"And now"—Dr. Fisher turned to Miss Worthing—"what do you make of it, Matilda?" he asked.

"Not much," said Miss Worthing dismissingly.

"What!" said both clergymen together, clearly somewhat shocked.

"Bishop, it's just another possibility. And, frankly, I should think a remote one.

"It's simply a question of complications," Miss Worthing explained to the nonplussed men. "Well, you see, when I couldn't get back to sleep this morning, I decided to go see one of our local witches, knowing full well she'd be up and about."

"What!" demanded the bishop.

"A witch, Bishop. A woman who worships the Great Mother and tends her land better than a whole lot of other people here in the Valley. I thought she might be able to help, and she did. Do you remember that thing Alan Brown told my aunt: that the timing was wrong?"

The bishop nodded. "Of course, I do."

"I don't know what you're talking about," said Father Reggie.

"Don't worry," said the bishop grimly, "there's no need for you to know." And turning back to Miss Worthing, he said, "So?"

"He was right. Bishop, there's nothing happening this weekend. We're plumb in the middle between Lammas and the equinox, and it was—my friend's definite opinion that although Satanists may be little more than upside-down

Christians"—Miss Worthing ignored the bishop's gobbling—"they tend to follow the old fire festival thing pretty much like the *Wicca,* which means: Nothing. Even if there were some group out to sacrifice priests and desecrate Hosts and demean the Church, it's just the wrong time of the year. Besides, judging from what Father has just told us, this group that seduced Jack was nothing more than a group of very silly people probably into some adolescent notion of sex magic.

"No, Bishop," she concluded, "I grant you it was an attractive possibility, but as far as I've been able to establish, voodoo in the vestry just ain't gonna cut it."

The bishop sighed and shook his head. "Oh, very well then. Disgusting as it is, it would have made things so much easier for us. But I'm sure you know what you're about. Time, meanwhile, creepeth on apace. I shall leave you both right now, head upstairs and into a cool shower, and hope against hope that my mind is functioning somewhat better by the time I get to church."

"I'm off, too," said Father Reggie, checking his watch when the bishop had gone.

"Where are you going?" asked Miss Worthing.

"I want to make sure that everything's ready for this morning."

"Elspeth already did that last night."

"I'm sure she did. But it will make me feel a lot better if I see to it myself.

"Before you go, Father, would you mind if I asked you a few questions?"

He frowned. "Not at all. That is, not if you can do it quickly," he amended.

"I'll be as quick as I can."

She gestured him to a seat, which, though visibly twitching to be up and out and gone, he took.

"First of all, you do have a full set of keys to the church and outbuildings, don't you?"

"Yes, of course. All the clergy have full sets."

"Okay. Now about yours. Do you keep it with you?"

"Hell, yes, I do," he said, and then gave a little laugh, "although actually, that depends on what you mean by keeping them with me."

"What do you mean?" she asked with yet another little sinking sensation in her solar plexus. "I meant do you keep them on your person?"

"Good heavens, no. I leave them in my office most of the time when I'm at the church."

"Why?"

"Because they're too damned heavy, that's why."

"And where do you leave them in your office?"

"On my desk."

"So anyone, essentially, could get into your office and pick them up?"

"I guess so."

"Would you have noticed if they had been moved?"

"Yesterday?" He looked at her as though she had taken leave of her senses.

"Sorry," she muttered, "silly question." And all but growling to herself, she glared at him a second and then asked, "Okay, Father, once more. Did you notice anything unusual yesterday? Anything at all. Most especially, was anything out of place? Was anyone where they shouldn't have been? Dear God, anything unusual?"

"Not a thing, Matilda. I'm sorry. Not a thing out of place and nary a soul either. Other, of course, than the whole mess and uproar the place was in generally."

"Well, I can't say I was expecting you to say anything else," Miss Worthing conceded grimly.

"Why?"

"Because it's what everybody's been saying."

"Really?"

"Among other things," said Miss Worthing, cutting the subject short. "Okay, let me ask you this: What was your reaction to the play's being canceled—to Dr. Cantrell's deciding to take it before the parish council and get it canceled?"

"Well—"

"Please be honest with me. Please."

"Frankly, I thought it would probably have been better for everyone concerned to postpone. Both for me personally and, I think, for the community at large. What with the harvest coming in so unexpectedly early, no one really had the energy to adequately devote to it. And maybe—who knows?—if we had had a little more time, it wouldn't have been quite the shambles it was. Although Elspeth's little bit of business certainly took care of that, didn't it?" he added dryly.

"But I mustn't get sidetracked on what I thought of that," he said, and frowned a bit as he explained his position. "I just could not stand by and let Dr. Cantrell have his way over it. Not after we've tried so hard to turn things around here. It simply was not to be borne that he should succeed in yet another attempt to drag us lock, stock, barrel, and banjo back into the fifties. And no, if you're going to ask, I would not kill him in order to prevent that."

"Not, perhaps, to secure production of the play but—and please, don't be offended; these are the kinds of questions we have to be asking—you are, in effect, acting rector of the Church of All Saints. Had these machinations succeeded, you would probably have been elected rector at the very next parish council meeting."

"That's probably true," conceded Father Reggie. "But for a number of reasons, it's a bit far-fetched. Not only would I remind you that I have not forgotten that passage in Scripture about gaining the world only to lose one's soul, but even were I to have abandoned my faith to provide such a post for myself, I can assure you that I certainly would not have left any concoction I'd contrived for Cantrell to be innocently swallowed by poor dumb Father Hughie, much less Philip Kesterson."

"Very well, Father. Thank you."

"Anything else?"

"Yes, there is—and this really is a delicate matter."

"Oh?"

"Father, you heard confessions yesterday afternoon."

Warily Father Reggie responded: "Yes?"

"I'm not going to ask who went to confession, nor am I going to ask what was confessed. But I want you, if your conscience will allow, to answer one very simple question."

Father Reggie's face had gone completely blank of expression.

"What?"

"Did anyone confess anything unlikely yesterday?"

"I can't answer that question, Matilda."

She sighed.

"I didn't think you could, but I thought I had to try. You see . . ."

"I know why you asked it. I know it would make things easier. I can't answer that question. Ever.

"And now, if you don't mind"—he stood up—"I really have to be getting to church."

"Of course," said Miss Worthing, rising also. "You go on ahead. If I think of anything further to ask, I'll get to you later. And yes," she added with a smile, "we'll bring Belinda Sue with us."

"Thanks for everything, Matilda. See you about seven."

3   After he had gone, Miss Worthing sat for a few minutes longer in a kind of stupor of astonished disbelief at the wasteland of disjunct, negative, and, generally speaking, useless data wherein she wandered. And the prospect of the day—perhaps many days—ahead of her was not a congenial one. She had already reached that stage of wondering quite seriously if she would ever feel rested again. But she had said she would do it, and by God, do it she would.

She rose, took a deep breath, and once more steeled herself to the fray. Out there in the kitchen was yet another of the principals in this peculiar little drama. Not that she had any real hope of getting anything useful from her. Nevertheless, squaring her shoulders, Miss Worthing went to see if anything intelligible, useful, or meaningful could be gotten out of Belinda Sue Morgan. . . .

. . . And a few minutes later, wandering in the heat devastation of the back garden, she came to the perhaps inevitable conclusion that no, this was not going to do anyone any good either.

She sighed.

"I'm sorry, Miss Worthing," said Belinda Sue gently. "I would like to help. And I do assure you that ever since the whole megillah began, I've been over and over it in my head, trying to think of something—anything—that just might be useful. But"—she shrugged—"*nada!*"

"Thank you, Belinda Sue," said Miss Worthing. "I was so hoping that you, at least, would have something to make what's coming a bit less unpleasant. You do know what's coming, don't you?"

Belinda Sue nodded. "Oh, yes. It means there's going to be a great big, stinking, public investigation that's going to give the Church of All Saints a very nasty black eye from which it will be a long time recovering. Poor Reggie."

"Why do you say that?"

"He really loves this parish. And I guess so do I. Nevertheless . . ."

"Yes?"

"You promise not to tell anyone?"

"I'll promise no such thing, young lady. And it's highly improper of you even to ask me."

Belinda Sue chuckled. "You're right, of course. Sorry."

They had reached a little bench sheltered by a bower of apple trees with a bed of variegated petunias underneath. Neither apples nor petunias were looking any too plump or vigorous, but the shade covering the bench was pleasant.

"Shall we sit a moment?" said Belinda Sue.

"Certainly."

"It's like this, Miss Worthing: Father Reggie wasn't planning to be here at the Church of All Saints that much longer."

"What!"

"Please keep your voice down," said Belinda Sue severely. "I'm sorry. But under the circumstances, I quite agree that you should know. But Father doesn't want people in general to know."

"All right, my girl, enough mystification. What are you talking about?"

"Father Reggie has received a 'call' from another church."

"Oh, no!"

"Why do you say that?" asked Belinda Sue tartly. "Because you like him?"

"Well, certainly that. He's been a more than usually bright spot among us these last years."

"But then why—although probably I shouldn't even ask that."

"Why didn't we get rid of Cantrell?" asked Miss Worthing, interpreting the interrupted remark.

Belinda Sue nodded.

"My dear, you know perfectly well that it is not, in the first place, all that easy to do. And secondly, please try to remember that there are a lot of people who genuinely like and respect Leo Cantrell. I can't even say that I actually dislike him—even if he is a bit of a windbag."

"There!" said Belinda Sue. "No wonder Reggie put out the news that he might be available."

"Did the bishop know about this?" asked Miss Worthing.

"He rather has to, doesn't he?"

"And you approve?"

"I neither approve nor disapprove. I do think Reggie's an awfully good priest, though."

"So he is," agreed Miss Worthing.

"The only problem," Belinda Sue continued, "is that, if

this thing erupts into the kind of scandal you think it might—I just hope that other church doesn't suddenly decide to withdraw its offer. I know Reggie's got that on his mind."

"So that's what he meant," said Miss Worthing, and elevated by a new thought, she rose and began to stalk back and forth along the path.

"Have I upset you?" asked Belinda Sue.

"Oh, no, my dear, not me. My calculations, perhaps."

"How's that?"

Miss Worthing halted and cast her eyes to the heavens and raised her hands as though in prayer. And laughed. "Oh, God, what do I do now?" and explained to Belinda Sue: "Every single avenue that I try is blocked to me. Here we are, stuck with a puzzle of dismal complexity. And at first I was just sure it was going to be as easy as could be. I thought every blessed one of you people—the folks involved in the play—had means, motive, and opportunity to have committed this crime. In fact, from what little I have been able to uncover, access to the means and opportunity have broadened out all over the place.

"But the more I talk to all of you, the more I find that, if I'm to believe what I'm told—and at the moment I have no reason not to believe it—no one really has a motive. And at the same time, I've learned about more snakes writhing just beneath the surface of this community than I ever dreamed possible—or certainly wanted to know. And where has it gotten me? Precisely nowhere.

"Well, I never liked motive as a *vae viae* anyway," she concluded grimly. "And now we're all just going to have to live with this wretched investigation that's coming and pray to the Lord above that our church can somehow survive a muckracking like it's never known before."

"I'll help in any way I can," said Belinda Sue simply. "I'm not much of a criminologist, but I have been trained in logic and the collation of data. And I can program a computer."

"Thank you, Belinda Sue. I just may take you up on it."

"But for now," said Belinda Sue, "I'm afraid we'd better get moving. Once we get this Sunday morning out of the way"—she stood up and took Miss Worthing's arm companionably—"let's just see if we can't cut through the crap with a judicious swipe of Occam's razor."

4 As Father Reggie had said, "around about seven" several automobiles proceeded at a reasonably decorous pace across the town of Jolliston toward the Church of All Saints.

The first to arrive was that of Neil Bonewarden, the only member of the parish staff allowed a parking slot in the clergy lot. Normally the very first to arrive on a Sunday, as he pulled in he could not help but notice that Father Reggie's battered old Buick was already in place.

Ordinarily, upon arrival, Neil's first order of business was to head to his office and brew coffee. Today, however, he decided that perhaps the best thing to do would be to look in and see if Father Reggie needed any help. It was going to be a hell of a day, and that poor priest had had the entire responsibility of the Church of All Saints thrust unexpectedly and altogether willy-nilly upon his youngish though able shoulders.

Pausing at the claustral entrance of the sacristy only long enough to check that the LED in the alarm system was on green, Neil went in and found there was no one in the sacristy.

"Father Reggie!" he called and walked through the door into the church—and came to an astonished halt at the scene confronting him on the ambo in front of the altar.

For a moment neither man said anything. That which lay between them would never say anything again.

Then, almost frantically, Father Reggie said, "I found her here. Just like this."

"You did? Then what the hell are you doing with that?" asked Neil, pointing to Father Reggie's right hand in which was clasped the bishop's staff, stained for fully half its length with blood.

Father Reggie looked down and, with a gesture of alarm and distress, cast the repugnant object from him to land clattering on the steps of the ambo. Even so, when it came to rest, Neil could plainly see the bloody imprint of Father Reggie's hand on it.

Father Reggie started toward him.

"Stay where you are!" commanded Neil, swelling up like an indignant bullfrog. "You just stand right there. Don't you go anywhere. Don't even think about moving."

Reluctant to take his eyes off Father Reggie even for a second, Neil backed into the doorway to the sacristy, clutching behind him to find the telephone. Presently his reaching fingers found it. He picked it up, cradled the receiver against his shoulder, and stabbed at random on the line buttons till he got a dial tone and, again by feel, dialed 911.

After a single ring, a voice said, "Jolliston County Emergency."

"Send a deputy. Church of All Saints. Quick. Come in through the cloister entrance to the sacristy. Send an ambulance, too," he added, though it took no imagination whatever to realize that the body prone upon the floor was that of a very dead person indeed. No human being could have survived that kind of damage to the skull. "And get onto the sheriff," he added. "And George Lorris, too."

"Who?"

"The district attorney, damn it! Tell them Fiona MacLaren's been murdered. Fiona. MacLaren. I'm Neil Bonewarden. I'm the organist here. And I'm holding a prisoner, so don't dawdle. Get them here now."

He hung up the phone and glared at Father Reggie. "You just settle down. You aren't going anywhere."

"Neil, I didn't do this."

"Yeah?" said Neil, his disbelief patent. "You're real good

with that thing," he said, pointing to the bishop's staff. "What did you think? After you'd poisoned Cantrell, they'd elect you rector? And then maybe bishop of something? Is that why you like using a bishop's staff so much?"

"I didn't . . ." began Father Reggie, then suddenly his face lit up. His eyes focused on something over Neil's shoulder as he all but shouted, "Oh, my God, Bishop! Thank God you've come!"

"Don't try that kind of shit on me," sneered Neil.

Whereupon, behind him, the bishop's voice said, "Would one of you care to tell me what's going on here?"

Neil whirled around in surprise. As he did so, the bishop saw what lay on the ambo.

"I see," he said softly.

"Bishop," said Neil, "I found him"—he pointed to Father Reggie—"standing over her, holding that." He pointed to the horribly discolored staff still lying on the steps of the ambo. "I called 911 already."

"Did you tell them to get George and Sam here?" Miss Worthing's voice called from behind the bishop.

"Yes."

Neil still stood guardlike in the doorway, his eyes glued to Father Reggie, who also remained, as it were, like a cornered rat, not moving, his eyes glancing rapidly from one to the other of those present, standing in a state of bewildered shock, a yard perhaps from the body.

"Neil, stand aside," said the bishop.

Reluctantly, Neil obeyed and watched as the bishop, almost, it seemed, indifferent to the presence of the younger priest, walked over to the body and squatted next to it. With a fastidious little gesture, he pulled the skirt of his cassock back and leaned down to touch the neck of the dead woman.

"She's dead," he announced, surprising no one, and blessing the body, chanted, "Go forth, O Christian soul . . ."

"I already did that," said Father Reggie.

"You better do it, Bishop," urged Neil.

The bishop snorted and shook his head. "No. It's not necessary."

"But he killed her," protested Neil.

"Even if he did, which has not yet been proved, he's still a priest, Neil. Let's not be little Donatists now."

Nevertheless, he said it all rather absently. He was still looking intently at the entire *situs* of the mess.

By this time Miss Worthing had long since pushed through the immobile crowd in the doorway of the sacristy. She came to a halt, standing over the bishop as he finished his examination.

"Bishop?" she said.

He glanced up and gestured her to join him.

With something of an effort, she lowered herself to her knees, avoiding the bits of spattered blood as best she might.

Without speaking, the bishop looked first at her and then pointed here and here and there.

It was fairly easy to read what the bishop meant—and that, for the moment, he wished it kept between them.

Gingerly she too felt that place under the jawbone. The cold and clammy texture of the skin told her what the absence of pulse only confirmed.

Standing up, she circled the body and came to a halt near the head. Again she lowered herself to her knees and peered at the head. There was not even the ooze of serum from the wreckage of the skull.

"Hmmm," she said and gestured to the bishop.

"Mmmm?" he said.

She pointed toward the curled-up left hand of the poor creature, which lay within a foot of the bishop.

He nodded and with the utmost gentleness reached down and tried to uncurl the fingers. They yielded not a fraction of an inch.

He looked up and shook his head.

In response to which Miss Worthing nodded and gestured to a pool of blood that had collected in one of the unevennesses of the ambo's stone surface, a depression perhaps half a foot from the head of the body and into which a quantity of blood had flowed from the woman's fractured skull.

It is a distressing fact that wounds to the scalp bleed inordinately profusely. At least while the person is still alive. The really appreciable amounts of blood scattered about on the ambo revealed two things, neither of them pleasant— that the attack had been of a savage, even maniacal intensity, and that long after she had fallen unconscious to the pavement, whoever had done it had gone on battering her until she was quite thoroughly dead.

Which, as it transpired, had been a serious mistake on the part of her assailant.

The blood in the depression worn in the stone of the ambo was still recognizably blood. But the bright arterial scarlet of fresh blood had given over to a kind of orange-brown color, which probably had to do with the fact that the red oxygen-bearing cells had settled to the bottom of the depression, while on the surface, as it were, floated a layer of a thinnish, faintly straw-colored fluid, thus filtering the color of the whole blood beneath.

The bishop sighed and looked up, his expression grim indeed. "Well, that certainly tells me all I need to know."

"Me too," said Miss Worthing.

Together, they stood up.

As they did so, a flurry of activity erupted in the sacristy.

"They do take their time, don't they?" commented the bishop. "But at least they're here. Well, let's just see if the cutting edge of police technology reaches the same conclusion we just did."

At which point, rather like a marionette all the strings of which have been suddenly jerked together, Miss Worthing blinked, lifted her head, and frowned with an access of utter malignance at the bishop.

"Matilda?" said that hierarch.

And presently, after a moment or two of aphasic gaping and looking not unlike a fish deprived of its native element,

Miss Worthing finally managed to ask, "What did you just say?"

The bishop repeated himself.

"Why?" he inquired, not unreasonably.

"Bless you, Bishop," said Miss Worthing, and smiled with unspeakable ferocity. "Bless you. Thanks to you—and Belinda Sue Morgan—I've just had a revelation."

"Oh, good!" said the bishop placidly. "I knew you would."

CHAPTER SIXTEEN

Perhaps a quarter of an hour later, Miss Worthing paused in the second-floor corridor of the church hall, took a number of long, slow breaths, and strove to calm herself. To the left of the double door by which she stood was a small plate of polished brass upon which had been engraved, and the engraving filled with black enamel, "Office of the Rector."

And presently, with a somewhat inarticulate prayer for guidance, she raised a hand, knocked, and without waiting for a response, depressed the handle of the right-hand door, pushed it open, and went in.

The office of the rector of the Church of All Saints is rather grander than that pedestrian word *office* might indicate. It had been, in the old days, the drawing room and dining room of the rectorial manse. Even now there was an archway with a sliding door, still functional, within it about two-thirds of the way down the length of the room, providing an alcove wherein it had been the practice of every rector since the renovation to have his office properly so called. In it were desk, typewriter, a scattering of chairs, more or less comfortable but distinctly utilitarian, filing cabinet, dictaphone, and all the other impedimenta of business.

The other two-thirds of the room, that into which Miss

Worthing now entered, was appointed as a sitting room, with couches, chairs, coffee and occasional tables, a good if rather timeworn carpet on the floor, high, wide windows with Irish linen draperies, and, ranged around the room, bookshelves stuffed with Dr. Cantrell's personal working library. A pleasant enough room, if perhaps a trifle fusty.

And as she had expected to find, both from previous experience and what she had determined, Miss Worthing, upon entering, found Millie seated on a sofa underneath a window, listlessly turning the pages of some ecclesiastical magazine, while, at the far end, Dr. Cantrell, already in cassock, sat at his desk intent on something that might well have been the sermon he had been scheduled to preach that weekend.

Both Cantrells looked up at Miss Worthing's somewhat precipitate entry. Neither was pleased to see her.

Dr. Cantrell left off his meditations and frowned. Millie was more forthright.

"Isn't it customary to wait to be invited to come in?" she asked rather sharply.

As he took his cue from his wife, Dr. Cantrell's mellow voice rolled the length of the room. "Indeed. I'm afraid we shall have to ask you to leave, Matilda. It is, of course, always lovely to see you, but I'm rather busy at the moment, and Millicent does need her quiet time before the nine-thirty."

Undaunted, Miss Worthing came even farther into the room. When, eventually, she spoke, however, it was with, considering the day, night, and morning she had had, with surprising gentleness. "I'm very sorry. I know you both must greatly cherish this time before your activities. Unfortunately, time is running out for me, too, and I'm afraid I have to ask both of you a number of questions. Rather badly, in fact."

At this, Dr. Cantrell frowned and lay down his pen. When he spoke, however, he sounded, not exactly angry, but irritated.

"But what's the point of asking questions?" he demanded.

"Dr. Cantrell," said Miss Worthing, refusing to be goaded out of reasonable speech, "I don't know if you were informed of it, but the bishop appointed me to be his deputy in this dismal affair. As a result—"

"I was informed of your—peculiar office," replied Cantrell, interrupting and rising to move around his desk. "But I was also informed that the perpetrator of this wickedness has been arrested. I believed that I was reliably informed—" He paused to look or, rather more accurately, to glare at his wife, who was looking just as puzzled.

"That was what I was told, Leo," protested Millie, rather snappishly. "It's what Elspeth told me when she called last evening."

"Well, then, there you are," said Cantrell, turning back to Miss Worthing with the brusque air of one happy to have cleared up a minor misunderstanding.

"I'm afraid," Miss Worthing began carefully, "that we—that is to say the police—have rather had to revise their thoughts on the matter."

"But this is nonsense," expostulated Cantrell. "Nonsense. Why, it's plain as can be. That—that person put those corrosive pool chemicals into the wine in the sacristy, wine that I would have been almost certain to drink. And then, when I took ill unexpectedly, dashed around in time also to poison my tea.

"And a brutal, sadistic crime it was, too. Leaving that foul stuff for Father Barnes to drink! But there, I'm sorry; we must remember to pray, even for Richards, wretched creature though he be. . . ."

Millie, long inured to pompous rodomontades, had turned to seek confirmation from Miss Worthing during her husband's fatuous peroration. And was clearly frightened by the expression on the older woman's face.

"Matilda," she started up, "what's wrong? Oh, do hush up, Leo!"

"I'm afraid," Miss Worthing repeated when Cantrell had come to a sputtering halt, "that there have been—developments."

"Dear God, what's happened, Matilda? Don't play with

me like this. I can't stand it." Millie ended on a note near hysterical with terror.

"Fiona MacLaren was found this morning. Dead. At the foot of the altar."

Millie went absolutely white, while her husband merely frowned. "An accident, surely. Or even perhaps (though it may be uncharitable so to speculate) suicide. Her fiancé, after all—"

"Her head was bashed in with the bishop's crosier," Miss Worthing cut off his maunderings.

And he, too, suddenly sat down. "Bless my soul!"

"It was—I can only thank God—most stupidly done," said Miss Worthing, crossing to pull the soft linen draperies back from a window to look out.

"Why do you say that?" asked Cantrell.

"Because at the time it happened, Julian—who was indeed our prime suspect—was in the county jail."

For a long moment Miss Worthing continued to contemplate the drought-sere grass of the playing field.

Then, "Are you sure it—the accident that befell Miss MacLaren—is connected?" asked Dr. Cantrell.

"I wasn't. But I am now," replied Miss Worthing rather vaguely, and turned back to look at the couple. "As you probably know, I have several times in my life been involved in the investigation of crime. More specifically, of murder. And one of the most depressing things in the world is when you only get a handle, *can* only get a handle on a murder when another murder is committed."

She returned to her contemplation of the view without, though in reality, she was acutely aware of the room and its inhabitants behind her.

"And that happened here?" asked Millie in a small voice.

"Yes, Millie, I'm afraid so," said Miss Worthing. "That was why I said it was stupidly done. If—whoever it was had been content, or, I'm sure, been allowed to remain content and let be with the poisoning of the altar wine, we should have been in a terrible quandary—as well as in the unendurable position of having virtually every leading parishioner of the Church of All Saints a suspect in what would have been a protracted and very public investigation."

After a moment during which no one spoke, it was Dr. Cantrell who asked, "And that won't happen now?"

Finally Miss Worthing turned around, her eyes still somewhat dazzled from the light outside, and said softly but firmly, "No."

"Why?"

"Because I know now who was responsible."

Overcome with a sudden access of moral and mortal weariness, Miss Worthing dragged herself to a chair and sat down gratefully, even though she remained poised on the very edge of the seat.

"Perhaps it might interest you to know how I reached my conclusion," she said.

Again there was no answer from either Cantrell or Millie. Both merely continued warily to regard her.

"Curiously," Miss Worthing began, ignoring the seeming lack of response, "my first real break, as it were, came to me up in the hills this morning. It doesn't much matter what I was doing, but I was actually clearing up a very bright red herring. And I heard some bells.

"You see, last night, Saturday evening, was so still and calm that even from where Martha and I live out on Jasmine Avenue we were able to hear the great bell ring the Angelus, followed fifteen minutes later by the same bell ringing for Mass.

"Later, after Julian had been—detained, I suddenly remembered that. And that Julian was almost certain to have been that bell ringer as he has been for months past. Subsequent inquiry confirmed that.

"Subsequent inquiry also provided me with another fact— that Julian and Father Hughie were, had become, extraordinarily good and close friends. Like brothers, I was told. Did you know that?" she suddenly asked Dr. Cantrell.

"No," he replied instantly. "I can't say that I much cared

who Richards palled around with as long as he left me alone."

"I see. Well, incidentally, I didn't know it either. About their great friendship, I mean. Indeed, I wasn't even certain that it was relevant. It was just another datum to be gathered. Until, that is, I was reminded about the church's intercom system. You see, Julian and Hughie talked, albeit briefly, when Hughie called the bell chamber to tell Julian to go ahead and ring for Mass last evening. And again, we have a witness to this conversation. Which means, of course, that Julian knew that Father Hughie was substituting for you. And then Hughie said Mass, drank the poisoned chalice, and died. And little Philip Kesterson came damnably close to going out, too."

Cantrell was equal even to all this. "Clearly, then, Richards was so depraved that, realizing his plan had gone awry, he abandoned even his best friend and that child to their fates. And then came and tried again at me," he added.

"It's possible," said Miss Worthing. "Or was, until Fiona was murdered, too."

"But what does that have to do with it?"

"Just so," said Miss Worthing. "I did ask myself that, of course. What did Fiona's death have to do with anything?

"Well, for starters, it eliminated Julian. For whatever reason Fiona was murdered, Julian simply could not have done it. Okay, Julian. But then, what about the others?"

"What others?" asked Cantrell irritably.

"Surely," said Miss Worthing, "it can hardly have escaped even your notice, Dr. Cantrell, that there are a number of people in this parish who do not love thee, Dr. Cantrell; the reason why, I cannot tell, but this I know and know full well, they do not love thee, Dr. Cantrell."

Resentment, hot and naked, was immediate. Nor had her impromptu adaptation of the well-known epigram of Martial helped anything.

"Come, come, Dr. Cantrell," said Miss Worthing deliberately, "you can hardly blame them, you know. You've always been a bit of an egomaniacal boor, riding roughshod over anyone who had the temerity to disagree with you. And then, on Friday night, without so much as a by-your-leave, you threatened a project upon which a number of people have lavished love, devotion, and a great deal of energy. And for which they cherished more than a few ambitions—frivolous ambitions, to be sure," she hastened to add, "but ambitions intensely real for all that, for—well, for things to come of the play.

"And a surprising number of those people all had"—she ticked them off on her fingers—"means, motive, and opportunity to see to it that, parish council vote or not, you would be eliminated from all further equations.

"Or so it seemed at first.

"So naturally, then, when the bishop asked that I investigate, I began to try to pin 'em down, figuring that one of them had to have done it and that by a standard exercise of investigatory routine, presently we would uncover the one responsible."

"But they'd already arrested Richards!" protested Dr. Cantrell.

"So they had," admitted Miss Worthing. "But I felt, and the bishop agreed with me wholeheartedly, that the arresting had been done with precious little in the way of anything other than purely circumstantial evidence.

"Now, circumstantial evidence has hung more than one felon in this wicked world. But given the wide field from which to chose, Julian was just one of several—and, as I said, as my own investigation proceeded, by no means did it seem at all likely that Julian had had anything to do with this.

"'Very well,' said I, 'we'll pin 'em down some other way.'

"The only trouble with that, of course, was that I couldn't pin 'em down on anything. Not a one of 'em. Either they had no real opportunity to lay hands on—the appropriate poison, or had no access to the sacristy, or did not—at least on their own say-so—have any real motive.

"Only Julian, it seemed, had it all.

"So you can see that I was more than a bit distracted when

I found out that Julian, too, wished to suspend production of the play."

"What?" said Millie.

"Precisely my own reaction," said Miss Worthing. "The perfect motive gone up in smoke. Then, of course, when Fiona was found this morning, he was definitely out of it.

"So I had to amend the question: Who would kill Fiona? Why would anyone murder Fiona? What could possibly be the point of murdering Fiona? Especially now that Julian was out. Elspeth was out. Jack was out. The Yateses were out of it, by my personal knowledge, and so too Neil, as well as was Father Reggie because of the—well, the circumstances surrounding the crime."

"I'm sorry to interrupt your fascinating exposition," said Cantrell sarcastically, "but what circumstances?"

"That was the stupidity of Fiona's murderer I told you about. Had he been content to bash in her head and leave her to die at some subsequent hour, all of the above would have remained as much under suspicions as before. Indeed, Father Reggie would probably be in jail right now on two counts of murder and two of attempted murder."

"Father Reggie?" said Millie.

"That's right, Father Reggie. But whoever killed Fiona made certain she was dead, and as a result, they're all in the clear. Oh, and incidentally, so is the last person who might putatively have had anything to gain from keeping Fiona quiet because—well, because of whatever: Bonnie Harris is in San Francisco trying to get a sufficiently nasty lawyer for Julian.

"So what do we have? The people who most dislike you, who had the most to gain, or garner anything tangible from the uninterrupted production of the play, the people whom you have sufficiently provoked that they might want to kill you, all are too remote, too restricted, or just plain too Christian to have done it.

"Of course, wouldn't you know it, none of this really registered with me. I just knew they were all lying. And why shouldn't I? I mean, conspiracies have occurred. I actually experienced one myself once, you may recall. So maybe, I thought, they were all in it, and covering each other.

"And then, after the bishop and I were finishing our examination of poor Fiona's body this morning, and the sheriff's posse finally arrived, he said something to me about wondering whether the 'cutting edge' of technology would come up with the same conclusions we had reached. Such a little thing, really. But it chimed like a bell with something Belinda Sue Morgan had said to me a bit earlier, about using Occam's razor to cut through the crap. Occam's razor, that wonderful old scholastic device which reminds us that the simplest theory that covers all the data is very likely going to be the right one.

"And suddenly I saw the whole thing in a completely different light.

"Like what if, in fact, the victim, the primary victim, which is to say poor simple Father Hughie, was not killed by inadvertence as we have assumed all along. What if he was the intended victim all along?"

Miss Worthing paused a moment to let the full import of that sink in before she continued:

"Needless to say, once the question was posed, the picture, hitherto inordinately fuzzy, got rather clear rather quickly. And a whole lot of things began falling into place.

"Because, you see, once you've done that, once the question is posed that way, there is really only one possible candidate for the murderer. Someone whose disdainful tolerance of Father Hughie was turned into virulent hatred by the poor ineffectual young priest, for perhaps the first time in his life, standing up and making a difference. And by so doing, of course, thwarting a fixed determination of our— murderer. Someone of no mean intellect who could almost instantly conceive of a plan that would not only eliminate Father Hughie, but implicate as the murderer Julian, another man for whom our man had at least as deep a loathing as he had for Father Hughie. Someone—the man for whom we are looking—who, furthermore, had keys to the entire plant and a man so ubiquitous that his presence in the sacristy, church hall, gym, what have you, was so normal that, of course, no one ever noticed anything."

"This is intolerable," raged Cantrell, rising to his feet, although his normally resonant baritone was a ragged croak.

"Is it? Well, you know, Dr. Cantrell, it is too bad then that your clericals got wet when, rather than risk being seen going into the shed through the courtyard in the normal fashion, you took advantage of the closed swimming pool, you went down to the pool area and let yourself into the tunnel to the shed basement. You didn't even have to go up to the main floor of the shed. You found a canister of the pool chemicals right there, providing you with what you needed.

"You then proceeded normally enough to the sacristy. Who was going to notice the very priest who was scheduled to say Mass? You added the chemicals to the jug and cruets and then were 'taken ill.' And, by the way, made another mistake. You didn't object when Father Hughie asked if Fiona could serve Evensong, resting no doubt content in your knowledge that he was soon to die anyway, and with him gone, you'd never have to worry about Fiona again. You know, if you're going to do something as serious as murder, you should be careful of mistakes like that. . . ."

"This is insane."

"Perhaps it was."

"You're saying I murdered Father Barnes because he crossed me in the council?"

"I am."

"Ridiculous. And am I supposed to have murdered Fiona MacLaren?"

"Who else? Dr. Cantrell, no one else could have. You were discharged from the hospital shortly after four this morning, and you were also seen driving away from your house at the right time to get you here at the right time to have murdered her. I don't suppose you'd care to tell us why you killed her? She was seen, incidentally, here in the church yesterday, puttering about. She told Bonnie Harris she wanted to see what it felt like to preach here. I asked Bonnie why, then, she hadn't gone into the pulpit. Bonnie replied that it was probably a failure of nerve. Fiona? A failure of nerve? Who would have been there to prevent her doing such a thing if she had really taken it into her mind to play preacher? Only you, Dr. Cantrell, who disliked her so intensely. But also, if she were dithering about at the lectionary, she would have been well placed to see directly into the sacristy. What did she see, Dr. Cantrell? And what did she demand of you in exchange for her silence?"

"This is nonsense," Cantrell continued to insist. "If I was seen driving from home, it was probably to get the Sunday papers. Besides, you've already said that you weren't certain this—the murder of MacLaren—was related to the other business yesterday."

"No, Dr. Cantrell, what I said was that I wasn't certain, but that I was now."

"Why?"

"Because you told me that Julian had put pool chemicals into the chalice wine. And I'm afraid, Dr. Cantrell, that we reserved that bit of information. At the moment you said that, Dr. Cantrell, the only people who knew what actually killed Father Hughie were the police, me—and the murderer."

"But—but I was attacked, too!"

"Yes, I know. And that was the reason for the amount of time wasted while I felt compelled to go along with the consensus that the whole thing was a series of determined attacks on you because of your intransigence about the play."

"And what changed your mind?" asked Cantrell with a sneer.

"The same thing that bothered me from the beginning."

"Which was?"

"That the poison in your tea was not the same as that in the chalice."

"And if it had been?" asked Millie, rather unexpectedly, in a strangled voice.

And after a moment of consideration, Miss Worthing replied, "It might have taken me rather longer to figure it all out. We might have wound up in our old scenario of a large-scale public investigation. Although maybe not. I might have come, for instance, to believe that Dr. Cantrell poisoned himself to put the scent off himself. The arsenic in the ant powder that was used was, after all, considerably less toxic than the chlorine mixture in the pool chemicals."

"This is outrageous!" shouted Cantrell. "I was poisoned and I didn't do it."

"Oh, I know that."

"Who did it then? Find that out and there you'll find your real—"

"Oh, stop it, Leo," Millie all but screamed at her husband. "Just stop it!"

"I think that's a good idea, Dr. Cantrell," said Miss Worthing. "I'm afraid it's all over. Posturing will do you no good."

"But someone tried to kill me, I tell you," protested Dr. Cantrell.

"I know," repeated Miss Worthing and, sighing, looked at Millie. "Do you want to tell us about it, Millie?"

After her outburst at her husband, Millie had seemed almost distracted. Now she folded her hands in her lap seemingly almost calmly. It was only, however, that each hand held the other so tightly that prevented them from wringing each other. Her head was bowed, but the back of her neck and the tips of her ears were pink. Nor did she raise her head as Cantrell, looking like a man who had just run full-tilt into a wall, addressed his wife in a stunned voice, "Millicent?"

Without a word, Millie stood up, ignored her husband, and eyeing Miss Worthing expressionlessly, marched to a silver butler's tray standing on an occasional table with several bottles on it with a number of glasses. Deliberately keeping her back to them, Millie poured herself a generous quantity of a sweet sherry and bolted a very healthy slug indeed.

"Oh, yes, Matilda," she said presently. "That was me. How did you figure that one out?"

"You were conspicuous by your presence here yesterday, Millie. You canceled your lessons. You were knocking about to no good purpose." Miss Worthing shrugged.

"I see," said Millie, once more gulping sherry.

"Millicent?" again asked Cantrell in a whisper.

It might almost have been funny. The man, having himself committed murder, was now outraged and shocked that his wife, whose son he had killed, had tried to murder him.

"Millie," asked Miss Worthing, "did Leo know who Hughie was?"

"Of course he knew." The woman's voice was ablaze with bitterness. "I told him."

"When?"

"Friday night. After he tried to cancel the play."

"Why?"

"Because he said that if Hughie tried anything funny—"

"Meaning crossing him?"

Millie nodded. "—that he would see to it that Hughie regretted it. Permanently."

She put her unfinished glass of sherry on the tray and groped her way to a chair, and sat down heavily, staring into her memory. "But I was too late. He'd—Leo had already done it. I didn't realize that until I came running into the church, thinking I had been so damned clever. But I was too late, Matilda. He'd already done it. I thought he was just going to have my boy fired. But instead he just murdered him. And now I've lost my son and my husband all at the same time and what on earth have I gained?"

For a moment Miss Worthing and Dr. Cantrell looked quietly together at the weeping woman. Then, gradually, their eyes met as they glared at each other with the level, unflinching regard of mortal enemies.

"What now?" asked Cantrell.

"That, Dr. Cantrell," said Miss Worthing, "is entirely up to you."

"Yes, it is, isn't it. Yes, I suppose you're right. Oh, very well." He squared his shoulders and shook his head as though to clear it. "Take her and go, will you? Now. Out."

"But what are you going to do?"

"What do you think I'm going to do?"

"You tell me, Dr. Cantrell," said Miss Worthing.

He paused at the sliding double doors leading to his office and began pulling them to.

"I am going to write out my confession and sign it. This isn't the way I imagined this whole thing resolving, but there it is. I was forced to it, you know. And I shall not lose the opportunity to say exactly what I think of what's become of this parish and the diocese under that—" He broke off in an access of rancor and asked, "I imagine the bishop and the law are downstairs waiting for it?"

Miss Worthing shook her head. "They're right outside in the corridor, actually."

"And they let you come in here alone?"

"I'm not as helpless as you might think, Dr. Cantrell," said Miss Worthing, patting a pocket of her suit.

She crossed the room to Millie and put a hand on her shoulder. "Come on, Millie. We have to go now."

Slowly Millie stood up. "What's to become of me, Matilda?"

Although the question clearly had rather an existential thrust, Miss Worthing chose to reply pragmatically. "It depends, Millie. You did attempt murder, didn't you? But, personally, I doubt there's a court in the land—at least in civilized areas—that will not consider that you've been most severely provoked. . . ."

They heard the double doors behind them slam as they emerged through the outer doors in the passage.

"Hello, Bishop," said Millie. "I'm so glad you're here."

"You need a rest, Millie," said that good hierarch.

"I know. I need a long, long rest. Leo's in there signing a confession now. He'll let you know when he's done. He killed my boy, you know."

"Yes, Millie. I know."

"I loved them both, you know."

"I know, Millie."

"I think I want to go now."

George Lorris wordlessly signaled to a deputy, who stepped forward and gently began to escort Millie away.

They had not gotten halfway down the hall when they all heard the sound, muffled somewhat by those well-made walls and doors but unmistakable for all that, of a gunshot. And the bishop's face became one of flint.

"Millie," he called down the hallway, "is that what you meant when you said that Leo would let us know when he was done?"

Millie turned, the deputy hovering uncertainly at her side.

"I wasn't sure, of course. But I thought it might be."

And, angrily, Lorris demanded of Miss Worthing, "Did you know he would do that?"

"No," said Miss Worthing. "The probability existed, of course. Leo Cantrell kept guns. I did know that. For protection, don't you know."

At which, Millie actually uttered what might have been a kind of laughter.

"The only problem, of course," said she, coming closer to speak to Miss Worthing, "was the things that haunted Leo were boggles that can't be dealt with with guns. It might have been easier for him if they had been. I don't know. But they weren't real. So few of the things that angered him were real." Again there was that little ghost of a laugh that contained nothing whatever of humor. "And maybe I'm being disloyal to say it, but I do have to admit"—she looked at the bishop—"that when Leo finally, and so foolishly, tried to deal with the real world, I can't say I'm surprised he turned out to be such a coward."

EPILOGUE

"So what do we do now?" asked Father Reggie several hours later.

To Lorris's and Marshall's enormous relief, his lordship had insisted that, when the main business of the day was done, a meeting be called in the church. Not the full plenary session of the whole parish which had been feared, but a gathering together of those who had been involved in the play or who happened to have been inconvenienced by the intricacies of the events.

"It is only fair that they should know," said Dr. Fisher, "having been under suspicion, that they're all free to go about their business without worrying any further."

And the sheriff and district attorney, whose behavior had not been at all exemplary, had wondered how they were going to be able to get word out to all those whom they had hassled. The culprit was dead by his own hand, and the law and popular sentiment took rather a dim view of trying a dead man, or even besmirching his name.

Whereupon, in sheer goodwill, Miss Worthing instructed the bishop to leave her out of it and give all credit to Lorris and Marshall. And their cup was full—even though they all knew that absolutely no one would be in the least fooled by such pretty fictions. It had been Miss Worthing, after all, who had done all the legwork, and virtually everyone knew it—most especially those who had been, however briefly, suspects.

And so his lordship, the bishop, had gathered the hundred or so people involved in the church directly following the eleven o'clock liturgy and carefully explained what had happened among them.

"And I have only one thing to ask," he concluded. "Nor do I think it too much to ask, either. And it is simply this: You will all please keep your mouths shut. There is no need for anyone to know. It is in God's hands, people, and there is nothing further for us to do, but to pray for the souls of Father Hughie, Dr. MacLaren, and Dr. Cantrell. To pray. And to keep silence."

Which was the point where Father Reggie stood up to ask his question: What now?

"Father d'Arcy and I," said the bishop, "will stay on for a while to help out both liturgically and administratively . . ."

And sitting beside Miss Worthing at the back of the assembly, Miss Shaw squirmed delightedly and muttered, "Oh, good. And I wonder what they'd like for dinner. Shall we ask Mrs. Fisher to come and stay, too? I do like her, don't you, Mattie?"

"Secondly," continued the bishop, "right now, all of you, police, players, congregation, and clergy, are going to assist me as I say a memorial for Dr. Cantrell. Julian?"

Sitting next to a positively radiant Bonnie, but looking himself rather the worse for wear, Julian stood up. "Yes, Bishop?" he asked.

"Will you ring the toll?"

"I should be honored, sir."

And while Julian stood up and began to slouch down the aisle on his appointed errand, once more the bishop leaned forward and addressed his little congregation. "And I want you all to go on with the play. Find someone who can take Hughie's part. Jack, surely you must have a friend at the college who would be eager to take on such a juicy role, the distressing Hincmar.

"What was the title of the piece again? Ah, yes. Thank you. *Death of a Heretic?* Dear me, how appro— Well, never mind that. Yes. Yes, and we shall make it a memorial to Father Hughie and poor Fiona, but most of all to Dr. Cantrell. I was his bishop, and when all is said and done, you were his parishioners and we can only hope in some measure his friends. Yes, dear people, do it. *Death of a Heretic* in memory of Leo Cantrell."

And presently they heard it, the sound reverberating through the great stone-bound space of the church.

Thrice times three the great bell rang to signify the death of a man. And then, when that had rung, a pause ensued of a full minute, after which the clear measured strokes began, one for each of the sixty-seven years the man had lived in middle earth, the solemn strokes ringing out to all the world—and those present contemplated, each in his or her own fashion, the life and death of Leopold Cantrell.

NOTE

Should anyone be further interested in the unfortunate history of Gottschalk of Orbaix, I would refer the reader, first of all, to Helen Waddell's *The Wandering Scholars* (London: Constable, 1927), and the same author's *Medieval Latin Lyrics* (London: Constable, 1946), the latter containing, admirably translated, several of Gottschalk's quite beautiful if rather depressing poems. Jaroslav Pelikan touches on the more specifically doctrinal aspects of the controversy in his *The Christian Tradition*, volume 3, "The Growth of Medieval Theology (600–1300)," pp. 80–98 (Chicago: University of Chicago Press, 1978). The treatises *Contra Gottescalcum* by John Scotus Erigena and *De Una et Non Trina Deitas* by Hincmar of Rheims can be found in Migne's *Patrologia Latina*, although the latter treatise actually refers to a trinitarian dispute several years prior to the Augustinian/predestination controversy referred to herein—Gottschalk certainly seems to have been a theological gadfly.

Finally, to anyone interested in such things, it will have been obvious that the Church of All Saints in Jolliston is like no church on earth. It has become something of a cliché in recent years to deplore the chasms that separate the "branches" of the Catholic Church. Nevertheless, they remain deplorable and, in far too many cases, as gaping and rancorous as ever. Accordingly, when I came to plan *Mass Murder,* I deliberately chose to employ Anglican church practice, Roman Catholic ecclesiology, and, except where it did not fit into the mise-en-scène, Orthodox liturgical practice. To a certain extent, this was done to fit the story, but it was also for fun and provocation: I created an "ideal" church—with which I most sincerely hope everyone with a party ax to grind will be thoroughly dissatisfied.

San Francisco
March 1990